A FAMILY AFFAIR

PATRICIA DIXON

For Grandma and Grandad Birdie

This book is inspired by true events.
Told to me in part by my mother.
The whole story remains a mystery.
A secret never to be told.
A family affair.

MARPLE, CHESHIRE. 2003

Beryl bounded down the stairs and swung open the front door to find the cheery district nurses waiting on the step. Never had she been so glad to see anyone in her whole life.

On a day-to-day basis they eased the sometimes-weighty responsibility of caring for her cantankerous mother, and dealt with the more unsavoury tasks involved. Today, however, they signified respite. Time and space in which Beryl could gather her wits.

In her opinion, they were real-life angels living there on Earth. And if the previous hour or so was anything to go by, they'd need every ounce of godly, or saintly power they possessed to deal with their patient. All Beryl wanted was a moment or two so she could process what she'd just heard.

Beryl hovered by the hall stand as the nurses snapped on rubber gloves and donned plastic aprons. They had no clue that, according to their patient, during the night there'd been a much-awaited visitation. Apparently, Walter, Beryl's long-dead father had popped in to tell his wife to pack a bag because her time was almost up, and he'd be back soon to fetch her.

With her eye on the hourglass, Mother Molly McCarthy – as

she was fondly referred to by family – had decided before Walter came back, to unburden herself, just in case the sands of time ran out. In her eagerness to free herself of sin, she had conveniently dumped all of her troubles on poor Beryl.

Waving the nurses onwards and upwards, Beryl felt duty bound to give them the heads-up so called out, 'She's on form today. And take no notice to her ramblings if she starts going on with herself. I'll pop the kettle on for when you've finished.'

To the sound of *thank-yous* and *not to worrys*, Beryl silently watched their ascent. The minute their black tights and blue tabards disappeared from view she headed through the kitchen and then straight outside, carrying the weight of her mother's secret like a sack of dirty washing.

She plonked her bottom on the wooden bench by the back door and sucked in great gulps of fresh air. But the tension didn't leave her body, and Beryl didn't think it ever would.

Surely it was all a lie. Or confusion, muddled events twisted by the passage of time.

Yet her mother's account had been so precise, her voice clear, her eyes looking upwards. Focused on a scene playing out on the bedroom ceiling as she spoke her truth. And that's what Beryl believed it was. The truth.

Beryl rested her head against the kitchen wall. After swallowing down the lump in her throat, she whispered her shock and exasperation. 'Oh Mum, what have you done?'

Closing her eyes for moment or two, Beryl waited for an answer. From where or whom, she had no idea. If she was hoping that when she opened her eyes the problem would have gone away, she was disappointed because, just like her view of the garden and life, nothing had changed.

The rockeries that ran around the border were weed-free, always well-tended and stocked with an abundance of perennials and alpines. The lawn, large enough for a kick-about or a game of

Swingball, was springtime-lush and not yet scorched by the approaching summer sun.

The wooden shed to her left still held all of her dad's tools. As her eyes fell on the handle, Beryl was tempted to fetch the key and take out the largest shovel she could find, then go straight upstairs and whack her mother over the head with it. Move things on a bit. She was due to shuffle off soon, anyway.

With a sigh and hoping to somehow divert her mind from the confession and murderous thoughts, Beryl focused on the pretty garden that hadn't altered since they'd moved there in sixty-five. The year Mother Molly finally made her yearned-for escape and dragged her family along with her.

Leaving their terraced house in Manchester had been a huge wrench but, according to Mother, the scrimping was worth it, not to mention the overtime Beryl's poor old dad was strong-armed into. Their arrival in suburban Cheshire and the purchase of their three-bed semi meant a fresh start and brighter futures for all of them.

All Beryl remembered about that time was being distraught and hating the neat little cul-de-sac, the prim neighbours, and the fact her mum thought she was better than everyone they'd left behind.

At sixteen, Beryl hadn't wanted a fresh start. She'd wanted to stay in Openshaw with her friends who were all going to work at the steel factory, in the offices like they'd planned. Mother would have none of it and said Beryl could be a typist anywhere. To prove her point, she secured an interview at the council offices for the Monday after they'd moved in. Beryl still worked there to that day.

Looking back, Beryl recalled that before the move, her mother had often behaved like the devil, or a debt collector, was on their tails. Always on edge, wary when someone knocked on the door, mistrustful of strangers and unyielding where privacy was concerned.

It was one of her many rules, rammed home to the point where you'd think they were the Openshaw branch of the Manchester Mafia.

McCarthy law advocated keeping themselves to themselves. Whatever went on under Molly's roof, arguments, trouble and strife, personal business, was never repeated outside the front door.

Molly was neighbourly, friendly but best-friendless, and avoided social events and gossips like the plague. And on a post-war street of housewives there were plenty to choose from.

'Private business is just that, a family affair. Like we used to say during the war, keep mum, she's not so dumb.' How many times had Beryl and her older brother Ernie heard that? Being almost nine years older and sharp as a knife, he'd tease their mum, saying she was a spy who was waiting to be called back to the cold. Now, Beryl knew it was nothing of the kind and the truth was so much worse than having a member of the KGB for a mother.

As if she hadn't enough to ponder on, another thought pinged into Beryl's beleaguered brain. Yes, Mother had seemed happier when they moved to Marple, but she never really changed. Or had they all simply got used to 'Mother's funny ways'? Beryl knew the answer was no.

Puffing out her cheeks then letting the air trapped inside them escape slowly, Beryl wondered how a morning she had expected to follow the same monotonous routine had turned into an earth-shattering epiphany.

As the live-in carer for her dying mother, in between her office shifts, nothing very much happened. But as dull as her life had become since her divorce, Beryl really could have done without her mother's revelation.

Regardless, she now understood why Mother had always been on pins and semi-reclusive, and what fed her desperate determination to escape Manchester. And yet in the wake of it all, Beryl was having trouble feeling sorrow or loyalty for her old mum. Instead, she had this dreadful sense of being let down and deceived.

Her view of the childhood home she had come to love, the average life she'd been content with and – most importantly – the mother she'd adored and respected, despite her sharp tongue and high standards, had shifted like a tectonic plate.

That was the only way Beryl could describe the previous hour, as she'd sat on the very uncomfortable dressing table stool, clutching the hem of her cardigan for strength, listening dumbfounded while Mother Molly bared her soul. It was as though the Axminster under her feet actually moved the foundations of her family's history.

God, Beryl was so flaming angry, she could feel it building inside. Not just for the decades of deceit and the ramifications that her mother's secret could have if it ever got out. Because before she'd made her unholy confession, Molly bloody McCarthy had extracted a promise and made Beryl swear an oath never to tell a soul, not until she was dead and gone, and only if she felt it was right to do so. *Cheers Mother. Thanks for that.*

Beryl thought she was going to hear something juicy, or of no real consequence. Had she known what was about to leave her mother's lips, Beryl would have sellotaped them firmly shut then ran a mile.

But it was said, never to be forgotten. And basically, her mother had very cleverly passed the buck, leaving Beryl to decide what to do about it all. It was up to her whether to keep the secret for the greater good, contain it like a killer virus, or explain it all and hope there was an antidote for the shock and pain she would unleash on the McCarthy clan.

Approaching footsteps forced Beryl to shake off her worries for a second and paint on a smile as the nurses popped their cheery faces around the doorjamb.

'All done, lovely. She's clean and changed and fast asleep

already. Must have worn herself out chatting to you, bless her heart.'

Making to stand and intent on serving them refreshments, Beryl was halted by a raised palm. 'You stay there, lovely, and enjoy the peace and quiet. We'll let ourselves out. See you tomorrow morning, bright and early.'

Before Beryl could object or voice the notion that actually she wouldn't mind a cup of tea and a natter, they were gone, and she was left alone with a thirst and a problem to solve.

'What the bloody hell am I going to do?' Beryl asked the little stone lion who sat beside the doorstep and stared, perhaps needing a tad more information to go on.

One thing she did know for sure is that she would keep her promise and not expose her *dear* mother. It would all be too much to bear. She had enough to cope with as it was, so a family bombshell followed by a funeral from hell was not Beryl's idea of fun.

Accepting that the stone lion was going to be of no use, Beryl looked skyward, instead, telling herself it was worth a try. 'Oh dear God in heaven, what the hell am I supposed to do now?'

A heartbeat or two later Beryl was still on her own. And in an attempt to be logical, focused on the subject of her mother's life-changing nugget of unwanted information.

Ernie.

Should Beryl decide to share, there was no way of knowing how Ernie would take the news. His relationship with their mother had always been strained, as far back as Beryl could remember, really.

There was so much to consider. The pros and cons of being the one who blew their past apart let alone the hurt it would inflict on Ernie. Because if she was reeling, knowing him, there was a chance he would spiral out of control. No, this wasn't something Beryl could fathom on a Wednesday evening and have it all sorted by the time *Corrie* started.

It was a biggie. Telling Ernie, her beloved big brother that their unassuming, bedridden, eighty-two-year-old mother was actually a fraud. That the foundations of their family were built on a tangle of secrets and lies.

And how could she – never mind Ernie – come to terms with the lip-numbing, brain-freezing facts about the past? Make sense of their lives? Everything she'd taken for granted for as long as she could remember. As if that wasn't enough, there was also one stark fact that made her stomach roil and her blood run cold.

Mother Molly McCarthy was a thief. The worst kind of thief of all.

CHAPTER 1

HONEY

Present Day

Looking up from the counter, Honey checked the time. She'd been replenishing her stock of French pastries since the first batch had sold out during the after-school-run-rush.

Midday approached and she was a man down. Actually a woman down, but it didn't have the same ring to it. Honey always imagined people manning the lifeboats when she said it or rushing about in a flap like the dinner ladies at school when it started to spit rain.

Lizzy, their waitress, had rung to say she'd be delayed on account of a traffic jam and one of her longest and most elaborate stories yet.

Something to do with a road-block by the mini roundabout near the humpback bridge, and at least ten police outriders escorting a huge entourage of mysterious limousines. Lizzy had been utterly convinced it was either the prime minister or a member of the royal family. Why they'd be passing through a sleepy village in the Peak District on a Wednesday morning was anyone's guess. Honey's especially.

Then again, Lizzy was known for gilding the lily. The customers loved her chatter, and tales of UFOs flying low over the Swizzles factory in the valley. Or the one about the big cat that roamed the tops of the peaks, descended from a leopard once owned by a batshit crazy Victorian mill-owner who collected rare species.

Lizzy could also shift their specials like no other, so as long as she arrived before they got busy, Honey would let it go.

It had been steady during the morning, and she'd managed by herself. The usual coffee-morning mums and then a flurry of hikers, and a couple of regulars from the marina who popped in for the all-day breakfast. Now the lull before the storm.

Behind her she could hear music, accompanied by Gospel, their chef, who she knew would be dancing to whatever was playing on Radio 1. Modern songs weren't her thing at all. For a start she could never understand the lyrics and found the chatter of the DJ a bit annoying. Gospel, Lizzy and their kitchen assistant Butch, loved it. She saw her café as a collective effort where they all had a say, and their opinions and ideas were respected and welcomed.

Honey checked the counter, and after a backwards glance, satisfied that the beverage station was prepped and ready for action, she took a moment to survey her pride and joy. Honey's Place. Her real name, Honeysuckle, had been ditched in favour of her shortened version during her schooldays to avoid teasing. In the present, having to pay a signwriter per letter sealed the deal.

Her best friend, Ziggy, had been adamant that Honeysuckle would've been a cool name above the shop. Honey's dwindling bank balance disagreed.

Regardless, it was, in her estimation, a unique eatery; different in many ways to the others dotted around the surrounding towns and villages in the picturesque Peak District. A welcoming destination where you could eat, drink, chat and, in the quieter moments, read.

To the right of the central doorway, arranged in three blocks were the sofas and armchairs, low tables in the centre, all reclaimed and getting a bit worse for wear. But they added to the laid-back ambience, the sense that many people before them had rested their weary bodies and taken a moment.

On the opposite side stood her beloved and – yes, rather eclectic – collection of tables and chairs, again reclaimed and upcycled, most of them carefully painted in pastel colours or sanded and varnished by her grandad Ernie.

An array of modern prints adorned the walls. Hung in no particular order, the art beneath the glass was actually pages sliced from gallery brochures, donated by a local art collector who had stacks of them in their garage. The frames, Honey had gathered from charity shops and car-boots.

Once combined with the colourful prints, the old, the new, and the quirky retro finds kept customers occupied while they waited. Honey often heard them commenting on the sea and landscapes, the still lifes and the curious pop-art posters with Beatles lyrics faintly etched into the background.

In the two years since she'd taken the plunge and opened the door, Honey had built up a regular clientele. At the start, her mother and grandfather had their reservations about ploughing her little inheritance into a run-down shop. They had expressed first their uncertainty about the risk she was taking going it alone; then their bemusement once she'd explained her philanthropic vision. Despite all that, Honey was doing okay.

Grandad Ernie said he was proud. Her mother was still on the fence, albeit from a nice safe distance in Marbella; and her stepfather stayed out of family affairs and basically did as his wife told him.

Dragging herself from daydream-land, she gave the counter another quick wipe. Honey's Place was quiet, but any minute the lunchtime service would start. It was her favourite time of the day, when the wholesome comfort food they served flowed from the kitchens to the tables. It made the team's hard work, and Honey's vision worthwhile.

She smiled, remembering Grandad Ernie's expression when she told him about her plans to run an enterprise where once she'd paid the bills, herself and the staff a wage, whatever was left over, would go to a charity very close to her heart.

Also – and raising her grandad's eyebrows even further – on Sundays and Mondays, when the café would be closed for her business, it would be used to help the community. So far, so good, and Honey's vision had become a reality, but it was time to take things up a notch, stretch herself a little and hopefully help a few more people at the same time.

Her mini-plan for Peak District domination was interrupted by the dingle of the silver bell above the door. It had been there when she bought the old haberdashery, and each time it rang, not only did it alert Honey and the team to a customer, the happy sound never failed to lift her spirits.

It was as though it too was glad that someone had stepped over the threshold and had graced Honey's Place with their presence.

She was further cheered by the sight of her next and most special customer. Grandad Ernie, one of her regulars and from his usually reserved table in the corner, her greatest critic. Not to mention supplier of organic seasonal vegetables straight from his allotment, a box of which he carried in his arms.

Moving from behind the counter she went to take the box but without fuss or any hint that a strapping eighty-three-year-old couldn't manage. Grandad Ernie fiercely guarded his independence, a proud man who took care of himself and Honey in particular.

'This is a nice surprise, Grandad. I wasn't expecting you. Here, I'll whip these into the kitchen; you grab your table. I haven't put the reserved sign on, but it'll get busy soon, so chop-chop. Bag a seat.'

Ernie nodded and passed Honey the box that had long stems of rhubarb popping out of the top and did as he was told.

As she rounded the counter, Honey couldn't resist a tease. 'And while I think about it, you're looking rather smart. Hot date? Back in a tick.' Ignoring the loud tut followed by the scraping of chair legs, she quickly deposited the vegetables into the arms of Gospel, and after giving him a wink, headed back into the café.

Minutes later, she was seated opposite Ernie who was tipping his second pouch of sugar into his tea, while she sipped the froth off her coffee. 'So, to what do I owe this unexpected pleasure?'

He didn't answer at first, stirring his tea instead. She noticed the frown that momentarily creased his brow, followed by the slight sag of his shoulders which caused her heart to drop. 'Is something wrong, Grandad? You look a bit mithered.'

When he spoke, his sentence began with a deep sigh, and when he looked up Ernie's brown eyes looked sad. 'Been to the solicitors. Our Beryl's affairs are all done and dusted, the probate. I 'ad to sign some papers and the like. Bloody depressing, I can tell you.'

Honey was taken aback, but only for a second. Her grandad's secrecy didn't really surprise her. He was a very private man. Not prone to flowery outbursts or great shows of affection. Saying it like it was when he needed to say it. Otherwise he kept his thoughts and feelings very much to himself.

Ernie showed you love in his actions.

A pat on the knee, or a nod when he agreed with you. A firm hug and the acceptance of a peck on the cheek when you said goodbye. And *love you, from Grandad* once a year in her birthday card. When he mended her leaky sink, or she came home from work, and he'd painted her garden fence as a surprise. It was the little things.

For Honey it was enough and now, apart from her mum, he

was her only alive-and-kicking close relative and she savoured every single thing about him, and every single minute.

Noting that she'd left enough of a gap for him to take a few slurps of his tea and read the specials menu, Honey decided to venture forth.

CHAPTER 2

'I would've come with you if you'd said where you were going, Grandad. Sometimes it's better to have someone with you at places like that… Mum came with me, when Dad… you know.'

Ernie lowered his voice and gave his forehead a scratch. 'Died? You can say it, Honey. No need to beat about the bush. It's a fact and you won't upset me by mentioning him. You should know that by now. It isn't going to make what happened go away. Just like I know Beryl's dead and I'll have to get used to it no matter how bloody fed up it makes me.'

'Brusque' was Ernie's default setting and he meant no harm by it. Honey moved on. Her heart sank as she asked, 'D'you need me to come to the house? You know, to help pack her stuff away.'

Honey dreaded going back to her great-aunt's. This thought, and the certainty that her offer would be declined resulted in a twinge of shame and the need to avoid her grandad's eyes. Instead, Honey focused on her coffee and swirled it around her cup. Almost all the froth had gone, and she'd lost interest in the bitter remains that sloshed about at the bottom.

Thankfully, she was quickly let off the hook by Ernie. 'It's all taken care of, don't worry. Our Beryl didn't have much, nothing that's worth 'owt. I've been round and taken her personal belongings and some knick-knacks, vases, paintings, and stuff. You can have a look through when you get time.'

Now Honey really did feel bad, imagining her grandad having to empty drawers and bag up his sister's clothes. Then Ernie offered more information.

'Mrs Taylor from next door did the honours with Beryl's what-nots, you know, the stuff in her wardrobes. She's taking most of it down to the Sally Army once she's had a root through.' He drained his cup and then slid it forwards, which meant he needed a refill.

Relief flooded Honey as she said a private thank you to Mrs T for being a good neighbour and friend to Aunty Beryl, and for getting Honey off the hook.

'And I've found a clearance firm to shift the furniture and heavy stuff, so this is your last chance to say if you want 'owt. They're coming next week then it's going on the market. I'm not buggering about doing it up. If someone wants it, they can have it as it is.'

Ernie stood. 'Right, I need to use the bathroom,' and tapping the menu, 'I'll have the shepherd's pie special and apple crumble for afters, custard please. Back in a mo.'

Honey watched him weave around the tables, nodding good naturedly if anyone caught his eye but avoiding conversation where possible. He wasn't what you'd call a chatty man.

Gathering the crockery, Honey headed into the kitchen and called out her grandad's order to Gospel who was busy with the last of the lunchtime prep.

'Is it for Ernie?' Gospel smiled as he spoke, in fact, Honey often thought her good friend and colleague never stopped spreading his own brand of happiness. There was even a hint of happy in his voice where the lilt of the Caribbean was slowly being twisted by the vowels of northern England.

'Yes, so a big portion and same with the pudding, or you'll be in trouble.' As Honey turned she heard Gospel chuckle, a deep throaty sound that she'd come to love.

Taking up her position at the counter, front of house being her favourite place, she thought of her dear aunty who she'd miss. Another hole in Honey's life that would be hard to fill.

She'd only been back to the house once, days after Beryl's 'good death' as Ernie had put it. Tucked up in bed with a Mills & Boon, half a mug of cocoa and three shortbread biscuits, she'd taken a bite out of one, then nodded off and slipped away.

It had freaked Honey out, being in Aunty Beryl's spick-and-span terraced home. It just wasn't the same without her there. The usually polished surfaces were dusty. The bright flowery furnishings – even her pale pink velour armchair – looked dull, saggy, and sad. The horse and cart in the print above the mantelpiece seemed to be even more stuck in the river, like they'd given up the ghost. And when the carriage clock below chimed the hour, instead of saying *time for tea*, Honey heard it say, *time to say goodbye*. The house had dimmed, as though Beryl had turned down the lights before she left.

Honey knew there and then she would never go back. Not if she could help it.

Growing up, Honey had spent a lot of time at her Aunty Beryl's. It had been a warm and cosy environment away from her own home. There, the atmosphere had, more often than not, been cold and tumultuous.

Aunty Beryl was the matriarch of the McCarthy family, an indomitable force who, in the absence of an errant husband, put everyone else first. She glued them all together. To Honey, her aunt was storybook perfect. She stepped in when things were bad at home, and when her mum had to work, and her dad was having 'trouble coping.'

School holidays were spent at Aunty Beryl's. Sleepovers, baking and sewing, taking picnics to the park and coach trips to the coast. Southport, Cleveleys, and St Annes. Honey was always the youngest on the trip by about fifty years, but she never minded. Had she not gone along, Beryl would have been without a partner, and that would've made Honey sad. She knew what that felt like: being the girl on the school trip who was looking out of the window and ignoring the empty seat by her side.

Seeing her grandad on approach, she heeded the call from Gospel saying Ernie's lunch was ready. By the time Honey had nipped into the kitchen and delivered a plate of steaming shepherd's pie to his table, her grandad was seated and unfolding his cutlery from the paper napkin.

'Here you go, Grandad, enjoy.' The look of pleasure on his face as he examined his lunch filled Honey's heart. 'I'll have to get on, so I'll leave you to eat in peace. Give me a shout if you need anything, okay?'

Ernie gave her a nod and was about to tuck in when he looked up, an expression of remembering something important caused Honey to stall. 'I meant to say, there's a box, for you, in my car.' Having spoken, Ernie got on with eating while Honey was left curious.

'What do you mean, a box? Who from?'

A swallow, a loud tut, then Ernie answered. 'Mrs Taylor found it in the spare bedroom. In the wardrobe. All taped up. Got a big sticker on it saying it's for you. It's in the boot. Looks like our Beryl saved some bits and bobs just for you. I'll put it in your car before I go.'

Honey wasn't shocked exactly, more touched that her aunty had taken the time to put things aside for her. Swallowing down the big lump that was obstructing her throat, and the threat of tears, she managed a wobble of her head before turning. Heading to the counter, her place of safety, Honey stood behind her barricade, waiting for the heat in her cheeks to subside.

And if she'd wanted to ponder on the contents of her

bequests, the dingle of the doorbell, and the arrival of Lizzy in a flap, followed by two customers, put paid to that. There would be time later. And then all would be revealed.

CHAPTER 3

LEVI

*N**ever again. Bloody never again.* That's what Levi told himself as he bashed open the pub door. He bashed it so hard that the heel of his hand throbbed as he marched across the almost-deserted hilltop carpark, yanked open his car door and as soon as his bottom hit the seat, slammed it shut.

Bloody well never again, bloody well ever!

God, he was so angry. And humiliated. What a prize pillock he was. Being lured – yes *lured* – to the back of bloody beyond to meet a woman who, if truth be told, he wasn't even that interested in. She wasn't even his type! Not in the flesh. On her photos she'd looked pretty, in a groomed and understated way. Long dark hair, minimal make-up, nice smile, some kind of flowery blouse.

When Wendy walked in, he didn't even recognise her. It was only when she tottered over to the table, giving him a 'who cares about personal space when we've spoken three times online' too-long-hug, that he realised yep, this is your date.

Jesus. He'd seen more subtle face contouring on the drag queens in the gay village in Manchester. And those lashes. And what the hell was wrong with her lips? It looked like she was permanently blowing him a kiss.

'My mate Steph just dropped me off. Been staying with her for a bit just down the road. In Marple. I'm between digs so it made sense to meet here. Now, shall we get the drinks in? My treat. What are you having?'

Levi had managed to mutter, 'Coke please,' then she was off up to the bar leaving him in shock.

He knew it was a mistake right there and then. He was the one that should've legged it but no, once again, soft lad was far too polite. Which was *precisely* why he'd been pestered into the date with that... that prosecco-guzzling lush who, after scoffing a three-course meal, and draining her glass, had excused herself and buggered off to the ladies. And never came back.

Why hadn't he realised what she was doing?

'Just texting my friend to say it's going great. It's what we do, you know, when we're on a date. Better safe than sorry. Not that I go on lots of dates, mind you. I'm very choosy, me.'

Levi should've known she was texting her friend, telling her to order a cab. And then Wendy (was that even really her name?) had the nerve, the bare faced cheek, to order a vodka and coke, presumably while she waited for her ride home to arrive. He remembered the ding, not fifteen minutes later, and Wendy looking at the screen and smiling. 'Ah, bless her. She says to say hi and hopes we're having a great time and she gets to meet you very soon.'

Yeah, right. More likely it was the Uber saying they were outside. He'd felt such a fool, sitting there waiting. Trying to be gentlemanly and not wondering if Wendy was doing a number two, and how they'd gloss over how long she'd been when she came back.

In the end, he'd asked the barmaid if she'd go and check on Wendy, just in case she wasn't well. For all he knew she might have been chucking up her garlic king prawn starter, her fillet steak and triple-cooked chips main, with an extra side of onion rings and her double-choc brownie and Cornish ice cream dessert!

Levi wasn't sure who looked more embarrassed. The barmaid or him. It was bad enough when she approached the table to say the toilets were empty, but when he had to pay the bill, she couldn't even meet his eye. Not that he'd wanted to because he could feel her pity-rays from where he sat, as she held the machine and the ping of his contactless payment chimed out, *loser*.

In the relative shame-free zone of his car, Levi rested his head and closed his eyes, taking deep breaths in the hope it would calm his smouldering temper.

He was usually a mild-tempered man, prided himself on it in fact, but some things just did his head in. Like customers being rude to staff in any situation. Litterbugs. Freeloaders called Wendy.

In testing situations, Levi's default was a tip he'd learned from listening to a radio interview with a motivational therapist. The woman had advised that in every negative you had to find a positive.

Like that morning when he'd run out of his favourite coffee and instead of it ruining his day, he'd said, 'But on the upside, I have my emergency bag of sachets I've collected from all the motel rooms I've stayed in this year. Waste not want not.'

It was all going great until he opened the fridge and the milk had gone off.

Not giving in to the thought that someone was trying to tell him something, or that he should've stayed in bed, Levi attempted some positive thinking.

So the date was an utter disaster, and his debit card had taken a bashing. But at least the pub had been empty and the two early birds in the corner left before Wendy did. The fish pie had been very good, one of the best he'd had in a while actually. And, during his wait, he'd read all the posters on the noticeboard and one of them was advertising a car-boot sale the following month. Levi liked a rummage. And... and... nope. That was it. No more positives.

Tutting, Levi decided nothing was to be gained from sitting in the car park of the aptly named Lost Stag, trying to conjure positives from a shitty Wednesday, stuck in the middle of bloody nowhere. Inserting the key in the ignition, he started the car and as he did, one more positive popped up.

That if this experience was anything to go by, never mind all the other useless dates he'd wasted his time on, he might as well ditch his dating app and resign himself to the inevitable. Being undatable. And at least he'd save some money.

Without further thought, Levi took out his phone and jabbed the app and after less than thirty seconds of navigating the site, had deleted his profile and cancelled his subscription. 'Bye-bye Wendy. Bye-bye pub on the hills. Bye-bye Levi the loser.'

Feeling proactive, he started the engine and decided to take the thirteen-mile scenic route back into the city. It was his week off and he had plenty of time on his hands. So, he'd wasted one day, but there were four more to enjoy before he went back to work and nothing was going to put a dampener on his well-earned break.

At the car park exit, seeing the sign for Marple to the right, Levi shuddered. No way was he going anywhere near Wendy-Ville. In the opposite direction was Valley Mills. It was a small, canal-side industrial town he'd heard of but never visited. Levi indicated left and headed there.

CHAPTER 4

Ignoring the hoots from the van driver behind him, Levi had just about managed to steer his limping, almost powerless car into the side of the road and after a juddering, spluttering last-ditch surge, it gave up the ghost and conked out.

Resting his head on the steering wheel Levi groaned, 'You have *got* to be kidding me. Here, right now, seriously?'

Looking up, he knew there was nothing for it and that someone somewhere really did have it in for him. So once again, he pulled out his phone. Scrolling, he found the number of the breakdown service and took his place in a virtual queue.

Forty-five very long minutes later, Levi knew he was in for another wait. Two hours approximately, the lady on the other end advised. Been a busy day, she'd said.

Puffing out his cheeks, he disconnected and with nothing else to do, took in his surroundings. On his journey along the meandering peak roads, Levi had become familiar with the sandstone mill cottages that dotted the route and the hillside, and the Victorian mills that nestled in the valley below.

He was parked slap bang in the centre of the high street and the shops that lined either side were a higgledy-piggledy mismatched row of sturdy retailers and later additions. One in particular caught his eye. Honey's Place. The exterior wood of the double-fronted café was painted sage green, the door a contrasting deep cream and hung in the upper glass pane, a sign. *Welcome.*

The little bell that tinkled above his head caused the woman wiping down a table to turn and smile, then wave her hand, indicating nowhere in particular, 'Hello flower, 'fraid there's only me on at the mo. I'll come over and take your order when I've done this. Find yourself a seat and I'll be with you in a tick.' Her voice had a Derbyshire twang, and her name badge told him her name was Lizzy.

There were only two tables taken and the far side of the café was empty, so Levi chose a spot by the window on a comfy sofa. From there, he could keep an eye on his car and spot the breakdown van when it arrived. His attention was then drawn to the rest of the café which had a quirky vibe. Colourful prints and furniture added to the ambience of what he imagined to be a popular venue in the town.

Lizzy was on her way back, tiny order pad in hand. 'So, flower. What can I do you for? We have specials on the board over there… I can recommend the lasagne. Only one portion left, it's a big slice, as well.'

Levi immediately double-regretted his fateful lunch because he only wanted coffee but maybe… 'Is it okay to just order a latte and a pastry? I noticed you had some on the counter.'

If Lizzy was disappointed at not offloading her last portion of lasagne she didn't show it. ''Course it is flower. We have…'

Levi, his conscience somewhat appeased, interrupted. 'You choose. Surprise me.'

Lizzy sucked in air. Her ample bosom that escaped from either side of her tabard rose, as though the responsibility of choosing a customer's pastry wasn't something she took lightly. 'Okey-dokey. I saw a nice big lad hiding at the bottom, so I'll fetch you that. You look like you need fattening up. Leave it with me, flower. I'll be right back.'

As he watched her weave around the rest of the seating on the way to the counter, Levi smiled. Lizzy had a twinkle in her blue eyes, and a messy blonde top knot that jiggled when she spoke like it was in on the conversation. She also had a bounce in her step, and an eagerness to please that told him she was someone who enjoyed their job. He liked people like that.

Returning his gaze to the window, Levi became lost for a few moments, his attention on the street outside. People watching: one of his favourite pastimes. Hearing footsteps and the clink of crockery, he dragged his eyes away and expected the return of Lizzy, only to be met by, *oh!*

Instead of the cheery blonde and bouncy waitress, before him stood well, for want a better word or phrase, a flame-haired goddess. Levi was struck dumb.

'Hi, your order. Sorry, Lizzy had to take a call; her son's school; bit of an emergency. Here you go. Latte and what looks like a mutant pain au chocolat!'

Levi watched as she placed his drink and pastry on the table, noticing that a sandwich and mug of tea remained on the tray. He had the incredible urge not to let her go, but how? Keep her talking...

'I hope it's not serious, with Lizzy's son.' That was the best he could do.

The goddess rolled her eyes and laughed. 'Oh no, just Tommy being Tommy. He got his head stuck in the school railings *again*, on account of his ears, you see. He's having them pinned back soon but according to the headmaster, Tommy likes making the other kids laugh but it's getting beyond a joke now. They had to buy a tub of Vaseline specially for him, so the dinner ladies can rub it on his ears and get him out.'

'Oh, I see.' Levi was fascinated by her and the image of a boy with big ears having Vaseline massaged into them, then being yanked out from between the railings.

The goddess continued. 'Anyway, the headmaster wanted a word with Lizzy about it. Apparently the dinner ladies have got better things to do. I only heard half a conversation, but I got the drift. Right, I'd best leave you in peace.' She made a half turn then, stopped. Levi almost cheered.

'I've not seen you in here before, have I? We've got a loyalty card, just so you know. You collect stars and when you've got twenty you get a free drink. You should pick one up on the way out, that's if you're planning on coming again.'

Speak, man. Speak!

Finally… 'No, I've not been here before. My car broke down. It's parked just there and I'm waiting for the breakdown van… they said it could be a couple of hours and it's chilly out there. I hope you don't mind me lingering in here. I promise to buy lots of drinks in the meantime.'

At this, the goddess plopped her tray onto the coffee table between the sofas and peered out of the window. 'Oh what a pain. Which one is it?'

'The black Golf, with the dint in the door. Not my fault I might add.' *Why did you say that? Like she cares. You big sad dork.*

The goddess took a moment, appearing to be in no hurry, and in the meantime Levi took her in.

The rays silver from the autumn sun, which hovered above the buildings opposite, lit her hair. Golden streaks against the softest auburn, like honey running through treacle, the red kind you got on toffee apples at bonfire night. Shoulder-blade length and tied back with a blue scarf. She was tall but not taller than he. And this made him feel ridiculously pleased, and somewhat previous. He also noticed that where her white T-shirt stopped, her long arms were scattered with pale freckles, and she wore dark blue skinny jeans that made her legs go on forever, and on her feet, mad rainbow striped socks and pink Crocs.

Finally she turned from the window and rested her gaze, hazel eyes focused on Levi who was acting like a gormless rabbit, totally entranced. But he couldn't help it.

'Well you're welcome to stay as long as you like. The midday service is over and we're usually quiet for a while, that's why I'm having my lunch now, while I can. Best leave you in peace, though, while you keep lookout. I've kept you long enough.'

When she bent to collect her tray, the goddess looked a bit startled when Levi's next words burst forth. 'No, it's fine. You're welcome to join me here... but if you don't want...' He looked around and cringed, seeing half a café full of empty sofas and tables, the heat in his cheeks a portent of impending embarrassment. Levi expected her to decline.

'Oh, really? Thank you. That's very kind. This is my favourite spot. My people-watching post.' With that the goddess plonked herself down opposite Levi and took a bite of her sandwich, then said, 'So, tell me what brings you to Valley Mills on this Wednesday afternoon? House hunting I expect. You're dressed too smart to be off hiking. And don't let your coffee go cold... drink up.'

Doing exactly as he was told, Levi picked up his mug and as he sipped, silently thanked the god of Match for sending him on a date to be rinsed by greedy Wendy. To the god of knackered old engines for making the one in his car conk out. And while he was at it, he asked the god of breakdown vans to make sure the one on its way to him took a very, very long time.

CHAPTER 5

ERNIE

Instead of going home, Ernie had taken refuge in his shed. Situated in the furthest corner of the allotment, it afforded him the privacy he required on what had been a bugger of a day. On arrival he'd kept his head down while he made his way along the path, not wanting to pass the time of day with his fellow gardeners. And unusually, he didn't want to work the land. Ernie simply didn't have it in him.

He just wanted to be.

Huddling into his armchair, left by the previous occupant most likely out of laziness more than kindness, Ernie pulled the old army blanket over his body. The leather that wrapped around his bony limbs was worn, threadbare in places. Over the years the stuffing had moulded to his shape, so comfy that many a time he'd nodded off and woken in the pitch black, stiff and hungry.

Hoping those fellow gardeners he'd nodded to earlier would take a hint and give him space, Ernie had chanced leaving the door ajar, allowing him to look onto the rows of vegetables that lined his precious allotment. This was his patch of happiness, and nothing gave him more pleasure than seeing the rewards of honest hard work.

Getting his lily-white hands dirty had always given him a perverse kick, be it tending the flowerbeds in his garden at home or pulling up weeds amongst his vegetables.

He knew it was ridiculous and contrary. Belligerent perhaps. After all, had he been given the freedom to choose his own path, would his unblemished hands look any different? Unlikely.

So was it fair to hold on to the bitterness he felt towards his mother and "owt for a quiet life' father? Yes, Ernie thought it was.

Okay, so Ernest Walter McCarthy was from working-class stock and would have gone down the pit, if that were his only option. And truth be told, he'd have preferred a profession that didn't entail a day of hard manual labour and getting muck under his nails. But he got on with it because he had to earn a living, just like his dad. Yet despite this, he'd always resented having his life steered and his options taken away. But in those days, the fifties, you did as your parents told you. Well he did, anyway.

And deep at the root of his long-held grudge was the fact that he resented himself, too. For not standing up to his parents or having the strength of personality to find a way to be who he wanted to be. The man he could have been. That was the real crux of the matter. The sense of failing oneself.

Ernie shivered: his feet were cold. Perhaps he should rest them on the stool but he couldn't be bothered to move. He wasn't dressed for the allotment but the lure of solitude, the four walls of his shed and the scent of earth and tomato fertiliser, were more tempting than an empty house. Again, he was being a contrary Mary.

Ernie didn't mind living alone and it was preferable to spending the rest of his days in sheltered housing or a care home. He prided his independence and guarded the luxury of being in control of his life, his mind, his meals, the telly.

Regardless of those positives, there was no denying that his bungalow seemed too big, now that Nancy was gone. And it was a shame because their three-bedroomed chunk of middle-class utopia had suited them well. A lawn to mow on Sundays, a conservatory to keep up with that snooty lot next door. A fancy drive that cost a sodding bomb and was basically concrete stamped with a pattern. It had made Nancy happy though, and that was all he'd cared about.

But nowadays, her beloved fitted kitchen – with the posh blinds she'd had specially made – didn't hum with activity and the waft of something cooking. The oven was never lit and instead the microwave pinged a lot. The kitchen echoed his footsteps, the click of the kettle, the clank of spoon against mug. The sound of loss and solitude boomed in his ears.

The lounge that Nancy dusted every day had become a Tardis where he sat alone in his recliner. The sofa and Nancy's wingback armchair openly mocked him when he looked, expecting her to be there, and she was not.

The bedroom – well, that was the worst. The chamber of thoughts. A cell decorated in florals. A summer meadow of memories. Hour upon hour of them. Even the bathroom with all Nancy's bits and bobs scattered around came second to that hell-hole.

Whereas there, in his creosoted shed, Ernie seemed to fit. Just enough room to make a brew or warm a tin of spaghetti on the camping stove. In winter he'd get the paraffin heater going and in summer, well he could happily stay there all night watching the sun set and rise over the treetops.

Come to think of it, he needed a brew, something to heat his insides, but he couldn't be bothered. Looking over to his shelf, Ernie managed a smile when he saw the row of caddies that contained tea, coffee, and sugar and next to them the biscuit tin. They were always full. Refreshed and re-loaded by Beryl who'd wander up once a week bringing slices of cake she'd made. Mince pies in the winter.

Ernie closed his eyes, just for a minute, and imagined he was waiting for her to arrive. It eased the ache in his heart. Beryl might have been his younger sister by nine years, but somewhere along the way their roles reversed. She became his guardian angel, the person he was closest to in the world before Nancy came along.

Beryl was the peacekeeper, the mender of bridges, the soother of hurt feelings and the one person who understood Ernie.

Then when her marriage broke down, and after their mum had passed, there was another shift in their brother–sister relationship. A kind of equilibrium. It was Ernie's turn to look after Beryl. Take care of the stuff she couldn't, like repairs to her house, running her about if she needed to go further afield. She'd never had the confidence to learn to drive, thanks to their mother who'd said it was a man's job and anyway Beryl only worked five minutes from home so what did she need a car for? Typical.

With Mother gone, their sibling bond grew stronger, and Beryl seemed to relax. The tension she'd always carried around Mother eased, and she seemed to enjoy life a little more.

She would come for tea one night a week with him and Nancy, who saw Beryl as a friend, not just a sister-in-law. They'd all holidayed together, too, so she wouldn't have to travel on her own. Beryl was there the night Nancy went. Keeping vigil. Holding her hand on the other side of the bed to him, and then right by his side at the funeral. He thought losing his wife was bad but now his sister... it was too much.

Keeping his eyes closed, Ernie listened to the voices drifting on woodsmoke from further down the allotment. His body relaxed and his head lolled as he allowed sleep to sweep him away, memories of Nancy and Beryl cushioning his head and his heart.

CHAPTER 6

'Ｗhat're you doing, sleepyhead? You'll get nowt done nodding off. I thought I'd pop by with this banana loaf and a nice packet of Garibaldis. Shall I pop the kettle on?'

Ernie roused and his heart lifted when he saw Beryl at the door of the shed, a wicker basket on her hip and a smile on her face.

'Sorry lass. I was having forty winks. Here, you take the chair and I'll have the stool. Flick the kettle on and I'll make us a brew.'

'You'll do no such thing. Stay where you are. I'm a woman so I can multi-task. Anyway I've brought us a thermos of cocoa so I only have to pour it out, then we can have a nice natter. It's getting nippy and me knees are aching so you can run me back home later. How's that for a deal?'

Beryl set about unloading her basket while Ernie, knowing not to argue, did as he was told.

Minutes later Beryl was settled by his side on the low wooden stool, sipping her drink and gazing round the shed. 'I hope you're not going to be a hermit in here, our Ernie. I don't want you moping about and being an awkward bugger now I'm not around to give you a kick up the bum.'

'I'm fine Beryl. And I'm not hiding, just came here to think, I s'pose. Can't get used to it... you know... not having you to talk to.' Ernie took a bite of his cake and swallowed the soft sponge, along with a lump that had formed in his throat.

'Then talk to Honey. And stop making out that you're doing fine when you're not. She can't help you if you don't tell her how you feel, and perhaps she's hurting too but trying to be brave for you. She's a good lass and only wants to help. You and every other bugger in the Valley.' Beryl gave him a smile, then held out the packet of Garibaldis.

Ernie shook his head, 'You trying to fatten me up? I know Honey is. Should've seen the portion of shepherd's pie she gave me at the caff. And you're right, she is missing you. I can see it in her eyes when I mention your name. But we both have to be strong. Me more than her. She's lost her dad and her gran and that flighty mother of hers is useless so I'm it. I'm all she has, and I can't let her down.'

Beryl nodded. 'That's as may be. But it does you no good bottling things up and you'll only get yourself into a state. Share the load, Ernie, that's all I'm saying.'

She was right. Beryl always was. She knew him too well because Ernie didn't know when to let things go. He'd spent a lifetime battling with his mother over stupid things. Her cloying ways, needy at times. Her possessiveness that suffocated him in his teenage years when he started to spread his wings.

Ernie had resented her stupid rules, too. Her obsession with privacy and mistrust of everyone she met. She'd even been cold with Nancy and suspicious of her and her family. It was as though Mother wanted to keep Ernie all for herself, and he often felt bad for Beryl who, despite being a good daughter, always came second to him.

Sometimes, Ernie really did believe his mother used to be a spy. Either that or she had serious issues, mental or otherwise. He didn't care to dwell on what they could be.

'Penny for them.' Beryl was folding the greaseproof paper that had wrapped the cake. She was from the era where nothing went to waste.

'I was just thinking about Mother, and how you always used to smooth things over. Remember when I got engaged to Nancy and her parents put an announcement in the *Manchester Evening News*? Mother went mad. Saying they should've asked her first. There was always something to complain about, wasn't there?'

Beryl just nodded and busied herself with the biscuit tin.

'You sorted it all out by saying she could do one for the wedding and would mention it to Nancy's parents. And after all the fuss she made, Mother never even bloody bothered!' Ernie finished with a jerk of his head and loud tut.

'Well, there's no point getting all het up about it now, and time's getting on. When you've finished your cocoa, how about we take a wander round your veggie patch and then you can take me home.' Beryl screwed the lid on the thermos then began arranging things in her basket.

'Okey-dokey. My pumpkins are coming on a treat. Wait till you see the beets. I've got a bumper crop this year of root veggies. I reckon our Honey and Gospel won't know what to do with it all.' Ernie drained his mug and passed it to his sister. 'And thanks for coming to see me, Beryl, it's been a tonic, it really has.'

The smoke from the bonfire one allotment over was wafting closer and infiltrating the shed, swirling around Beryl, making it hard to see her. He could still hear her voice though.

'Well you mind what I said, or I'll not bother coming back. And make sure you go and see our Honey more often. No squirreling yourself away in here. Now get up lazy bones, I need to go.'

Ernie started. Opening bleary eyes he looked around the shed for Beryl. She was nowhere to be seen. He realised immediately, as sadness overwhelmed him, followed very quickly by something else: love. A warm swell of it washed over him.

Okay, so it hadn't been real, but he'd enjoyed chatting to Beryl, if only in his memories and dreams, and perhaps his sister had a point. It was time to go home.

CHAPTER 7

CLARISSA

Leaning heavily on her walking stick, Clarissa tentatively made her way towards the top of the stairs. Taking hold of the brass banister she caught her breath, and then gingerly lowered herself onto the waiting seat, grateful to have the weight of her birdlike body lifted.

Forty-five steps. That's how far it was from her bedroom chair to the top of the landing. Eleven from the bed to the chair. Sixteen from her ensuite bathroom to her bed. Clarissa had counted each excruciating one of those steps. Being able to make them symbolised the last vestiges of her self-respect and mobility.

She'd hated the stairlift at first. An abominable contraption that the mere mention of left her feeling humbled and humiliated. Neither emotion came naturally to her. It wasn't in her blood.

However, despite the rest of her body being incapable of obeying her commands, her mind was still firing on all cylinders. Hence, she had begrudgingly reasoned that the 'contraption' would enable her to move freely around her beloved home.

Otherwise she'd end up with one of those up-and-down hospital beds in the lounge. But she needed to go upstairs so she could visit her dear sister.

Footsteps on the parquet flooring drew her attention to Jennifer, her kind and attentive aide and confidante who took up her post by Clarissa's side. 'Righty-ho. I'll meet you at the bottom. It's kippers for breakfast, your favourite. See you in a mo.'

'Thank you dear. I'll race you to the bottom shall I? First one gets extra brekkie.' Clarissa produced her best cheery smile for Jennifer who seemed to relish their morning banter or indeed any sign that her patient was in good spirits. Clarissa's fakery was a small price to pay if it made her smile.

With the push of a button, Clarissa began her undignified descent, banishing memories of the times she'd raced down the stairs, fleet of foot, to meet whichever eligible chap her mother had roped in to take her dancing. The thought made her cringe.

Gripping her walking stick, tilting her chin, she commenced the second phase of her daily routine and as she glided by, said a polite 'good morning' to each of her ancestors.

The old guard in the gilt frames were complete strangers, connected only by genetics; but in some there was definitely a hint of resemblance to relatives she'd actually met. Her uncle's almost imperceivable sneer. Her father's eyes, brooding and black. Or her fierce grandpapa, his eyebrows bushy and grey.

While the staircase was lined with portraits of those one could, without guilt or remorse, choose to acknowledge or ignore, the remainder of the house was thankfully filled with faces that spoke of happy times.

Bygone eras. Links to her past. No images of love – for there had only ever been one, forbidden and gone forever. Definitely her losses.

Clarissa could, if the mood took her, reach out and touch the faces of those captured in black and white, in time immemorial. And instantly, those days, those people, the feel of their skin, how she loved some of them despite their faults, others not so much. It all came flooding back.

Fanciful, yes. Clarissa knew this. Being compos mentis had its drawbacks and even she couldn't deny there had been bad times. Drown out her mother's tears; smother her father's anger; and her uncle… well, she certainly didn't want to think about him. Not today or ever.

Chamberlain Manor, Clarissa's home for ninety-one years, had seen such happy times, yet, as with all families, they'd had their share of bad times, too. Things never spoken of, swept under the Persian rug in the dining room.

Thinking of which, she had landed, and now all she had to do was force her knees and spine to do her bidding and make it to breakfast. When did standing upright become such a chore? Clarissa pondered this often. And why did she insist on making the fifty-four steps to the dining room table that would be set for two? A tray on her knee in the drawing room would do.

She was hanging on, that's why.

As if by magic, Jennifer appeared and her timely arrivals often reminded Clarissa of a cartoon, one she'd watched with Timmy, the old Cookie's grandson. Now what was it called? Where a jolly chap went into a male outfitter, or was it a fancy dress shop and poof, the owner would appear and send the unsuspecting man off on a wonderful adventure.

'And what, may I ask, is amusing you this morning? You look positively chipper. Have you been pulling faces at those portraits again?' Jennifer held out her arm, and as always it was Clarissa's decision to accept it, or not. Today was a not.

'It's nothing dear… it'll come back to me, I expect. Now, breakfast. Do we have eggs as well as kippers? Or is Cookie Beattie being a meanie? I quite fancy an eggy soldier.' All of their many cooks were referred to as Cookie with their name tagged on. It was a Chamberlain tradition.

'You're in luck; she's in a good mood and we have both.'

'Excellent. Now you scoot ahead and pour me some tea. I'm parched.' Clarissa preferred not to have an escort as she shuffled along, but admitted it was comforting to know Jennifer was there, within reach day and night.

And it was the nights that were becoming the hardest. Interminable hours between saying goodnight to her loyal aide, and hearing the doorknob turn at 7am on the dot. They stretched endlessly.

'Tea's up.' Jennifer's cheery way made even a cup of Darjeeling seem like a treat, so after taking the last four steps, Clarissa lowered herself into her seat by the fire, and smiled.

Clarissa had many negative attributes, obstinacy being quite near the top of the list, but being churlish towards those who worked under her roof had never been one of them.

Those days were long gone, when the Chamberlains – her father and uncle in particular – looked down on others. An entitled class who meddled, and set standards and their own rules, wreaking havoc, causing great distress, all in a vain endeavour to uphold their name and – at all costs – avoid a scandal, making sure their dirty little secrets remained a family affair.

The day had crawled by as the clock struck two and soon the autumn evening would start to draw in. There was a chill in the air and before they knew it the vast rooms would become a challenge to heat. But Clarissa was used to it. Nothing a shawl and a few layers couldn't solve.

Jennifer had settled Clarissa by the fire in the parlour while she'd headed into Chester to do some shopping. Wool and books: the lifeblood of her dear aide. And horses. Jennifer adored them as much as Clarissa did.

From where she sat in her armchair, she could see the fields that surrounded the house, bathed in early afternoon sunshine, white and bright with a hint of gold.

How she longed to go outside and hike across the Cheshire plain, or ride Spirit just one more time, taking hedgerows at a gallop, his hooves pounding the dark earth.

Spirit was long gone. Grazing in a field somewhere over the rainbow. Thoroughbreds didn't live for ever, but for the time he had been part of her life, he'd been her soulmate. He'd taken the place of the human, listened to her woes as they hacked for miles in the rain and kept her head above water during the darkest of days. But it had been touch-and-go, almost losing her precious Spirit to the will of her father.

She had never been prone to tears or tantrums, yet on the day her father told her he was going to sell her beloved gelding, Clarissa thought her heart would break. But there was a deal to be done; the trade-off was one love for another. Shame versus living in the shadows, family loyalty, the unbearable tears of her mother, loving someone enough to let them go, being brave enough to do the right thing, making the hardest choice of all.

Never since had she felt panic and grief like it. Then relief, followed by hate tempered by anger. Both she wore like a badge of honour. Never letting go.

Not wanting to linger there, she had enough on her mind as it was, Clarissa rearranged the blanket over her knees and fidgeted until she was comfortable. On the footstool below, her feet were warming nicely, and the fact she could still feel them brought a hint of comfort, or was it irony.

Clarissa knew that time was running out. There was nothing she could do about it. She wasn't getting any younger. It was just a pity that the doctor, when asked, hadn't been able to give her a timescale, some indication of when she'd be checking out. Didn't he know she had things to do? Decisions to make.

Loose ends. Clarissa hated them. In particular, the overwhelming responsibility of what to do about Chamberlain Manor. It had been in her family for 300 years and its future rested on her shoulders. Apart from some tenuously linked third cousin twice removed, or something like that, she was last in line. The female heir with an uninspiring legacy. A life utterly wasted, with no way to turn back the clock and put things right.

But worse than that, the thing keeping her awake at night, gnawing away like a mouse behind the skirting boards, were the unanswered questions. And those gave rise to a terrible sense of unease that something wasn't right. Thoughts she'd buried for years, suffocating her instincts like her parents had suffocated the woman Clarissa wanted to be. Who she really was.

She dreaded the night. In the darkness of her room. The velvet drapes pulled close, the sounds of the countryside and life beyond the squares of glass kept at bay. Along with her breathing, a very comforting sound, there was something else.

Strains of a heated conversation, overheard by nine-year-old ears; questions batted away by her mother, just before she was unexpectedly batted away to school.

There, each time she played rounders, the thud of the ball against the bat seemed like another punch in the gut. *Keep running Clarissa. One more time around the pitch, old girl, and you'll soon forget.*

Later, more cruel words that her adult ears would never forget and would understand completely. Hurled her way. Hitting home like a cricket ball to the face. Designed to cause deep shame, strengthened by the fear of the unknown and the threat of being cast out.

Keep running, Clarissa. Do as you're told. Deny your heart and you'll soon forget.

Somewhere in between fact and faded memories, Clarissa feared there was a truth. Swirling in a grey mist, was a murky family myth. Protected by stiff – or stitched-up – lips. Fuelled by a class system and a belligerence honed by a generation. All in the guise of post-war stoicism.

What if her parents had done something really bad, and then buried their secret forever? It was driving her quite literally mad.

CHAPTER 8

The slam of the front door, the shrill ring of the phone in the grand foyer, followed by the clip-clopping of Jennifer's 'nice town shoes', as she called them, applied the brakes to Clarissa's train of thought.

Inclining her head in order to hear better, she listened to the one-sided mumblings of a conversation. Clarissa owned a mobile phone but rarely used it. Her friends, those who were still relatively able bodied, were like her. Talkers not texters. If they wanted to chat, they rang her mobile or called in for tea unannounced.

You didn't need an appointment to be a friend. You just were. Anyone else used the landline number which told Clarissa that it was either the land agent, the solicitor or one of those annoying people selling annoying things. Jennifer would see to it.

Not that Clarissa didn't mind dealing personally with the staff who came and went. The nice ladies who came in the little white van that had pink bubbles painted on the side were a hoot. They always brought a bit of life to the house, with their chatter and humming and hoovering. She took tea with them once they'd finished their twice-weekly cleaning and made sure they had a bit extra in their wages at Christmas, and a hamper from the farm shop, too.

Matheson, the land agent and general estate manager, was very diligent, and she looked forward to their monthly meetings where he kept her abreast of estate matters. The tenant farmers and cottage dwellers weren't any trouble and he and his team managed the swathe of acres around the house very nicely. Tidy hedges and well-maintained stone walls gave her an immense sense of pride, and she admired the craftmanship of those who tended them.

Clarissa suspected that Matheson came just to keep up with tradition, or out of respect. Or maybe he was indulging a batty old lady who lived in the big house, and in the past. It was very kind, though, and much appreciated.

What a contrary Mary you are, Clarissa Chamberlain.

It was true. She was. One minute she railed against the injustices meted out by her parents, and the next, she was lost in times gone by, hankering after her carefree childhood.

She was often absorbed by the images of her teenage self: lithe and lovely, courted by the sons of the Cheshire elite, because that was what you did back then, what was expected. She knew no different. Not until she went away to Switzerland, where her life changed forever in the time it took to take the ski lift to the top of the run, and down again, racing to the bottom with the love of her life by her side.

And then the light always faded and the shine of being a Chamberlain wore off.

The door of the drawing room opening restored brightness to Clarissa's day as Jennifer breezed in, her face aglow with excitement.

'Oh, Clarissa, you'll never guess.'

Clarissa played along. 'I probably won't unless you tell me, so sit. Spill the beans. I could do with some excitement.'

Jennifer sat, unwinding her scarf and unbuttoning her coat as she spoke. 'Well, it was your solicitor, the old Mr Henderson, not *him*, the young one.' Jennifer, for no other reason than his eyes were too close together and he wore far too much aftershave, had never taken to Tristan Jnr, 'the young one'. Anyway, he wanted to speak to you, but I said I'd pass on a message.'

'And the message was?' It sometimes took a while with Jennifer.

Jennifer swirled her scarf into a coil as she spoke. 'Well the old grump wasn't going to tell me at first. Said it was a matter for you. So I reminded him that I *am* your personal confidante and that you were having a nap.'

'I was wide awake!'

A roll of the eyes. 'Well I didn't know that; and anyway, did you really want to get up from your cosy warm chair to talk to grumpy pants? Could've been something totally boring for all I knew.'

'Well, no. You have a point, so continue.'

Jennifer leant forward and gave a little clap before opening the tin and spilling the beans. 'Well first off, your long-lost relative, the one the young Mr Henderson tracked down, is coming over to meet you. How exciting!'

Jennifer's expectant face left Clarissa wanting, so she pretended. With her dear aide it was often easier.

'Well, it will be interesting, I'm sure. And when does he arrive? Please tell me he's not expecting to stay here you know I'm not fond of stran–'

When Jennifer held up her hand, Clarissa came up for air.

'No, apparently Tristan has made the arrangements and will be in touch in due course to facilitate a meeting. I do wish solicitors would speak like normal people, don't you?'

On hearing this, Clarissa relaxed slightly and her shoulders slackened. 'Very good. I shall wait to hear what he has to say, hopefully in normal-person-speak. And as for the other news?' She winked at Jennifer who was raring to go again.

'Well, it seems that a local news programme want to do a piece, all about Chamberlain Manor and other grand homes in Cheshire. Turns out some rich chap – old money according to Mr Henderson – invited the PM to stay at his pile over in the Peaks. It's sparked a bit of interest in the press. There's rumours about the old school tie network doing dodgy deals and planning new transport links, so the local countryside protection league aren't happy. He says you need to call him back first thing.'

Clarissa hadn't expected that. And was there even such a thing as the local countryside protection league? Possibly not. And why had they rung the solicitors and not her directly? A question for Jennifer that was answered simply.

'Oh, apparently they contacted the estate office first – the email is listed online – and they said to direct any enquiries via Mr Henderson. I suppose they were just protecting your privacy.'

'Ah, I see.'

Jennifer, however, was eager for an answer. 'So, what do you think? I know you saw off those loony ghosthunters and you were right. Who wants some nutters wandering around with the lights off while we're tucked up in bed? But this is different. They'll show off your lovely house and… and it'll be nice, won't it, to have a record. Something to watch over and over, whenever we want.'

When Jennifer's cheeks flushed, Clarissa's heart went out to her. She knew exactly what she was getting at and maybe she was right. Perhaps it was time outsiders saw the inside of Chamberlain. Heard the story of her forbears.

Finally, Clarissa would have something to leave behind. A little snippet. Not a reel of film but the modern equivalent, a digital footprint on a memory stick. She might not be forgotten after all and her philanthropic efforts not in vain.

But there was something holding her back, those voices again, the ones that came at night and they advised caution. 'I'll give it some thought. Decide in the morning. It's a lot to take in, having strangers snoop about our home.'

At this, Clarissa saw Jennifer smile, because it was her home, too.

'Now, did Cookie Beattie leave us something nice for dinner or shall we be very naughty and ring for a takeaway? We can share a bottle of wine.'

Jennifer's eye's widened. 'Takeaway. On a Wednesday! And wine. Whatever next. Okay, I'll go and peep in the fridge then we can decide. I have a dreadful feeling I spotted her making liver and onions earlier.'

'Oh dear Lord, not liver. No matter much how much I hint Cookie insists it's good for me and I don't like to offend her when she's being kind. If you find any, chuck it in the bin. I do miss having dogs because they come in ever so handy when liver is on the menu, and kidneys. And Jennifer, bring the menus.' Not needing to be told twice, Clarissa watched as Jennifer scooted off, carrying her coat and scarf, all talk of documentaries wiped away by the threat of offal.

Clarissa had made it alone. Along the hallway, enduring the seventy-nine steps to the farthest room on the corridor.

Standing under the dim light of a flickering bulb inside a lampshade unchanged for over eighty years, Clarissa stared at the portrait of Eleonora. It hung above the fireplace that had been devoid of warmth since the day her beloved big sister left home forever.

The bedroom had become a shrine. On her mother's insistence everything inside remained as it was. Never touched. In a similar way, the day of the big fight was engraved on Clarissa's memory; the only time in her whole life that her mother stood up to her father.

Like a needle scratching a record, the screeches of Mother's hysteria had been etched into Clarissa's ten-year-old brain. Her face still went hot when she pictured the servants, as embarrassed as she by the scene, avoiding eye contact as they removed Eleonora's portrait from the wall in the drawing room. Clarissa, concealed behind the grandfather clock in the foyer, listened, eyes wide and filled with tears, to the scene being played out in the drawing room.

Father said that Mother had lost her mind and ran to the door, bellowing at the butler to call for the doctor. Then the door slammed shut and Mother had screamed at Father, saying she'd tell everyone what he'd done. Silence. Then Father stormed from the room and straight out of the front door, yelling for the groom to saddle his horse.

Mother got her way. And instead of Eleonora and all her belongings being banished to the attic, her portrait was hung in her room and Father forbidden to enter.

Clarissa took two steps closer. It was all she could manage: the pain in her hips was almost unbearable and she needed her energy for the walk back to her own room.

Eleonora would have been 102, had she lived. All those years without her. As she stared into her sister's soulful hazel eyes, not for the first time, Clarissa asked the portrait the question that played on a loop in her brain.

Clarissa's voice was barely a whisper 'What did Father do? To make you run away. Was it like what he did to me? Forbade your love? You were braver than I. But I wish you hadn't been. I wish you'd stayed. Then we could have fought them together. And you'd have lived. My beautiful big sister. Oh, how I adored you and how I cried for you when you left. I hope you know that. That you were missed.'

Clarissa was so tired and needed to lie down. But before she did, had one more message for Eleonora.

'Not long now, dear one. We will be together soon and then you can tell me your truth. And I will tell you mine.'

When she reached the light switch, Clarissa flicked it off and, without looking back, the pain of parting always raw, worse than that which riddled her bones, she closed the door, leaving Eleonora alone in the dark.

CHAPTER 9

HONEY

F air hair, cut close at the sides, which accentuated a mop of curls that flopped and flapped as he spoke. Deep brown eyes, the colour of horse chestnuts, were framed by round, tortoiseshell glasses that slowly slipped down his nose. Each time they did, he pushed them back up again.

His fingers were long. No wedding ring – praise be – and the back of his hands showed signs of a faded, sun-kissed tan. She imagined he was the type to turn golden-brown and wondered where he'd been on holiday. Honey wondered a lot of things as she took in every detail of the man seated before her.

His tan corduroy jacket went out with the ark but the fact he wore it meant he didn't care, and she liked that. It was a teeny bit worn where the collar met his neck that was cleanly shaven like his face. The dark denim shirt looked newish, buttoned to the top, and his jeans, skinny fit. She'd guess extra-long leg, thirty-four inches at least.

Finally, his watch. Manually wound, and with a battered brown leather strap, the glass of the round face slightly dulled. It was an heirloom. She just knew.

They'd made polite conversation as they ate. About the

weather and how worried he was his old car might not be fixable. Levi – such a cool name – unabashedly made short work of his mutant pastry, not self-conscious at all as the flakes fluttered onto his jacket and jeans. She watched as he flicked them into his hand and then his plate, not the floor. Very polite: she liked that too.

Eating in front of strangers was a problem for some people. Her dad had hated it, and her grandad preferred his meals in the company of his family to that of strangers. Honey didn't care a bit and wolfed down her sandwich, talking between mouthfuls about what a nightmare the street outside was if it snowed, which it often did in winter, and her cottage was on a hill and a death trap.

Honey was a chatterbox. Her capacity and desire to fill in quiet gaps had done her previous boyfriend's head in. The fact that Levi seemed comfortable was a sign. Honey was sure.

'So, why are you here, in High Peak? It's a long way to come from Manchester to get cake and coffee.' Honey took a sip of her drink. After he'd told her his name and where he lived – in the city centre, thirteen miles away – she'd reciprocated, explaining her family were from Marple, three miles away, but she'd settled in an old mill terrace on the far side of Valley Mills. A doer-upper.

At her question, Levi sat back, his body relaxed in the sofa, but his face wore a wary expression, like he was wondering what to say. 'Do you really want to know? Or more to the point, do I really want to tell you?' He stroked his chin, affected a ponderous look, and there was a hint of amusement in his eyes.

'Go on, tell me. I'm intrigued now.' Honey hoped he'd share and it was a *really* long story and also, that Gospel and Lizzy weren't getting peeved with her for not helping out in the kitchen.

'It's really embarrassing. A very sorry tale of woe so maybe we should move on and talk about you.' Both his eyebrows rose in an expectant kind of way.

'Go on, be a devil. And then you can ask me something. Anything you want.' For another coffee which will be extra hot. Or for a date. *Did she just think that?*

Levi puffed his cheeks then sat forward and grimaced, before starting his sad tale. 'I'd like to make up some random story about lord knows what, but I hate fibbers so, here goes. It all started with a dating website...'

By the time he'd finished, Honey felt incredibly sorry for Levi and at the same time, even more smitten, simply because he told her the truth. Not many people would admit to that, probably not even her.

'Oh that's awful. What a horrible thing to do. And then you broke down. But at least it happened outside here, and you could come out of the cold.' Honey looked on the bright side wherever she could and from the look on his face, Levi agreed.

'Yep, every cloud and all that. But my date from hell is history now, *and* that dating website. Have you ever used one? Or are you happily, you know, involved, so have no need.'

Honey's heart did a happy dance inside her chest. That was a first. Being glad to be single. 'Nope. Me and dating don't go very well together; and neither do the hours I work here to be honest. My last boyfriend took the high road over a year ago, literally, and moved to Edinburgh. Couldn't get away quick enough.'

'I'm sure that's not true. So, tell me about your café. How long have you been here? I love the décor; it's really chic and homely, too.'

Honey was about to answer when movement to her left distracted her. Expecting Lizzy, telling her to get her finger out and come and help with the prep, she was surprised to see her bringing over more drinks, which she placed on the table.

'There you go, chickens. Thought you might like a refill.'

Addressing her next comment to Honey she said, 'We've got everything covered out the back, so you relax. I'll watch the shop.'

And in true Mr Benn style, as if by magic, the little bell rung and three regulars entered the café, causing Lizzy to shoot off, but not before giving Honey a sly wink.

Honey turned to Levi. 'I love that woman. I don't know what I'd do without her. Right, the café, where should I start?'

CHAPTER 10

Minutes later, Honey had given a brief version of how, after her dad died, she'd used the money he'd left her to put down a deposit on her little cottage terrace and take out a lease on the café. There'd not been much left over to furnish it so she'd improvised where she could.

'What made you decide to run a café, though? Are you a trained chef?' Levi reached for his drink and waited.

'I went to college and studied hospitality. After I graduated, I realised that the corporate side wasn't for me. I don't think I'm suited to a big chain and was looking for an opportunity to change career. Just after dad died, I saw this place when I was cycling with Ziggy – she's my best friend. It was all closed up and looked really sad. By the way, I think inanimate objects have feelings and I swear this one had tears in its eyes because it had been neglected. You can join the dots after that, and ta-da. This became my history, or my future, I suppose.'

Levi sank back and took another look around. 'Well I think you've done a brilliant job and I bet your dad would be really proud of what you've achieved.'

Honey felt a familiar prick of tears that often welled

whenever she talked about her dad, and the last thing she wanted was to start blubbing in front of a virtual stranger. To fend them off she focused on the café. 'I've got loads of ideas for the place, but it's baby steps for now. We're doing okay, though. I just need to be patient.'

Levi nodded. 'Agh, the impatient type. My mum says I'm too laid back for my own good, but I bet you're the opposite. Do you open every day? You said you worked a lot of hours.'

Levi seemed genuinely interested... unless he was really a burglar, trying to work out when he could rob her chest freezer of Gospel's stash of curried goat; or a lying con-man, who'd just rinsed some rich widow in the Lost Stag and now had his sights set on a trusting, slightly lonely thirty-three-year-old who liked crocheting blankets in her spare time. Still, his curiosity made a pleasant change.

'We're open Tuesday to Saturday. Sunday is our day off, but on Monday it's open for the community – the elderly to be precise. I gave the vicar a spare key and he does the rest.'

'Really?!' Levi's eyes were wide, not a unique response. Kind of like her mum's and grandad's when she pitched her idea to them.

'Yes really. Look, you'll probably think I'm mad, but I have this theory, or maybe it's a dream and a theory, or is it an ethos? Well, anyway, I once heard an interview on the radio with a millionaire businesswoman who, as she approached retirement, decided to change her life completely.'

Honey always got fired up when she told the story, as if the spark she'd felt when she first heard it were reigniting. 'This lady worked out how much money she would need to live comfortably for the rest of her days, put that aside, and then gave the rest away. She bought a forest, and then started a charity that trains people who have struggled in society, or been in prison, in forestry skills, carpentry, stuff like that. I just thought it was so cool and it made me think about what I want from life.'

Honey took a breath while Levi stared. So she continued. 'I have my little cottage that I'll do up at my own pace. A decent wage from this place that pays my bills with a bit left over, so apart from maybe having a couple of weeks' holiday a year somewhere warm, I don't really have a big list of wants or needs. For me, it's enough. I've never wanted to be a millionaire and I don't crave fancy things; but I would like to help people if I can. Give more than I take, I suppose. My mum thinks I'm naïve and will get hurt or used, and that I should be looking after my future first. Grandad has come round a bit now he's seen phase one of my plan work, and he helps by supplying veg free of charge from his allotment. I want to do more, though.'

'I think that's amazing.'

'Really, do you?' Honey was taken aback. She didn't often get that reaction to her crazy ideas.

'Yep, totally one hundred percent, but tell me what phase one is?'

Honey was thrilled he'd asked, and that he thought she was amazing. 'Well for a start, I wanted to employ local people because so many have to leave the area and find work in the cities and bigger towns. Then, once I've paid Gospel and Lizzy, and the other overheads, I give the profit to charity and use some of it to help local people.'

Levi had sat forward, arms resting on knees, hands clasped together, totally focused on what Honey was saying.

'You know how cold it was last winter, and that people struggled to heat their homes and pay their bills?'

Levi nodded.

'I couldn't bear the thought of old people freezing and going hungry, so I had a word with the vicar who was totally on board and put the word out for volunteers. I thought that even if it was for one day, they'd have somewhere they could come and keep warm, have some toast and tea, and at lunchtime a bowl of soup and a roll. A warm hub to meet up with people if they were lonely too. Gospel makes it all in advance and the vicar's volunteers dish it up. I come in and help too, but the others have the day off.'

'And was it a success?'

Honey smiled. 'Oh yes. I had posters made and put them everywhere and contacted the community nurses, and anyone I could think of who came into contact with people that might want to come. It was a slow start at first, but gradually word spread, and we were soon full. It was such a success that we've carried on throughout the year, but then I hit a problem.'

'Oh no. What happened?'

'It wasn't a problem as such, more of a dilemma because one day, I spotted a young mum hovering outside. She had two little boys with her and eventually she came in and asked if the Warm Hub was open to anyone. I felt so bad. I sensed it had taken her a lot to pluck up the courage to ask, and that she felt embarrassed. Long story short I invited her in and gave them something to eat and later, she told me that during the school holidays she struggles to feed them. It killed me inside, hearing that. Later, Lizzy explained that a lot of parents rely on free school meals in term time but during the holidays, it's a worry. So we decided to do something to help.'

'What did you do?'

'There wasn't enough room in here for mums and kids, and our elderly guests, so I did the next best thing and during the Christmas break, on Mondays, we made up packed lunches that parents could collect. We do it during all the holidays now, but it's a drop in the ocean really, one day a week, and now, with winter on the doorstep people are going to be dreading the cold again. I just wish I had the money to do more because, like I said, I have loads of ideas. I can only do so much, though, and I don't want to stop donating to charity to fund my grand plan. It drives me crazy, you know. And keeps me awake at night. I'll just have to learn patience I suppose.'

Honey could feel her passion and frustration as she talked. Like a ball of fire in her chest and, sometimes, it got too much. Desire to do something thwarted by the same old problem, money, or lack of it.

When Levi smiled, at first Honey wondered if he was amused by her, but when he spoke, she realised it was for another reason entirely.

'Well, as it so happens, it's looking like my earlier catastrophes may have been worthwhile after all.'

Honey scrunched her face, then stopped, knowing it made her look like a chipmunk. 'How so?'

'Because it so happens that I might have the solution to your problems, or at the very least be able to help.' Levi picked up his mug and smiled. 'Drink up, it's going cold. And then you can tell me a bit more about these donations you make, and I'll explain where I come in. This really is turning out to be our lucky day!'

Bemused and intrigued, Honey obeyed. She also hoped so badly that the kind-eyed man seated before her was for real, and that somehow and totally unexpectedly, he'd be the answer to all of her prayers.

CHAPTER 11

MR TRISTAN HENDERSON JNR

M r Tristan Henderson Jnr tapped the walnut desktop, impatient as always. It was 5pm UK time and midday in New York as he waited for his transatlantic call to connect. He wasn't particularly impressed with the man at the other end, and for some reason the lackadaisical and unfamiliar ring tone sought to irritate him further.

Finally, he heard a drawling voice at the other end ask, 'w'sup man' and even the 3,334 miles that separated them did nothing to calm Tristan's ire.

'Where are you? Please tell me you're on your way to the airport because if you miss this flight…'

'Hey dude, relax. I just got here. About to check in with plenty of time to spare. Jeez, you Brits really are uptight. I hope you're gonna be more fun while I'm over there because I ain't spendin' time with a guy who acts like my pa. I was wonderin' if we could go to the races. Horses are my fav'rit thing. I checked online and I saw that there's a track in Chester; we could go there.'

Chuck Chamberlain's tone might have been jovial, but it didn't wash with Tristan who'd paid for his ticket, and the rebooking fee after Chuck missed his earlier flight, and not a chance in hell was he going to the racecourse with the man.

'Funny. Just make sure you get on the plane. Someone will pick you up at the airport and take you straight to your hotel. It's all arranged. And we can see about the races if we have time.' Tristan attempted to be convivial, swallowing down his dislike of the human waste of space who he was speaking to like one of his children. Although at least they were intelligent.

Chuck had been a major pain in the arse ever since he'd tracked him down, but Tristan needed to keep him on side and play the game. Because that's what all this was. A game where, if all went well, he could make some serious money off the feckless loser at the other end of the line.

Chuck responded in his far-too-laid-back way. 'S'cool. I'll text you when I'm through security and airside. I'm kinda lookin' forward to kickin' back and relaxing on the flight and hey, spending time with you and my new fam when I land in good old England. Gonna be a blast.'

Tristan cringed. It was going to be hell, chaperoning this utter moron, but needs must. 'Well, you just get here and then we can focus on the job in hand and hopefully have some fun at the same time. Mix business with pleasure, so to speak. Ring me when you're airside, then I can run through arrangements with you, okay?'

'Sure thing man. Back soon.'

The line disconnected and Tristan felt nothing but relief. Chuck was everything he despised about the lower echelons of society. And now, he'd have to babysit the utter moron while he tried to ingratiate him with his long-lost second cousin – removed more times than Tristan cared to think about.

There had been moments when he'd pondered the wisdom of his little scheme and whether it really was worth his time and effort. But as the weeks had gone by and he'd made more enquiries amongst his diverse group of business contacts, Tristan was reassured. If Chuck did as he was told, there was a very good chance they'd both be laughing all the way to the bank.

Patience would be the key.

Although Clarissa's days were numbered, nobody knew exactly how long she had left on this mortal coil and once she did shuffle off, there'd be the probate period to get through. All this was doable though if – and only if – Clarissa was enamoured enough by Chuck, would she leave her entire estate to her only surviving relative.

Once this was the case, Tristan intended sending Chuck back to Brooklyn on the first plane out. He could wait it out in his cess-pit flat amongst his cronies, the low-lifes from the hood.

The private detective Tristan had hired stateside to track Chuck down had given him a very detailed and – thanks to the digital images that had pinged onto his laptop – a vivid and lurid image of Clarissa's kinsman. Tristan doubted she'd be impressed. In fact, smelling salts might be required.

Antsy, and imagining Chuck wandering around JFK like a lost dog, Tristan sighed, stood, then made his way across the office to the drinks cabinet. After pouring himself a two-finger measure of his favourite malt, he leant against the window frame, looking onto the streets of Chester. Tristan never swigged, he sipped and savoured every mouthful.

Below, office workers and shoppers mingled on the cobbled streets of the city, and soon Tristan would be amongst them, heading off to Alderley Edge and his elegant mews house. It was a thing of beauty, his home. The interior designer who'd come highly recommended by a premier league striker made sure of that.

Tristan had no time in his life for sub-standard, be it food, wine, lovers, dogs, holidays and cars, children even. He often wondered what he'd have done if either of his sons had inherited an ugly gene. After all, he'd hand-picked his wife but with offspring, there was an element of doubt. Always the chance you'd be lumbered with a throwback. And to be fair, his mother-in-law must have fallen out of the ugly tree and hit every branch on the way down. Procreation was a bit of a lottery.

Tristan drank the last of his malt and glanced at the bottle. One more finger? He needed it to calm his jangling nerves before Chuck rang back.

The man was an imbecile. A wannabe hoodlum who'd relocated from Kentucky with his lap-dancer girlfriend, only to be dumped as soon as she found a better prospect higher up in the food chain.

Since, Chuck had ducked and dived, taking part-time jobs in bars and, currently, a car wash. Tristan shuddered and decided to chance one more finger. As he poured the toffee-coloured liquid, the finest malt, he pondered his current predicament. On top of his penchant for the white stuff, life was getting expensive. He needed an injection of funds, or the promise of one, to hold those he owed at bay. When the solution had landed in his lap some months earlier, Tristan could barely contain his glee.

It began when Clarissa Chamberlain summoned Tristan and his father. During the meeting, she announced that due to her declining health and on the advice of her doctor, matters of her estate needed to be finalised.

It was here that she requested Henderson & Co make enquiries with regards to any long-lost family she might have mislaid along the way. There were cousins, on her uncle's side, who'd struck out for the Americas in the sixties. Clarissa had lost touch with all of them but maybe they could be traced.

Previously it hadn't been of concern, but, feeling her mortality, it seemed that Clarissa had done a spot of soul-searching. As a consequence, when she signed her final will and testament, the lady of the manor wanted to be sure she'd done the right thing. Otherwise the lot was going to charity and the National Trust.

Tristan had been present at the meeting and, seeing as they'd require a comprehensive list of relatives for probate purposes anyway, Mr Henderson Senior tasked his son with the search. It was a brief Tristan was rather grateful for. Anything beat the dross and drear of his daily grind. And by that he wasn't referring to his wife, Diana.

Tristan checked his watch and wished Chuck would hurry. He didn't want to get stuck in rush-hour traffic and he hated talking shop in the Jaguar. That was his time. To savour the luxurious interior, the power of the engine and listen to Supertramp on the stereo. He also didn't want to antagonise his wife by being late for dinner.

Demanding and high maintenance in the old school style, Diana ran their lives meticulously. They lived by the laws of the Cheshire set and she made damn sure that the standards set by her parents' generation were met. Which meant private schools for their two teenage sons; the latest model Range Rover; three foreign holidays a year, including the ski-season in the French Alps. The usual stuff expected of his class.

Not that Tristan was complaining, because he loved his life. Who wouldn't? If it meant pushing a pen from behind his desk, in his plush office, situated in the grand building owned by the family firm for the past century, then so be it.

Henderson & Co gave him respectability and that respectability provided the perfect cover for his more lucrative and interesting pursuits. And the key to expanding Tristan's wealth and enhancing his enjoyment of life, was Chuck.

CHAPTER 12

The streetlights flickered on outside. The yellow glow from the lamps gave the quaint, black-and-white timber-framed shops opposite an olde worlde edge. Chester was simply beautiful with its Roman walls and the river that ran through its core. Tristan preferred to remember it from his childhood rather than accept the march of time.

Sub-standard elements of society were a blemish on the picture postcard city, so he often tried to imagine it cleansed of the scruffy people, like the homeless guy and the *Big Issue* seller, and anyone from the Blacon council estate. In fact, if he had his way you'd require a pass to enter – social housing tenants need not apply.

Grimacing at the thought, Tristan smoothed the collar of his jacket. He relished the feel of sheer quality. Was smug in the knowledge that the suit label resting against his Saville Row shirt said Henry Poole & Co. Tristan prided himself on his appearance as much as he did his accomplishments, which were many.

His law degree to begin with, marrying into Diana's family, producing two sons, his platinum client list, but the thing guaranteed to make his trousers feel a tad too tight in the groin area was his other triumph – his property portfolio.

It had made Tristan a small fortune, and having experienced the thrill of landing a deal and seeing the figure on his bank statement increase exponentially year on year, he wanted more. The sticking point was that property was future capital, earmarked for his retirement and what he needed now was a cheeky little tax-free cash payment.

Chuck was the key to that.

Tristan had seen the draft copy of Clarissa's will. If a suitable heir was not found or approved of, and by no stretch of the imagination could The Kentucky Kid be described as that, Tristan's plan was doomed. Because apart from personal and very generous bequests to members of her staff, it was looking like Chamberlain Manor would end up as another tourist attraction.

What a waste that would be. Especially when one of his cohorts, a certain Romanian billionaire was looking for a new home befitting of his nouveau-riche status. Somewhere out of the way where he could entertain his guests *and himself* however he wanted. Tristan had been to Ion Pavǎl's parties and sampled everything on offer, so knew only too well why privacy was most definitely required.

And while Ion was not the type of person Tristan would choose to associate with in the company of Diana –because they both found people of his ilk and background most distasteful – needs must.

Tristan fastidiously kept his shadier acquaintances in the shadows and well away from his life with Diana. For all appearances, he was the epitome of respectability and soon, fingers crossed, his standing would go up another notch, in both of the worlds he inhabited.

Tristan's father was due to retire and finally Henderson & Co would pass down the line to him. So, if he could smooth the way and ensure that Clarissa left everything to Chuck, once the probate period was over, Tristan would have sole control of the Chamberlain estate's legal affairs. Perfect.

All being well, Chuck would see dollar signs and take the first deal that landed on the table and no need to guess who that bidder would be. Ion Pavăl.

A very nice commission awaited Tristan as a reward for brokering the deal. In cash. Also included in the gentleman's agreement between Tristan and Ion was the purchase of a row of tenanted cottages, for a knock-down price of course. These, Tristan intended to transform into luxury homes. Their prime location on the banks of the River Dee guaranteed a premium return, once he'd ejected the tenants.

Which was why everything hinged on Chuck. And why Tristan had forked out for a first-class seat on the British Airways flight – to give the Kentucky Kid a taste of the high life. Why a limousine would collect him at the airport. And, after wrestling with the idea of dumping him in the Travelodge on the Chester Ring Road, why Tristan had booked him into a boutique hotel. And by some strange coincidence, it was just down the road from the land of milk and honey. Chamberlain Manor.

It had to work. Ion Pavăl had deep pockets and rewarded those who he trusted and were of use. Tristan was on the edge of the inner circle. Who knew what opportunities getting a foot into the centre of Ion's world would bring?

But what if Clarissa hung on for years? The dark thoughts he harboured with regards to that little glitch in his plan sent Tristan's heart racing. Would he have the guts to arrange a little accident? Perhaps a stumble at the top of that very elegant staircase at the manor. No, not for a second. But Ion would.

The mobile on his desk began to trill. The one in his pocket remained silent, which meant Diana was occupied elsewhere and didn't require his presence. Striding across the room, depositing his glass on the way, Tristan snatched the phone and answered.

'Hey dude, we're all set and thanks for setting me up in this fancy bar. It's real swanky. I could get used to this.' Chuck had obviously been directed to the first-class lounge.

'Well, you'd better get used to it, my friend,' Tristan cringed. Over-familiarity wasn't his thing, but in for a penny. 'Because if you play your cards right, this could be your life every single day of the week. All you have to do is follow my lead and you'll be sitting pretty. I can assure you of that. No more wiping tables and washing cars for Chuck Chamberlain.'

Tristan had begun to relax into his part, the tension of earlier receding now he knew Chuck had made it through security. And once he was on the plane, Tristan could forget about his new best friend for a few hours. Which was a blessing, because he really couldn't bear the sound of the man's voice. Why did he talk *so* loudly? Did he think he was on a ranch and needed to drown out the sound of hooves, or be heard in the next state?

'You can rely on me, dude, but for now I'm gonna get a drink and enjoy the hospitality. You want me to tell you when I'm on the plane? I'm still getting that old poppa vibe down the line.' Chuck was laughing, a strange hee-heeing sound that was bound to be attracting attention.

Feeling his blood pressure rise again, Tristan called time. 'Just a quick text, when you're seated, so I know you didn't get smashed and miss the call for your flight. Then you can enjoy some more pampering while you're in the air. Okay?'

'Dude, you're a legend. I'll text soon. You be good now.' And with that, Chuck cut the call.

Dragging his hand down his face, Tristan felt anything but a legend, in fact, he was drained just from the effort of keeping his patience. Chuck was hard work, and in comparison his teenagers were a walk in the park. Even Diana for that matter.

Tristan glanced at the notepad on his desk. He'd jotted down Chuck's flight number and arrival time. He was due to land in the early hours of the following morning. Tristan had appointments all Thursday, so intended leaving Chuck alone to get over his jet lag.

They were going to meet up on Friday to run through a few things and then all being well, Chuck could meet his dear cousin over the weekend. Diana wouldn't be happy about him working but he'd fob her off with a spa retreat. They always did the trick when he was in her bad books.

A rap on the door to which Tristan responded with an *enter*, and the prim face of his secretary appeared. Punctual and predictable as ever, Ms Forbisham gave her 5.30pm speech.

'I'll be off now, Mr Henderson. Have a good evening.'

'Jolly good. Take care on the way home. See you in the morning.' Sometimes Tristan wanted to say, 'Good for you. Now fuck off, you boring old crone, and don't slam the door on the way out.' Imagine.

Tristan massaged his temples and, not having the patience to wait for Chuck's text, decided to head home too. There was nothing more he could do, and if the imbecile missed his flight again... he'd hire a ruddy nanny.

Swiftly closing down his laptop, he then switched off his desk lamp, grabbed his briefcase and, after a flick of the light switch, closed the office door on tedium and Chuck.

CHAPTER 13

LEVI

A stiff breeze was blowing down the hill and whipped Levi's body as he waited for the AA man to print the repair report. The temperature had dropped in the past hour and, even though it was mid-October, he could imagine the harsh winter weather up there on the peaks.

While he was grateful that the mechanic had fixed the problem, Levi was eager to get back inside and finish his conversation with Honey. She never got to tell him about her donations to charity and he still hadn't explained how he might be able to help her.

Levi seriously couldn't believe his luck in meeting someone like her, who ticked all the boxes. He'd only known her for a short while, but she was perfect. Ripe for... not the picking, that sounded wrong. Honey was just the type of person he and his associates looked out for. Today's quirk of fate had certainly made his job a hell of a lot easier.

So far, he'd been genuinely impressed by her business acumen. He was trying to ignore how she made him feel inside. Keep that separate.

She owned her own home and the lease on the café; ran a solid enterprise with cash-flow to spare so on paper Honey McCarthy was a sure bet. Actually, *proposition* sounded better. He doubted she would need much persuasion.

All he needed to do now was get back inside and see if she'd agree to going for a drink with him, maybe a bite to eat. He'd been about to explain what he did for a living when a large group of walkers turned up, so Honey had to get back to work. She'd insisted he remained in his seat and over the next hour or so had refilled his coffee while he occupied himself on his phone or read magazines from the bookshelf.

Then the cavalry arrived in the form of the AA man, and Levi had spent the past fifty-five minutes chatting with him while his car was fixed.

Honey had popped out and asked if they'd like a warm drink, which AA man accepted. Levi was so full of caffeine he reckoned he'd be able to run all the way back to Manchester, so declined. When she returned with hot chocolate, Honey told Levi she'd be working late in the café, so to let themselves in, if they needed the loo or anything. He'd taken this as a welcome hint.

Levi had seen Lizzy and the chef, who he knew was called Gospel, leave. And noticed Honey turn the sign on the door to closed, giving him a little wave as she did do. He returned it with a smile.

'Here you go, mate. You keep that for your records and remember what I said, about checking the oil now and then. You were lucky the engine didn't seize up. Those flashing warning lights on the dash are there for a reason.'

AA man gave Levi a cheeky wink as he passed over the paperwork. 'Say thanks to your girlfriend for the brew. You take care now.' And with that he headed back to his yellow van.

'Thanks mate, and she's … Okay, I will. You take care too.' Folding the sheet of paper and stuffing it in his pocket, Levi headed straight for the café where he found the door open but Honey nowhere to be seen.

The bell announced his arrival and then a voice, 'Won't be a min,' and true to her word, after a bit of pacing and hovering, Levi was greeted by a huge smile and Honey. Wearing her coat. Levi's heart dropped. Maybe she wasn't interested in what he had to say after all, and she was just being polite earlier.

He'd soon find out when she booted him onto the street and locked up and that would be the end of that.

Stop being a quitter. Ask her out. Just do something you big wimp.

Honey beat him to it. 'Is it all fixed?'

'Yep, all sorted. My fault mainly. I'm not very mechanically minded.' *Is that it? The best you can do.*

'Oh good. Now, you wanted to tell me something... about an idea? D'you fancy going to the pub? There's a nice one on the corner and we can talk there. I've been here since seven and as much as I love the place, I could do with a change of scenery. No pressure if you have to get off.' Honey had hooked her rucksack over her shoulders and waited for his answer.

It was a no-brainer.

They sat not quite opposite one another. More side by side but not touching. A circular table made a sturdy chaperone, although now and then their knees knocked together. This brief contact made Levi go 'all of a doo-da' as his granny Iris would say.

Sometimes, he wished that he was as confident in his personal life as he was professionally. It was always the same. When he was talking money, he didn't feel self-conscious or worry about making a fool of himself. He knew his job inside out. He enjoyed it too.

When it came to conversing with the opposite sex – and by that he didn't mean the lady on the till at Tesco, or the female members of his family; he meant dates, or anyone he found attractive or who showed the faintest glimmer of interest in him – he became a dithering wreck. Struck dumb and devoid of personality. Like he had regressed into his teenage self but with slightly better clothes, no spots and minus the braces.

No wonder the new 'for when I get lucky' duvet set he'd bought well over a year ago was still in its packaging in the airing cupboard of his flat. The only reason he'd got this far, to a half pint of lager shandy (which looked so wimpy) and a glass of red wine (large), was because Honey was a chatterbox. All he had to do was ask a question and boom, she was off. Like a whippet out of the starting gate, and that suited him just fine.

She was currently telling him all about tomorrow's special; Lancashire Hot Pot, which apparently was a favourite with her customers, but Gospel hated it. He said it lacked soul and colour, which was why once a week he got to make whatever he wanted. That Friday they were serving Jamaican beef patties. You could tell that Honey respected Gospel's culinary skills and appreciated his input. Levi had also gleaned that Gospel was Leeds born and bred but stayed true to his roots and had the potential to be a great and innovative chef. It was also clear that Honey adored him, which left Levi feeling pathetically jealous.

She was currently describing the patties, which was good because at least they'd moved away from St Gospel the Great. 'They go down really well, and we always sell out. You should try them. Now, it's your turn to talk because I'm rabbiting on as usual so I will sit here nice and quiet and drink my wine. It's lovely by the way. Good choice.'

Caught in Honey's gaze Levi had one of those moments from school where it was his turn to read something out loud in assembly. He could even feel the kid behind nudging him in the back.

Get on with it!

'Oh right, me… well. I didn't choose the wine, by the way, the guy behind the bar did. I'm more of a real ale drinker but I'm glad you like it.' Deciding his strengths lay in asking questions Levi went with, 'You were going to tell me about the charity that's close to your heart.'

And she was off.

CHAPTER 14

Honey was opening a packet of crisps as she spoke and began eating them like she'd never been fed, and Levi found her unconscious enjoyment and lack of self-consciousness endearing.

'Well, it's all down to my best friend, Ziggy. She's a nurse at the general. A&E to be precise, but that's not really got anything to do with it. I just thought I'd tell you because I'm well proud of what she does. She might come down later. This is her parents' pub. I texted to say I was here.'

Honey took a breath, ate a handful of crisps and Levi took a drink, trying hard to focus and keep track.

'We've been best friends since year seven when we met at secondary school. I'd been a bit of a loner up till then and meeting Ziggy was the best thing that ever happened to me. She's totally bonkers and brought me out of myself. I bet you can't imagine that I was once shy.'

Nope, Levi couldn't.

'She's like a firework, or one of those birthday candles that re-lights itself. Ziggy was the one who thought of mad pranks, wasn't scared of anything or anyone, would join an after-school club even if she didn't think she'd be any good at it, just to see what it was like. To tick the box. She's really bad at singing and didn't make the choir – thank heaven – but was captain of the netball team and played rugby at weekends. My grandad used to say she was built like a brick shi– strong and sturdy.'

Then Honey fell silent and raised her glass, taking a sip, suddenly thoughtful.

Levi hated awkward silences and always felt the urge to fill the gap so said the first thing that came into his head, and he meant it.

'Ziggy. That's a cool name. I take it she's a Bowie fan. Or her parents are.'

At this Honey brightened.

'Neither actually. Ziggy is a mad Bob Marley fan and that's his son's name, who she also had a long-distance and unrequited crush on. Never shut up about him so, in year nine we started calling her Ziggy and it stuck. And to be fair, she does look the part. Sorry, I'm going off track again.'

Honey put her glass down and turned her body so she was facing Levi.

'Right. Just after her fourteenth birthday, Ziggy got sick. She was what her mum described as "big-boned". She *loved* her food, but suddenly lost her appetite and started to lose weight. Ziggy didn't care at first. I mean, what teenage girl complains about shedding pounds; but soon it became really noticeable. And she was tired all the time and had no energy. I remember her falling asleep in lessons and saying the whiteboard looked fuzzy. And she was always thirsty.'

Honey pushed a loose strand of hair behind her ear then continued.

'It was the summer term, and we were doing track and field for PE. I was by Ziggy's side and heard her say, "Honey, I can't do this. I need to tell sir I don't feel well." And when I turned round she wasn't there. She was sprawled on the floor unconscious. I thought she was messing about at first but when I couldn't wake her I knew something was badly wrong and then, all hell broke loose.'

Honey looked like she was going to cry, the memory of that day etched on her face, so Levi tried to make it easier for her.

'I think I know what you're going to say... she had diabetes, didn't she?'

Honey nodded. 'Yes, Type 1. And that's why I give to a charity that supports anyone with the condition because I saw first-hand the effect it has on someone.'

Levi wanted to touch Honey's hand because it felt right but then chickened out so instead asked her to go on.

'From the moment they took her off in the ambulance, Ziggy's life and all the stuff we'd planned and talked about changed forever. She went straight into re-sus at A&E, then spent a week in the critical care unit, where they slowly got her better; but really, that was just the start of her journey. And it wasn't easy.'

'What do you mean?'

Honey looked thoughtful, as though she was going back in time, to her teenage self, trying to remember and get the words right. 'It's sometimes tough being a teenager, isn't it?'

Levi nodded, knowing exactly what she meant but not wanting to admit he was still feeling the aftershocks.

'Imagine you *and* your parents having to have lessons – I suppose you could call them that. They had to have them in hospital, before Ziggy could come home. Learning how to manage a condition for which there is no cure. One that through no fault of her own, or anyone's, struck out of the blue and attacked her immune system.'

Levi was there with them. 'Awful, what a nightmare. How did they cope?'

'It was a total mind-bomb. For Ziggy and her family. The days of getting a bag of crisps after school or raiding the cupboards whenever you felt like a cheeky chocolate bar were gone.

Mealtimes, days out, hanging around with your friends, meant weighing and calculating how many carbohydrates were in your food. While the other kids at school legged it to the corner shop and wolfed down a 50p mix-up, Ziggy had to inject insulin first. Each time she ate, an apple, a glass of milk, a biscuit out of the tin.'

Levi was genuinely shocked. 'Really, I didn't know.'

'Yes, they told her she could eat anything she wanted, and it wasn't like she could never eat sugar again, but each mouthful came at a cost if you didn't follow the rules. But that was just part of it.'

Levi's heart sank as Honey carried on.

'One evening just after she came out of hospital, I went round to her house and found her crying in her bedroom. She told me her life was ruined. That she hated T1. She said it was the first thing she thought about as soon as she woke up, and the last thing at night. Like a voice in her head saying, "I've got diabetes, I'm different." She'd also been looking stuff up, and convinced herself she was going to go blind, or have her feet amputated and die young. All sorts of hideous things and, basically, she was terrified.'

'Poor Ziggy,' and Levi meant it.

'It was so sad. She asked me, "Who's going to want a girlfriend who has to stick needles in her body every time she eats?" And no matter what I said, she didn't believe me. She was also adamant she wasn't going back to school. "There's no point, not now". I remember it like it was yesterday.'

Levi could tell from Honey's face that her friend's pain had affected her deeply. 'That's terrible. Why didn't she want to go back to school?'

Honey answered. 'Ziggy's dream was to be a medic in the armed forces. She'd set her sights on it; took the right options, even going down to the army careers office to get all the info. We got the bus into Manchester, and she was *so* excited on the ride home. Despite being a bit of a rebel, she always worked really hard at school, and I truly believed that she'd do it. She was even going to join the army cadets the following term, but she never did.'

'Why?' Levi hadn't even met this Ziggy person, but he could picture a young girl, lying in her room feeling like her life had been trampled on.

'Because the Armed Forces are the only organisation exempt from discriminating against a person with diabetes. Ziggy would never be able to join-up. So, in her eyes, there was no point in joining the cadets, either. Even learning to drive would be different for Ziggy. A new set of rules and regulations to follow. In her head, it seemed everything set her apart from her friends. Made her the odd one out.'

Levi shook his head. 'I honestly had no idea or even thought about the impact it would have on someone, getting a diagnosis like that. Did things get easier for her?'

'Yes, they did, but it wasn't plain sailing and we had blips because–' Honey didn't continue, her attention was drawn elsewhere. 'In fact, talk of the devil, here she is now.'

Honey nodded in the direction of the bar. As she approached, Ziggy's electric pink dreadlocks bounced with each stride she took in her flowery Dr Martens. Waving tattooed arms that held a stack of jangling bracelets, her smile was broad, with an upper lip adorned with a piercing. As was her nose and both ears, many times over.

Ziggy spoke first. 'Well this is a nice surprise. What are you doing drinking on a school night, Miss Honeysuckle?' She pulled up a chair and extended her hand to Levi, her focus fully on him. 'And *hello* ... I don't think we've met.'

He extended his hand too, managing, 'Hi, I'm Levi...' then thankfully, before nerves took over and his words dried up, he was saved by Honey, who took over the conversation.

As she waded in, explaining about his car, thankfully omitting the date from hell part, then onto Lizzy's son's ears, and then something about Beryl and a box of stuff her grandad had dropped off earlier, Levi relaxed.

It was also hard to keep up.

Still, he was happy to sit back and observe Honey and Ziggy. He could tell they were a proper double act, finishing each other's sentences, talking fast and furious, only coming up for air. They were amusing and real so after he offered to get the drinks in and they accepted, he left them to it.

Ordering a pint of snakebite and two cokes because he and Honey had to drive home, Levi accepted that his pitch might have to wait. It wasn't a problem, and meant he would have to meet Honey again. That was a bonus and, for what he had in mind, there was plenty of time.

CHAPTER 15

CLARISSA

C larissa was nervous. And that wasn't a state of being that she was altogether familiar or comfortable with. Her life was so perfunctory that there was little room for anyone or anything upsetting the equilibrium, yet here she was, waiting in the drawing room for a researcher from the production company. Clarissa was discombobulated.

It had been a bit of a whirlwind since Mr Henderson's call, but as dear Jennifer said, it gave Clarissa less time to dither and back out.

She had provisionally agreed to meet 'the cousin' the following day. They would have lunch there at the Manor. Reassured that Jennifer and young Mr Tristan would be in attendance, she'd managed to put that potential trauma to the back of her mind.

Clarissa was dreading the encounter. He was probably a very nice chap, the American. On the other hand, if he was a descendant of her uncle, there was a very good chance the nasty-gene flowed through his veins.

Don't think of him, not now. Focus on today and not the past.

Doing just that, Clarissa turned her attention to the television people, or whatever they were, who it seemed had strict schedules and time slots and were eager to get the ball rolling. Hence, an early morning meeting on a very sunny Friday had been arranged.

Clarissa could see the driveway from where she sat and was watching like a hungry hawk for what she imagined would be some kind of Winnebago with a satellite dish on its roof. She'd seen them on the news. A hoard of eager beavers would pile out and begin scouting around her grounds, trampling on her flower beds and peering in windows.

Stranger danger. The phrase that popped into Clarissa's head, along with an information advert from way back. Charley the cat and his little friend who warned children everywhere of the dangers that lurked out there in the big bad world. *'Charley says...'*

The arrival of a dusty hatchback, shooting along the tarmacked drive, followed by the disembarkation of only two bodies coincided with the click of a door handle.

Jennifer's excited voice replaced Charley the cat's. 'They're here! Shall I show them straight in?' Jennifer cocked her head and gave Clarissa a concerned look. 'Now remember, they're just here to have a look around, not open all your closets looking for family skeletons.'

At this, Clarissa's tension level dropped a notch. Jennifer had the knack of reading her charge well, and she'd spent much of breakfast reassuring Clarissa that she could still change her mind and put a stop to filming whenever she wanted. With this in mind, Clarissa straightened her back and said, 'Show them in.'

They were getting on like a house on fire. Penny the researcher was a delight. Most affable, despite being a bit on the scruffy side, with her tangled fair hair, hoody and baseball boots that had seen better days. Clarissa presumed it was how young folk dressed these days.

Despite lacking in the appearance department, Penny was an intelligent scrap of a thing who informed Clarissa she had a modern history degree and fascination with all things gone before. She had a habit of blinking and clasping her notebook while she spoke, like a shield – maybe a nervous tic. So, as was Clarissa's way, she resolved to put the young woman at her ease.

Terry, the photographer was the opposite. Gregarious and enthusiastic but polite with it and, while Clarissa and Penny chatted, after seeking permission, he got on with clicking away, zooming in on this and that, taking shots of the grounds from the window, his long limbs crouching and twisting, lost in his own artistic world.

Feeling much more comfortable, Clarissa decided it was time to get on and as previously agreed with Jennifer, would be pushed in her blasted wheelchair along the marbled corridors and around the vast reception rooms. There was absolutely no way she would be able to walk all that way.

'Come along. Let me give you the grand tour and afterwards we can have some tea and biscuits. We will start with the dining room…'

It had been most pleasant, showing off her home to Penny, who appeared to soak it all up, asking very intelligent questions, even spotting and naming antiquities, the odd painting and artist, even some of the first editions in the library. It was as they returned to the foyer that Clarissa saw Penny glance upwards, her eyes taking in the beautiful staircase and then downwards, to the stairlift.

'This has been such a treat for me, it really has, and I wouldn't want to intrude on your privacy by going upstairs, so perhaps we could focus on family history now. Get some background detail

about your ancestors. Shall we go back to the drawing room?'
Penny flipped a page in her notebook, pen poised.

As Jennifer began to turn the wheelchair, Clarissa made a
snap decision and raised her hand to indicate they should remain
at the foot of the stairs. 'Actually, I would like to show you the
first floor, and afterwards you and Terry can have a wander up to
the servant quarters in the attic – but before that, there's a special
room I want you to see.'

They were standing before the portrait of Eleonora. Clarissa had
insisted on walking there once she alighted the stairlift. Jennifer
hovered at the door while Terry took more snaps.

Penny just stared. 'Who is it? She's very beautiful.'

'That's my elder sister, Eleonora. She was ten years older than
me. I was a surprise baby after mother had lost two in between. I
idolised Eleonora. She would be one hundred and two, had she
lived, and there isn't a day goes by that I don't miss and think of
her.'

Penny asked, 'What happened to her?'

Clarissa felt suddenly weary. No doubt all the chatting and
pointing had worn her out so feeling the need to sit, she took
the few steps to the bed and sat, indicating that Penny should
do the same. Clarissa rarely disturbed the damask quilt and
now felt she was doubly invading Eleonora's space; but needs
must.

Looking up at the portrait, Clarissa considered the question
before giving an answer. The urge to talk, to explain, to open her
very own Pandora's box was immense yet at the same time,
Clarissa had no desire to air her family's affairs to all and sundry.

Turning to Jennifer, she suggested, 'Jennifer, would you take
Terry downstairs and ask Cookie Beattie to prepare him some
elevenses. Penny and I will be down shortly.'

Always reliable in picking up the beat, Jennifer nodded, 'Of course, come along, Terry. I'll lead the way.'

Also good at taking the hint it seemed, Terry glanced momentarily at Penny then followed Jennifer out of the room. Once the door closed, Clarissa spoke, but kept her eyes firmly on the portrait, while the young woman by her side listened attentively.

'This part of my family history is between you and me, not the masses who watch your programme. I will tell you it all because I sense in you a kindred spirit, someone who respects the past and hopefully my privacy. Do you understand?'

'Yes, yes of course.' And as if to reassure Clarissa, Penny clicked the top of her pen and closed her notepad.

It did the trick and encouraged Clarissa to tell Eleonora's story.

'The last time I saw my sister was in 1940. May the 2nd to be precise. I wrote about the day she left in my diary. It was such a strange time because everything around us was changing. Young men marching off to war, young women wanting to do their bit; and it seemed that Eleonora was no different.

'It began, I'm sure of it, when her friend, the village schoolteacher Mr Jones, was killed in Belgium only days after he'd arrived. He was a lovely man. Had a kind face and was so tall and handsome, like a film star. I used to see him at church each Sunday where he'd lift his trilby and say hello to my parents and make Eleonora blush when he smiled at her.

'I didn't blush when he bowed theatrically and said, "and good day to you, Miss Clarissa," but I did wish I could go to the village school. Cookie said Mr Jones was the best teacher they'd had for many a moon and her nieces and nephews thought the world of him.

'I'd heard the news at breakfast from Mother and later, I found Eleonora crying in the rose garden. She was reading letters, dabbing her red eyes with a soggy handkerchief and when

I asked her what was wrong, she said, "Bloody Hitler has ruined my life, that's what's wrong." I remember being so shocked that my perfect sister had said a swear word.

'One of the letters got caught on the breeze and fluttered away so I chased it and nervously handed it back to Eleonora. As I did, I glanced at the signature which said, "ever yours, Robert."'

Clarissa paused and Penny asked, 'Do you think it was from Mr Jones, the teacher? And they were lovers?'

'Oh yes, most definitely. Not that I made the connection right away, because to me he was simple Mr Jones. In those days I didn't even consider that my governess had a first name. She was just Miss Cleves. It was later, when I saw his gravestone at the church, that I realised. Of course, they'd kept their affair secret because my parents were terrible snobs and lived by the rules of their class and station. And whilst I was an inquisitive child, I was also naïve. I lived my happy life inside the Chamberlain bubble. One that my sister was about to pop.'

Penny inclined her body slightly, clearly intrigued. 'How so?'

'Not long after I saw Eleonora crying, there was a terrible row. As always, I'd been sent to my bedroom while my parents and Eleonora were at loggerheads in father's study. And as always, I disobeyed and crept downstairs to eavesdrop. I was a terrible ear-wigger. There are secret passageways all over the house and I was always creeping about, but none in his study unfortunately, so I listened at the door.

'My sister wanted to do her bit and join the Women's Auxiliary, the ATS as it was known, and father flipped his lid. Mother was distraught and begged Eleonora not to go. Eleonora was adamant she would, insisting it was only delaying the inevitable. There were rumours that soon, women would be drafted into all sorts of roles to make up for all the men being sent to war.'

'Did she get her way?'

Clarissa allowed herself a rueful smile. 'Oh yes. Eleonora was a fiery redhead and had a temper to match her flaming locks, and lord, could she scream and shout when the need arose.

'Before I knew it, she was packing her things and, once her papers came, she was off to begin her basic training. Before she left, she entrusted me with some of her most precious jewellery, and the books that Mother said were deviant and had banned from the house. Eleonora had hidden them in her room. I still have them now.'

'Which books were they?' I love the old classics.'

Clarissa chuckled, 'They're not Brontës, let me see. There's *Lady Chatterley* by DH Lawrence, *Chéri* by Collette, *Mrs Dalloway* by Virginia Woolf... oh and *Ulysses* by James Joyce and many more. Mother would've had a fit if she'd known they'd been saved from the bin.'

Penny seemed in awe. 'She was quite a one, wasn't she, your sister.'

'Oh, she was. And I cried so much when she left that day. Clinging on to her hand, eliciting promises that she wouldn't go anywhere near Mr Hitler and would write every week. You'd have thought she was going to the other side of the world forever, but that's how it felt. And in a way, I was right, because it was forever.'

'How so?' Penny was focusing on the portrait once more, not a note had been made and her pen lay idle on top.

'She kept her promise and wrote every week for a month, telling me all about the camp and the horrid mattresses they had to stuff with straw. The drills and the food that wasn't too bad but not a patch on Cookie's. I used to rifle through the post when it arrived and then for no reason whatsoever, her letters just stopped.'

Penny hugged her notebook to her chest and turned to Clarissa. 'Do you know why?'

Clarissa wished more than anything that she could say, yes. Instead, she told a half-truth. 'You have to remember that it was a long time ago and I was so young. And after all these years what happened seems dreamlike, I suppose. But I can put it all together. A sequence of events that began with a phone call.'

'Would you like to tell me about it?' Penny's voice was gentle, encouraging.

Clarissa though for a moment, her breath caught in her chest, then she said, 'Yes, I think I would.'

CHAPTER 16

Gathering her thoughts, Clarissa closed her eyes. Like a reel of film playing before her eyes, she went back to that rainy August day in 1940 and watched her nine-year-old self playing in the hallway. Hopscotch on the black and white floor tiles, her patent shoes tapping each square. And while Penny listened, Clarissa narrated the scene.

Outside, the deluge was showing no signs of abating. Her parents were in the drawing room reading. When the phone in the hall began to ring, Kingsley the butler appeared and with nothing more interesting to do, Clarissa watched and listened. His back was turned but whoever was on the phone had a profound effect because his stoop became ramrod straight. After telling the caller to hold the line a moment, rather than his usual sedate gait, he scurried to the drawing room, his face set in alabaster flecked with pink.

Knock. Enter. Then mutterings and in a flash her father appeared, followed closely by her mother. Clarissa might well have been invisible from where she sat on the third step up, peering through the spindles. Father told Kingsley he would take the call in his study. He *was not* to be disturbed.

Whether he wanted Mother there or not, from the way she raced after him, wide-eyed and ashen faced, her presence was not an option. After the butler disappeared, no doubt to pass on events to Cookie, Clarissa crept over to the door and pushed her ear to the wood.

'No. You will not come here. I will come to you. I won't have you upset your mother. Be at Piccadilly Station at noon. I will meet you outside. No, Eleonora you may not speak with your mother! For once in your life do as you are damn well told. Until tomorrow.'

The force with which Father slammed down the receiver of the phone made Clarissa jump, but it was the words of Mother that caused her heart to constrict.

'Tell me, George. For the love of God tell me what she's done. Why is she in Manchester? I don't understand.'

'Francesca, leave it to me… Why do the women of this house persist in disobeying me? Just do as I say, woman.'

Her mother gasped and stormed from the room, slamming the door behind her.

Clarissa didn't sleep a wink that night. She was banished to her room and ate tea alone, with only her dolls for company. The hours dragged and dragged, while her mind whirred and whirred. Maids came and went. Clarissa wished Miss Cleves the governess hadn't gone to Kendal for a week's holiday at her sister's.

The following morning, Mother took to her bed, Father left in the Daimler to catch the 11.40 train to Manchester, telling Kingsley he would be back by two. Clearly he didn't intend spending long with Eleonora. Clarissa held on to the vain hope that he would return and by his side would be her sister. All friends again.

It was not to be. Clarissa waited at the long window on the landing. Her heart flipped when his car appeared at the gates and raced up the drive. Even his Daimler looked angry.

When father alighted the car he was alone. And after he spoke to Mother in her bedroom, there were tears, the wailing kind and the slamming of doors. Another long night loomed for Clarissa, and she had to wait for three days before somebody deigned to explain what was going on.

Summoned to the orangery by her mother, Clarissa wavered between nerves and curiosity as she scrutinised the pinched face and tired eyes before her, the painted lips as they said the words.

'Darling I'm terribly sorry for neglecting you but truly, I have been so utterly distraught...' Mother paused, gripped her handkerchief, affected a wistful look before gathering herself. 'Your sister has done a very foolish thing but, under the circumstances we must support her decision. Merely because it is for the good of the country and despite breaking my heart.'

Clarissa just stared and waited, like when she wanted seconds and Cookie said there were none, then gave in. Instead of a dollop of apple crumble and a spoon of custard, Clarissa was served a tale of the unexpected.

'Eleonora has volunteered to go to London, to the war office where she will do very secret and important work. Which means she won't be coming home for a while. So you will have to be brave and pray hard for her, and I shall do the same.'

Panic set in. 'But Mother, what if one of Mr Hitler's bombs drop on Eleonora... you must make her come home, right now. It isn't safe.'

Mother fought to maintain her composure which resulted in a steel-edged response. 'Well I am sure many mothers across this land wish they could demand the safe return of their sons, and indeed their daughters, but it isn't quite so simple. We all have to make sacrifices in order to win this war. Now run along. I'm getting another of my headaches and need to lie down.'

Clarissa was used to being dismissed or dispatched and knew when a conversation was over so as she turned, was surprised when Mother added, 'And please, Clarissa. This is a family affair, and you mustn't go telling your friends. We all know what the posters say, don't we. Careless talk costs lives. And we can't have that.'

Registering the stern look, Clarissa simply nodded and fled to her room where she lay on her bed, thinking of Eleonora. Even at nine, Clarissa understood why her parents were cross, because she was too. Then again, Mother was right, and sacrifices had to be made. By the time the bell rang for lunch, Clarissa had rallied and was determined to wait patiently for news from London, in a letter Eleonora had promised to write.

By November Clarissa had given up checking the post. She was hurt beyond belief that Eleonora had let her down despite Mother's assurances that it was due to the secret nature of her work. Clarissa had no concept of what 'secret war work' entailed and, in the end, had no other option than to trust her elders. After all, the soldiers at the front probably didn't get to send letters home every five minutes, so wherever Eleonora was, the same applied.

Which was why Clarissa got on with it. Just like everyone else. Tried to understand what was going on outside Chamberlain Manor in a world ravaged by war. She listened to the radio and read Father's newspaper once he'd finished with it. Looking for news, a clue to where Eleonora was. In the meantime she waited and prayed.

~

Clarissa was exhausted and parched. Desperately needed a cup of tea and a break from her memories. It was time to curtail her stroll down memory lane. She was, however, expecting Penny's question when it came during the lull.

'So Eleonora never came back?'

Clarissa merely shook her head and allowed her guest to fill in the gaps.

'I think she joined SOE, Special Operations Executive and was sent to France as a spy or to work with the Resistance. Could Eleonora speak French?'

'Oh yes, extremely well. The benefit of a governess and boarding school. Before the war we holidayed with Mother's cousin in Cannes.'

'That'll be it then. I suspect she was captured by the Nazis and...' Penny glanced sideways then fell silent, as if realising how painful her next words could be.

Clarissa was grateful for pause and patted Penny's knee, chivvying her along. 'Well I think that's quite enough for now. Shall we hunt down some refreshments and then I will tell you all about my forefather's contribution to the Industrial Revolution. It's a fine day and I'm sure Terry will be chomping at the bit to explore the grounds with that fancy camera of his.'

Penny followed Clarissa's lead. 'Of course, that would be lovely. And thank you so much for sharing Eleonora's story with me, and I promise to consult you about the content of the film. I won't mention anything about her without your approval.'

For this, Penny received a smile and then a request. 'Marvellous. Now, I don't suppose you could heave me up? These old bones won't do as they are told these days.'

Within minutes they were heading downstairs. Penny on foot, sent to find Jennifer, while Clarissa descended slowly on her chair.

As she passed, Clarissa looked each one of her ancestors in the eye, sure to that day that they were privy to the secrets her parents kept and the lies she was convinced they had told. At the time she'd been too young to fathom it all but with the passing of time Clarissa had questioned her version and memory of events.

She was still no nearer to the truth, though.

~

One week before Christmas 1940, Clarissa had spotted a new pile of correspondence on the little table by the fireplace in the drawing room. It was where Kingsley left Mother's mail each day. There had been a raft of jolly festive cards that adorned the surfaces of the room and still daring to hope that Eleonora might get in touch, Clarissa sneaked a peep.

It lay almost at the bottom of the pile, addressed to her parents, but Clarissa would have recognised her sister's handwriting amongst thousands. It was with utter glee that she ran from the room and after taking the stairs two at a time she burst into Mother's bedroom giving her a start.

'Mother look. It's from Eleonora! I knew she would write I knew it. Open it please, quickly.'

Infuriatingly, Mother slowly took the envelope that shook in her pale manicured hands. Clarissa saw this as a sign that Mother was excited too and waited, her heart pounding, eager for news. And then the unexpected.

'Perhaps we should wait for your father. Let him open it.'

'But mother that's *your* job, silly. Father says so and you always open cards and this one is from our dear Eleonora. Please open it. Father won't be back until dinner, and I can't wait that long.'

Clarissa saw Mother swallow and with trembling fingers she silently opened the envelope, slowly sliding the card from inside. On the front, a red candle surrounded by holly and ivy, the words *season's greetings* in a swirling decorative font. Mother stared and Clarissa grew impatient. Without thinking, in her excitement perhaps, Clarissa plucked the card from Mother's hands, raced to the window to catch the light, and flipped the cover.

'Clarissa how dare you? Give it to me at once.' But Mother's words fell on deaf ears so engrossed was Clarissa in the words which read.

Mother, Father, and my beloved Clarissa.

I am thinking of you all and wish I could be there with you.

My greatest hope is that one day we will be reunited and that I may return home.

Please stay safe.

Happy Christmas.

With love always,

Eleonora.

x

Feeling the card torn from her grasp, and while Mother read the curious words inside, Clarissa moved back to the dressing table and picked up the envelope for no other reason than to touch something that Eleonora had. Feel a connection.

And while Mother placed the card to her heart and wandered over to the window where she became lost in thought, Clarissa folded the envelope and slid it into her pinafore pocket.

Clarissa didn't think it was odd, Mother not displaying the card with the others in the drawing room. Instead she kept it inside her journal that rested by her bed. Remembering the words of the radio announcer who reminded everyone that spies could be everywhere, Clarissa thought Mother prudent to keep the card out of sight. It was, after all, from someone who worked at the war office. Mother was doing her bit, too.

Then three days before Christmas, the most terrible thing happened. Something that brought Mr Hitler and the war within touching distance. The date was written in red in Clarissa's diary, December 22nd, 1940.

That night, German planes flew overhead, skimming through the sky above the Cheshire countryside. Their target lay only a few miles north. While terrified Clarissa covered her ears and imagined the devil in the cockpit, the Manchester Blitz had begun.

For two nights, bombs rained down on the city, killing hundreds, decimating large swathes of the city centre, homes, hospitals, factories and docklands. It was a terrible time, and many people lost their lives and their homes. The horror of it was replayed in Father's newspaper, the terrifying images on the front page were seared into Clarissa's memory.

As was the final scene of the reel inside Clarissa's mind. It occurred two months into 1941.

Clarissa was reading in the library. Father took a call in his study. Then Mother was summoned by Kingsley. The quick-time sound of her heels on the tiles and the closing of the heavy mahogany door. This time Clarissa couldn't eavesdrop from the foyer, not with one of the maids busy polishing the banister. Instead she hovered just inside the library and strained her ears to the muffled sound of voices next door.

Over an hour passed after which Mother shot from the room, handkerchief clasped to her mouth as she ran up the stairs, the sob that escaped was loud enough to cause the maid to make the sign of the cross.

A terrible dread gripped Clarissa's heart as she slunk back inside the library, too scared to venture out and ask what was going on. This time she didn't want to know.

When Father sought her out, and seated himself opposite while he explained, Clarissa couldn't meet his eye. That would have made it all too real and she would have had to face facts, that Eleonora was missing, somewhere overseas, and presumed by the war office to be dead.

While Clarissa forced back the tears, Father said they all had to be brave and try to carry on, like so many other families were doing right across the world. Perhaps had Clarissa lifted her head and looked into her father's eyes she might have seen tears. Or maybe, along with the flames of the fire and the glow of the reading lamp she may have seen something else.

The hint of a lie.

Because once she was excused, and fled to her bedroom, Clarissa went straight to her wardrobe and from her box of secret things, she pulled out the Christmas envelope. She cried alone in her room for hours, praying that if she held the paper close enough to her heart she would receive a message from Eleonora.

It was later, when no message came through, as she was placing the envelope back in the box that she took one last look at the writing on the front, taking in the wiggly lines where the stamp had been franked. And that was when she noticed it. The postmark. It hadn't been sent from London, where Eleonora worked at the war office.

The black ink was clear and told Clarissa exactly where and when the Christmas card was posted. On the 9th of December. In Manchester.

CHAPTER 17

MR TRISTAN HENDERSON JNR

What had he got himself into? That was the question whirling around in Tristan's head ever since he'd clapped eyes on cowboy-Joe-from-Mexico, AKA Chuck Chamberlain.

The skipping song that the girls at his boarding school used to sing in the playground was lodged in his brain, an annoying earworm that he couldn't shake out. It pinged into his head the second he spotted Chuck in the lounge of the hotel, wearing skin-tight jeans, a blue and red checked shirt, cowboy boots and on his head...

Surely, thought Tristan as he'd approached, Chuck hadn't worn his cowboy hat on the plane – or maybe he had. Perhaps first class was used to eccentric passengers and knew how to deal with them, but Tristan really didn't think a boutique hotel in Cheshire would.

Chuck stood out like a sore thumb amongst the plush wing-backed chairs, potted plants and dramatic drapes of the Victoriana styled lounge. What had he been thinking? Tristan knew the answer to that. He was dangling the carrot, giving Chuck a taste of how it could be if he played the game. So what if the other guests turned their noses up when they heard Chuck's brash, southern drawl. Or if he'd ordered half the room service menu. The firm would pay and recoup the cost when they invoiced Clarissa.

Tristan smirked, ignoring the curious look from the receptionist as he hovered behind one of the marble pillars. From there he could spy on Chuck, who was engrossed in his phone, and for a millisecond, considered bailing. The thought of associating with the likes of cowboy Joe for half an hour, never mind days, resulted in an involuntary shudder.

Would Tristan have to be a chaperone for the whole time Chuck was in the UK? Possibly. Just to make sure he didn't step out of line and most importantly, *somehow* ingratiated himself with Clarissa. It wasn't going to be an easy task. Certainly not dressed like that!

On the other hand, if old Clarissa took a shine to her long-lost cowboy cousin, maybe Tristan could drop the hint that Chuck could bunk up at the manor. She'd never struck him as a snob, in fact, his father always remarked that Clarissa was far too friendly with her employees and didn't know the meaning of the word boundaries.

With this in mind, Tristan felt better already. Fixing his best 'be nice to the client because they're paying you a fortune' face, he took a fortifying breath and headed towards Chuck.

Tristan waved over to the waiter and, with two fingers, indicated that they required more drinks. After the introductions had been made, Chuck acquitting himself admirably in the firm handshake department, he hadn't stopped talking about the flight and the food and the limo, how swanky his room was and how many times he went back to the buffet table at breakfast. Apparently, Chuck thought he could get used to a life like that.

Excellent.

Still, as much as he'd been amused by Chuck's boyish wonder, they had business to discuss.

'So, you understand how important tomorrow's meeting is. We need to tread very carefully at first and treat Clarissa with kid gloves. Gain her trust for a start. She's very old but wily, and she doesn't suffer fools.'

Chuck stretched out his legs and crossed his arms behind his head, oblivious to the odd looks he was attracting.

'Dude, how am I going to do that? She's like, related to the King so how the heck can I impress her? She's royalty. And anyway, just because we're distant relations it doesn't mean she has to leave me anything... or does she? Like, is it the law over here?'

Tristan sucked in his irritation. 'Actually, for a start, she's not related to the king, so I don't know where you got that idea from.'

Chuck shrugged and gave a thumbs up sign to the waiter who brought over his beer, whipping it off the tray before he'd had chance to put it on the table.

'Seriously! I thought she was a lady or something and anyone who lived in a castle was related to the king.'

'No. Well I mean yes. Her mother was a lady but the title died with her although Clarissa is descended from those very well connected to royalty. However, Chamberlain Manor isn't a castle, even though the surrounding walls and façade – the front of the building – do give it that appearance.' Tristan took a slug of his whisky then, 'And it's entirely up to Clarissa who she leaves her estate to because she was the sole beneficiary when her mother died many years ago. You would only have a legal claim if she died intestate – that means without making a will – and there's no chance that is going to happen. That woman is nothing if not meticulous.'

'So who is she going to leave it to, if not me?' Chuck was about to put one of his cowboy boots on the table until the withering look Tristan gave him registered.

'Truthfully, I'm not sure because she changes her mind like

the blasted weather, but last time it was amended it was various charities and that would be a crying shame in my opinion.'

'Jeez. Sure would be a wasted trip if that happened. I ain't had no fun yet.'

Acknowledging the understatement of the year, and Chuck's hint about having a good time, Tristan moved on. 'Don't you worry about that for now. You just have to focus on being polite and friendly. Get her to think you're genuinely interested in your heritage, and her, obviously. Can you manage that?'

Chuck drank and nodded his head once he'd swallowed his beer. 'I can certainly do that for you, dude, and hey, I am interested. Until that PI gave me the fright of my life I had no idea I was related to any Brits. Hell, I had no idea about nothin' if I'm honest. And I'm a lone wolf. My daddy's dead and my mama's gone nuts so I like the idea of havin' family somewhere in the world.'

Well there's a big surprise, that your mother is a lunatic and you are an annoying ignoramus!

Tristan held that thought and his temper then wondered whether he should broach the subject of Chuck's attire. At least get him to ditch the hat.

Then an idea. 'Do you have any formal clothing with you?'

Chuck looked downwards at his shirt and jeans. 'This is formal. These are my best. Bought 'em for the trip. Not the Stetson. Had this beauty for years.'

God give me strength. Tristan tried to curb his sarcasm, but it was big ask. 'Hmm. I was thinking something less... ranch-like; you know, ditch the cowboy look when we go for lunch with Clarissa tomorrow.'

'Oh, I get ya. Like a suit. Nope. Don't own a suit. Sorry man.'

Tristan puffed out his cheeks and resigned himself to the inevitable. 'Well, in that case drink up. It looks like you and I are going shopping.'

CHAPTER 18

Tristan's temples throbbed. His anxiety levels were through the roof. The urge to throttle Chuck was increasing by the minute. Their luncheon with Clarissa and the ever-watchful Jennifer reminded him of similar afternoons when his boys were toddlers.

He and Diana would take them to a local but very upmarket carvery for Sunday lunch. Carnage, that's how he'd describe it. Stuck in a heaving restaurant with other foolish parents who'd also believed that their little darlings would sit nicely, eat with a knife and fork, and not have a tantrum because they couldn't have ice-cream before their main.

For the past hour and a half, Tristan had skilfully guided conversation, kept the subject matter jolly, given Chuck the evils when he knocked over a crystal glass as he fumbled for the salt and pepper, and wanted to die when he'd dipped his bread into his soup. How he'd resisted rapping him on the knuckles when he asked for a beer instead of wine, Tristan had no clue. It was exhausting.

As was the trip to Cheshire Oaks, the designer outlet village where Tristan had bought Chuck some new clothes. He'd objected at first, to the smart casual blazer, shirt and slacks, and outright refused to wear a tie but, in the end, Tristan cajoled and bribed, and Chuck had seen sense. First impressions counted so even if the loafers pinched a little, all he had to do was grin and bear it then he could go back to his cowboy boots. Tristan would have to endure a trip to a karaoke bar, that was the bribe. While the incentive of bagging a fortune had not only worked on Chuck, it had helped steel Tristan's resolve. He could do this. It would be worth it.

To be fair, Chuck had scrubbed up well. If only he'd stop fidgeting with his collar and tie, like it was his first day in school uniform. God, the man was irritating.

And to her credit, Clarissa had been the perfect hostess: greeting Chuck warmly with a smile and handshake when they arrived; putting him at ease when he asked how he should address her. Tristan had advised going for overkill, and using the title, Lady Chamberlain, even though by rights she wasn't actually a lady, just acted like one. Chuck, overcome by nerves or amnesia, had ignored this, despite practising in the car on the way over. Instead, in his lazy drawling way he called her ma'am while Tristan cringed as he listened to vowels that he thought would go on forever.

She'd insisted he call her Clarissa, thank goodness. And as Tristan orchestrated, winced, glared, and gritted his teeth, he'd also observed. By the time the meal was at an end and Jennifer served coffee, a blessed relief in Tristan's opinion, he was somewhat assured that their host was neither offended nor bored by her guest. In fact, she appeared to be amused. He hoped this was a positive sign.

'So, Chuck. You've heard all about our family tree and Chamberlain Manor so now it's time to hear everything about you. Tell me, what do you do for a living and how on earth did a gentleman from Kentucky end up in New York City?' Clarissa lifted her coffee cup and waited.

Tristan pounced, not wanting Chuck to go full-blown honest. He'd had three beers, politely decanted by Jennifer. At least they'd not had to watch him swig from the bottle and belch like he had the previous day in the hotel bar.

'Well, Chuck has had a varied...' The sight of Clarissa's raised hand immediately silenced him and while he flushed, she turned her attention to Chuck and waited.

Chuck, now comfortable in his surroundings and no doubt buoyed by alcohol and an encouraging smile from Jennifer, told all. 'Well, it's very simple really. I was a fool for love and followed a lady, my girlfriend at the time, to the Big Apple. One of her friends got her a job and she thought she'd hit the big time so, rather than be alone in Kentucky, I packed up and headed out. I drove her north, and used my savings to get us a place to live. But within a month she met a new guy, the owner of the joint where she worked and kicked me to the kerb.'

Tristan was tempted to translate but fearful of the hand-signal and being made to feel like a naughty boy, he remained silent. Anyway, it seemed that Clarissa was fluent in Chuck-speak.

'Oh what a shame. And how horrible to use you like that. But why didn't you return to Kentucky? Were you not happy there?'

'Ma'am, I love my hometown. Owensboro is in my heart. I love that place so goddamn much.'

Give me strength, Tristan said to himself while he threw imaginary daggers at Chuck's head.

Oblivious to the invisible attack, chatty Chuck continued, 'But I'd given up my apartment in Owensboro and used what money I had for the new one in New York, so decided to stay in the city until I had enough to go back. There was plenty of work, in bars and the car-wash and other...' Chuck paused, side-eyed Tristan who was holding his breath, then continued, '...delivery jobs here and there. I was doin' okay and planned to head home before Christmas when the PI turned up and told me I had a family on the other side of the pond. And well, here I am.'

Again, Clarissa sipped, then gave Chuck what Tristan hoped was a benevolent smile before she asked, 'And what do you plan to do, when you go back to Kentucky? Do you have a trade, a profession other than what you do in New York? And tell me about Owensboro. What it's like there.'

A smile lit Chuck's face and for a second, Tristan saw a glimmer of the person he hoped Clarissa might take under her wing.

'It's the home of Bluegrass, my favourite kinda music, and we have bourbon distilleries and manufacture chewin' tobacco like you ain't ever chewed in your life.'

At this Tristan saw Jennifer stifle a chuckle while the corners of Clarissa's eyes crinkled in what he took as amusement, rather than disgust.

'And then when you head out of town and hit the highway, there's miles and miles of green pastures and cattle ranches on every hill. I got me some photos on my phone if you'd like to see.' Chuck reached into the inside pocket of his jacket and was soon flicking away, showing Jennifer first, who then passed the phone on to Clarissa who needed her glasses, that were somewhere, oh yes, hanging around her neck.

Ten minutes later, after an interminable period where Tristan thought his face had frozen into a fake rictus grin and he was losing the will to live and the ability to summon any more enthusiastic adjectives, Chuck put his phone away.

'Well, I must say it looks like a lovely place to live, but what is it you do there? Well, before you left for New York.' Clarissa waited and Tristan felt the weight of expectancy, realising that while he'd focused on Chuck's New York lifestyle, he too had no clue what he did in Owensboro. Again, Tristan held his breath and to his surprise, he saw Chuck blush.

'Well, y'all might find this amusing... heck you might not even know what Bluegrass music is... well anyways, before I shipped out I used to work in a bar by day and at night and during the summer months I was a dancer.'

You could actually have knocked Tristan down with a feather but then a thought, followed by creeping dread, followed by another bloody question from Clarissa.

'A dancer, how marvellous and no, I'm not sure what Bluegrass music is but perhaps later you can show us, on Jennifer's laptop but first, what kind of dancing do you do?'

He's going to say erotic, I know he is...

Chuck quickly and in a rather bashful voice, proved Tristan wrong. 'Clog. I'm a Bluegrass Clog Dancer.'

Tristan was getting agitated again and no sodding wonder. After they'd all relocated to the drawing room where Jennifer found video after endless video of Bluegrass country music. Then, as if that wasn't bad enough, after being told to pull back the Persian rug, he'd hidden a grimace as Clarissa clapped like a deranged seal, thoroughly delighted by Chuck's clog dancing routines. Tristan had literally wanted to die, again.

And now, to add insult to injury, while Jennifer caught up with the utter dross that was *Coronation Street,* and he fended off another angry text from Diana wanting to know where the hell he was, Tristan wondered if the day could get any worse.

Scanning the grounds from the drawing room window, Tristan watched for signs of Chuck and Clarissa who'd insisted on showing him the stables, albeit from her wheelchair.

Okay, so the afternoon had been sheer torture, and if Chuck held him to his promise of hitting Manchester to find a karaoke bar, he'd be in deep doo-doo with Diana. While on the other hand, rough and ready Chuck the Clog-Dancing Cowboy appeared to have won Clarissa over, so it hadn't been a complete waste of time.

During the impromptu cabaret, Chuck had also divulged that it was his heart's desire to open his own bar and restaurant in his hometown, where the sound of Bluegrass and clip-cloppingcloggers could be heard night and day. Hence, Tristan had the most perfect carrot to dangle.

If Chuck inherited the lot, once Chamberlain Manor was sold, good old Chuck could bugger off back to Kentucky and open a chain of bars should he so wish. It couldn't have been more perfect if he'd planned it himself.

Hearing the front door opening and the shrill sound of Clarissa's voice, accompanied by guffaws from Chuck's, Tristan scooted into the hallway, followed by Jennifer.

'Well, I must say you've got some colour in your cheeks. Did you enjoy your walk?' Jennifer was removing the blanket from Clarissa's knees as she spoke.

'We most certainly did. We've taken a stroll down memory lane, and both learned a bit more about each other and our family history and, we have some news, don't we, Chuck?' Clarissa looked up and gave him a beaming smile.

Chuck was still holding onto the wheelchair but looked to Tristan, who tried his best to look casual. 'Oh really. What's been going on?'

'Well, Clarissa has kindly asked me to come and stay here, until it's time to head home and I've accepted her mighty fine offer. So I'll need to get back to the hotel and pack. I said I'd stay there tonight and make my way here tomorrow.'

For a second, Tristan was speechless, and only one word sprang to mind. *Bingo!*

CHAPTER 19

HONEY

Honey eyed the cardboard box on her coffee table and was hit by a wave of guilt because she still hadn't had chance to open it. As she fastened the zip of her boots, she spoke to the photo on the sideboard, knowing that her great aunty Beryl would forgive her anything.

Still, she felt bad, and it never hurt to say sorry, did it?

'I promise I will have a good look through your bits and bobs later, after I've been to see Grandad. It's been so busy the past few days and I really want to appreciate whatever you've got stashed in there.'

The photo of Aunty Beryl smiled back, her silver perm bobbing as she shook her head, arms crossed over her ample bosom as she sat on Morecambe beach, resting against the promenade wall. Honey easily imagined Beryl's voice saying, 'Don't be worrying yourself, love. There's no rush, and it's only a few bits and bobs I thought you might like. Sunday is your day off so enjoy it.'

There, conscience clear.

Grabbing her rucksack, Honey gave the box lid a couple of taps and headed to the front door of her cottage. Since she'd said goodbye to Levi on Wednesday evening it was as though she'd been holding her breath, waiting, wishing the week to go fast and for Monday to arrive. Just thinking back to being in the pub with him sent a fizz of excitement running through her veins.

He hadn't stayed long after Ziggy joined them for a drink, but he'd amiably chatted away until she saw him check his watch. She knew from his expression he had other arrangements and her heart had sunk, immediately wondering who, where, why. But he'd sworn off dates, he'd told her so, which was why she believed him when he explained.

'I'm really sorry but I'm going to have to head home. I'm going away for a few days with my family, so I need to get organised. And before you say, yes, I have left it late. But I hate *packing*. Can never decide what to take and the weather forecast is always wrong, and I end up either freezing, getting soaked or baking to death.'

Honey, always the nosey mare, asked, 'Ooh, where are you going?'

'Anglesey. My mum and grans love it there so I'm taking them… she has a minibus… for all of them and the wheelchairs… long story.' Levi had faded off, as though he'd caught himself out oversharing or rambling, then he was back. 'I'll be back on Sunday night.'

Honey held her breath and crossed her fingers because if he didn't ask, she would.

Levi homed in on her and she could tell before he spoke he was nervous, which she thought was sweet. 'You said your day off was Monday? Unless you help with the warm hub.'

Honey nodded enthusiastically.

'Well, I was wondering, if you're not busy… I'm back in work but I could… we could… meet for lunch if you like…'

'That would be great. Let's swap numbers.' Before he could change his mind, Honey had whipped out her phone and passed it to Levi who dutifully tapped in his number.

Within seconds, the deed was done, and Honey had relaxed. The worm was on the hook and no way was he wriggling off.

'I'll text you over the weekend, then, if that's okay.' Levi was hovering, looking hopeful.

Honey watched as he backed away from the table, once again awkward, as if he found goodbyes as troublesome as hellos. 'Yep, no problem. And I'm intrigued. You said you had an idea about the café, but you can tell all on Monday.'

He left after saying bye to Ziggy and with a wave to both of them, and no sooner was he out of sight than Honey felt a sharp dig in the side.

'Bloody Nora, mate. Talk about gagging for it! The poor guy has no chance does he?' Ziggy didn't do subtle.

'I have no idea what you mean, young Zigster. Now go get a round in, and order me a chip butty. Lust has made me hungry.' She had given her pink-haired friend a cheeky wink because Ziggy was in fact correct. Honey was smitten.

Since then the week had flown by, and even though she'd been rushed off her feet, her thoughts had often strayed to Levi. Sundays always came around so quickly and after dropping off Grandad Ernie, who was in great need of a nap by the fire, Honey headed home. She could hardly move after the roast from the local carvery, and was looking forward to a glass of wine and an afternoon of doing absolutely nothing.

It was getting chilly, but not cold enough for the central heating, so after bringing in some logs from the garden and lighting the wood burner, Honey settled in the lounge. In her hand was the promised glass of wine and as she reached for the TV remote, something caught her eye.

'Okay. I give in. I'm all yours.' There was no putting it off and she *had* promised so, reaching forward, she slid the box off the table and onto her lap.

It had once contained a Christmas food hamper. Honey knew this because Aunty Beryl ordered one every year and the name of the company was printed on the side. After picking at the brown packing tape that sealed the lid, Honey stripped it back and opened the two flaps to reveal a layer of newspaper. Again she recognised it: the *Manchester Evening News*. After glancing at the date, she realised that her aunt must have packed the box almost eighteen months earlier.

'Always organised, weren't you, Aunty Beryl… now what have we got in here.' Honey removed the items one by one, with care. They were, after all, things her aunt regarded as heirlooms, special enough to warrant passing them on to Honey.

Half an hour later, after smiling and blubbing her way through three battered photo albums, she unwrapped a trio of china vases decorated with peonies, a tea set for two and some empty but beautifully intricate photo frames. They would all look perfect in the cottage.

She knew instinctively that Beryl had saved items that wouldn't burden Honey; and that she had not wanted her niece to feel obliged to take them. A memory floated in, of Beryl giving Honey some sage advice.

And when I'm gone don't you be thinking you have to keep all my tat. Just send it to charity because most of it is worthless, basic bits and bobs I've bought from Wilko's or Tesco. I remember sorting through my old mum's house, and it was a blooming nightmare, deciding what to chuck and what to keep. Weighed heavy on me for months it did. Not a nice job at all, so I don't want you having to do it.

At the time, Honey had thought the conversation morbid and

depressing, but Beryl had meant what she said. Which was why by the time she passed away she had de-cluttered and left very precise instructions for whoever she left behind. In the event, it had been Honey's grandad and he followed her words to the letter.

That was why the items in the box meant even more to Honey, because they had been hand selected. Wrapped in tissue, a woollen cat and rabbit, knitted by Beryl's own fair hands, and bless her, two matinee sets for a baby. A hat, bootees, and a cardigan. One pale yellow, the other white.

'Are you trying to tell me something, Aunty Beryl?' Honey smiled through her tears and swore, if she ever did have a child, maybe children, they would wear the traditional woollen clothes lovingly knitted for them.

Next, she picked through a little red velvet jewellery box that contained, amongst other things, Beryl's wedding and engagement ring, a gold chain and a rather ugly brooch.

Covering what Honey thought was the bottom of the box lay a hand-embroidered tablecloth, decorated in an array of summer flowers entwined in pale green foliage. As she touched each one, Honey could imagine the hours it must have taken Beryl, who loved to sew and craft, and those hours suddenly meant the world to Honey.

'Oh I do miss you, Aunty Beryl.'

After taking a sip of her wine, Honey pulled the tablecloth from the box so it could be stored in the spare room, and as she did, spotted the A4 manila envelope at the bottom. There was nothing written on the front but there was really no need, seeing as the contents were meant for her, anyway.

'Ooh, what's this?' Honey was intrigued and lifted the envelope that was sealed with a strip of sticky tape.

She unpicked it quickly and tipped the contents onto her lap. Two more envelopes, marked one and two. This time her name was written on envelope number one, slim and white. Envelope number two was much thicker, manila and when she gave it a squeeze, Honey could tell there was something else inside. A hard bump and the sound of tissue crinkling under her touch.

For some reason, Honey was overcome with nerves, and she took a moment, just gazing at the contents of her lap.

So many thoughts. *Why were they hidden at the bottom and why are they numbered? This isn't like Aunty Beryl, to be secretive and mysterious. Just open number one, for heaven's sake.*

Following her own orders, Honey tore open the envelope and unfolded the lined paper inside, recognising her aunt's neat writing instantly. She swallowed. Curiosity accompanying a sense of unease as Honey began to read Beryl's words.

CHAPTER 20

Dearest Honey. My beloved niece. Wonderful companion and friend,

Before I explain why you are reading this, I want to remind you of how much you mean to me, how much I love you. You were the daughter I yearned for, my little helper and attentive student. The hours we spent together baking and sewing, sticking, and gluing all sorts of crafty things were a gift, a true joy.

I am immensely proud of the young woman you have become, and I know that you will continue to make a success of your life, in your own kind and giving way.

The bits and bobs I left for you are just tokens, really. Little nods to you and me.

I hope you like my choices but if not, please don't feel you have to hang on to them.

Honey paused and looked over to the photo on the side, 'Oh Aunty Beryl. I love you too and I'd never throw them away. I'll treasure them always.'

With a sigh she returned to the letter, still curious, and tentatively read on.

Now, to the reason for these letters. I trust that you have opened *them in order and inside envelope 2, you will find a smaller package. Please open that when you have finished reading the contents. It will make more sense then.*

As you know, family means everything to me and I have always done my best to keep us all together, bind the generations through good times and bad. I felt it was my duty. I must add it was one that I loved. Never a chore. I suppose in the end it became my quest.

At the time your great grandma Molly died, I had just divorced, and I admit, I was extremely lonely and cast adrift. The future terrified me, having to start again. Navigating life as a single woman was not something I'd envisaged.

I suppose I was quite a solitary figure and only had a handful of friends, all married, so I was quite the odd one out once the decree absolute came through. My husband got on with his life with his new woman and, for want of a better definition, I became stranded.

Your Grandad Ernie and Grandma Nancy, and your dad, were all I had. They were my safety net and I needed them in my life. Which is why I made the decision I did.

I had to choose between sharing a terrible secret and risk losing my brother or protect his feelings and keep my mother's confession to myself.

Honey gasped, 'Oh my … Aunty Beryl, what have you done? What did Granny Molly do that was so bad?'

Looking at the beautifully written words, knowing they were about to expose something shocking and potentially life-changing, Honey faltered, embroiled in a battle between fear and intrigue. The latter won.

At the heart of my decision was the fractious relationship between Ernie and my mum. For as long as I can remember they had been at loggerheads. Never saw eye to eye and it was as though when Mum pulled one way, Ernie instinctively pulled the other.

As a child I didn't think too much of it. It was how they were. I thought that was how big brothers behaved. Our rebellious, independent Ernie was my hero, so whatever he did was fine by me.

I do remember sometimes feeling second best, because Mum smothered Ernie with affection and attention which he rejected and resented without fail. Then when I became a teenager, I was actually glad to be second best. That her focus was elsewhere, and I began to understand – or I thought I did – why Mum's clingy ways and ridiculous rules drove Ernie to distraction. She wanted to protect him from the dangers of a man's world, or the clutches of an unsuitable wife. How wrong I was.

But Ernie was my world and without him in it, I don't know what I would have done which is why when he married your grandma, I was scared. Scared of becoming second best, again.

Honey's heart dipped on reading that line. 'Oh Aunty Beryl, that's so sad, that you felt like that.' Going straight back to the letter, desperately hoping for good news, she read on.

They were so in love and for a time I felt abandoned, stuck with a bossy mum and a subservient dad. You don't remember either of them, but Mum ruled the roost and Dad adhered, and stuck to his philosophy of "owt for a quiet life".

I truly believe my dad had no idea how much, or why Mum controlled his life, our lives, and maybe it was for the best.

In the end I needn't have worried about losing Ernie or becoming second best. Because he and Nancy always welcomed me in, made me part of their new life and for that I was so grateful.

So, to the confession.

I hope that when you read the notes that Mum insisted I wrote down word for word, that as they did for me, things will make sense and you can piece it all together.

And as God is my witness – well, I hope he is because otherwise it means I've gone downstairs and not upwards to the pearly gates – there were so many times, especially in recent years, when I tried to pluck up the courage to speak to Ernie. Make my peace before I died.

And then I would imagine his anger. It would turn on me, in the absence of Mum and I truly could not bear the thought of him being cross or hating me. I knew I'd left it too late. That the time for telling was back then, after Mum passed. I was so wrong. So stupid.

And now an apology.

For being a coward all these years. And for burdening you with a secret. Just like Mum did to me, I am about to do the same to you. It's so very unfair of me.

Why?

The answer is simple.

I cannot go to my grave knowing that our family secret will be buried forever. That Ernie won't know the truth. Or, if you choose to keep it to yourself for whatever reasons, at least I passed it on.

Please know that I have thought all this through, agonised over it. But I believe it is the right thing to do. To give you the choice. Just like Mum did with me.

I know I was selfish. And for that I am sorry. I put myself first, over Ernie, and that was wrong, too.

I don't expect or ask that you put it right. That is not my intention.

Merely that something Mum always regarded as a family affair, our personal business, remains so. Our history. You will soon know the truth and then it is for you to do with as you wish.

Once again, please try not to be angry with me. But if you are, then I understand.

One last thing.

Will you please tell Ernie that I am sorry. And that what I did was borne from love and nothing else.

Goodbye and God Bless, dearest Honey.

From your loving aunt,

Beryl. x

Honey was stunned. And she hadn't even opened envelope number two yet. To know that her precious Aunty had kept some terrible secret for so many years, one that had caused her such heartache, was unthinkable. Unfathomable. Did Honey want to know what her great grandma Molly had done? And once she knew, would she want to tell her Grandad?

Then a sobering and welcome thought occurred. Aunty Beryl, let alone her great grandma, were from a generation who thought you had to take down mirrors in a thunderstorm, and closed their curtains when someone in the street passed away.

Perhaps, whatever this secret was had been blown out of all proportion by two old dears who would have the vapours if they read what went on social media these days.

Feeling her anxiety dial down a notch, Honey tutted. Beryl wasn't the type, capable even of keeping something terrible hidden for all these years. So expecting nothing more shocking than a case of hiding love letters to her grandad, sent by an unsuitable girlfriend, Honey peeled open envelope number 2.

Molly's big secret was about to be revealed and, if truth be known, now she'd chilled out, Honey couldn't wait to see what it was.

CHAPTER 21

BERYL

Marple, Cheshire. 2003

Beryl nudged the bedroom door open with her hip and, spotting her mother was still sleeping, placed the tray onto the hospital-style table that arched over the bed.

Moving over to the dressing table, Beryl lowered herself onto the stool and waited. Hopefully once sleeping beauty awoke, ate her toast and drank her sweet tea, she could get on with telling her the 'great McCarthy family secret.'

The ramblings had started earlier that morning when Beryl heard Molly calling her name: 'Beryl, Beryl! Hurry I need you!'

And in those bleary-eyed moments when she'd noted the clock said 6.30am, and panicked that her mum was ill, she'd stumbled into her bedroom to find Mother McCarthy wide awake and sitting upright, pointing at the wardrobe door.

'There you are at last. Your father's been. He came out of the wardrobe to tell me it's time to go... I need to pack a bag. That's what he said. Have a look inside and see if he's still there.'

At the time Beryl was part-relieved and part-freaked out. 'Mum, what on earth...'

'I knew he'd come and get me, when it was my time, so we have to prepare and I'm not ready. I haven't told you my secret and I can't go before I confess.'

'Confess what? And may I remind you, Mum, that you're not Catholic so don't even think about asking me to ring for the priest. I don't know any for a start. Now, seeing as you're awake I'll go and put the kettle on.' Beryl yawned and headed for the hall but only made it as far as the door.

'And then when you come back I'll tell you my secret. I want you to write it all down, so you don't forget … so find some paper and a pen. Look in the bureau. Hurry up Beryl, go on, time's running out.' Molly raised her arm and flapped her hand, ushering Beryl from the room.

By the time she returned with a cup of tea, Molly had fallen back to sleep but knowing she'd never be able to do the same, Beryl decided to get on with her day and tackle the subject of ghostly apparitions and the secret, later.

The thing was, while she went about her morning routine, Beryl's mind had wandered. And the more she thought about her mum's outburst, and as the clock ticked, her curiosity was piqued, and her imagination ran wild.

Which was why she was perched on a green velvet stool, like an impatient lady-in-waiting, for Molly to wake up.

Beryl gave a small cough, hoping it might nudge her mother awake, but nothing. Then she shuffled on her seat and gave a loudish sigh. Still no joy.

Should I let her sleep?

Yes, really you should.

But the toast will go cold.

You can make some more, just leave her.

While conscience won the day, Beryl sat, part-mesmerised by the rise and fall of her mum's chest. This was accompanied by raspy breaths that emitted a faint hooting sound from between her thin, barely open lips.

Molly was a dozer and took naps throughout the day, yet as each passed, Beryl could see she was becoming weaker, more frail, less present. Like she was dissolving into the beige duvet set. Being absorbed by the wool of her white cardigan. Sucked into the down of her pillows until poof! One day she'd just fade away and be gone.

It was how Molly McCarthy had lived, really. Fading into the background like a bit-part player in a theatre production of her own life. Never wanting to take centre stage, draw attention, make a fuss. Not on the outside anyway. In public. Whereas between those four walls, in their family home and lives, Molly had ruled the roost. Her word was law.

Still, Beryl thought, a gentle dimming, like the switch that controlled the light in the lounge, would be a nice way to go. Better than how her old dad went, anyway. So if Beryl had one wish, for Molly, it was that when the time came she would just slip away, but *not* before she'd divulged 'the secret'.

Tipping her head to the side, Beryl gave a gentle sigh and thought, *I bet whatever this is, it's going to be a right load of old rubbish.*

Nevertheless, and as instructed, before being dispatched to make a cup of tea, Beryl had searched the bureau in the lounge and found a notepad and a biro, both of which were in the pouch of her apron, ready and waiting. It had to be said, much more patiently than she was.

Perhaps catching the aroma of buttered toast or being woken by her very obedient body-clock, Molly began to stir and stretch, before turning her head towards Beryl. 'Ah, there you are. What time is it?'

'8am, just like it always is when I bring your tea and toast. Here, let me raise the bed.' Taking the remote Beryl pushed the button that gracefully lifted Molly into a sitting position. After which, she plumped pillows, smoothed down the duvet and refastened a button on Molly's cardy.

Flicking away Beryl's hand, Molly's characteristic impatience and forthright manner had her daughter retreating, but not before she'd slid the table along the bed and checked the pot was still warm. Ignoring the irritable huffs and puffs by her side, Beryl poured the tea.

'Oh do stop fussing Beryl. Sometimes I wish you'd just sit. You make me anxious with your constant tidying and to-ing and fro-ing.' Molly ended her reprimand with a loud tut, then proceeded to get stuck into her snack.

'The butter isn't runny. It's soaked into the bread again and this tea is stewed.' But still she ate and drank, her back arched and her shoulders hunched over the table.

Beryl sat as instructed and rolled her eyes because her mother's tetchiness was the norm. Her pernickety and sometimes ungrateful attitude was water off a duck's back. She was no better with the nurses.

So while Molly nibbled and slurped, Beryl fought the urge to tap her foot and tell her mother to hurry up. To be fair, caring for Molly meant nothing more than making numerous little snacks and keeping her company, which was a doddle, seeing as since the divorce Beryl had been forced to move back home. It wasn't like she had to traipse across town or go out of her way. She now resided in the second largest bedroom, the one that used to be Ernie's when they all lived under one roof, many moons ago.

Silence and inactivity and slow-eating eighty-four-year-olds were the enemy because they allowed Beryl time to dwell on her circumstances and the shame she felt about all of it; her husband's dalliances; splitting everything down the middle and ending up with half of nothing she really wanted; becoming the odd one out; morphing from contentedly married woman to the spinster; the ultimate loser who'd run back to Mum because she had nowhere else to go. Apart from Ernie's, but that wouldn't be fair on him and Nancy. So there she was.

At least she had Ernie's son, Kevin, her grown-up nephew.

And his little gem of a daughter, Honey, who she adored. Kevin's wife, Astrid, was an acquired taste and not particularly enjoyed by anyone in the family. The thing was, Beryl took immense comfort in her kin, and cherished them. And once her mum was gone they would be her everything; all she had.

CHAPTER 22

The clatter of crockery rescued Beryl from her lonely meanderings and her attention was drawn elsewhere. Molly drained the teacup, and after a dab-dab of the lips, she slumped. Her shoulders sagged and her head flopped onto the pillows as though it was too heavy, or the mere act of eating and drinking had been an immense effort.

Beryl knew why: the doctors and nurses had explained it all very simply and with kindness. Her mother's body was slowly shutting down and therefore they should make the most of the good days, when Molly was on form and present. On the bad days, when it was touch and go if she was about to slip away or manage another episode of *Countryfile,* they should hope for a peaceful end.

Today had been a good day and Beryl knew she had to grasp the nettle and chivvy Molly along, otherwise the not knowing would drive her mad to the end of her own days. She had to find out, one way or another, what on earth her Mother Molly had been rattling on about, before the nurses arrived to bathe and change her.

'So, Mum. About this secret you mentioned earlier... do you

still want to tell me about it?' Beryl removed the tray and set it on the dresser, not sure whether to get out the pad and pen just in case she appeared too eager. Which she was.

Molly shifted her gaze to the window 'No, not yet.'

Beryl angled a look at her mother, irritation buzzing like wasps in her head. *I knew it, she's just being melodramatic.'*

But before the wasps could settle, she was swiftly corrected by Molly whose voice, often brusque, always clear with perfectly formed consonants, had taken on a softer tone. Tentative tinged with sadness. 'First I need to explain why I'm telling you. And why now. And I need to apologise, too.'

Beryl was more intrigued than ever. 'Apologise for what?'

Molly pulled at her cardigan, wrapping it around her sparrow-like body as if for protection before she spoke. 'For being a coward. For burdening you with my secret because if I tell you, that's what I'll be doing. And now I'm thinking it's not right, to do that… so maybe I'll stay quiet. Take it with me to the grave and have done with it. Might be for the best.' She sounded wistful as her words trailed off but even that didn't quell Beryl's mounting irritation.

Talk about dangling a carrot!

'Mum, listen. Whatever it is, it's clearly bothering you so perhaps sharing it will make you feel better; and let's face it, this big secret hasn't had a terrible effect on your life has it? You've been happy, had a nice home and husband, and a family that loves you, so it can't be that bad, can it?'

Beryl was very confident about her general appraisal and even gave her mum's hand a pat, as if to offer extra reassurance. In the grand scheme, and even considering the Ernie-blips along the way, they'd had a decent enough family life. However, going by the look on Molly's face, mother-ship didn't agree.

'And what would you know about it?'

'Pardon?' Beryl was stung.

'I said what do you know about the things I kept in here,'

Molly tapped her liver-spotted forehead with a bony, yellow-nailed finger. 'I hid it all from everyone, what I did, so I could keep this family together, so you and Ernie would have a home and a family. I'm telling you, if your dad'd found out he'd've chucked me onto the streets.

'Mum... I don't underst–'

'No of course you don't. None of you did. None of you had a clue what it was like for me back then... always, every day of my life. But I did it for you. That's what I need you to understand because I couldn't take it back, couldn't change what I'd done, and I've had to live with it all these years.'

Beryl swallowed, and tried to ignore the dread that was building inside, but she had to ask, 'Mum, what did you do? Please tell me and then I can help you sort it out.'

Molly only shook her head and pulled a handkerchief from her cardigan sleeve and dabbed her rheumy eyes.

Beryl pleaded. 'Mum, Mum! Look at me.'

Molly turned and Beryl's heart contracted when she recognised anguish on her old mum's face.

Beryl pulled the stool closer and gently took Molly's frail hand, stroking the tissue-thin skin that crinkled under her thumb. 'Let's take it step by step. Why don't you explain what happened. No matter what it is, I promise I'll stand by you. Then once I understand, we can work out a way to fix it. Is that what you want?'

She waited.

Molly remained deep in thought for a moment or two then sighed before answering. 'I don't know that you can fix it, not now. Nobody can. But I do know one thing.'

Beryl stopped stroking. 'And what's that, Mum?'

'I want all this to be over. All the worry. Looking over my shoulder and... and for you to know I'm not a bad person. I'm really not. If I could go back I'd've done things different. But I just can't take it to the grave, Beryl. I just can't.'

Molly was getting worked up and that wasn't good for her so Beryl sought to soothe her with words. 'Mum it's okay…'

'No, Beryl, love. It's not. I should've told the truth. To your dad for a start and…' her voice trailed off, as though she'd thought better of what she was about to say, 'But I was a coward and as the years went by I lost my nerve, told myself we were fine but most of all, I didn't think he'd forgive me.'

What could Beryl say? Without knowing what on earth her mother was going on about how could she even begin to imagine what her dad would've done, never mind if he'd forgive. There was only one thing for it.

Reaching inside her apron she picked up the pad and pen and then, adopting a stern but not unkind tone, made a suggestion. 'Mum, you have to get this off your chest. I'll write it down like you wanted and then once you've halved your troubles we can decide what to do. And if that means throwing this notebook in the bin and me swearing never to tell a soul, then so be it.'

Without warning, Molly reached over and gripped Beryl's wrist with such a force it made her gasp. She also remembered her mum's temper and how as a child she'd been wary of a backhander. But it was the panic in Molly's eye that actually chilled Beryl, and made her wish she hadn't pushed it. Suddenly she didn't want to know.

'No, you have to swear now that you won't breathe a word of this till I'm dead and buried and then you can do what you want. I'll leave the decision in your hands. Now promise, or I'll take my secret to the grave.'

Beryl gulped and while a voice in her head shouted *NO*, the one she found somewhere in the back of her throat said, 'Okay, yes. I promise.'

And that was all it took to elicit a curt nod in the direction of the pen that Beryl held in trembling hands, and for Molly McCarthy to speak her truth.

CHAPTER 23

MOLLY MCCARTHY

Manchester. December 1940

They said it was the stress that did it. Made my baby come early. The terrible bombings and my Walter being overseas. Not knowing whether he was dead or alive. I blamed the Germans. The first wave of bombers had swarmed over the city the night before, on the 22nd, and we'd spent a night of terror in the air-raid shelter. It was 6am when it stopped, and the 272 tons of bombs that dropped from the sky had decimated parts of Manchester.

Hitting cities on consecutive nights was a Luftwaffe tactic to inflict maximum disruption and destruction. The second wave came the following night when another 195 tons of explosives hit the city. Over a two-day period, 684 people lost their lives and more than 2,000 were injured.

I know all this by heart because my dad kept the cutting out of the paper and put it in a frame. Every year on the 22nd, he'd read it out, to mark the anniversary of losing family and friends, so we wouldn't forget. Not that I ever would; how could I?

It was about four in the afternoon of the 23rd and even

though it was almost Christmas, nobody apart from the kiddies felt any festive cheer. Not when such grim stories were filtering through about the death and destruction from the night before.

Mam had sent me to the corner shop, insisting that a daily constitutional did me good, and I was usually glad to get out of the house, but not that day. As soon as I stepped onto the street, I had to cover my face with my woolly scarf because the acrid smell of smoke and lord only knows what burnt my nostrils.

We lived in Ancoats back then, within walking distance of the city centre, in a little two-up two-down with an outside lavvy, a few doors away from my mam and dad. I loved living there. Me and Walter knew all our neighbours. A right little community it was. Walter used to drink in The Hat and Feathers, round the back of the *Daily Express* building where my dad worked. That's where we'd all go after the Whit Walks, and on Boxing Day, too, because it was Mam's birthday. I miss those days.

Only a couple of miles away, Beswick had taken a battering. Dad's older sister and her family lived there, and we didn't know at the time, but her house took a direct hit. We found out they were dead on Christmas Eve when a bobby came with the news.

As I made my way along the street I feared the same fate, if my house got hit, and Mam and Dad's. I wondered how the poor souls who'd been bombed out would manage and how many had been killed. It was bitterly cold and so many of us were struggling to make ends meet and the thought of having nothing, no home, no belongings made me shudder.

My mind then wandered to my Walter, who was God knows where, and I hoped with all my heart he was okay. Not cold or hungry or scared. It didn't do to dwell, that's what Mam said, so I shook away the images in my head and pushed open the shop door.

It was full, but I squeezed inside, out of the cold and the stench, and listened from the back of the queue. Naturally the talk was of the air raid and the women up ahead were all unanimous in their hope that the bombers wouldn't return.

I remember standing there, trying to ignore the horrible lump of dread that was lodged deep inside my chest. I didn't join in but nodded my agreement because I hated going down to the shelter. Scared that I'd go into labour and give birth while everyone looked on.

And that's when it happened. While I waited in line, worrying myself half to death as I listened to second-hand reports of how badly damaged Manchester was, horror stories of people being buried alive and burnt to death. I felt the first contraction, almost four weeks early. And then, while I clutched my stomach and tried not to cry out, my waters broke, right there in the corner shop. I was so ashamed. I also knew something wasn't right.

Someone ran to get Mam, and two of our neighbours helped me to a chair while Mrs Baines, the shopkeeper, went to get a mop. I didn't want to go to hospital. The midwife was supposed to be delivering my baby at home when the time came, but when Mam arrived she insisted. Said the baby might be in trouble and that panicked me more, so I did as I was told.

Anyway, Mrs Baines had a phone, so she rang for the ambulance and before I knew it I was on the way to the hospital. Mam didn't come with me because she was minding our Linda's three kiddies. Little buggers them lot were. Our Linda worked in the Avro factory as a riveter, same as me before I had to give it up because I was preggers.

So I went to hospital on my own. I'd just turned twenty-one and even though I was a married woman, about to become a mother, in those moments I felt like a terrified little girl who only wanted her mam.

I can't remember much about arriving because it was all such a rush. I was in a big panic; everyone seemed to be from the second we got there. I was thrust into a wheelchair then pushed at speed along the corridors by a nurse who told me how busy they were, with the casualties from the air raid, and that everyone had everything crossed the Jerries didn't come back.

'I've not been home yet... was here all night and managed to get some shut-eye earlier but we're dreading another raid... last night, well I saw things you can't imagine and won't want too, either.'

I wanted to tell her to stop, but reminded myself that was selfish and maybe she just needed to talk. Along the way, in between contractions that were getting stronger and made me howl, I passed people on stretchers and the walking wounded. Some of them had been patched up and hobbled along, others waiting to be seen. I felt like such a fraud despite the agony.

But I did as I was told, like Mam said I should. And I tried to be brave, like she wanted me to be. I can still feel her kiss on my cheek and her words as the ambulance doors closed.

'Just listen to the nurses and do what they tell you. It'll be okay, I promise. And be a brave girl. I know you can do it, love, and I'll be waiting with a nice pot of tea when you bring our new baby home. Then you can write your Walter a letter and tell him he's a dad.'

I hung on to those words through it all. The labour that just went on and on. Where I thought I was going to die from the pain and humiliation, my legs in stirrups and mess and blood all over the bed. Then when the air raid siren went off, I thought I'd die at the hands of the German bombers and my Walter would never see the little baby boy who lay quietly in my arms.

My baby was barely minutes old. There was pandemonium outside and I could tell the nurse was torn between me and rushing off to prepare for the worst. She appeared unconcerned by his weight and size even though I knew he needed longer in the oven, as Mam would say. The nurse had patted my hand and told me he had a good set of lungs on him, and not to worry. She'd seen plenty of little ones do well and after she'd done what was necessary down below, and tried to help me feed my little boy, she went off to fetch me a cup of sweet tea, telling me to rest a while. She never came back.

I was in a side ward, in a tiny room with a partition, and I presumed on the other side was another patient, perhaps sleeping because they made no sound. I was scared, sore and achy. Hungry, and thirsty. But the sight of my sleeping son wiped it all away. He was all that mattered.

The blood-curdling wail of the sirens outside seemed to heighten the sense of urgency beyond my room. I blanked it out at first and focused on my baby, Joseph. Before he went to war, me and Walter made a list of names we liked. Two choices for a girl or a boy but Walter said I should make the final decision when I'd had the baby. He reckoned I'd know what suited them once I'd seen their face.

Walter was right. Our baby definitely looked like a Joseph, after Walter's dad. And he was already being a good boy and hadn't cried since he was born, or suckled, but the nurse assured me he'd feed when he was ready. I told myself he was like his dad, a dozy bugger who liked his kip.

Before long it was impossible to ignore the nausea-inducing sound of the sirens and to be oblivious to the hurried footsteps on the corridor. Nurses gave terse instructions to orderlies who were moving people into the basement. Those who could walk were being told to make their way unaided and others I imagined being wheeled out in their beds. I was feeling fine and without being told, decided to get out of bed and find shelter.

When the door burst open, the ashen-faced nurse barked an unnecessary order, 'You need to go down to the basement immediately, there's no time to dress. Go as you are, now hurry.'

Before I could respond, another nurse appeared behind her and asked, 'What about the lady next door? She can't possibly walk, she's too weak.'

I heard the first nurse tut and reply, 'Come with me and we'll take her in a wheelchair. You carry baby.' With that they left me alone. No way was I going anywhere in that gown with my bottom showing. I'd had enough embarrassment for one day.

Joseph was in the little cot, swaddled in his blanket so I hurriedly dragged off my hospital gown and dressed in the clothes I came in with. Wincing as the anaesthetic down below began to wear off and the stitches made their presence felt, I told myself not to panic. Me and Joseph just had to get to the basement, and we'd be okay.

I'd just put my bag on the bed, slipped on my shoes and had one arm in my coat when the first bomb hit.

The noise was like nothing I'd ever heard before and the blast reverberated within me, rattling by bones and teeth. And the strangest thing – the room vibrated, the air wibbling and wobbling like a jelly on a plate. Maybe I imagined it, or my brain went a bit peculiar for a second but that's how I remember it.

Then came the screams and noises that mingled together, mushed up alien sounds that translated into fear. Whether it was instinct or the voice in my head, I obeyed both and took cover in the only place available. I grabbed Joseph and, oddly, in the midst of it all, my handbag which I threw under the bed, and with my free hand pulled at the mattress and chucked that under the steel frame, too.

Holding Joseph tightly I crawled underneath, using the mattress as an extra layer of protection over our bodies. I yanked the pillows towards me, one of which I laid my baby on, then placed the other under my head. All I could hope was if anything fell on us, the sturdy metal bedframe and then the mattress would take the impact.

And there I lay, throughout the longest night of my life. Me, my baby boy, and my handbag.

CHAPTER 24

When the next bomb hit, all the lights went out. We were plunged into darkness, and I remembered the woman in the shop earlier, recounting the sight of the buildings in Piccadilly gardens glowing orange, as shrapnel pinged off the bricks and peppered her coat and body. That's what I imagined to be happening outside to all those poor people caught in the raid.

From the black abyss under the bed, as the bombs rained down on my lovely city, not caring who or what they hit, I sang Joseph nursery rhymes. And told him all about his brave daddy who was going to be so proud of his baby boy.

'He'll take you to the park and teach you how to play football, and when you get big you can go with him to Maine Road to watch a match and after, meet Grandad in The Hat and Feathers. No drinking, mind. Just lemonade for you. I know what your grandad's like.'

About his grandma who couldn't wait to see him, 'She makes the best pea and ham shank soup in all of Manchester, and she's knitted you some lovely things. We unravelled a couple of your dad's jumpers, so it'll be like he's close to you when you wear them. You'll be snug as a bug in a rug you will, because it's blooming cold out there at the moment. Brass monkeys, your daddy would say.'

And his naughty cousins who'd look after him when he went to school. 'They're so excited to see you. And you'll be our Christmas baby now. An extra present for the little sods to fight over. P'raps I should put you under the tree with a bow on Christmas morning. Imagine their faces.'

I didn't allow myself to think about not being home for Christmas morning. Instead I held Joseph tightly and stroked his face, marvelling at the peach-soft feel of his skin and wishing he'd wake up so I could feed him. I told myself not to worry. That he was content, snuggled in the pillow, cocooned in my arms while the heat from my body kept him warm. Hoping my heartbeat made him feel safe.

I didn't feel safe, though. I wanted my mam. I wanted to ask her what to do and if it was normal for Joseph not to feed. I wanted to go home.

I think that maybe part of the roof above us had collapsed because I could smell burning and hear the sirens outside more clearly. That's probably why I heard the bomb before I felt the aftermath.

It whistled and whined, a horrid sound that tormented me as it approached, like a school bully heading across the playground in my direction. I imagined the tip pointing downwards seeking out a target and prayed so hard and held Joseph tighter, scrunching my eyes as I waited for it to hit.

It was like I imagine an earthquake to feel. The ground beneath me rumbling on impact, and then above me objects falling on the bed, splattering it with debris. A creaking and groaning, like a monster awakened from a cave or a giant, straining to hold the weight of a beam, the burden pressing down on his shoulders. And then he gave in.

Something very close had collapsed. I knew because it

sounded as though someone was hurling bricks onto the bed and two or three made their way under the mattress and hit my legs. Then the dust. Again instinct kicked in and I pulled my coat over our heads and around us, using it as a shield, like a tent, trapping the remaining clean air inside.

I waited. I held my baby. For how long I don't know. For the dust to settle and the bricks to stop falling. The stories from the women in the shop came back to haunt me. I was petrified that the whole roof and ceiling would come down and we'd be buried alive. That fire would ravage what was left of the hospital. Thoughts, none of them good, swept through my mind like poison.

Then after a time the room seemed to quiet and settle. There was still the odd creak and groan, muffled noise from outside became confused with that within. Cries for help, sirens, fire and ambulance, voices that came and went. It was the darkness I hated the most and then later, a new noise. A baby cried.

Not Joseph, he was still and quiet in my arms. And then the sound of someone coughing, close by. I realised it must have been whoever was on the other side of the partition. It lifted my spirits somewhat to know I wasn't totally alone, so I called out. 'Hello, are you all right? Can you hear me?'

There was nothing for a moment and then a voice, weak, female. 'Yes, yes I can hear you.' She sounded nicely spoken, not like me.

The baby cried and I wondered when she'd had it, perhaps before I came in. And then because I wanted to talk to someone, a mother in the absence of my own who could perhaps give me courage I asked, 'Is your baby all right? Is it a boy or a girl?'

Nothing again, and when she did speak I sensed it was with difficulty and I became scared that something had fallen on her, so laboured was her voice.

'Yes, he seems fine. I need to feed him, but I don't feel very well.'

Suddenly *I* became mother and tried to offer advice, remembering our Linda feeding her brood each time one came along. 'Can you put him to your breast. I think he'll work it out for himself.'

In the silence that followed my mind wandered to Joseph who had shown no such inclination when I'd tried earlier, and a tingle of fear prickled my skin. Absorbed by the surrounding noise it was hard to hear if she was moving but my hopes lifted when the baby stopped grizzling and she finally spoke.

'I did it. He's feeding…'

Something told me that I needed to keep her talking, whoever she was, so while I snuggled under my coat-tent, not wanting to suck in dusty air, I did my best to chivvy her along. She must only have been feet away from me and the urge to reach out my hand and take hers, was immense.

'What's your name, love? Mine's Molly.'

The waiting seemed like forever and then, 'Nora.'

'Hello Nora. And what's your little one called? Is he named after his dad? Mine's overseas in the army. Where's your old man? I bet he'll be proud as punch to see his little lad. I know my Walter will be.' The nervous gift-of-the-gab had possessed me, so I told myself to shut up and give Nora chance to speak. I soon wished I'd kept talking.

'His father's dead… but I know he's watching over him…'

I gasped. The tears came quickly but I forbade a sob. I had to be strong for all of us. That's what everyone said you had to do. Stick together at times like that. 'Oh you poor love. But your family will be pleased, especially his daddy's side and he'll remind them of your husband. That's a good thing.'

It was then that I heard her crying, so loud that it cut through everything going on around us. 'Oh love, don't cry. It'll be all right. We're going to get out of here I promise.'

I don't know why I said such a stupid thing and it reminded me of the promise Mam made before they carted me off to hospital and I instantly regretted it. Like I'd tempted fate and Mam had, too.

I pushed my coat away so I could hear better, still shielding Joseph underneath I listened. Within seconds my nose was invaded by dust, and I began to cough as my airways filled with the stuff. My face felt grimy and dry, and my eyes stung and watered but finally, once my coughing ceased, to my great relief, Nora spoke.

Just hearing the voice of a human close by gave me such comfort until her words sank in.

'We're not married.' A pause, and it must have taken such courage to say the next bit. 'And my family have disowned me. I'm in disgrace. I wouldn't get rid of my baby or have him adopted so my father told me never to darken his door. I have nobody. Not anymore. It's just me and my baby.'

All I could think of, right at that time was how lucky I was to have a husband, far away but – God willing – alive. A good mam and dad waiting at home for me and baby Joseph. Even our Linda and her lot, and Walter's annoying parents were bearable while just across the way, was a woman and her child with nobody at all. The gift of the gab took hold once more.

'Well you've got someone now. Me. When we get out of here you can come to ours. It's only small and nowt fancy but we can squash in together till you get sorted. And my mam and sister will look after you, too. We can all muck in and our little lads will grow up best friends. It's going to be alright. I'll take care of you, Nora… you're not on your own no more.'

This time, when she spoke Nora sounded a tiny bit stronger but at the same time disbelieving. 'You'd do that for me. A total stranger?'

'Course I will. We women have to stick together, and you never know, once your mam and dad see the little one, they'll have a change of heart.'

'They won't. My parents are ashamed of me, that's what my father said but thank you, for your kind offer.'

I smiled at that, even though my mam would think I'd gone daft, inviting a stranger, but I knew she'd understand, too.

Thinking of Mam gave me strength, 'Well let's not worry about that just now. Let's focus on them bloody Germans and hope our lads in the RAF are giving them what for. We just have to hold on till morning then someone will come and get us out of here. And I can't tell you what I'd give for a brew right now. Two big sugars and a slice of toast and dripping. What do you fancy, Nora?'

When there was no reply I held my breath and my stomach turned, and then when she answered I could breathe.

'I'll have what you're having,' she said, and I imagined she was smiling, my friend in the darkness. It made me smile too.

And then, 'Molly…'

'Yes love.'

'If I don't… if I'm not here in the morning will you look after my baby for me? His name's Robert, after his father. He has nobody else, and he deserves to be loved. I can't bear the thought of him being alone, not having family.'

I bit my lip and forced out a reply. 'Let's not be talking like that. We have to keep our spirits up, that's what Vera and Gracie would do. You're going to be all right just hold on.'

I listened in the darkness to the sound of nothing and it was the worse sound of all because I felt I'd let her down.

'Nora, Nora… stay awake Nora.'

She didn't answer.

I was so angry because I should have promised when I had chance, but that would have been admitting defeat and I couldn't do that. So along with listening to the sounds of Manchester burning, the sky falling in and heroes trying to do their best against the odds, I focused on good things. My son's breath on my face. The feel of his body. My husband and my family.

It was getting colder by the minute, and I shivered under my coat and wished I'd had a blanket and warm boots because my feet were freezing. I had to keep Joseph warm so pulled him closer and tucked my coat around him.

There, in the midst of panic, despair, and dogged hope, I entered a surreal state somewhere between sleep, nightmare, and reality, and waited for morning.

CHAPTER 25

When I opened my eyes, instead of black I saw grey, and as I slowly lifted the mattress a dim shard of light peeped through a hole in the roof. It allowed me to take in the floor of my room that was covered in thick dust and all manner of debris. It was morning and we'd made it.

And then I realised.

It was and still is the most dreadful, most terrible moment of my life, and I think in some ways I knew. I knew during those hours of fitful sleep and lip-numbing terror that my Joseph wouldn't make it.

That him and me, we were never meant to be. That he'd never meet his daddy. That his grandparents wouldn't take him to The Hat and Feathers on his eighteenth birthday, and his cousins would have no need to stick up for him in the schoolyard. I'd never hear him call me mummy, and his daddy would never hold him in his arms.

He was so beautiful. The silver-morning light lit up his face. And I took him in. The scent of him. His eyelashes, long and dark like Walter's. His perfect little fingers and hands. His cherub lips that I kissed as I drenched his cheeks in tears.

Somewhere between the bombs and the fires, the sirens and the cries for help, Joseph had slipped away and left me behind. I cried for… what seemed like forever, until at some point another sound interrupted my grief. A baby crying.

Robert.

Still holding Joseph, I wriggled from under my hospital bed fortress and waited while my eyes further accustomed themselves to the light and, when they did, I realised I was lucky to be alive.

Above my head, a steel girder dangled precariously, and the ceiling flopped, plasterboard and tiles sagging under the weight of whatever had been above it. Then sheer horror when in the corner of the room I spotted legs, and then a body spattered with blood, and as my eyes travelled further upwards the dead, unseeing eyes of a patient. Stripped bare in their moment of exit from this world. Their dignity snuffed out by a German bomb.

Averting my eyes, because that was all I could do for the person who once inhabited the broken body that lay in the corner, I took Joseph and crawled toward the gaping hole in the partition wall and the hospital bed covered in debris.

I had to scramble over bricks and shards of wood and whatever had fallen from above until I reached Nora and her baby and, although I was weak from the cold, thirst and hunger, I dragged myself onto the bed.

I was exhausted and my arms ached from holding Joseph while my legs felt like jelly, but I had to see Nora. She was covered in dust but, what struck me the instant I caught sight of her, was that beneath the grey, I saw red. She had the most glorious auburn hair that tumbled around her face while the rest of her locks flowed onto the pillow behind her head.

With a trembling hand I slowly wiped away the layer of fine particles to reveal… a beauty. A pale yet perfect complexion, pastel pinks lips, fine cheekbones. Her eyes, shuttered by lids, but I imagined them to be green.

'Nora, Nora wake up. Baby needs feeding, come on. Robert needs you. He's hungry and wants his mam.' My heart was breaking for the baby I held in my arms, and I wanted nothing more than to lie down right beside him. Join him in another world so it wouldn't hurt any more. Instead I remained upright.

I waited a while and tried, once, twice, and just when I was about to give up I caught my breath when her eyes opened. I was right. Eyes clear and green as the shamrock leaf on my dad's lapel pin, stared back.

'I can't. I'm sorry, I just can't.' Nora's voice was barely audible, and I noticed that as she tried to lift her arm, and move Robert who lay in its crook, her limb flopped back onto the bed.

Her baby cried out for nourishment, but she was deathly pale and as she closed her eyes again I remembered one of our Linda's gruesome stories. About a neighbour who bled to death after giving birth. Shifting my weight slightly I pulled back the filthy sheet that covered her to reveal the horror beneath. The crimson-soaked mattress told me all I needed to know. Without a word, I hid the truth and sucked in courage.

Looking down on my little boy I knew there was nothing I could do for him so, after laying him on the bed, I picked Robert up and unbuttoned my dress to feed him. He was tiny, like my Joseph, and I wondered if he'd come early, too.

He latched on immediately and whilst I was overwhelmed with a sense of relief I was racked with such immense guilt and disloyalty towards my own baby who lay silently on the bed.

I'd only just buttoned up my dress and placed Robert back by Nora's side when she roused. I picked up Joseph and hugged him to my chest as her eyelids flickered. When she revealed her emerald eyes, I noticed they had dimmed. No longer intense.

'Thank you...' Nora's free arm rested on her midriff, and I saw her fingers twitch, so I reached over and took her hand in mine.

'Shush, rest now. They'll start searching soon...' but Nora interrupted.

'He's a good boy, your little one... not a peep. They'll be like brothers, best friends.'

I swallowed and nodded. 'Let's rest now. The danger's over. You sleep and I'll watch Robert... it's been a long night.'

'Please hold my hand, don't let go. I don't want to be alone when...' she didn't end her sentence but drifted off, not away, and I thought she might be able to hang on. Just for a few more hours till they found us.

I did as she asked and, although I was dog tired and my body could barely hold itself up, I kept vigil, watching her chest rise and fall. I closed my eyes and jolted awake, no idea how long I'd slept for, seconds or minutes. Eventually I couldn't stay upright so lay back on the bed at an awkward angle, holding onto Nora's hand, with Joseph on my chest while Robert slept by his mother's side.

My eyes didn't respond at first to what my ears were hearing. Disobeying my brain that demanded I woke up.

'There's someone down there, I can see. Hello, love, can you hear me?'

And then Robert began to cry, and I heeded that voice rather than the one from the Home Guard who'd found us. I forced open my eyes and listened.

'I can hear a baby crying. Hello, hello! Can anyone hear me?'

Finding my voice as I let go of Nora's hand I raised my aching body and called out, 'Yes, I can hear you.'

And then the words I'd waited all night to hear. 'Don't you worry, love. We're going to get you out... I'll be back soon with help.' And then he was gone, his footsteps sending a cascade of dust and earth from above.

My attention turned to Nora and Robert, the baby first, who grizzled and waved angry fists. And then to his mother whose lips were tinged with blue and the gut-turning grey pallor of her skin.

Whether it was the cold, or lack of sustenance or horror but the combination made the room spin and as I gasped for air, I clung to Joseph and waited for it to stop. When it did, I gathered what strength and courage I had left.

'Nora, wake up. They've found us.' Reaching out a shaking hand I touched her face that I knew would be cold, and then I tried her wrist, feeling for a pulse like the nurse had done when I was admitted. Nothing.

In desperation I gave her a nudge and begged her again to wake up, but Nora didn't hear me. She was gone.

While Robert kicked his legs in temper beneath his blanket, I sat and stared at the woman who had no friends, or family or home and in it all, surrounded by destruction and mayhem, that's what made me cry. The futility of it all. Because there I was, ready and willing to take her in, be the friend and share the family she so desperately needed. I would never have the chance to show her kindness, love. Whatever her own kin were incapable of.

And then I looked at my little baby boy who would be missing out on the same. Joseph was gone too. Which is when I realised I couldn't help either of them anymore, but I could help Robert. He had nobody, that I knew from what Nora had told me. All I could think was he'd end up being adopted when I could love him as much as the next person, more. Neither baby wore a name tag, perhaps due to the state of emergency, but it made it all much easier.

I was on auto-pilot. And what happened next I could argue was a result of many factors. My mind being unbalanced by trauma. A body overflowing with hormones and confused further by fatigue. It wasn't. I knew exactly what I was doing.

I pulled Robert towards me on the bed, and then gently kissed my Joseph goodbye, telling him I would love him forever and remember him always. I placed him in the crook of Nora's arm and wrapped it around him. Then I picked Robert up and fed him.

While he guzzled milk, I waited for the rescuers to return, and gazed upon Nora and Joseph who slept side by side, him tucked into her arm, and I asked a favour. One mother to another.

'Will you look after my boy while I look after yours, Nora? Take him with you to heaven. I'll take good care of this one, I promise. He'll want for nothing, and I'll love him as my own.'

The sound of the Home Guard returning interrupted the tranquillity of the moment, but there was nothing more to say. So I sat on the bed, keeping Nora and Joseph company right until it was time to leave.

I asked the foreman to fetch my handbag from under the bed, because it had my ration book inside. Once he'd retrieved it, I handed him my new baby and watched as he climbed up the ladder and took him to safety.

Before I followed, as I gripped the wooden rung I steeled myself for what I was about to do. Because I knew it was wrong, but at the same time right.

I took one last look at the sleeping angels on the bed, then turned my head and focused on the hand that reached out from the hole in the roof, ready to guide me to the surface and the future.

When I stepped out into the frozen morning, the fireman handed me back my son and my handbag, while an ambulance man wrapped a blanket around my shoulders and steered me away.

I refused to go to another hospital and get checked out. I insisted on going home and said I'd walk if nobody could take me, and I would have. That's how determined I was.

I told the ambulance man my mam would be waiting with a nice pot of tea and later, I was going to write my Walter a letter and tell him he was a dad. It would give him hope, even more to fight and stay alive for.

While the ambulance man nodded kindly, the firemen went back to bring out Nora and what they thought was her baby. I walked away from the rubble and didn't look back. Instead, I left Joseph behind, and held my new baby very tightly. Sleepy precious Ernest, named after my dad. Then I took him home to meet his family.

CHAPTER 26

HONEY

The vibration of her phone which lay on the kitchen table beside her was a minor distraction and not enough to drag her away from the task in hand. Staring out of the window.

That, and making a cup of strong coffee, was all that she could manage, mainly because her brain was fried, and her eyes looked like pee-holes in the snow. Being reminded of one of her grandad's favourite sayings didn't even raise a smile like it normally would, because thinking of him made it all worse.

What the hell am I going to do?

This, and a hundred other questions, had plagued her throughout the longest of nights where the bedside clock reminded her with each passing hour that she'd be knackered by morning. And she was.

Her thoughts then roamed to Ziggy, who she pictured zapping around A&E saving lives and making people smile. Ziggy was adamant that after hearing some of her patients' stories, and seeing some of things they'd done or, had 'accidentally' inserted into various bodily orifices, nothing would shock her.

Well, have I got news for you, mate!

What Honey was also having great trouble with – what Molly had done, what Beryl had not done, and what she was more than likely going to have to do, was that *this*, this bloody awful family secret affair was happening to her. Them. Her and her grandad.

It wasn't some tacky daytime telly show where you could roll your eyes at the participants who were more than willing to air their dirty laundry in front of a studio audience and millions of viewers. This was her life and her poor Grandad's.

Her body felt like lead and, when her phone buzzed again, it took herculean effort to look downwards at the screen. She saw two names. Gospel and Levi.

Oh God... I can't go and meet him. Not today.

Honey had too much on her mind to fake it, and this pissed her off even more because she'd been so looking forward to seeing him and hearing all about this advice he was so desperate to impart. Never mind the fact he was as fit as... and Ziggy would string her up if she stood him up.

Bloody Molly McCarthy, and Aunty bloody Beryl, too!

Her big mistake was opening Levi's message because she knew as soon as she read it, she'd have to go.

> Hi, hope you're still on for today. Bought you some rock from Wales. Will meet you at Piccadilly at midday. Lunch is on me. L x

One kiss. He'd added a kiss. None of his other texts had kisses. As far as Ziggy was concerned that was like supergluing your lips to a love letter and Honey knew if she didn't obey the Zigster, shit would go down. And who was she kidding anyway? Honey wanted to go. Had even chosen what to wear – but that was before she'd opened the box.

Before she could change her mind, Honey fired a message straight back and felt a little lighter for doing so. Lunch with Levi would take her mind off things.

Hi, ooh. I love rock and yes, we're still on. See you later xx

She jabbed the send arrow, then opened Gospel's message that was all about Aki and the ingredients he'd picked up at the wholesalers. He got a 'yum' emoji in return although she did wonder if the diners at the café would have the same response come Friday lunchtime.

Pushing back her chair, Honey then deposited her mug into the sink and headed for the lounge where the offending box was waiting. The pile of lined paper was still on the coffee table, as was the smaller envelope, its contents safe inside. With a tut of irritation, Honey folded the sheets quickly and placed everything inside the flaps, then pushed them shut. She'd had enough of other people's mess.

Before she could return to the dilemma of if, and what to say to her grandad, Honey turned and made her way upstairs to the shower, desperate to wash away her irritability and waken her sleep-deprived eyes.

Getting away from the village and the café would do her the world of good and, on the train journey home, she would make a plan; but until then, the next few hours were going to be about her and Levi.

They'd walked from the train station up to the Northern Quarter where Levi had booked a table in a quirky fusion restaurant where the onus was on relaxed and informal. The staff were friendly and chatted away as they took their orders, two giant burgers and sweet potato fries. Honey saw this as a sign. Especially when they both chose halloumi cheese on top.

I mean, how could we be more in tune?

This, and the way Levi made her feel like she'd known him for ages, helped spread some much-needed calm through her tense body.

Honey, never one for dressing up unless it was absolutely necessary, was glad she'd stuck to her uniform of jeans – her best pair, her precious vintage Sex Pistols T-shirt showing a blacked-out face of her ex-majesty the Queen, and her beloved flowery Dr Martens.

He was wearing a similar jacket to the one he had on when she met him, but this was dusky blue, or maybe just faded, and underneath a grey paisley shirt and deep blue jeans. He clearly had his own style and it suited. They matched in a fashiony way. It was another good sign.

'I like your jacket, Levi. It looks retro. Did you get it from one of the shops around here?' The area was known for little boutique stores and the well-known antique and designer centre, Affleck's Palace, was a stone's throw away.

'I do pick up bits and bobs from Affleck's, but this is one of my dad's old jackets. There's a room at my mum and dad's that's used for storage, and I found loads of his stuff in the big wardrobe. Mum's a hoarder of family things and those four walls are like a shrine to tat and useless objects. I was actually in there looking for a snorkel and found a treasure trove of retro clothes. I'm glad you like it though.'

Honey saw from Levi's face this was so, and she was glad she'd commented. 'So do you still live at home?'

He shook his head. 'No, I moved out about a year ago. Broke Mum's heart and all my grandparents' too, but I wanted my own place and thought it might get me out of mini-bus duty. I was on call twenty-four-seven. Not that I minded too much, but it was getting to a stage where I was reverting back to my teenage self and being sent on daft errands by my loony family.'

Levi must have picked up on Honey's bemused expression and let out a sigh. 'Right, I haven't explained about our home for grannies and grandads, have I?'

Honey shook her head, eager to hear what he meant.

'So, bear with me, because there's a few of us, and you might need to stop me if you get confused...' he paused then continued when Honey gave a nod.

'We lived in what used to be Mum's family home. It's in Chorlton, it's a bit trendy now but wasn't always, anyway, it's huge, eight bedrooms, built in the Victorian era. Melba Villa, that's its name. It was inherited by my maternal great-grandma who ran a bed and breakfast lodging house for travelling salesman and single, professional ladies. All very respectable and above board.'

Honey interrupted. 'Ooh, I've seen dramas like that, set in the fifties, where the landlady was really strict, and you had to follow the house rules or else.'

'Yep, that's the kind of thing. Well, that great-grandma is no longer with us, but then my Grandma Birdie took over. My mum worked in a care home most of her life, but helped out a lot at the B&B. When Grandma and Grandad Birdie retired...' Levi stopped when Honey raised her hand.

'Why are they called Birdie? Is that their surname?'

At this Levi chuckled. 'Nope... it's because they had a budgie, well a few actually and when I was little, I got confused which set of grandparents was which, I mean let's face it, there was so many people coming and going I wasn't sure where lodgers and family ended. So I called my grandparents after their pets.'

'That's priceless, so go on... what are your paternal grandparents called?' Honey was loving this glimpse into Levi's family dynamic especially when he grimaced.

'They were Nana and Grandad Kitty-cat.' Levi immediately hid his face in his hands to conceal his embarrassment, but she could see he was laughing behind his fingers.

'That's just brilliant. I love it! Do you still call them that?'

Peeping out he said, 'NO! I'm not *that* sad.'

Honey would have thought it endearing, not at all odd or sad, if he'd said yes. Anyone else might have been another story. 'So, go on. What happened when they retired?

Levi reappeared from his finger-shield and rested his arms on the table. 'Well, me, Mum and Dad lived there anyway. I grew up in that house and loved being around my grandparents, and seeing the guests come and go.

'They worked for as long as they could, neither of them wanted to retire, but Grandad Birdie had a stroke and Grandma refused to let him be cared for anywhere than at home. Shortly after, she had a fall and broke her hip, and struggled to get about after that. Long story short, Mum left work and became their carer.'

Honey sighed. 'That's very sweet and I bet they preferred it to be your mum, rather than a stranger.'

'Oh definitely, and then, when the Kitty-cats became infirm, they moved in too. We also have my Uncle Norris – he didn't have any pets thank God. He was one of Grandma's lodgers who had nowhere to go when she closed. And then there's Great-grandma Pins who's actually my step-grandma on my mum's side and as old as the hills but that's another *huuuge* story and hurray, saved at last, our food is here.'

Honey watched as the waitress placed their meals on the table, but the second she walked away, simply had to ask, 'Please tell me why your great-grandma is called Grandma Pins. I won't be able to settle until I know.'

Levi rolled his eyes and grimaced before answering. 'Well, this is a corker… she used to have a black poodle called… wait for it… Pins The Knicker Ripper.'

Honey was in tears before she managed to ask why. Luckily, Levi filled the gap.

'He was a really giddy, naughty dog and whenever anyone wearing a skirt came to visit, he would jump up and try to bite their bums and rip their knickers. Apparently my mum was terrified of him. When she told me the story, my great-grandma instantly became Grandma Pins. Now, eat your food and stop laughing at me, okay!'

Levi pointed his fork, his eyes full of mirth and a smile on his face so, Honey nodded and picked up her knife and fork, still curious about his odd-ball family but at the same time, starving.

As she tucked into her lunch, she realised her earlier angst had eased and that her decision to meet up with Levi had been sound. At least someone in her family could make the right choices, but then again, lunch with a fit bloke was a lot different from deciding whether to steal a baby, or not!

While they ate, Honey skilfully moved the conversation on from family, suspecting Levi would at some point ask about hers, and that was the last thing she wanted to discuss. Today wasn't for talking about what happened to her dad, or why her mum now lived in Spain and God forbid they got onto her grandparents and those no longer with them! Talk about walking through the mire in leaky wellies.

Instead, Honey thought it best to be practical and ask Levi to explain how he could help her plans for the café because, after all, that was supposed to be the reason for their meeting which actually felt more like a date.

Focus. Don't go imagining stuff that's not there, and do not get your hopes up about anything.

'Right, so, are you going to stop being mysterious and tell me how you can help with my ideas for the café? I'm intrigued because you could've explained by text or called so I'm thinking you're going to persuade me to help rob a bank, unless you're a secret billionaire and you want to invest in yours truly.' Even though it sounded okay on the outside, inside Honey was cringing because she was just fishing for confirmation he wanted to see her again.

'Well, I can wholeheartedly confirm it's neither of those options but you're right, I could have emailed the details over but then I would've missed out on seeing you again, and after taking the tribe to Wales, I needed something to look forward to. Believe me, there's only so many times a human being can sing ten green bottles, and that, is a fact!'

Even though he'd made a joke of it, and he'd blushed a bit in the middle, Honey had got the message loud and clear. Pushing her feet to the floor to stop them doing a giddy under-the-table jig, she smiled her best smile, agreed about ten green bottles and settled back to hear Levi's idea. As long as she could see him again, Honey really didn't care what it was, even robbing a bank was doable.

CHAPTER 27

Honey couldn't believe her luck. If she and Ziggy hadn't believed in fate, karma, the tooth fairy, angels, aliens, pixies, the bogeyman under the bed and the Loch Ness Monster, she would have converted right there and then to all of them. Because for more than one reason, Levi was meant to be. She just knew it.

Someone somewhere had rolled lucky dice or cut the pack and Honey had turned up trumps. Why would anyone – after a failed blind date – break down right outside her café – of all the streets in the Peak District – and turn out to be someone who could help make her philanthropist dreams come true? And he was fit. That was a mega bonus.

'So, this is what you do for a living? Help businesses set up a not-for-profit charity and you reckon I can do it too?'

Levi clasped his hands together on the table, his expression eager. 'Yep. You're already on your way, with the warm-hub and giving back to the community but this way, by registering as a charity, it opens up opportunities to apply for government funding and grants so, your idea to expand next door could become reality.'

Honey sat back in her chair, 'I honestly had no clue... but it sounds perfect because I have so many ideas. My head is full of them.'

When Levi reached over and gave her hand a squeeze, then didn't let go, she wasn't sure who flushed pink the most.

'That's why I knew I had to help, because I could see how your eyes lit up when you told me about the café and you are exactly the type of person we are looking for. The way you spoke about your school holiday club, I could see the passion in your eyes, and it really resonated because I know through my contacts at work and the data I see, more kids are going hungry than ever before. I think what you've done so far is amazing, but we can do more, if you let me help.'

Oh, Honey was going to let him help alright! And no way was she letting his hand move so, to make sure, she put her free one on his. 'I'd love that, and the holiday club is going to be my main focus this winter, but I also need to tell you about another idea, and Butch who came to do work experience last year. He was always in so much trouble at school and on the verge of expulsion so the teachers didn't think anyone would take him. Lizzy knows his mum who was dreading him being kicked out and dossing around all day.'

They were interrupted by the waitress who came to clear their plates and offer the dessert menu, which meant letting go of Levi's hand. Honey didn't have the guts to reach over and take it again, so left hers on the tabletop as she chatted on.

'So I offered, gave him a chance, and you know what, he was a flipping star. Hit it off with Gospel straight away and now he works on Saturdays, and during the holidays. After his work experience he decided to do catering at college and got his head down and tried really hard. He scraped five GCSEs but he's at college now. So that's one of my ambitions, to get kids that have given up on education, and education's given up on them, interested in cooking. Give more Butches a chance.'

'I love that story. And I reckon we can make this a reality. It's not a quick fix as applying for grants et cetera takes time, but we can get the ball rolling, setting you up as a charity whenever you're ready. I can introduce you to my colleagues and contacts who are all on the same page as us, and if you want to bounce ideas off me anytime, don't be shy.'

Honey took a sip of her Coke, not wanting to think about bouncing on or off anything, so tried to focus and be business-like. She could do it if she really tried. However, being shy was not on the agenda, so Levi had no worries on that score. While she tried to work out how to prolong their 'meeting', Levi snapped her out of the lurid depths her mind was wallowing in, with a question.

'Do you want dessert? I'm three-quarters full but we can share something if you like. I've got plenty of time because my next appointment isn't till three.'

Honey also had room for more, of desert and definitely spending more time with Levi, so nodded vigorously, 'Oh yes, pudding it is – but you choose because it'll take me ages! And... seeing as you don't have to be in work for a while, I have a question for you.'

'Okay. Ask away while I ponder.' Levi glanced at the menu, his attention spilt between dessert and Honey who asked...

'Do you like donkeys?'

Half a banoffee pie and a short bus ride later, Honey and Levi stood in the grounds of the donkey sanctuary, the pungent aroma of wet hay and manure singeing their nostrils.

It was going to rain, tiny splats of the wet stuff were leaving their mark on her parka and Honey wondered whether it had been a good idea, dragging Levi out of the city.

She was stroking the mane of her adoptive donkey, looking into deep brown eyes that made her heart swell as she introduced him. 'This is Honker, isn't he gorgeous?'

Levi stretched out his arm and ruffled the donkey's mane. 'He really is. And that's quite a name! They're all really cute and I still can't believe I didn't know about this place. I mean, who would've thought there'd be a farmyard right here in Manchester, let alone a donkey sanctuary.'

Honey smiled because it was slap-bang in the middle of rows and rows of terraced houses, not far from a sprawling secondary school, and as urban as you could get. Then in contrast, a thin stretch of green-belt cut through the industrial and domestic landscape to create a paddock just big enough for grazing.

'I know. I found it by accident when I was having a gander on Google, looking for some old photographs of where my aunt and grandad grew up. They used to live just up the road in Openshaw, in a little terraced house like the ones we passed on the way here. Before that they lived in Ancoats, near to the Northern Quarter where we just had lunch. I always feel close to my heritage around there; it's weird, like I can picture them all going about their lives before I was even born.'

It was as she spoke, the truth, or invalidity of what she'd just said hit home. That those people who she'd once considered to be her ancestors actually weren't, and that made her a fraud. Imagining stuff that was impossible. No connection to her at all. Her heart slumped, but she didn't want to ruin the afternoon, so ploughed on with her explanation, resolving to leave the past behind for a while and focus on the present.

'I wanted to buy my Aunty Beryl some prints and while I searched the local archives I stumbled on this place. I've always loved donkeys so on my next day off I made my way here. I was blown away when I saw it and after speaking to the staff here, I decided to adopt a donkey and I pop in whenever I can to see him. If I'm in the car I bring a sack of veg from grandad's allotment. The other gardeners contribute too, which is kind.' Again, thinking of her grandad caused her mood to dip, knowing that she still hadn't decided what to do about the letter.

'It's such a great place and I'm going to ask one of my lot to donate, instead of getting me a Christmas pressie, because otherwise one of them will knit me something hideous or go crazy on the shopping channel and buy me another useless kitchen gadget. Bless 'em, but they're all loopy and out of control most of the time, especially where yours truly is concerned.'

Honey loved the way he spoke about his family because even though he teased, there was great love for them. She could hear it in his voice and see it in the wicked glint in his eyes. 'Are you their golden boy then?'

'Oh yes. I've got loads of cousins on the outlaw side of the family, that's my grandma's name for the in-laws by the way. But where my lot are concerned, I'm it. The one and only, and because we all lived together for so long, we do have a special bond. They also think I'm their slave and was born to run errands and talk them through getting off a page they're stuck on. I do often wonder why I taught them to use the internet. But I don't mind really.'

'I'd love to meet them... they sound like good fun.' *For fuc– did you really just say that out loud?*

'Well that can definitely be arranged, and I might even bring my batty-old-grannies here in the Batty Bus; they'd like seeing the donkeys.' Noticing Honey's bemused look he explained, 'Mum's minibus that she uses to transport them all to their various appointments and activities. Wheelchairs, Zimmers, walking stick and picnics. You name it, it goes on the Batty Bus, full of my batty rellies.'

He gave her a wink, to which she replied, 'Well you'd best bring them sooner than later because come next year, the donkeys might not be here.'

'Oh no, why?'

A sigh. 'Because the lease is almost up and rent's going up to an astronomical amount so unless they get a massive injection of donations, it looks like our little donkey friends might be on the move.'

As if to add to a dip in mood, a chilly gust whipped around the stable yard and the rain started to fall in earnest causing Levi to look skywards. 'That's totally crap… bloody landlords. I'm sick of hearing stories like this… and I also think we're going to get very wet if we don't take cover.'

Honey agreed and checked her watch. Time with Levi was running out. 'I wish we'd come on a nicer day and had longer, but you're right, we're going to get soaked so shall we head back? Let's get a cab, my shout, and we can wait in the station until it's time for my train. You'll need to go to your meeting soon anyway.'

Flipping off her rucksack, Honey delved inside for her phone and after giving Honker a peck on the head and promising she'd see him soon, they headed back towards the entrance. But as they did, Levi raised his arm, indicating she should link up and, without missing a heartbeat, Honey threaded her hand through the gap and fell into step. The maudlin fingers that had begun to wrap around her heart quickly lost grip, and for that Honey was grateful. She didn't want anything to spoil their last few minutes together.

They waited side by side on the station concourse, watching the announcement board. They sipped takeaway teas – he had no sugar, Honey took two. For strength she told herself. Because no matter how much she'd enjoyed being with Levi, her thoughts insisted on straying to her grandad. A nudge from Levi soon did the trick.

'Penny for them. You keep drifting away and I'm starting to worry you're bored of me already.' He gave her a grin and raised his eyebrows.

'No, I swear I'm not. I just have things on my mind, that's all. I need to go and see my grandad and can't decide whether I should get it over with today or leave it a while.' She realised too late that she'd spoken her worries out loud and would have to explain.

'Sounds ominous. Is everything okay? I mean, you don't have

to tell me and I'm not being nosey but every now and then your face clouds over and I did wonder if it was me... I seem to have that effect on women lately.'

His wink told Honey he was going for glib, but deep down, might be speaking the truth. 'I swear it's nothing to do with you. I've loved everything about this afternoon, even my foolhardy excursion to see Honker. It's just a family thing that I need to sort out, and it'd take too long to explain now, which is a shame because if I'm honest, another set of ears would be appreciated.'

'Well, why don't I give you a call tonight. I'd offer to drive over and chat in person, but I've got a five-a-side match later and I'd not live it down if I bailed. But we could talk afterwards if you like.'

Honey didn't have to think twice. 'I'd like that, I really would. Ziggy is my go-to agony aunt but she's on three late shifts this week and there's no getting any sense out of her after a twelve-hour stint. Lots of yawns, but not much else.'

'Right then. It's a phone-date. I'll be back about eight-thirty, so I'll call you then.' His attention then diverted to the departures board, 'Looks like your train is in. Come on, my little Miss Mysterious, I'll walk you to the ticket barrier.'

Knowing that he'd not binned her off and had suggested they talk later made saying goodbye much easier than she'd thought it would be. As was the moment, just before she went through the ticket barrier, that Mr Shy and Awkward from Chorlton gave Miss Mysterious from Valley Mills a very nice kiss goodbye.

CHAPTER 28

LEVI

It had been ages since he'd felt this buoyant and as he wolfed down a Bombay Bad Boy Pot Noodle, Levi took stock of his rather magnificent day.

Not only had his five-a-side team won 3–1, his date with Honey had gone brilliantly, *and* he would be speaking to her in six minutes and forty-two seconds precisely.

There had been moments, right at the beginning, in the restaurant, that he thought he saw a shadow of a frown cross her face. She'd done it a couple of times. Kind of drifted off and then he saw it, her eyes looked a bit sad and worried then she'd be back in the room. At first he thought it was him and he was boring her, but after a while, as he regaled her with embarrassing stuff about his family, she seemed to relax, and they'd had a laugh.

He was mightily pleased when Honey asked him to go to the donkey sanctuary because that proved she wanted to spend a bit longer with him *and* she'd dropped a hint about meeting his family, so it was all good. Maybe she could go with him to his great-grandma's big birthday at the end of the month.

Two minutes and ten seconds to go. Levi wiped his mouth of

Bad Boy sauce, reached over for his laptop and booted it up. That way he'd be ready to send over the file of info he'd collated when he went back into work. Once he'd given Honey a brief rundown, he'd leave her to look through it herself, and then they could talk about other stuff.

He had so many questions to ask and wanted to know everything there was to know about her. Levi picked up his phone, seven seconds and… it rang… it was her… she rang him… it was a sign. He jabbed accept.

'Hi, I was just about to ring but you beat me to it.'

Honey laughed. 'You snooze you lose, mate. So, are you going to whizz this info over to me? I'm ready and waiting. Do you want my email?'

Levi was prepped and ready to go.

Half an hour later, they were done with the business part of their call or so Levi thought, but Honey had one more question.

'So I can definitely use my profits to support my favourite charities because Ziggy's… well, I call it Ziggy's, but you know what I mean, and then the donkeys. Both are really special to me.'

Levi was nodding even though she couldn't see him, which was when a thought occurred. 'Yep, it's all good and you know what I've just realised, we should've Facetimed. I could swap to my laptop. You don't have to if you don't want… it's just an idea and I warn you, I'm in my Hogwarts pyjamas.'

'You are not! I don't believe you.'

'Try me!'

And she did.

After Honey had booted up and connected, and their faces appeared on their respective laptop screens, she pointed out a stray noodle that was stuck to his chin and complemented him on his very fetching wizard tee-shirt and tartan lounge pants, Levi moved the conversation on.

Honey was eating a bag of crisps, noisily, but he didn't mind. At least she hadn't seen him slurp his pot noodle. 'What have you got planned this week, apart from work? I'm stuck in the city until Friday, training and meetings which will be *so* boring.'

And there it was again, a faint flash of worry then it was gone.

'The same old. I've got Ziggy coming for tea tomorrow night, just whatever is left over from the café, but it'll be nice to see her. She's a right busy bee. I swear she never stops for a minute. She says it's because she's powered by insulin, and I do wonder if that's true.'

Levi had taken to Honey's best friend the moment he met her, which reminded him. 'You were going to tell me what happened when she was at school, remember, last week. But she came and joined us, so you didn't finish. I've been thinking about what you told me a lot, especially while I've been at work. I want to understand more in case I ever come across anyone with the same condition.'

Thankfully, Honey had stopped munching so answered with a question. 'Oh yes, where did I get up to?'

Levi smiled. Her head was constantly all over the place. Not quite scatty but close. He found it endearing, though, part of her personality. 'You said that being diagnosed with Type 1 made her the odd one out and that it wasn't plain sailing and she had blips along the way.'

'Yes, I remember now. Do you fancy a brew? I mean I can't make you one, but we could both get a cuppa and meet back here… won't take long. I wish I'd put my jamas on now!'

He knew there was no point in resisting and that there was every chance she'd come back to the screen in her jamas, and there'd be more snacks.

He was right.

When she returned with a 'ta-da' and was dressed in her old-fashioned button shirt pyjamas and carrying a tray loaded with enough snacks to feed customers on one side of her café, Levi settled back into his sofa, hopefully far enough away from his laptop speaker to avoid the crunching, munching and wrapper crackling.

Honey, once settled cross legged on her sofa, got straight back into her story. 'Right, where were we…? Well, to start, it was baby steps I suppose, for Ziggy and her family and even her close friends who rallied round. She missed the end of term, but when we went back in September the real problems started. Kids can be so cruel and at our school there were some monsters.'

'Oh no, what happened?' Levi wasn't sure he wanted to hear but the words just came out.

'Well, at lunchtime and breaks, Ziggy would go and inject her insulin in a welfare room, but it didn't prevent some kids calling her nasty names. Like junkie, and diabetes girl, and then some went one step further and said she was disgusting, she made them sick, and they hoped she'd get cancer and die.'

'Seriously… they were that cruel? That's awful.' Levi had been a recipient of school banter, but this was another level.

'Yes, they were that cruel and it was an awful time especially when she was getting used to her new way of life. It was like everything was conspiring against her. Even the weather – because extreme heat or cold would send her glucose up or down, hormones took their toll, too. Then she decided not to eat, because that way she didn't have to inject. Honestly it was a tough time until we had a breakthrough.'

Levi felt instantly relieved, knowing that there was some light in the tunnel for Ziggy, a girl he'd weirdly started to care about, and others like her.

'What happened?'

'She was offered counselling by the diabetic team at the hospital who were brilliant. They suggested Ziggy joined a forum specially for teenagers, on Diabetes UK. She wasn't keen at first but with a little encouragement, she did, and it helped her so much. Talking to other youngsters who were in the same boat, seeing how they were coping and taking inspiration and comfort from people who were making a huge success of their lives gave Ziggy hope.'

Levi relaxed into the sofa. 'I can't tell you how glad I am you said that. So, how is she now?'

'Well, in a nutshell, Ziggy got back on track and although there were blips along the way, she passed all of her GCSEs and got three excellent A-levels, then did a degree in nursing. She is, and I hope always will be, the most bonkers, confident, and wonderful friend I could wish for. Nothing holds her back now. And I'm sure you've guessed already where my main donations go.'

Levi laughed. 'Yep, I think I've worked it out and it's a very worthy cause, so well done you.' He raised his mug of tea to Honey who smiled at the screen and did the same.

'No wonder you two are such good friends, helping her through all that.' Levi was watching Honey open a packet of biscuits as he spoke.

'It goes both ways, because she was there for me a few years later when my dad–' Honey stalled mid-packet-ripping, and looked at the screen, her words had dried up, as though she'd spoken out of turn.

'What? Are you okay?' Levi could tell she wasn't and it had something to do with Honey's dad.

So when she put the biscuits by her side and picked up her mug, holding it in front of her like it was putting distance between them, he waited until she was ready to speak.

CHAPTER 29

Levi wondered if Honey was stalling as she shuffled and made herself comfy. He hoped she wasn't going to tell him anything really horrible, not that he'd mind but it was hard to comfort someone through a laptop screen.

'I know we're going to be mates, so I want you to know... about my family and how we tick because to put it mildly we're what I'd call a bit odd and depleted right now.'

Honey took a breath. Levi waited because what could he say apart from, *oh really?*

Then Honey added, 'There's just me and my grandad now. I had an aunty, Beryl, who died not long ago, we were very close, and she was so lovely...' At this point Honey did the wandering off thing she tended to, then wandered back again, 'Anyway, my mum lives in Spain with her new husband and although we chat every week, our relationship is a bit strained, I suppose on account of what happened to my dad.'

Oh, oh, thought Levi. *This isn't going to be good.* And with that in mind, gave Honey the opportunity to keep her family history to herself. 'Look, if it's painful you don't have to...'

'No, no I'd rather tell you. I think it'd help because I have tons of other stuff going on right now and it might help to clear my head a bit.' Honey took a sip of her tea, then explained.

Astrid, her mum, wasn't the most popular member of the McCarthy clan and wasn't the kind of woman who they'd have chosen for Kevin, their one and only son, grandson and nephew. By all accounts even Kevin's friends weren't keen on his choice of girlfriend and were even less impressed when Astrid became his wife.

Apparently Great-Grandma Molly had her down as 'flighty with ideas above her station' which according to her Grandad Ernie was rich coming from the woman who thought living in Marple meant she'd 'arrived'.

Anyhow, Astrid and Kevin's marriage was beset by argument after argument. Nothing was ever enough, and the rot set in early on. The arrival of Honey healed the rift but only for a time and they stumbled through life, falling out and making up. Kevin, for reasons none of his family could ever fathom, continued to make promises that an accountant, unless he put his hands in the till, could never fulfil.

And in the middle was Honey, who couldn't actually remember a time when her parents weren't at war.

Astrid was adamant there'd be no more children even though Honey longed for a sibling because being the glue in her parents' relationship, the weakest, watery kind that they use in schools and barely sticks tissue to paper, wasn't fun. Looking back, Honey was sure that her mum was simply marking time. Waiting for the moment she could leave, and that time was just after Honey's A-level results came in and she was all set for the future.

The moment Astrid told Kevin she was leaving as she stood in the hall with her cases already in the boot of the car was, according to Astrid, civilised and mature. What happened after the door slammed and her car roared towards freedom was another matter entirely.

Kevin simply lost his mind. Couldn't work, sleep, exist

without Astrid, so turned to the bottle, which was not a pleasant sight for anyone to see. And that's what was the hardest to deal with, in Honey's mind. The last pathetic images of living with her drunken, sobbing father, who looked like a vagrant living in his own home that despite Honey's efforts was becoming a pigsty; of him staggering to the off-licence for more booze, despite her pleading with him not to go out.

The part where he staggered into the main road as he shouted abuse at the shop owner for refusing to sell him whisky, was based on eyewitness accounts, but it was easy enough to picture. As was the car hitting him at speed, ending his misery, silencing his sobbing there and then.

'So, that's why I have a difficult relationship with my mum because there's always this big thing between us. Like I have trouble hearing what a wonderful time she's having over there because I can't get over the fact that her freedom and lovely sunny life came at the expense of my dad and yes, I know that he chose to drink and all that, but it's the sequence of events that bothers me. What led to that night.' Honey looked into her mug before draining the contents.

'And it changed my grandad because he's, shall we say, a very complex man as it is. Some say he's an acquired taste, but it made him so bitter. He's never spoken to my mum since. Not even at the funeral. Totally blanked her. It was so awkward. So once again, I'm in the middle but very glad she lives in Spain. It makes life easier and now, it's just me and Grandad. There. My family skellybobs are out of the closet.' Honey paused, as though there was more to say, but then perhaps to divert her attention or the need for sugar overwhelmed, she continued to open the packet of biscuits, fiddling with the cellophane wrapper.

Levi didn't know what to say but was, at the same time, sure Honey didn't need his platitudes or advice. Clichés wouldn't cut it so instead; 'And I thought *my* family was complicated, but I appreciate you telling me… and yes, we are going to be friends, but this mate wants to ask you something.'

Honey ceased fiddling, and eyes wide, asked what.

'Can I take you for dinner? I'll drive over to yours and you can pick the venue as long as it's not that pub on the hills where losers go.' That, for him was bold and even though he knew there was a chance he'd overstepped, and that she might just want him for his dossier and contacts, he remained hopeful.

'Yes, I'd love that, and I know some great places around here. When?'

Result! 'Whenever you're free… weekend perhaps. Just let me know.' Levi was relieved and the serious mood had lifted.

'Weekend will be fine. Saturday is best because I have to be at the café early that morning as it's our busy day. I'll book us a table somewhere but nothing fancy. I'm not into fancy, are you?'

Levi shook his head vigorously. 'Not in the slightest. I prefer places like yours or where we ate today – but I trust you to choose.'

He watched as Honey squinted at her phone, 'I've got your email by the way…so your surname is Robinson. I've been meaning to ask about your first name. It's unusual and I wondered if it was a bible name. I love quirky names, don't you… so now you're going to tell me you go to mass every Sunday and that your dad's called Moses, or Noah.'

Levi shook his head again, 'Nope, nothing of the sort. My mum picked my name off a telly advert from the eighties.'

Honey's eyebrows lifted. 'No way! Which one?'

'Well, my mother had a massive crush on Nick Kamen who, I'm reliably informed, was hot back then – by the way my mum overshares – but she didn't like the name Nicholas, it's too boring apparently so…'

By this time Honey was holding her stomach and laughing, 'I know what you're going to say, it was the jeans advert, the famous one in the launderette where he takes them off and stands there in his boxer shorts.'

'Yep, yours truly is named after a pair of Levi 501s. Thanks entirely to my mad mother's crush on a supermodel. And moving swiftly on, how did you get the name Honey?' Levi actually quite liked his name and the story that went with it and the fact he'd made Honey laugh.

'Oh, mine's a lot more boring. My mum's favourite plant is Honeysuckle and then, when she was pregnant with me, she had a craving for honey – swore it was the reason she never got morning sickness or stretch marks. She's always attaching importance to random stuff, so when I was born I had whisps of hair that was actually the colour of honey, even though it darkened to auburn as I got older. Mum named me Honeysuckle which I hated when I was little because it took ages to write in my schoolbooks, so I shortened it to Honey. Either way I suppose my name does suit me.'

Levi loved Honey's hair colour and told her so. 'I think it's a lovely colour. In fact, my great-grandma used to have hair the same colour as yours.'

'Do any of your family members have it, too? Passed down the line?'

'No, because she's my step-great grandma. I don't know the full story, but she couldn't have kids and brought up her husband's children as her own. Their mum died in childbirth, I think, during the war. My great-grandad was a doctor and was left with two little children to care for and, because his occupation was protected, chose not to enlist. He was scared his children could be left orphaned. When he met my great-grandma, she took them under her wing. Everyone adores her. She's quite a character too. Very vocal about what she believes in and who she doesn't like. The Conservatives are right up there on that list, and royalty … you should have heard her banging on about how much the King's coronation cost. Refused to watch it on the telly but went to the street party because she likes a bit-of-a-do. Once she gets something in her head, though, she sticks to it.'

Honey had moved closer to her laptop screen, soaking it all up. 'I love her already, tell me more.'

Levi was proud of his grandma and happy to oblige, 'Well, back in the day, she burnt her bra by all accounts. Went on ban the bomb marches, camped out at Greenham Common, collected money for the miners' strike, that kind of thing.

'And she totally embraced the whole yoga and vegetarianism vibe in the sixties and seventies, still meditates and drinks vile green concoctions that Mum blends up for her. Rattles from all the vitamins she takes and has hardly anything wrong with her medically. She does struggle a bit to get about but her mind's as sharp as anything. She's probably healthier than me. Oh, and guess how old she is.'

He watched as Honey tried to do the maths so helped her out. 'She'll be a hundred and two at the end of the month. How ace is that!'

'Oh my. That's really ace. I've never met anyone that old.'

Levi didn't miss a beat. 'Well you can come to her big birthday as she calls it. The last two were called the same, when she was one hundred then one hundred and one. She reckons that she deserves a fuss, so we're having another party. It'll be full of oldies, but you'd be very welcome.'

Honey was beaming. 'I'd love that so yes, I accept. I'll look forward to it.'

The sound of Levi's phone ringing interrupted and once he'd located it under a cushion, saw it was his mum and after signalling to Honey he'd be one minute, answered, 'Hi, Mum. I'm just on a Facetime call at the mo, can I ring you back? Is everything okay?'

After swerving the question about who he was talking to, otherwise she'd want to interrogate him, he listened patiently as his mum told him it wasn't urgent, but could he definitely call her back as she needed to pencil him in on the Batty Bus rota, she finally hung up.

'Sorry about that, I'll ring her in a bit.'

'Hey, it's fine and it's getting late, so I'd best get on. A girl has to look her best when she's serving all-day breakfasts and as much as it's a big cliché and totally not an excuse, I need to wash my hair.'

He would've talked all night, but they'd covered quite a bit of 'personal stuff ground', so it was a good place to leave it. A weekend date was in the bag, and she'd said yes to meeting his family, so he couldn't grumble. After re-affirming their plans, because he was a worrier like that, and promising to drop her a text the next day… and every day after that even though he didn't actually say that thought out loud, they signed off.

Levi took a moment to take stock and congratulate himself on not messing up for once, and then with a sigh picked up his phone and rang his mother, vowing that no matter how much she twisted his arm, he would not be driving the Batty Bus anywhere on Saturday. Fact.

CHAPTER 30

HONEY

Hump day had arrived. And as she lay in bed snuggled under the duvet with her eyes closed, Honey knew that this Wednesday's hump was a biggie. Worse that the camel's hump bridge they'd had to cross to get to primary school. Even though it spanned the canal below, it wasn't actually that steep, not when seen through adult eyes, but to a child, it looked like Mount Everest especially in winter.

Honey used to be terrified because the smooth cobbles were often covered in ice and if it snowed – which it always did back then – it was a death-trap. When she looked back, she did chuckle at the image of mums and little kids, gripping onto the wall of the bridge, taking tiny sideways steps upwards, desperate not to slip. Going down was like taking your life in your hands – a white-knuckle slide. The number of times Honey had slipped and gone to school with soggy knickers and a bruised bottom was nobody's business.

As her alarm came to life and she reluctantly pushed back the duvet and whacked the button hard, making the racket stop, Honey knew that the next few hours were going to be like going over the camel's hump bridge.

First she had to get to the top without her grandad losing his mind, or his rag, or both, knowing him. Then they had to get down the other side in one piece and work out what to do next. Most of all, she didn't want to fall out with him over someone else's mistake.

Her grandad Ernie was a grudge-holder and prone to belligerence. Her grandma used to despair of him, saying she'd lost count of the times he'd cut his nose off to spite his face. Never backing down once he'd made a decision, he would rather be stuck in a corner on his own than admit he was wrong.

She'd always thought he was so like Great Grandma Molly, who Honey only remembered via other people's memories, but now she wasn't so sure.

But if his difficult demeanour couldn't be attributed to nature inherited from Molly, could it be nurture?

Not wanting to begin the day just yet, her mind wandered to the previous evening when, after bringing Ziggy up to date with all things Levi, and Ziggy had reciprocated with her racier exploits with the new registrar, Honey explained about Aunty Beryl's letter.

She hadn't really wanted to tell anyone at all, but bearing such a huge secret was eating her up inside and she trusted Ziggy with her life and her family's affairs.

They were halfway through a plate of leftover steak pie and mash, and Honey had got to the crunch part, describing the moment Molly had walked out of a crater with someone else's baby and then went off to start a whole new, fake life. To say Ziggy was shocked was an understatement.

Her fork, filled with gravy and mash, hovered in front of her mouth that was making a wide O-shape and not for the purposes of shovelling in food. 'Oh my God! You are kidding me... you're not, are you?'

Honey had lost her appetite so put down her cutlery and

answered, 'Nope. Deadly serious and now I'm left with a decision and then a task. Should I tell Grandad? Because it will totally mess with his head and fuck knows how he'll react. Or do I spare him the heartache and keep schtum but that way, I will have to reconcile myself to the fact that I denied him the truth. Just like Molly and Aunty Beryl did. Either way I will have to live with the consequences, won't I?'

Not one to let anything stand in the way of food, Ziggy continued to eat, but Honey could see by the look on her face she was mulling it all over and once she'd swallowed the mash, she gave her verdict.

'There's no way round it, mate. You are going to have to tell him. You of all people cannot go through the rest of your life overthinking this decision and I'm telling you now, you'll regret not telling him far more than being honest. It's not going to be easy but it's definitely the right thing to do.'

Honey knew Ziggy was right. It was what her conscience had been telling her since Sunday, when she'd read the letter, and even if she had confided in Levi during their Facetime, she was sure he'd have said the same.

The only reason she hadn't spilled her guts was because she'd have felt disloyal. First to her grandad and then to Ziggy who was the original keeper of Honey's secrets. Not that there were any juicy ones, sadly, but it was the law, one of the many they'd made up when they were thirteen. As yet, Honey had kept the faith and felt better for it.

Resigned to the fact that hump day *and* her task couldn't be avoided, Honey flipped the duvet aside and with a yawn, headed for the shower. She'd get work over with and go to the allotment if the café was quiet mid-afternoon, leaving Lizzy and Gospel to manage. Never had she wished for a mad rush more. In fact, bring on three coach parties and every member of the Peak District Rambling Association. That'd do nicely.

~

Honey watched him from the gate of the allotment. He was fixing some netting to poles with cable ties, lost in his own gardeners' world. When her next thought hit, it was like an unexpected wave that gets you from behind and sweeps you off your feet and when you get up, stunned and covered in sand, eyes stinging from the salty sea, it takes a while to get your breath.

This was one of those waves and these were the last few minutes of her Grandad Ernie's life as he knew it, where ignorance had been bliss, of sorts. He'd accepted his lot in life and was pottering about, marking time as he called it, until he saw her grandma again. He said it often.

The sting in her eyes wasn't from the sea, but from the tears that swam as she looked at her beloved grandad.

Honey shivered and she was glad she'd worn her parka because the afternoon was turning chilly and already her feet were cold inside her pink wellies. Or was it fear cooling her bones and heart?

Again, the doubts crept up on her, whispering that she should leave him be.

Then another voice, firmer, telling her this was her duty, and it was down to her now. To right a wrong and speak up for those who'd missed their chance, or absolved themselves and passed the buck. There were so many ways to look at her situation she thought her head might explode and splatter like a pumpkin. Seeing him like that, in his special happy place, made her regret her choice of venue. She shouldn't sully it. This was his refuge and she'd made a mistake.

Honey decided instantly that she'd wait for him at his. Go round and make him some tea and tell him there in the privacy of his own home. What had she been thinking? She was about to turn and flee when one of his buddies called over to Ernie and pointed in her direction, alerting him to her presence. Bugger.

There was nothing for it now. She'd have to get it over with so returning her grandad's wave, she took a deep breath, flicked the gate catch and invaded his world.

CHAPTER 31

ERNIE

They'd told him to get to the hospital as soon as possible, because Nancy's condition had deteriorated and to this day, he couldn't remember the journey there. He must have been on auto-pilot.

There was a glimpse, a recurring memory of him buzzing the intercom like crazy, then after hearing the automatic click that allowed him entry, barging through the doors of the ward and racing towards her bed. Then being hijacked by the male nurse who barred his way and in the kindest, most reverent way you can break anyone's heart, told Ernie he was too late.

The next scene is the curtain being drawn back, and the sight of his beloved Nancy who looked like she was sleeping, having a nod, as she used to say. And then Ernie sat, by her bed, in a state of anaesthesia. Not exactly blissfully unaware, that was the wrong word entirely, but Ernie was sure that they could have chopped off his left leg, and he'd have felt nothing. Heard nothing. Was oblivious to those on the other side of the curtain, as though the rest of the world had been muted and the only two people in it were him and Nancy.

He must have breathed in and out, his heart kept beating

while he spoke to his precious, most beautiful wife who listened patiently while he stroked her hand and touched the rings on her wedding finger. But Ernie couldn't remember what he said, or the feel of Nancy's skin under his. All he could remember was the numbness. Being detached from reality.

That was exactly how he felt in that moment as Honey sat by his side, holding the sheets of lined paper in one hand, gripping his own hand tightly in the other. He could see movement in the corner of his eyes as her fingers stroked his skin, but he couldn't feel them. Ernie couldn't feel anything.

He kept his gaze straight ahead and looked out onto the allotment where normally he saw patches of land, ordered rows of planting, his fellow gardeners toiling away.

Today there was nothing. He looked but didn't see. Just stared through the mist that clouded his eyes. One thought repeating on a loop.

How could she?

Before he could answer his own question, a voice, one that held a hint of panic, jolted Ernie into reality.

'Grandad, are you okay? Please say something.' Honey had huddled further into her parka, like she was shrinking away from the hurt she caused him while her hand kept a firm grip on his.

Ernie spoke his thoughts. 'How could she?'

'Who? Do you mean Aunty Beryl or your mum?'

'She's not my mum and how I feel right now I don't even want to call Beryl my sister.' He instantly regretted his harsh tone but the anger… he'd never felt anything like it.

Not even when he'd railed against God and the inept doctors who he'd blamed for taking his Nancy from him. He'd had to blame someone then and after, much later, he'd realised he was being unreasonable. But this time, oh this time he really did have a target for his hatred, two in fact.

'Both of them. *Her*, for stealing me in the first place and then living a lie for her entire life and Beryl, for not telling me when she could.'

Honey's tone had softened when she replied. 'Grandad, you're right to feel angry and hurt and so many emotions because I was too when I read the letter. I think I was in shock to be honest, that's why it's taken me a few days to get my head around it and pluck up the courage to tell you.'

'Well, at least someone in this family knows how to do the right thing and their moral compass is set straight, because those two certainly didn't, did they?' Ernie turned and even though he saw Honey's eyes widen, reflected in them was the sheer rage that he was struggling to contain.

They sat in silence for a moment or two while his comment settled, like an early mist on the allotment, seeping into the soil and his bones and heart.

They'd lied to him, for all those years.

First *her*, Molly, that's how he would refer to her now because she wasn't his mother, not anymore. And then Beryl. His sister who he'd adored. Had meant the world to him. The rock of the family. She was a liar, too.

And then a confession. 'I aways knew. Deep down. I think I always knew I didn't belong. It was this... this sense of not connecting, of being an outsider when there was absolutely nothing to indicate that I was. You know, when you think about it, an instinct that strong, no matter how contrary, was trying to tell me something but I just didn't listen. I've been such a fool.'

'But why would you? It's totally understandable that you believed that they were your parents because your birth certificate told you so. You'd been brought up by a family you had no reason whatsoever to doubt so you're not a fool, Grandad, nothing of the kind.'

It was Honey's well-meaning words that caused Ernie to slip his hand from her grasp and bury his face in his palms, resting his elbows on his knees to prevent his whole body from slumping in a heap.

'Oh dear God… everything, everything was fake… my birth certificate, my heritage… I don't even know who I really am.' As soon as he said the words he felt an arm go around his shoulder and a head rest against his left arm.

'You're my grandad and I love you just the same today as I did yesterday. Nothing will ever change that. You're you, that's what matters, not the past.'

Ernie wasn't placated, in fact Honey's words lit another spark and it took all his self-control not to raise his voice. 'How can you say that? I'm not the same and I never will be, not now! And the past does matter. To *me*. Can't you see that, Honey?'

Another lapse into silence.

Honey was the braver of the two and broke it with a confession of sorts. 'Yes, yes I do. And if I'm honest I'm angry too because I'd hate to find out that any of my family had kept something like this from me, and now I can see how much it's upset you. Which makes me feel terrible for telling you… and it makes me see why Aunty Beryl might have predicted this kind of reaction so kept the info to herself.'

Ernie's head snapped up, annoyed again. 'Don't make excuses for her, Honey, because she doesn't deserve it. Neither of them do. And don't feel bad either for telling me because at least I'll go to my grave and up there,' he pointed towards the sky, 'if such a place even exists, knowing who I'm not! And you never know, once I've met my Nancy again, my real mother will be waiting; because if *she's* there, and Beryl, they can both bugger off.'

He heard Honey sigh, and then through the corner of his eye watched as she stood and, for a second, he thought she was going to go. Part of him wanted her to, so he could be alone with his thoughts; while another needed her to stay so he could talk it through.

Honey placed a hand on his shoulder. 'I'll make us a brew. Then we can try and work out what to do next.'

Ernie nodded but couldn't ignore the swell of irritation or contain the bitter response that leaked from his lips, allowing poisonous words to pollute his perfect organic world.

'Next... there is no next. My mother, the woman who gave birth to me, is dead. So is my father. I'll never know who they were, what my real surname should be. All I know is the poor woman who died in a pile of rubble had her baby stolen by a thief and a liar. That my birth mother was called Nora and for a few hours she loved me. The rest is history. All fake. All lies. What's there to work out?'

He was glad when Honey didn't reply and instead she turned away and went into his shed, leaving him alone with his thoughts and a melting pot full of bitterness, and hate.

CHAPTER 32

They sat in silence, sipping scalding sweet tea from tin mugs. Perhaps his fellow gardeners had sensed tension in the air, or taken the hint when Ernie just about managed a curt nod when they attempted to pass the time of day, but he and Honey had been left alone. Him to seethe. Her to wait.

Eventually, the need to vent took over.

'It's funny, isn't it, that if you tell someone something often enough they start to believe it.' Ernie was glad when Honey remained quiet and let him ramble on, 'Like the colour of my hair for a start. Auburn it was, when I were a lad, just like Nora's was in the letter. And yet they all convinced me... *her*, and my supposed grandparents, put it down to the Irish genes coming through.'

Ernie could hear Molly now, rhyming off the same old story. That over in Enniskillen there was a whole load of relatives with the same colour hair as him.

'She got away with my eye colour because my dad's...' he stalled on that word because Walter wasn't his dad.

Jesus, that cut him to the quick because he was a good man. It also wasn't his fault he'd brought up another man's son, so Walter couldn't be held accountable or hated. Neither could anyone who wasn't duplicitous. Right then, the only person he blamed was *her*, Molly, and then Beryl.

'Not one other person in our family looked like me. I was tall and lanky, whereas dad was short and stocky. I stood out like a sore thumb at gatherings, weddings and the like, but nobody, as far as I know, questioned it. Everyone believed Saint Molly.'

A gentle nudge was followed by, 'Well wherever *we* get our hair colour from, I'm glad I share it with you, or I did until yours went grey.'

He glanced at Honey and saw her nervous smile and was instantly awash with shame. This wasn't her fault, either. And it must've taken guts to be the one to speak up. He might be a fool, but he was an honest one and Ernie accepted he could sometimes be gruff and spoke his mind too much about too many things. Still, that didn't make it right to be so with Honey.

'I'm glad too, lass. An' I'm sorry for being a grumpy bugger but it's knocked me sideways, has this.' He wished Nancy was there because she'd have known what to do and made it right, and it was thinking of her that brought on the strangest sensation, like he might cry.

He wasn't having none of that so took a gulp of his tea. The sweet hot liquid burnt his tongue and throat as it went down, but did the job, washing away the emotions that were on their way up.

'It's okay, Grandad. I'm used to you being a grumpy bugger and I had a feeling you'd react this way and I get it, I really do. But if we can, let's try and keep calm and talk it through. It's rocked me too, you know. So just tell me what you're thinking because the worst thing you can do is bottle it all up.'

Ernie huffed out a laugh. 'What, like I do everything, you mean. About your grandma and your dad. That's my safety mechanism, lass. How I cope and I don't see how being all airy-fairy and letting out my inner-mardy will help. Won't change nowt.'

Honey sighed. 'Okay, I get that's your way, so how about I tell you what I think because this is about me, too, you know.'

'Aye, you're right… so go on. What are your thoughts on this great big mess?' Ernie hoped that she wouldn't try to defend his so-called mother because that would be like a betrayal of the hurt he was experiencing, a physical ache inside.

'I never knew her – Molly – so I don't have this physical person in my mind's eye that I can be angry with which makes it seem weird, you know, being cross with a photo that was on Aunty Beryl's sideboard.'

'Only she wasn't your aunt was she? And that woman on the photo is no better than a stranger, especially now we know the truth of the matter. So be angry with whoever you want, lass. It's fine by me.' Ernie took a glug of tea and let his erudite statement settle.

He took a peep at Honey who puffed out her cheeks before speaking. 'What I'm trying to say is, it's easy to be annoyed with someone who isn't here, not to have to look them in the eye and tell them what we think about them. But what if that's why Molly and Aunty Beryl… and I know you have a problem with me calling her that right now, but to me that's who she was, and I loved her a lot.'

Ernie nodded. 'Fair dos, carry on.'

'What if they knew how you'd feel and were simply too scared of facing up to that? Looking you in the eye and telling you something that would rock your whole world. They might have thought it was easier, for them and you, to say nothing.'

Honey made it all sound so simple. It wasn't, not by a million miles, and again this thing inside him surged, like a wild beast trying to claw its way out and the only way to contain it was to remain silent. Until the swell in his chest abated.

Across the way, Old Tommy was chopping wood and each

time his axe fell, it was like an inaccurate marking of time, but it helped. The thud, thud, thud soothed him and, by the time Tommy had filled his basket with logs, Ernie was able to speak.

'Thing is, lass, it wasn't for them to decide whether I should live in ignorance or not. It was my life they both messed with. First *that woman*, and then Beryl. They had no right to do that to me to save their own feelings, or keep their lives in order, but that's what they did.'

Ernie turned his head towards Honey who met his stare as he asked, 'That letter you read said so, am I right?' She nodded and he responded with a loud tut. 'So, they put themselves before me. *She* was scared that she'd be found out, so kept shtum. Then Beryl was lonely so didn't want to risk tearing her family apart and me losing my temper or digging my heels in or turning my back on the little family I had. Well thanks for that, sister dear. For having so little faith in me, in the bond we'd built up over the years, that Beryl actually believed that if she told me, I'd disown her! I think that hurts more, you know. That she felt like that about me.'

'I'm sorry Grandad. You're right. In all of this, Aunty Beryl had the weakest reason for keeping the secret and I'm disappointed in her, even though it kills me to say so. Then again, it was a horrible thing for Molly to do in my opinion. Dump that on her shoulders just before she died and leave her to decide what to do.'

Ernie gave a loud and sarcastic humph, 'What, just like Beryl did to you? Must run in the bloody family, being cowards and liars.'

To this, Honey didn't respond, and through the corner of his eye he watched her fiddle with her fingerless gloves, worrying a loose thread of wool.

Ernie occupied himself by swirling the dregs of his brew around the bottom of the cup and from nowhere, remembered a trip to Morecambe with Nancy and Beryl.

They'd walked along the pier and, at the end, was a stripey

tent, and inside, a woman who could read your palms and the cards and whatnot. Beryl denounced it all as utter nonsense and ushered them on. He could actually see her pulling Nancy away and rolling her eyes at Ernie. Now he wondered if Beryl was so scared of the truth coming out, that she even feared a fortune teller. And, if he'd had his tea leaves read, would Gypsy Rose have seen something that would have given him a clue?

'We were so close, me and Beryl. She was Nancy's best friend. And all I can think is that every day we spent with her, all that time, she was lying to me.' Ernie threw the rest of his tea onto the path beneath his feet, a hand-jerk reaction to a spike of anger.

'You see, I think that's the key to it all, why she did it. From what I know of Molly, she ruled the roost and maybe because she was such a strong personality, she controlled Aunty Beryl more than you know, kind of destroyed her confidence. She told me she'd worked in the same place all her life, doing the job Molly got for her when she left school. She only had a few friends and by her own admission, her divorce left her isolated, and her self-esteem massively dented. I don't think she dared risk losing you and Grandma, and even me and Dad. It's as simple as that.'

Ernie wasn't anywhere near absolving Beryl, and despite not wanting to agree with Honey, her words had made sense, but he just couldn't allow the ball of fury that was swirling in his chest to be extinguished. It was fuelling him, allowing his brain to tick, his heart to beat and keeping him upright when he actually wanted to crumple into a heap on his row of brassicas.

Instead of acknowledging Honey's wisdom, he chose to swerve the subject of Beryl and focus on Molly. 'It's just all too much to take in. The whole thing beggars belief. I mean, *she*, that cold-hearted woman, actually took another woman's baby and didn't even have the decency to keep my name, the one my real mother gave me on her deathbed. If she'd had any goodness in her soul at all she'd have honoured Nora's wishes and called me

Robert, but no, Mrs Selfish McCarthy wanted a brand-new baby and a clean slate. She disgusts me.'

'Grandad!'

'Grandad, what?' His head swivelled to look Honey in the eye.

Ernie felt the beast inside and it had almost reached his throat and he knew if it escaped he'd say something terrible, and all of the allotment would hear, so he reined it in. 'Don't you see that if she'd told me, when I came of age p'raps, then I could have tried to find my family, like they do on the telly. You know that programme wi' that chatty lass. Big nose, dark hair, does Red Nose day.'

Honey sighed, 'Ah, Davina, yes I know the programme you mean.'

'It's one of my favourites is that. I record it and I swear, whenever I watch it, it's like something is telling me, calling out that I'm the same as them on the telly. We have a connection. I understand it when some of them say they never felt like they belonged. I thought it was just me being soft, getting old and nostalgic I suppose. And don't go telling anyone but I always shed a tear when they finally meet up with their mams and dads, or their sisters and brothers and find out who they were and where they came from.'

'And you didn't get the chance, did you?' Honey sounded wistful.

Ernie was glad she got it. 'That's right lass, they took that chance away from me. I could have had aunties and uncles, cousins, grandparents who would have been able to show me photos of my parents. I don't even know what they looked like.'

When Honey sat a little straighter, and sucked in a breath, Ernie sensed something else was coming.

'Actually, Grandad, that's where you're wrong because I was saving this for the next part of the story. I practised how I'd explain it to you, in stages so you could take it in...'

'What do you mean... what next part? And what have you

got?' Ernie's heart was bouncing around in his chest and he wondered if he was going to have a coronary before he found out. Instead of pegging it, he watched as Honey took a small envelope from her pocket and passed it to him.

'Look inside, Grandad.'

Ernie's hand trembled as he obeyed. The flap was open and when he shook the envelope, a silver locket, the size of a ten pence piece, slid onto his upturned palm. Carefully, he prised it open with a fingernail edged in soil and there they were. Two faces looking from beneath the glass. A man and a woman and he knew instantly who they were. His words when they came were soft, carried on wisps of woodsmoke.

'My mam and dad.'

Honey leant against his shoulder and looked down onto the locket. 'Yes, your parents. It was inside the envelope with Molly's account of what happened. So now you know their names and what they looked like, but you don't know the rest of the story. Grandad, you're going to have to be calm…'

'The rest? I don't understand.' Again Ernie's heart picked up pace and he noticed that Honey looked nervous, far more than when she arrived earlier.

'The thing is…' She twiddled the thread of wool on her glove and wouldn't meet his eye and this made him feel bad. That whatever it was weighed heavy on her young shoulders and none of it was of her making.

Ernie gently placed his hand over hers, 'It's okay, lass. Just tell me.'

Honey nodded and dipped her hand into her pocket and pulled out more sheets of lined paper and after a glance upwards, receiving a kind smile and a nod, she began to read Beryl's notes, and the words of Mother Molly McCarthy.

CHAPTER 33

HONEY

Her heart raced and her stomach roiled as she carefully unfolded the sheets of lined paper that had lain waiting in her parka pocket. Honey knew almost every word because she'd read them so many times, trying to get the enormity of it all straight in her head, never mind working out how she felt about her great-grandmother.

Whether she could find a way to forgive Molly's actions and see beyond the act to the heart of the matter. A woman who made a decision when she was at her lowest ebb. Alone, frightened, and only hours after giving birth, possibly in pain and suffering from shock. After all, bombs had rained down and almost killed her; and then Molly's baby had died in her arms.

No matter how hard she'd tried, there was no way Honey could put herself in that situation, because it was so alien. And another thing: she couldn't be judge or jury, it wasn't her place to lay blame or have recriminations because what Molly had done hadn't hurt or affected Honey. Not personally.

Yes, she'd been left with a huge dilemma and could have done without it and was still a bit peeved with her Aunty Beryl. That was a totally different matter, the whys and wherefores of how and when she'd decided to divulge the family secret.

How her Grandad would react was a different matter entirely. Time to find out.

Honey turned to face Ernie. 'Before I read what's in here, I don't want you blowing your top until I've finished, okay? Please promise me you will stay calm.'

His eyes bored into hers, seemingly cool and unmoved by her warning and request, but at least he responded. 'I'll do me best, lass. Now get on wi' it.'

Focusing on the sheets in her hand, Honey obeyed. 'Okay, I'm just going to read it out, in Molly's words, as Aunty Beryl wrote it.'

Sucking in her courage, or nerves or whatever the horrible sensation that had taken hold of her body was, Honey did as Ernie said, and got on with ruining his life.

CHAPTER 34

MOLLY MCCARTHY

Manchester. February 1941

Nobody batted an eyelid. No one realised that the sleeping boy in my arms wasn't the one that had grown inside me for the past nine months. Why would they?

I'd arrived home in the back of an ambulance and the sight of me and baby Ernie, alive and well, was cause enough for celebration, never mind my family surviving the blitz.

I can't describe how relieved I was when we turned into our street and saw our row of houses still in one piece, and you know all I could think about was being with my mam and having a cup of sweet tea. Those two things would put my world to rights, and in a way they did.

The blitz spirit, the mindset of everyone who was living through those war years, meant that we got on with it. Babies were born, the washing still had to be done, kids went to school, men were dying on the front, rationing was the norm, we were cold, scared, hungry, but at the same time stoic, jingoistic, making the best of a bad world. Me and baby Ernie were just a tiny part of all that and what I'd done slipped under the radar.

Just like I'd slipped the locket I'd found in Ernie's blanket into my pocket. It was while we were in the ambulance and as we rumbled along, avoiding craters and potholes, swerving obstacles in the road. It was the first time I'd been alone with him really, so I'd opened the swaddling to look better at the baby in my arms. Not having had chance to do the counting of fingers and toes that I'd seen Mam do when our Linda's babies were born, I just wanted a peep.

That's when I saw it. Wrapped around his hand. A silver locket on a delicate chain. Carefully, I removed it and hid it in my palm. I knew it was something private and personal, and would hold a photo, and that Nora must have put it there during the hours we laid in the darkness. I couldn't look at it then. It was too much.

Days passed before I found the nerve to open it and when I did I looked into the eyes of Ernie's real parents. A handsome young man and a very beautiful woman. On the back was an engraving, the letters R and E, encircled by a heart. This threw me slightly because Ernie's mother told me her name was Nora, so perhaps it was a nickname, or a shortening of something.

I didn't dwell on it. I couldn't. He was my baby now and that was all I cared about. Looking after him and waiting for my Walter to come home. Getting through the war and being a mum was my priority.

As for the locket, I couldn't bear to throw it away because I convinced myself it would be bad luck. And that if I kept it, hidden but close to Ernie, I'd be respecting Nora and she'd know I was looking after her boy – my boy now. It was like a talisman, and in some ways it eased my conscience.

I won't lie, but every now and then my mind did wander, and I couldn't help wondering if they'd given Nora and my Joseph a proper burial. I'd heard some horrible stories, about folk being put in mass graves because of the sheer volume, but I comforted myself that they'd be together, and Nora would be looking after him in heaven.

Two months passed by and there'd been no more bad raids like the night Ernie was born, so me and Mam ventured into the city. It was only a short walk, and even though it was a bitter cold February day, Mam said it would do us good to get outside and away from the house. We headed for Piccadilly, and I remember being shocked by the destruction of such a central part of Manchester. It was barely recognisable.

We couldn't afford to buy anything, so window-shopped instead. It took our minds off things I suppose, chatting and seeing folk going about their business, like there was hope and purpose to everyday life.

Mam, after all her bluff about exercise and varicose veins and getting rid of baby weight, decided she needed a sit down and sent me to fetch my dad's tobacco ration. I left Ernie with her, in his pram, and headed towards the newsagents.

That's when it happened. When my whole life was ruined. If Mam hadn't needed a rest. If my dad hadn't smoked like a chimney. If I'd chosen another shop. If I'd looked left not right.

It was her hair that caught my eye. I knew instantly it was her. Nora. Deep auburn locks flowed down the back of her coat that looked three sizes too big. She was standing slightly to one side staring into, or actually, at the window display.

I thought I was going to drop dead from heart failure right there and then. In a panic, short of breath, I took two steps to the side and hid behind a poster stand and from there I watched her. I can see her now. Everything about her.

She looked perished and was deathly pale, gaunt too. Her bare legs poked from the hem of the baggy coat and were like sticks. On her feet shoes that I could see were also too big because there was a gap between the leather and her heel. Her arms hung by her side and in one hand the bag, the same one that was by her bed in the hospital. I recognised the lovely oyster clasp. But it was her eyes that got to me. It was as though she was looking but not seeing, just being, a lost figure outside John Lewis, captured in time and in my memory.

It hit me, the hideous, hideous truth, like a punch in the stomach. Winded me right there on Market Street and made me sick to the core. Because I knew what she was thinking, what she'd been through and what she'd lost. And it was all because of me.

There, right in front of my eyes was a woman I truly believed had died. She'd lost all that blood. I saw it. Her lips had been blue; her body stone cold. I listened, my ear to her mouth and she wasn't breathing. I was sure. I felt for a pulse. There was none.

And thanks to me getting it wrong she was alone in the world, grieving the loss of her lover and her baby. That dreadful night, she told me she had nobody. So I'd offered her a roof over her head. Friendship and support. Love and a family.

All I had to do was go straight over to where she stood, place my hand gently on her arm so as not to startle her, and with a few gentle words and a smile, bring some light back into her life. It would have been the right thing to do. To make everything right.

And then I thought of Mam and Dad and my Walter out there fighting the Nazis. What everyone would think of me for doing what I did. They'd never forgive me for telling such lies and deceiving them. For putting someone else's name on a birth certificate. Having Ernie christened and standing there in front of them all, saying prayers and listening to promises. For taking someone else's baby and leaving my own behind, to be buried God only knew where.

My feet, that had been welded to the spot, followed orders from my brain and suddenly took flight. I dared one last look at Nora then turned away, making sure she didn't spot me before I almost ran back to Mam, who was where I left her with Ernie.

Before she could protest, I told her that the shop had run out of tobacco and that I didn't feel well and we needed to get home, into the warm. She must have told me a hundred times on the way home that I looked a funny colour, and asked if I was all right and would I slow down because she was getting out of puff.

I remember telling Mam I'd be fine in my home, and she went off in a bit of a huff to get Dad's tobacco. When I reached my little terraced house, once I'd pushed open the door the step seemed too high and the gap too narrow to get my pram in and I nearly screamed with panic and frustration. All I wanted to do was get inside where it was safe, away from Nora, away from the shame of what I'd done.

Finally I was in the hall and after I slammed the door shut I leant against the wood and tried to control my breathing and waited for the shaking to stop. When it did, I left Ernie sleeping in the pram and made myself a cup of tea and sat at the kitchen table, sipping, numb to the core as I tried to process it all.

By the time I heard the familiar cries of my hungry boy, I'd more or less worked it out. There was no turning back the clock, no chance of redemption. The fear of prosecution, persecution and public shame was too much so I resigned myself to what I knew would be my future and I suppose in some ways, my punishment.

I would have to look over my shoulder always, and live the life of a criminal avoiding justice. Because that's what I was. Me, Molly McCarthy. I was a baby thief.

CHAPTER 35

I never went into Manchester again. I told Mam that it made me upset and reminded me of the night in the hospital and the blitz. I suspect she thought I was being a bit mard because we didn't have words like post-traumatic stress in those days. We just got on with it.

I was a nervous wreck inside but put on a front, stiff upper lip and all that. If I did have a wobble I blamed it on worry, that I was scared for Walter and by the news on the radio. I told myself that all I had to do was stay on our street, keep Ernie by my side and we'd be fine. And I also had a plan that I put into practice as soon as Walter came home from the war.

I'd decided that we needed to keep moving and get away from Ancoats and the city where Nora was. She could be anywhere. Lurking. Living in the next street, working in a shop. And all it would take was for us to bump into each other and I couldn't take that chance. What if I had Ernie with me? What if she saw some family resemblance?

I comforted myself with the assurance that she can't have known what I'd done and must have been unconscious, maybe close to death when I swapped the babies. If she had seen, or even worked it out somehow, surely she'd have alerted the authorities who could have easily tracked me down. Perhaps her memory of that night was blurred. Facts and conversations lost in a haze of pain and fear. Or as result of losing so much blood that was quietly seeping from her, draining away her life force. If they were going to come for me, they'd have done so by then.

Walter came home, thank God, and he was overjoyed to see his son; they bonded immediately, and Ernie seemed to glow and gurgle more in the presence of his dad than he did with anyone.

Seeing this only made me more resolute. Or was it simply my way of justifying my actions? Probably.

Imagine how I felt when his hair started to grow. Auburn locks of baby hair sprouting from his head and a constant reminder of the woman at the shop window. Nora and her beautiful red hair. Thankfully, everyone wore rose tinted glasses and the family were overjoyed that the Irish genes had filtered through. Enniskillen Ernie was a great hit on St Patrick's Day down at the Hat and Feathers and had he been older wouldn't have had to buy his own drinks, I can tell you.

It took a while before I could put my self-preservation plan into action because after the war everything seemed to move at an interminably slow rate, and I had to bide my time. And inevitably, what I'd done, the fear I constantly lived with, sensing the spectre of Nora everywhere, changed me. Mam said so often enough yet again, I batted away her concerns and told her the war had changed everyone and I was no different.

Eventually we moved away from Ancoats, to Openshaw, which felt like a step in the right direction, although with a logical mind and hindsight I know I was kidding myself. No matter how far I ran, the law of averages, coincidence, bad luck, or fate meant that at any time Nora could step into my world.

But my fearful heart always ruled my head. I'd brainwashed myself into believing that the further away from Manchester I was, from that shop window where in my nightmares, Nora would always be waiting for me, the better.

So I became that wife, the one who always wanted more. Who pushed her husband to do better. I developed a protective shell, took control in order to keep all of us safe. It wasn't about possessions, but nobody seemed to notice that. Family had me down as a pain in the arse, that's what my dad used to call me. Our Linda said I had ideas above my station and Mam, well she just felt sorry for Walter who worked all the hours God sent and was lumbered with a nagging wife called Molly.

That's how I was perceived. The thing is, they were wrong. It wasn't that I wanted to be better than the family in the next-door terrace and actually, my kids were no worse dressed or fed than the next one. All I wanted was to be safe.

And there was something else. I had to make it right by giving Ernie the best life because I couldn't bear the thought that he'd have been better off with Nora, so I had to try harder.

And to achieve that, we needed savings and someone with a vision. Me. I did my fair share too. Taking part-time jobs and scrimping to put money in our savings account, which was also my secret escape fund.

It wasn't long though, before I realised that running away was actually the least of my problems. There's a phrase, nature or nurture, and looking back, that's what came to bite me on the bottom and punished me in a way I'd not imagined or prepared for. Because no matter how much I loved Ernie, how hard I tried in my own way to make up for what I'd done, to give him a good life, there was always something missing between us.

I'll never know whether something in his genes made him the way he was, that nature shone through no matter what, or his upbringing, me to be precise, had an adverse effect on him. It hurts to think it was that. And I suppose what's worse from my point of view is that whoever Nora was, whatever made her tick, something in her personality, the blood that swam through her veins, that swam in his, made Ernie who he was.

Oh, don't get me wrong, I loved him with all my heart, and nobody would dare think or say that I wasn't a good mother. Dear Lord, I put everything I had into it. If there'd been the time and I'd have been clever enough, I could've written a book on how to be perfect. Run the house, prepare the meals, starch shirts, work at the bakers, shine shoes, bleach the nets, scrub the step, back in the yard with a smile on my face for home time. It didn't make Ernie love me though.

I saw it more clearly when our Beryl was born because it was there from the start. A bond that went both ways. And it shone a light on what was missing between me and Ernie.

As he got older, he came to resent me even more. It was like I could feel it and so could he. We didn't fit or match and because I knew why, I overcompensated and in doing so, pushed him away little by little.

If I said black, he'd swear it was white. Even from an early age there was this inherent streak of stubbornness in him. So strong willed. Often belligerent. If Ernie made up his mind about something then *nothing* would change his mind. He'd cut off his nose to spite his face if you let him.

He also had a propensity to buck trends, stand up for other people's rights, be a bit of a rebel. I worried he'd do something stupid, become a hippy and live on a commune, shun society or become a troublemaker, or, God forbid, join the Labour party.

I think it was his stubborn streak that saved him from all that, or the desire to escape me which was why he was determined to start his own life, on his own terms. I'll always regret not supporting him when he wanted to go to university. We said we couldn't afford it, but I think we could. I just didn't want to let him go and, once again, had to stay in control. Manage him from the side lines because the 'what ifs' ruled my world. No wonder he grew to despise me.

His dad had moved up the ladder a bit at the railway company and was a supervisor, so he got Ernie a job working on the lines. It was how we did it in them days. Left school on a Friday and started work on a Monday. Ernie hated it, but in his own stubborn way he got on with it.

It was as though he knew deep down, by some invisible but finely tuned sense, that he didn't belong with me, and that makes me so sad. That he was loved so much but it wasn't enough. I'm sure that the father–son bond he clearly had with Walter was the only thing that anchored him, settled his soul. Even now it baffles me how he could have loved his dad unequivocally yet where I was concerned there may as well have been a concrete barrier and barbed wire between us.

But what could I do? I'd made my choice, or choices, and had to get on with it the only way I knew how. Guardedly, for a start. Always fearful of walking into a room, or a restaurant, or, God forbid, a schoolyard and her being there. And then there was the overthinking. What if, by some cursed quirk of fate, one day Ernie would bring home a girlfriend, with auburn hair and it'd come out in the wash her mother's name was Nora...

That was how my mind worked. Always on overdrive. Always on alert. Because I never knew where Nora was, if she'd married, had more children. I was tempted to search for Joseph though. Go into Manchester to the town hall and see if I could find out where he was buried. I had visions of going to his grave and laying some flowers. Telling him that I was sorry he didn't make it and that I thought of him and would never ever forget that I held him in my arms. But I was too scared, and truthfully didn't have much clue where to start.

And you might be surprised to hear that I did think of telling Ernie. Many times. When he was sixteen, eighteen, twenty-one, before he married Nancy, but I knew if I did he would hate me forever and I couldn't risk losing him. And I was terrified that the police would find out and come for me. Lock me up. That it would be in the papers, and everyone would know and hate me. That I'd lose everything. Walter, Beryl, my home, my family.

I'm such a coward. I accept that. I've lived my life feeling the mark of a big yellow streak running down my back and what I'm doing now just proves it. Because telling you this, passing my shame and burden on to you, is another cowardly act. But I can't go without telling the truth, just as much as I can't look him in the eye, say the words myself and see his pain and disgust and hate. That's what I've always imagined and it's what I deserve.

I'm so tired of it all, though. It feels like I've lived a hundred lives and carried this secret through all of them. It's weighed me down and I'm glad to have shed it. The choice now, is yours. Whether to tell him or not. And whichever you choose, please know you have my blessing, and I will understand either way.

There is one thing more, that regardless of your choice, I'd like you to say to Ernie. Tell him from the moment I took him in my arms, he became my son, and I did my best. That I loved him, and I always will. And that I'm sorry.

CHAPTER 36

HONEY

Nothing. He'd said nothing at all. Not one single word all the way through the reading of the letter. Perhaps he was in shock. What if it was too much and he had a heart attack or a stroke and then it would be all her fault and that bloody Molly bloody McCarthy's?

Honey chanced a glance at her grandad. He did look a bit pale but not like he was about to keel over, just staring straight away, like he was frozen. She couldn't stand it anymore.

'Grandad. Say something, please.'

His chest heaved and his shoulders rose then fell. Good, he was breathing. When he reached over and took her hand, Honey was flooded with relief and gave it a squeeze which reciprocated. His voice when he found it sounded hoarse yet with a softer edge than before.

'Thank you, lass. For telling me. That took some bottle and I want you to know this, that I'm glad someone in this family knows right from wrong because them words you read out have eased my soul.'

This, Honey was not expecting. 'What, you're glad about it all?'

'No, not glad. That's not the right word. More relieved I'd say. Because it's made sense of it all, everything I felt and knew, deep down. So many thoughts that I couldn't put into words about how *she* was, the way she behaved, how I felt about her I s'pose.'

Honey clung onto his hand, comforted by its warmth, which meant his heart was beating just fine. 'So you forgive her then? Molly.'

When his head whipped around so fast it might fall of his neck, Ernie startled Honey and the anger in his expression made her eyes widen.

'Forgive her? NO. Never. I'll never ever forgive that woman for what she did... dear God, she's a monster, can't you see that?'

Honey opened her mouth to speak then changed her mind because truthfully, she didn't know what the hell to say for the best. Ernie had plenty to get off his chest, though.

'She had the chance to put it right. To save that poor woman from whatever it was she was going through but oh no... Molly thought of herself first as always. That selfish, self-obsessed woman was evil and took me away from my rightful mother. Someone who I can tell from that letter was mourning the loss of me and my father, both of them I never got to meet, and I know there was nowt anyone could do about my dad, but she robbed me of the chance to find my mum, to tell her I was alive, and she hadn't lost me. That's the cruellest thing of all.'

Honey felt him let go of her hand and watched as he sucked in a breath of dusky air then stood and began to pace. This was not a good sign.

'You're right. The fact that she knew your mum was alive and the poor woman didn't know you had survived, never mind having to bury a baby she thought was hers, is very cruel.' Ernie paced and Honey braced herself for the fallout from what she was about to say. 'The thing is, Grandad, she explains in the letter why she did what she did, even in the hospital that night and later, when she saw Nora in Manchester. She was scared of saying something; and she was only young, what, very early twenties, and didn't have anyone to confide in. Perhaps if she had, maybe, told her mum or her sister, they could've found a way round it.'

Ernie put both hands on his flat cap as if to hold in his brains that were about to explode and splatter all over the allotment, and all Honey could think was, *That'll be good for the soil and the birds will love it.* She was losing the plot, too.

'But she didn't did she? Instead she deceived everyone, the whole family, and you know what?' he pointed his finger at Honey, who could see his hand was shaking, presumably and hopefully from anger, 'She made a choice between her and me, and chose herself. If she'd loved me, truly loved me like the son she said I was to her, then she'd have put me first. Simple. As. That.'

He began pacing again and when some late afternoon feasters swooped onto his plot to peck for food, he rushed across the soil clapping his hands and stamping his feet. Honey watched relieved that he was taking it out on the birds and not her. They could fly away. She couldn't and wouldn't. She had to weather the storm with her grandad.

Then the idea she'd had after reading the letter for a fourth, maybe the fifth time, popped into her head then out of her mouth. 'What if we looked for her, online. Like on that programme you love watching.'

Ernie's tut was so loud Honey was surprised he didn't crack a tooth. 'What's the point? She'll be long dead now. I'm eighty-three so she must have been in her late teens or twenties when she had me which makes her over a hundred. She's dead and buried and that's the end of it. All you'll find, even if you knew where to look because all we have is a couple of names, is a death certificate.'

Honey had already thought of this. 'Yes, that's all very true but you might have a living relative or loads of them that you can connect with. Would you like that? To meet some of your real kinfolk?'

Ernie answered immediately. 'The only person I'd like to have met is my mother. The person who gave birth to me, the one that will fill this gap that's been right here,' he tapped his heart, 'all my bloody life.'

Honey's lip wobbled and when Ernie's chin fell to his chest and she saw his eyes close and his shoulders begin to shake, she leapt from the bench, wrapping her arms around him and holding him tight.

She sobbed too, as the weight of someone else's secret took its toll, on her and her grandad. Her heart hurt, too, because there was nothing worse, in her mind, than seeing a grown man cry. She'd seen her dad like that and never ever wanted to witness such despair in her hero, her Grandad Ernie. But there was nothing she could do other than stay and comfort him. Wait for the tide of tears that were wetting her hair to ebb.

Once they did, Honey guided Ernie back to the bench where they sat, and she asked if he'd like another brew, reminding him of Grandma Nancy's belief that the strong sweet taste of sugary tea always did the trick. And a biscuit of course. She'd hoped to make him smile but had failed miserably.

'If it's alright with you, lass, I'd like to go home and be by myself for a bit.' Ernie took out a tatty handkerchief, wiped his eyes and blew his nose.

'Of course. I'll take you.' No way was she leaving him there. She expected resistance because, as Molly said in her letter, he was stubborn to the core.

'That'd be appreciated. I feel jiggered after all that. Come on then, let's be going. It'll be dark in a minute and it's going to be a cold one. I'll lock up. Two ticks.' Ernie stood slowly, resting his hands on his knees while the joints clicked into place.

While he fiddled with the door of his shed and fastened the padlock, Honey folded the letter, and when he returned, silently passed it to Ernie. He accepted it and put it in his pocket and as he did, she spotted the silver chain dangling from his palm that clutched the locket. Her grandad's only link to his parents.

Feeling tears threaten and not wanting to be apart from Ernie, Honey suggested, 'I think I should stay the night at yours. I've not done that for ages, and it'll be nice. I'll get us some fish and chips and we can talk some more, or not talk, whatever you want to do.'

Ernie swung his arm over her shoulder and began to walk as he answered, 'I won't say no to a bag of chips. Then you can get off home and have a rest.'

'I don't want to leave you though...'

Giving her a squeeze, Ernie assured her he'd be okay. 'If I need company I promise I'll ring you, but I really will be okay. I just want time to take it all in and then we can talk tomorrow. I'll pop to the café for breakfast. Is that a deal?'

'And perhaps we can talk about doing a bit of digging, you know, join one of those sites that do family trees, it's worth a try.'

She couldn't help thinking that somewhere out there, there might be a relative of her grandad's who would love to meet him and be able to join the dots up. In fact she'd like to know herself because at the end of the day, she wasn't a McCarthy either. Same for her dad. Maybe curiosity and her ancestors were nudging her on. Calling out, waiting to be found, never giving up.

Ernie wasn't as enthusiastic. 'We'll see. Now get yer finger out lass and take me home. My bones are aching, and I've done enough chatting this afternoon to last me till Christmas.'

Honey sighed, nodded then hugged him back, knowing when she was beaten by the belligerent gene that ran through his marrow. She never wanted her grandad to change, because no matter whose blood he carried in his veins, who fed him his tea and read him bedtime stories, he was who he was. His own man. The best grandad in the world and someone she loved and admired more than anyone, ever.

CHAPTER 37

CLARISSA

She had surprised herself by asking Chuck to stay. Apart from agreeing to the documentary, which did entail some humming and hawing, her invitation was probably the most unreserved thing she'd done in a long time. And rather than worry about it afterwards, something told Clarissa it had been the right thing to do.

She'd followed her instincts, and it wasn't often that they were wrong. She was a people person. Of that she was sure and proud. Her ability to read the room, relate to folk from all walks of life, make them welcome or wither according to the situation and their behaviour, was a skill she had honed over many years. Being mistress of Chamberlain Manor and the legacy that came with it had taught her many things.

And she had to face facts – it wasn't like she had anything else to do. Having nobody to love or love her back, or even relatives, someone she had a genetic connection to, Clarissa accepted that she was blessed to have good friends, but they were popping off left right and centre. That was why having Chuck around had brought her a sense of... what was it? Kinship, perhaps. Like when you make a good friend and wish they were a relative, and that you could click your fingers and banish the bad apples and have them replaced by nice people.

If only it were that simple.

Then again, those bad apples, the maggoty, black-hearted-to-the-core relatives who were long gone, had shown her how not to be. The way to approach life and business and human beings. With respect. Being fair. Kindness never hurt anyone, and this was a lesson she'd learnt the hard way from a father and uncle who were the antithesis of the word.

Which was why Clarissa had chosen to make the most of a bad job. A job that had occupied her for most of her adult life.

That life was coming to a close and, whether she had another ten years or ten minutes remaining of it, she had to make sure that her house and the estate were in order.

With that in mind, after observing Mr Henderson Junior over lunch, Clarissa's sixth sense had kicked in. Not liking the scathing looks; the barely concealed irritation towards Chuck; the giveaway pulsing just below the solicitor's ear, warning bells had sounded in her head and Clarissa had the immense desire to rescue her long-lost cousin. From what she wasn't too sure; but something definitely wasn't right.

He'd been there for three days, and his presence had lifted the mood in the house. Jennifer had certainly taken a shine to him, as had her cleaning ladies. They'd flustered when they'd been introduced, and he removed his cowboy hat and called them ma'am. Clarissa chuckled at the memory, and them telling her later that he looked like Clint Eastwood.

It'd be all round the village now, that a cowboy had moved into the manor. Clarissa loved a bit of gossip, and it tickled her that on this occasion she was the cause of it, or rather Chuck was.

The week had flown by. On his first day, she'd arranged for Matheson to give him a tour of the estate, which Chuck seemed to enjoy – especially meeting one of the dairy farmers – then lunch in the village pub where apparently he drew quite a crowd at the bar.

Tuesday, Jennifer had taken him horse-riding at the Equine Centre. It was her hobby and passion. Jennifer preferred four-leggers to two-leggers, categorising horses and men respectively because the former had never let her down in her forty-one years on the earth. Clarissa was moved to agree. Her loyal aide usually rode alone so she'd been thrilled to have a companion to hack across the Cheshire plain with. And since, Clarissa had also wryly noticed a definite spring in Jennifer's step.

Cookie Beattie was another one who'd been rejuvenated by their guest and had produced some special English dishes for Chuck to sample. Mealtimes were much more fun with another person at the table, and Clarissa welcomed not having to dupe Jennifer into thinking she was having a wonderful time, and that she was looking forward to her porridge or chicken broth for lunch. She could just sit back, listen, and observe.

Wednesday had been bright but breezy, and Chuck had been out and about with Yosef, the groundsman. Apparently he liked being in the fresh air and wanted to pay his way. Clarissa knew there was no point in persuading him it wasn't necessary, so left him to it.

She was currently in the library, reading in front of the fire and, on hearing Chuck descending the stairs, pricked up her ears. He was whistling, something he did a lot, but she couldn't catch the tune and then his phone rang. He'd been clip-clopping along the hall in his cowboy boots, but so unbridled were his vocal cords that she heard the one-sided conversation quite well.

She knew that Mr Henderson Junior had invited Chuck to play a round of golf at his club and have dinner in town afterwards. Clarissa had been rather surprised that Tristan had even entertained the thought of socialising with Chuck in broad daylight because if ever she'd met a thoroughbred snob, he was it. His father was the same.

It seemed that Tristan had called to confirm arrangements, however, Chuck had other plans.

'Well thank you kindly for the invitation Mr H but I've been asked to take an English afternoon tea with Miss Jennifer tomorrow and anyways, I'm not sure I'd be any use with a golf club, and Cookie is making me her special vegetarian suet pudding. I ain't got any clues to what it is but I'll give it a go.'

Clarissa smiled as she listened to Chuck listening to Tristan and then, 'Yes, it's going well, and Miss Clarissa has made me mighty welcome here... No, no there ain't no need in going over anything... yes, I know. You made it all plain as the hand in front of me.'

What. What did he know, and why did Chuck sound slightly peeved? The answer came shortly after.

'Well that's as may be, but I can't help feeling you're being kinda previous here, Mr T, because there ain't nothing agreed yet. And anyways, I don't feel comfortable talking like this while Miss Clarissa is fine and dandy and being a very nice hostess so if you don't mind, I'll be getting off. I wish you a very good day.'

And that was that. Next thing Clarissa heard was Chuck clip-clopping in the direction of the kitchen no doubt to sweet-talk Cookie into making him a pre-dinner snack. That man had a huge appetite!

Clarissa was perturbed by what she'd heard, and placed her book on her lap, then rested her eyes. Gazing into the flames she recalled another conversation with Chuck where certain facts had come to her attention. It was during their impromptu sojourn around the garden on Chuck's first visit.

The information had been given freely once Clarissa asked the right questions, following her instincts and relying on the observations she'd stored during lunch. Hence her suggestion they took a little walk together.

It had turned overcast, and the temperature had dropped, so while she had been bundled up like a newborn, Chuck was exposed to the elements as they trundled along, he pushing her wheelchair, she pointing to this and that. 'Are you warm enough, Chuck? Maybe I should have asked Jennifer to find you a Barbour. There must be some that will fit you in the boot-room.'

'I'm fine, thank you ma'am, apart from this darned shirt that Mr Tristan bought for me.'

Unseen by Chuck, Clarissa gave a wry smile. She had noticed how uncomfortable he'd looked during lunch. Pulling at the collar of his smart shirt with the monogram on the cuff that screamed Cheshire set; and as for the jacket, well, the poor man looked as though he'd jumped out of a window display on the rows on Chester high street. It was clear as day that Tristan had dressed poor Chuck for lunch, even down to his perma-pressed slacks and very shiny new shoes.

The man was from the heartlands of Kentucky, via New York. And from what she'd gleaned from their conversation over roast beef and Yorkshires – or in his case lots of veg and minus the meat – Chuck was a thoroughbred cowboy, or at least he'd like to be.

No way on this earth had he brought the glaringly smart-casual middleclass outfit with him and, no way was she going to be taken for a fool.

'Why on earth didn't you just wear your own clothes, Chuck? We don't stand on ceremony here and I would've preferred you to feel comfortable and be yourself.'

At this Chuck laughed. 'Well I don't think Mr T wants me to be myself. Don't get me wrong, the hotel he put me up in is very swanky and so was the plane… jeez, I ain't never seen nothin' like it, but it ain't really me.'

Again, the warning bells sounded. 'So you travelled first class?'

'Yes-sir-ee. Sure did. He even sent a limousine to take me to the airport and then I waited in a fancy lounge. Felt like I'd hit the jackpot, that's the truth of it.'

Hmm, thought Clarissa, *I bet you did*, and then made a note to self to check the invoice when it next came from Henderson's. As much as she'd agreed to Tristan's suggestion that they bring Chuck to the UK, a first-class celebrity-style package was not necessary. So why all the fuss?

'So, enlighten me. What has dear Mr Henderson Junior explained, about the reason for your visit?' Clarissa thought it best to be direct no matter how unsavoury the subject. 'Has he hinted that I'm after naming an heir to the estate and you're in the running and wants to make sure you don't mess up?'

She indicated to a bench set into an arched stone arbour, a place she'd hidden herself away many times to read or rage, depending on the circumstance. The resting place looked onto the sloping plains: the land she owned was green and fertile, two things she had once been. The first a curse, the second a waste and a regret.

Chuck sat beside her wheelchair on the carved stone bench and Clarissa suddenly felt bad. She'd put him on the spot, reacting to what she suspected could be a conspiracy; a betrayal by someone she'd trusted with her affairs and another who she'd hoped to forge a bond with.

Whatever the outcome, she would bet her horses on being correct in her assumption about Tristan.

'I'm sorry if I've made you feel uncomfortable and it was very rude of me to put you on the spot like that, so please forgive me. You don't have to answer that question because I agreed you should come here and it's not a secret that I'm going to die without an heir, so you would've put two and two together eventually.'

'Hey, it's okay. I get it.' Chuck paused a while then asked, 'Can I be honest with you?'

This eased Clarissa's heart immediately. The prospect of a truthful exchange. 'Of course.'

'Mr Tristan has explained about your family and circumstances and yes, he has hinted that if we get on well, then there's the possibility that you could leave this mighty fine place to me. But that's not the real reason I came here.'

Clarissa angled her body so she could watch him more carefully. 'Oh, really. What was it, then?'

Chuck dipped his head and twiddled his thumbs, one circling the other until he looked up and when he did, Clarissa spotting something she recognised immediately. Not a family resemblance because there was none, she'd already scrutinised him for that. What she saw, was sadness.

CHAPTER 38

Seconds passed before Chuck spoke but when he did it was to her face, looking her in the eye where a moment of honesty passed between them.

'You probably don't know what it's like, not to fit in, comin' from your fine family but I never have, not ever.'

Clarissa was tempted to disagree but replied instead, 'You'd be surprised, but do go on. Why do you feel this way?'

'I'm not sure how much you know about my family, if the PI explained about my parents and how I'm related to you, but truth is, I'm from rotten stock either side of the tracks. Whichever way you look at it.'

That had been a revelation because there'd been no hint of this from Tristan. According to the report she'd seen, that gave a genealogical rundown of where and who Chuck came from, the American connection began with her cousin, Quentin. He'd married an heiress, Mirabelle de Haviland, from Chicago.

Clarissa remembered the wedding like it was yesterday. A truly magnificent affair that would have financially crippled her Uncle Oscar. As it happened, Mirabelle's father was happy to show the Brits how it was done, and *dear* uncle was off the hook.

Clarissa could imagine him on one, hanging in the cold store in the cellar like a side of beef, because he was an animal. A beast of the worst kind.

Shaking that image off, Clarissa took the opportunity to fill in the gaps and speed things along, eager to get to whatever Tristan was up to.

'I do know that after my cousin Quentin married Mirabelle they headed for Chicago and you are descended from the male line who, by all accounts had a marvellous time squandering their wealth and making a total hash of things. Your grandmother married Ronald Chamberlain, who'd relocated to Kentucky after being made bankrupt. Your mother, Delilah married Hank Chamberlain. So we can pick up the story there if you like. Tell me about them.'

Clarissa saw Chuck's chest heave a sigh, so she sought to reassure him. 'Chuck, please know that I'm not going to judge you by your parents because my father has a lot to answer for, as does his brother, but that's another story for another day. I don't care what Delilah and Hank did, I'm actually more interested in you. So please, relax.'

Chuck gave a nod and a smile then began. 'My daddy was a man's man. A drinker and nasty with it. Too handy with his fists, especially where I was concerned, because according to him and his warped view of the world, I was a big sissy. That's what he called me all my life. I swear when I hear his voice and imagine his face he's mad and snarling and calling me that name.'

This made Clarissa sad. 'Oh Chuck, I'm so sorry but why did he call you that?'

He shrugged. 'Simple really. I hated violence, never got into a fight, and would rather get beat up than defend myself. Wasn't into sport so much, although I got real good at pretending I was. But what marked me out as a sissy was my love of music, and movies and getting lost in another world where singing and dancing took me to another place. And animals. I love animals so having a pa who worked at the abattoir and liked to bring his work home, verbally and in a plastic bag, wasn't a good mix.'

Clarissa thought back to earlier when Cookie Beattie proudly brought out the silver platter and the awkward moment everyone realised a non-meat eater was about to throw up. 'Ah, now I understand. You were most polite at lunch when you turned down the meat and had I known you were a vegetarian beforehand I'd have catered for you – but let's blame Tristan for that. It's easier and more fun. Please continue.'

'So my daddy was a chauvinist and a bigot, and I used to thank the lord that I wasn't homosexual, not that I'm against them, mind. I've met some great guys in New York who're gay, but my life wouldn't have been worth living. But my mama was worse. He was scared of her and that's the truth of it.'

'Oh you poor man. I'm almost scared to ask why.' But she did, because Clarissa was nothing if not thorough, which was why Chuck explained.

'Mama was the real mean one. She's gone crazy so they locked her up in a home, and when my daddy died, I didn't shed no tears. I've had time to think on it all and I suppose Mama was bitter. About everything and everyone who had more than her. My daddy came from people who had money and she thought she'd backed a winner, but they ended up on the bad side of town in a trailer park. My daddy was no stranger to jail and Mama spent a few nights behind bars, too. I forgot to mention that, sorry.'

At this Clarissa shook her head, by means of telling him there was no need. Chuck picked up the tale.

'Well, it made her bitter and I was her whippin' boy in the true sense of the word. She didn't defend me when my daddy was mad. I think she enjoyed it, seeing him act that way. That's what used to hurt the most. Not my daddy's fist. The fact that my mama never stood up for me because she should've.'

At this remark Clarissa inhaled. Suddenly overwhelmed by a

memory. Of that sense of injustice, a soul-destroying moment after being incredibly let down by the one person who should have stood by you. Your own mother.

Clarissa was becoming bogged down by the past, hers and Chuck's, and they'd had such a lovely lunch, she didn't want it all ruined by their memories, so sought to lift them, quickly.

'Yes she should have protected you. But I can tell this is making us both feel sad so let's move the story along. I know they're gone, one way or another, and how and when is of no consequence anymore. You're here now and that's what matters.'

Chuck's shoulders relaxed slightly and he rested against the arbour wall. Perhaps remembering his past and his parents had exhausted him.

'You know somethin', that's the nicest thing anyone said to me in a long while so thank you, ma'am. And I'm very glad to be here, too. Meeting some decent family for once in my life, so I hope I haven't' disappointed you in any way and that we can become good friends. Because I'd like that a lot.' Then when he gave her a rueful smile and laid his hand on her arm, it almost made Clarissa gasp.

It was such an unfamiliar gesture, the touch of another, one reserved only for Jennifer when she sought to reassure or give assistance.

Thankfully, Clarissa resisted the urge to recoil or react in a negative way and was forced to swallow a little lump in her throat, dismissing it thoroughly with a cough and a statement.

'And so would I, Chuck. Now, you should know that I'm not used to meeting new people or opening my home to strangers, and most of the time my guard is up. I'm a very mistrustful old lady and I'd really prefer it not to be that way. So let's get going and start again, shall we?'

Chuck stood and looked decidedly brighter. 'I'd like that a lot, thank you, Miss Clarissa.'

She was about to suggest he dropped the 'miss' but then again it was endearing and part of who he was, so she remained silent, and waited patiently while he manoeuvred her onto the path.

As they set off towards the house her thoughts returned to the start of the conversation and the niggle of doubt she'd had with regards to Tristan. He'd clearly omitted certain facts from his initial report. Whilst Chuck had a less than salubrious backstory, which hadn't put her off one bit, she should have been told. About the no-good, jailbird parents at least.

Had Tristan doctored the report from the PI and if he had, why? Was he that desperate to provide her with an heir? Maybe he wanted a bonus for doing so, but it was all very curious, which made her ask one last question.

'Chuck, I was wondering about Mr Henderson? Do you like him? I've known his father for many years and have no reason to distrust him as he's served our family loyally and well. But soon, Tristan will take over the reins and I don't know too much about him, apart from he's an incredible snob and, according to my dear cleaning ladies, who heard it via one of their colleagues, his wife is much the same.'

Clarissa let that thought settle and waited. Yes, it was a test, and she had no way of knowing if Chuck would pass or fail because she was merely following a hunch. So when he stopped pushing and came around to sit on the dry-stone wall by her side, she sensed a victory.

'All I know is this. He's very, very, keen for me to win you over and not mess up. He says he's looking out for my interests and wants me to have a better future.' Chuck then gave his forehead a scratch and said, 'Heck, I don't know the guy well enough to work out if he's genuine or not. I did kinda wonder if maybe he's gettin' a reward for finding me, because he was real pushy about flyin' me over here. I think that must be it... he's wantin' to get on your good side before he takes over his daddy's job.'

With that, Chuck stood, and they were soon on their way but

while he thought he'd solved a mystery, Clarissa wasn't so sure. What if Tristan was a puppet-master in disguise and if he was, could someone else be pulling *his* strings? But who and why?

Unease bloomed and as she jiggled in her chair, the pebbles on the path disturbing the smooth roll of the wheels beneath her.

The sequence of recent events didn't sit well with Clarissa. It had been Tristan's idea to hire a genealogist and that had led them across the pond; then a private detective to pursue the trail. And he'd been full of the joys when he'd found a prospective heir, alive and well in New York. It was his idea to bring Chuck over, insisting he'd handle it all.

Had she, in her desire to secure her estate, allowed Tristan to manipulate her? Clarissa hated that notion more than anything. It had happened once before, when she was young and naïve and under her father's thumb and look how that turned out.

For all she knew, Chuck could be an imposter. *Oh dear lord*, she'd thought, *he could be anyone*. Schooled and planted with only one purpose. To get his hands on her money. They were in it together.

And then as soon as it arrived, her terrible suspicion faded with the sound of Chuck asking her what the peacocks ate and why they made such a terrible sound. And she remembered the look in his eye. That innate sadness that only one who has suffered would recognise in another and was instantly ashamed.

Which was one of the reasons she decided to invite Chuck to stay at the manor. It would also do no harm to extricate him from the influence of Tristan, either. Or was it so she could keep an eye on him? Perhaps. Or because she actually rather liked him. Most definitely.

~

Clip-clopping on the hall tiles and Jennifer chattering away, accompanied the unmistakable rattling and squeaking of the hostess trolley. Knowing it would be carrying her pot of tea and – fingers crossed – a slice of cake, Clarissa re-opened her book and reposed her head. She would appear to be napping when they entered and from behind closed eyelids, took stock while she waited.

Over the past few days, any worries about Chuck had been banished and the one-sided conversation had strengthened her belief in him. As for Tristan Henderson, that was another matter entirely and no way was Clarissa going to sit back and do nothing. If he was up to something, then she needed to find out exactly what it was.

But how? Then it came to her, the solution. And it was right under her nose. Chuck.

CHAPTER 39

HONEY

In the end Lizzy lost her patience and snatched the notepad from Honey's hands and told her to go and sit at the table in the corner and face away from the customers in case she put them off their food. Knowing not to mess with Lizzy, Honey did as she was told.

'I'll bring you a pot of tea and then you can tell me what on earth is wrong. You've been neither use nor ornament all day and at this rate you're going to curdle the milkshakes, so sit.'

Honey sloped off to the corner and the table with the reserved sign that had been waiting for her grandad since they opened at eight that morning. He'd not turned up for breakfast and it was approaching 10am, so she was getting worried. His phone just rang out and she'd decided that if he didn't reply to her message by the time the big hand reached the top, she was going round there.

The evening before, as promised she'd bought him a bag of chips, lots of salt and vinegar – he'd refused a fish, saying he wasn't that hungry. It had killed her, watching him walk up the path with the carrier bag scrunched in his hand the way he always did. He never held them by the handles. Another thing she loved about him stored in her memory bank.

All evening, she'd tried not to imagine him being sad, definitely not crying and thankfully unlike her dad, not drowning his sorrows in drink because two pints of bitter was Ernie's max. He'd texted to say he was fine and was having an early night, so she'd done the same and, exhausted from the whole day, conked out as soon as her head hit the pillow.

She'd given him the benefit of doubt when he didn't reply to her 7am text, or her 8am one, thinking he was as tired as she. But once the breakfast trade faded away and he hadn't turned up by nine, an uneasy feeling began to settle.

'Here you go. One pot of Earl Grey for the lady with the smacked arse face. So, what's up? If it's man trouble and you don't want to say, fair dos – but as you know, I am the speaker of sense where the male species is concerned so fire away.' Lizzy had plonked herself opposite Honey and was pouring two cups of tea.

'I swear it's nothing to do with men, or a man, or Levi, because I know that's what you think and, before you ask, it's all going very nicely there. He's helping me with a little project that should benefit us here at the café, we've been for lunch, he's met Honker and we had a very nice kiss at the station and a Facetime later that evening. We're going out on Saturday night, and I don't intend letting him drive home back to Manchester or letting him sleep on the sofa, either. Does that satisfy madam's curiosity?' Honey gave Lizzy, who to put it politely had had her fair share of romances in her life, a wink.

Lizzy's painted-on eyebrows had risen an inch higher above her wide, kohl-pencilled eyes, and she wore a satisfied smile. 'Yes, that's excellent news and it's about time you started courting again.'

Honey nearly choked on her tea. 'Courting! Jeez Lizzy. You

sound like my grandma and you're only forty-one. Where've you dragged that one up from?'

Lizzy tutted. 'So, go on. Why the moody face?

'I'm just a bit worried about Grandad. He should've been in early for breakfast and he's not answering his phone and that's not like him.'

Lizzy opened her mouth to speak just as Honey's mobile began to ring in her back pocket. 'Thank goodness, at last.' Twisting her arm behind, she yanked out her phone and answered without looking at the screen but the voice on the other end wasn't Ernie. It was the vicar who she knew well from events he'd attended at the café.

Two minutes later Honey was racing out towards the door, her arms one-in one-out of her parka and her rucksack flapping everywhere, banging against tables and customers in her panic to get to the car.

What had her grandad done that caused the vicar to ring and tell her to get to the church immediately? Apparently, there'd been an incident with Mr McCarthy, who was asking for Honey. He was okay – not ill – but she should get there as soon as she could.

Never had the three miles to Marple seemed so far away, and never ever had there been as many cars driving at five miles an hour right in front of her. By the time she pulled up outside the church, Honey's head was pounding, and her heart was racing, but at least there were no police cars attending the 'incident'. So that had to be a good sign.

After being pointed in the right direction by one of the groundsmen, Honey ran along the path and between the neat rows of gravestones, realising she was heading towards their family plot. There, gasping for breath, she found the vicar and Ernie.

The vicar stood, one hand on Ernie's shoulder in a supportive rather than restraining gesture. By his side, sitting on the grass, was her grandad, his arms resting on bent knees, his head bowed.

'Oh Grandad, I've been so worried. What's happe–' It was as her eyes strayed from Ernie to the vicar, who dipped his head to indicate she should turn around, that she spotted it. Her hand flew to her mouth while she stared.

'Grandad, what have you done?' There, amongst what was left of her great-grandmother's headstone, lay the lump hammer that he'd obviously used to smash the memorial stone to pieces.

Ernie remained silent and, reading the room, or in this case the graveyard, the vicar kindly said, 'I can see this is a sensitive issue, so I'll leave you in peace. I have no intention of informing the police as it's clearly a family affair, but we will need to discuss the damage. I'll wait in the church. Take as long as you need.'

After a shoulder pat, a quick nod and a kind smile for Honey, he picked up the lump hammer, obviously keen on damage limitation, then scurried away, leaving Honey and Ernie alone.

Sitting beside him on the damp grass, Honey waited for an explanation, even though she knew more or less what had happened and why.

Seconds passed then, 'I'm sorry, lass.'

She reached over and placed her hand on his arm. 'I know, Grandad. So am I. And I wish more than anything that you weren't feeling like this, or I could take it all away. In fact I wish I'd not told you now.'

Ernie lifted his head to reveal an unshaven face and bloodshot eyes that must have shed a fair amount of tears overnight. Either that or he'd not slept a wink.

'Don't say that lass, because I stand by what I said yesterday and I'm glad I know the truth. I swear it as my oath. But I just lost it and had to do something with the anger inside. There's just too much of it to keep locked up and if I didn't let it out, show her how I feel and how much I hate her, I reckon I'd have gone loopy.'

Biting her tongue, she didn't mention that smashing a

gravestone to bits in broad daylight with the biggest hammer she'd ever seen wasn't exactly normal behaviour and instead pointed to the grave on the left of Molly's.

'I see you left Beryl alone then.'

Thankfully that headstone was intact but, at that moment, Honey didn't want to read the words inscribed in gold. She always did. Every time she came to lay flowers on special days but right then, they would have sounded hollow and that loss of faith in her aunt made her incredibly sad.

'Hmm. Only because the gardener bloke saw me and came over and talked me down. Nice man. I know his dad from the bowls club. He took the hammer off me and rang the vicar. When he came, I thought he'd ring the police, but he remembered I always bring a box of veg for the harvest, so I reckon he took pity. The power of carrots and turnips, eh?'

Great, thought Honey, *now everyone at the bowls club will think he's lost the bloody plot.* Still she was glad someone had come along, and that Beryl's gravestone was intact, because she was still on the fence where her aunt was concerned. The happy childhood memories counteracting confusion and disbelief.

As for Molly, that was even tougher to get her head around, and the scales of truth and justice tipped dramatically. Honey had a feeling that where both of them were concerned she'd never truly be able to decide how she felt about what either had done.

Still, she had to ask, 'Were you really going to smash Aunty Beryl's, too?'

Ernie shrugged. 'I don't know, lass. I don't know about 'owt anymore. What I do know is my whole family, apart from you obviously, is here, in this bloody place. Look,' he pointed at the plot of neat graves, 'There's them two liars, then my old dad who has nowt to be ashamed of at all, and our Kevin.' At this point his voice cracked and he took a moment before he continued, the words a strangled sob. 'And my Nancy.'

Honey rested her head on his shoulder and let him cry. It was all she could do. He was in shock. She was sure of it, and whether he liked it or not she was going to stay with him for a few days. There was no way she could leave him alone in this state.

It was as her eyes roamed the words on the stones of the good guys in the plot that something occurred to her. And even though it probably wouldn't make the whole bloody mess better, it was something she'd needed to say out loud for a long time.

CHAPTER 40

When his body became still, and after she felt the movement of him wiping his eyes, even though he continued to gaze at the grass beneath his feet, Honey tried to break through the barrier she could tell he was building around himself.

'Grandad, can I tell you something that's been bothering me for years and years. Ever since Dad died and I know you find it hard to talk about it, but I just want you to listen.'

Ernie remained silent. His head bowed again so she continued. 'I used to think it was my fault, that Dad died. I still do deep down.'

Ernie lifted his head slightly and tilted it so she could just see his eyes. 'Why lass? You know that's not true.'

Honey shrugged. 'Maybe, but I'll never know, will I? If my selfish actions could have changed the course of history.'

Her grandad just looked and waited so she explained. 'Twice Mum tried to leave him. That I knew of anyway, but maybe there were more. I remember her disappearing a lot, only for a day then coming home very late and I could tell she'd been crying. Perhaps she'd lost her nerve or had nowhere to go. On the occasions I stopped her it was because I couldn't bear the thought of them splitting up.' She raced on: if he interrupted, she'd lose her nerve.

'The first time, I was about six. She picked me up after school and, as we walked home, she explained that daddy was making her very sad, and she was fed up of fighting all the time. So she'd packed our bags and we were going on an adventure, somewhere we'd both be happy.' Even after all those years, remembering that day made Honey's heart constrict.

'Anyway, I kicked up the biggest fuss and started crying in the street which only got worse when she opened the front door and I saw two cases in the hall. I was hysterical and begged her not to take us. Pleaded for her to give daddy another chance and when I ran to my room and hid under the bed refusing to come out, kicking and screaming, she eventually gave up.'

The next part killed Honey because, with a few years under her belt, and after hearing Ziggy's stories of women who turned up battered and bruised for A&E care, only to go home afterwards, she didn't know if her mum was hiding more than just her sadness.

'I can see her now, sobbing quietly as she took the neatly folded clothes out of the cases and back in the drawers then went downstairs to make tea. It happened again when I was twelve. I remember that exactly because it was two days after my birthday. I think she'd waited until after my party.' And there they were to taunt her: images of balloons and a cake and jelly and ice-cream. Her mum doing the right thing for Honey. Wearing a brave face so she'd have a happy birthday.

'This time we actually went, but it wasn't till we got to Aunty Nicki's that she told me we were staying. I went mad, then did a terrible thing and rang dad and told him where we were, so he came round. It was awful. I was in bed, top and tailing with our Aileen and I heard a commotion downstairs, banging on the front door then a row in the hallway.' The part that followed always made her insides turn.

'Dad was calling my name, asking me to come downstairs and go home with him. I froze. Not because I was scared of him, because I didn't know what to do and his voice sounded so sad, pleading with me. I was in that awful position of having to choose between them. All I'd wanted was for him to come and get us both and for them to make friends. Eventually he went home, and I cried myself to sleep.'

Ernie took her hand in his and sounded sad as he said, 'I never knew all this, lass, and I'm sorry you went through that.'

Honey continued, 'Don't be sorry, Grandad. It was their mess and I got dragged in, I see that now. And I suppose when you're in a mess like they were, they lost sight of stuff. I wasn't going to give up on them, though so when my aunts convened the next day, there was talk of me moving schools and I lost the plot. I was like a wild thing and refused to eat or speak and said I wanted to go and live with dad.'

Ernie shook his head, a wry look on his face. 'Bloody hell, lass. I can't imagine you bein' like that. Mind, lookin' at the state of this place I'm not one to talk. That temper of yours must come from me. So what happened next?'

Honey glanced at the pile of stone and silently agreed, they were both similar in many respects, stubborn and, when pushed, prone to flares. 'Mum lasted a day and a half before I wore her down and convinced her we should go back. I even got Dad on the phone and made him swear he'd change and make it all right. So we went home.'

'It's not your fault, lass, the problems in their marriage. None of us could help them. Me and your Grandma did try but really, they were never suited.'

Honey knew that, but what she didn't know drove her mad. What if she'd been brave, not selfish; realised how unhappy her mum was for years and years, and not interfered. There was a chance that her dad would've found someone else, someone suited to him, and he'd have been happy. And her mum could have got on and met someone too.

Instead, she'd marked time, for Honey's sake. When her mum was finally able to leave without conscience or Honey stopping her, her dad spiralled out of control and went to the off-licence that night. If Honey had behaved differently, would her dad still be alive?

'I hated Mum for leaving for good, and I blamed her for Dad dying. The things I said to her around that time make me ashamed. I think it was my way of hiding the guilt I felt, and not facing up to what I'd done all those years before. And I know you're going to say that I was just a kid, and I was. I get that, too.'

Honey sucked in courage for the next bit because how it was received was anyone's guess, 'But what we both need to focus on is this… everyone makes mistakes. Everyone does stupid things, acting on knee-jerk reactions,' she nodded towards the pile of stone, 'that they can't change, and say horrible things they can never take back.'

It was hard to steady the wobble in her voice, 'And that's a killer. To have to relive a moment in time over and over and wish you could do it differently. Or say you're sorry. Tell someone you love them. So many lost chances and wrong turns. I've got to live with the memories of making Mum stay. And as much as you're going to hate it, Molly and Beryl had to live with what they'd done, or not done, whichever the case may be.'

Ernie remained silent and impassive.

Honey ploughed on. 'And that's why when I get home I'm going to ring Mum and say I'm sorry and tell her I love her. I can't say that to Dad, but I hope he knows, somehow. But I'm not going to be like Molly or Beryl. I swear from now I'm going to do what I think is right, no matter if it means taking the hardest route. Or speaking out or being a bit brave and honest every now and then.'

She flicked away a tear and held in the sob that was building in her chest and waited for something – anything – from her grandad.

Finally he lifted his arm so she could rest in the crook of his neck, and once he'd pulled her close, asked her a question. 'So, my little wise owl. What do you suggest your daft old grandad does now because apart from writing a very big cheque to the vicar, I'm buggered if I know.'

Honey smiled and sniffed, laughing at the thought of him getting his cheque book out. *Did anyone even write cheques anymore?*

'I don't know, Grandad. Apart from actually getting an online bank account that you've been promising you'll do for years, let's just take it one day at a time, eh? It's all too raw, this news about Molly, and it's stirring up a lot of stuff for both of us. Let's work through it together. It's just us now, me and thee, and we make a great team, don't we?'

She felt him kiss the top of her head. 'Aye, lass. We do that. And I'm sorry you've felt like that about your dad all this time and not been able to talk to me about it. So I promise I'll try not to be a stubborn old bugger and listen more and stop shutting you out. How does that suit?'

'It suits me fine, and I get it, by the way, that you were hurting too and trying to cope in your own way. So along with everything else please don't go beating yourself up about it. I'm fine and we're both going to *be* fine, as long as we stick together and keep talking.'

Ernie tutted. 'Well that's never been a problem for you, has it lass? You never bloody shut up and that's a fact.'

Honey gave him a nudge. 'Oi.' She looked at the mess he'd made of the plot and sighed, 'Right, come on. Get your bottom off this soggy grass and we'll go and see the vicar, or do you want me to? You can wait in the car if you prefer.'

Ernie gave her a sheepish look, 'Can we start togetherness

tomorrow? I feel a right daft bugger and I'd rather just try and forget all about it.'

Honey rolled her eyes. *Tell that to the bowls club*, she thought, but didn't say. And even if he wasn't going to be brave, she was sticking to her own promise and would face the vicar alone.

'Here,' she fished inside her coat pocket for her keys. 'Go and wait in the car, ya big mardy. I'll make your excuses and meet you there in a bit. Come on, best get this over with.'

Ernie took the keys and then remembered, 'And I'll need that hammer back… it's me favourite. Don't let the vicar keep it.'

Tutting, she linked his arm and pulled him along, her mind already racing ahead. Packing an overnight bag, moving back into her bedroom at her grandparents that hadn't changed since she was a teenager. Seeing Levi at the weekend and then, maybe, she'd start searching for long lost relatives online.

Would the name Nora be enough to track someone down? A living link who could fill in the blanks about who she was, who they were. And there it was again. A voice in her head, someone giving her a nudge and telling Honey loud and clear that she had to try. Someone was out there. She just knew it.

CHAPTER 41

MR TRISTAN HENDERSON JNR

I on Pavăl smoothed out invisible creases on his trouser leg in silence as the waiter arranged the paper coasters, then their drinks and a miniscule bowl of appetisers on the table before moving to the next. There, sticking out like sore thumbs and conspicuous by their nonchalance, Ion's bodyguards were also served refreshments which they barely acknowledged.

Rude, thought Tristan, who prided himself on his manners, but then again what could one expect from thugs. At least his drinking partner knew how to behave – well, in public anyway. What he got up to in private would make anyone's eyes water.

Tristan had been summoned to the bar inside the airport hotel. Ion was flying out to a location undisclosed and wanted an update on progress at the Chamberlain Estate.

It was how he liked to do business apparently, face-to-face, however, Tristan did wonder if the whole scene was meant to intimidate. He could understand why it would have this effect, the meatheads in the shades. And while it was all rather theatrical and, no doubt, bolstered Ion's ego, it had to be said Tristan also got a huge kick out of being around someone like that.

Finally, the man himself spoke. 'So, where are we at? Is she ready to sign her will at long last?'

Tristan had prepared for this question and hoped to get away with a bluff because Chuck was being a proverbial pain in the butt. 'We're all good. I'm going to go over there and have a word with Chuck sometime this week.' If he could get the imbecile to stop fobbing him off, that was. 'Primarily a social call but I have it on good authority that he has our spinster eating out of his hand.'

Ion nodded and leant forward to take his drink and then check his phone, followed by a lot of screen tapping, giving Tristan's heartrate a chance to settle slightly.

It was true, that Chuck was doing better than expected in the schmoozing department, but where Tristan was concerned, the man was being evasive, ignoring his calls and texts and turning down countless invitations.

The plan to get Chuck on side via whisky and women hadn't turned out to be the great temptation Tristan had envisaged and instead, the redneck preferred life down on the farm, or wherever that damned irritating horsey Jennifer took him. He'd never liked her, and he suspected, from the withering looks she doled out, that the feeling was mutual.

Then there was Clarissa. She wasn't responding well to his tactful hints that the will was drafted, and they just needed a final decision. He'd even enlisted the help of his father, who she clearly preferred dealing with, and even he got short shrift. It didn't bode well. Not that Ion needed to know any of that.

Finally, the texting ceased, and business resumed. 'I am pleased to hear the American is making progress, but how can you be sure that once he has... What is that expression you English have about a table and feet?'

'Ah, you mean having one's feet under the table.' Tristan was nothing if not quick off the mark.

'Yes, that. Very stupid saying but continue. How long can I expect to wait? I have other properties on my radar, so it had better not take forever. And how sure are you that the American will sell? Perhaps he will want to be king of his castle and stay on. Then this will have been a total waste of time.'

This was exactly what Tristan feared. He'd planned to work on Chuck once he'd arrived, dropping hints and bamboozling him with promises of great wealth. Chamberlain Manor was worth many millions and then there was Clarissa's even more substantial investment portfolio. Chuck would have absolutely no need of a country pile once he inherited. The problem was, he'd been ostracised and for all he knew, Ion might be correct, and the redneck buffoon may have ideas well above his station, a bit like the man seated opposite.

Breathe, play the long game, think of the rewards.

'I assure you there is no need for alarm. Chuck would be a fish out of water if he took over the estate. I mean seriously, what would someone like him do? The locals would never accept him.'

Tristan inwardly cringed, knowing that Ion probably wouldn't appreciate the fish idiom. But it was the dark look that washed over Ion's face in response to his scathing comment about Chuck, that had Tristan backtracking like he was on speed.

'What I mean is, the chap looks like he's just stepped out of a rodeo and he's not exactly...' Tristan refrained from using another idiom about bright buttons or sharp knives, especially not with the meatheads sitting close by, '...not exactly in your league. He's unsophisticated and I doubt he has a gram of your business acumen so it would be a no-go.'

He saw a nerve twitch at the corner of Ion's lips and, even though he wasn't sure if it was the hint of a smile or the beginning of a smirk, Tristan hoped he'd got away with it and changed tack.

'I can one hundred percent assure you that Clarissa is extremely eager to tie up all her loose ends and not die intestate but, as one would expect, she wanted time to get to know Chuck and make her decision. He's only been there just short of a month so perhaps we should be a tad more patient.'

Checking his watch, Ion raised an eyebrow, drained his glass then put Tristan straight. 'Unfortunately, patience isn't a quality I possess. Time is almost up. If you don't secure the American as heir by the end of November – two weeks' time to be very exact – the deal is off, and I will move on.'

Tristan quailed. Reminded of the time at boarding school when he and a some of other boys had been caught mid-jape in their dorm. It was just a bit of harmless fun, back then. Lots of boys did it, or so he was told.

Dressing up in the St Trinian's costumes they'd borrowed from the drama department wasn't a crime. But what his right hand was doing to Lord Jonty, the Home Secretary's son, was. And the threat of his father finding out had made Tristan keel over. Right there in the head's study. In front of the kinky-whipping-desk, as they all called it. Spark out on the Persian rug.

Tristan was not about to repeat the rug thing so inhaled through his nose and tried to steady himself. He also focused on the rewards of attending one of Ion's parties where nobody gave a fig about that what you did and who with. And then there was his big juicy commission. Failure was not an option.

'Ion, leave it with me. I'll have everything tied up well before then, you have my word,' and then just to be sure, 'but you do understand that you could be in for a long wait, for Clarissa to, you know, be on her way.' He gestured heavenwards with his eyes. 'And then there's probate. Six months at the very least.'

Ion raised his hand and silenced Tristan. 'Just get the signature and I will do the rest and I assure you, Mr Henderson Junior, that apart from your ridiculous probate laws, I won't be waiting for Clarissa to,' he pointed upwards, 'leave the building. Just do your job and leave the finer details to me.'

With that, Ion stood and so did his bodyguards, but there was one more thing on Tristan's mind and he wouldn't sleep if he didn't ask. 'And our agreement still stands? The figure we discussed and the properties.'

When a sly smile spread across Ion's face, for a second Tristan thought he'd gone too far and forced down a gulp and the memory of waking up face down on a rug.

'You know, I like you, Tristan. You are my kind of guy. Not afraid to ask the awkward questions so yes, you have my word. We will shake on it, again.' Ion proffered his hand which Tristan gratefully took.

The brief exchange and firm manly contact over with, Ion turned and flanked by his men made their way out of the bar, Tristan watching on. He'd almost done it. This deal would be the making of him and there was no way on this earth anyone would get in the way, so taking out his phone, he found Chuck's number, prodded the screen, and waited.

No more being polite. It was time to get things moving so he'd be seeing Cowboy Joe ASAP, whether he liked it or not.

CHAPTER 42

CLARISSA

I t was bitterly cold outside thanks to a front blowing in from the Atlantic, and while she didn't appreciate the weather, she was glad that via a similar route, dear Chuck had landed on her shores.

He'd been there almost a month and during that time Clarissa had learned much about him. Most importantly that he was a good man, kind, funny and self-deprecating. Pure of heart and, she gleaned, easily led, and that had rendered him alone and rather lost. Which was why she'd decided to help him find a home, a place to belong on his own terms, be it there in Cheshire or at home in his beloved Kentucky.

And that annoying Tristan Henderson had rang Chuck earlier saying he was calling by tomorrow. Couldn't that man take a hint? She'd had Jennifer fob him off countless times. And it had irked Clarissa immensely when he'd got his father to intervene with regards to her finalising her will. They were turning into a pair of vultures. She'd soon put a stop to that.

Turning her thoughts away from irritants, they'd had a busy few days at Chamberlain, hosting the crew who were making the television documentary that was soon to air. Dear Penny, who Clarissa had become rather fond of over the course of her research and during filming, had fluttered about in her anxious and studious way. Waving her notes, advising the crew and reporter who conducted the interview but, most of all, making sure that Clarissa was comfortable with it all. And she was.

Hearing the parlour door open, and Chuck return with their cocoa, his new favourite evening drink, and a packet of biscuits tucked under his arm, Clarissa smiled as he took a seat beside her on the sofa.

He began to unwrap the packet. Picking at the tear strip as he spoke. 'Miss Jennifer has gone up for a bath. I said I'd make her some cocoa when she comes down. I'm getting the hang of that old range now! Cookie's a good teacher.'

Clarissa smiled. Chuck had cast a spell on every female who crossed his path, herself included. She was so grateful for his company because not only did he lift her spirits, he'd given Jennifer a little break too and it was nice to see her relax. She dedicated her days to caring for Clarissa and sometimes, if she was poorly, nights too.

'Did you enjoy watching them make the documentary and seeing your ancestors' story unfold? I thought they did a very good job, especially the section about Eleonora. I was so undecided about mentioning her, you know, but I'm glad I did. And you even got a little mention too. I found it all rather exciting.'

Chuck seemed more interested in dunking his biscuits but between mouthfuls, managed to answer. 'I thought the part about Cousin Eleonora was the best... got me right in the heart, hearing you tell her story.'

Clarissa was pleased about this, and have her sister referred to as cousin, like she'd never really gone away and part of her remained at Chamberlain. She also didn't want to stand in the way of Chuck and his food so let him eat while she chatted on.

'And dear little Penny has offered to do some digging about Eleonora, but wanted my blessing first, but she also told me something rather interesting.' After receiving a 'uh-huh,' from Chuck which translated meant *carry on*, she did just that.

'It seems that not so long ago the MOD released the details of special operatives who were sent to France. Penny said that not all records are intact or complete, but it's worth a look, don't you think? We might be able to find out where Eleonora died and maybe visit or if I can't make it send someone on my behalf. You and Jennifer perhaps.'

Chuck had taken an eating break and looked surprised by her comment. 'You'd want me to go, kinda like your family representative?'

'Yes, exactly like that. But let's wait to see if she comes up with anything after her hols. She's off to visit her family in New Zealand, but said she'd make a start when she gets back.' Clarissa sipped her cocoa and lost herself in the flames of the coal fire while Chuck ate his way down the packet of biscuits.

The silence was companiable for a while until Chuck asked, 'You know what I've been thinking these past few days but didn't like to ask, in case it caused offence?'

Clarissa paused mid-sip, intrigued. 'What on earth could cause offence... go on, ask away. I'll have you know I'm quite unshockable.'

She watched as he considered for a moment, and she was expecting another rummage in the packet, however, he did in fact surprise her with his question.

'Thing is... I know how you like your tea, and your toast and which programmes are your favourites, but I don't really know anything about *you* and why you live here on your ownsome. I know you have Miss Jennifer and that makes me real happy, but I've wanted to ask you about your younger life but thought it might offend and no way would I go behind your back and ask anyone else. Our stories are private and ain't no business of other folk. But you told us about Cousin Eleonora, and I can't help wondering why you didn't tell us about you.'

Clarissa thought for a moment, not wanting to rush in, and then suddenly she didn't care and realised she was relieved that he'd asked.

'I told Penny that I didn't want to include my early life in the film because it was more important that I told Eleonora's story. I suppose I wanted to say her name out loud. There's an old black and white film about a famous secret agent called Violette Szabo. *Carve Her Name With Pride* and it always makes me think of my sister. It's such a sad story and my sister's is probably the same.'

Clarissa banished that thought and pulled herself together. 'Maybe that's a touch melodramatic on my part but it felt good especially when they filmed her portrait. I wanted everyone to see how beautiful she was. My life is nothing compared to hers and of little interest. I'm here. I inherited an estate created by my forbears, did my bit for charity and now someone else looks after it all for me. Totally boring.'

Chuck nodded slowly and then scratched his chin. 'That's maybe how you see it, but I've told you my story and I don't care if yours is all about sewing those tapestry things I've seen around the place. I'd still like to know.'

At that, Clarissa laughed and gave him a gentle tap on the arm. 'I'll have you know that I've never done a tapestry in my whole life! *So* boring – much to the chagrin of Mother and Miss Cleves. But I would like to tell you about myself and why I'm here on my ownsome because I see some parallels in our lives. Perhaps it might help us going forward, into the future together.'

On hearing this Chuck twisted the biscuit wrapping to seal the pack and, after placing them on the nest of tables, turned his body so he was looking directly at her.

It was as he waited that Clarissa realised something. A fact that had never occurred to her before then. That she had never told another living person her story. Only the portrait of Eleonora knew Clarissa's truth, and it was about time someone else listened. And if she was going to tell anyone, it had to be in her own words, and to Chuck.

CHAPTER 43

Chamberlain Manor, Cheshire. 1941

A cloud hung over Chamberlain Manor for months after the news that dear Eleonora was missing in France. Mother took to her bed and whenever she did venture downstairs, she insisted on being left alone to whatever thoughts made her cry so much.

I never gave up hope though, and it became an obsession, watching for the postie and checking the mail as soon as I took it from his hands. Spring and summer dragged, and in the July we had a visit from Uncle Oscar, my father's younger brother.

He resided in London, and he too worked at the War Office so I prayed that he would bring news of Eleonora. I didn't much care for Oscar. He had a handlebar moustache and greased back hair and piggy eyes that fixed you with a stare if you dared speak before being spoken to. He had no time for children, or, it seemed, women, and often spoke in a dismissive tone to my mother.

I think Mother tolerated Oscar to keep the peace. That was her way. Especially because the merest thing, like a grubby thumbprint on the silver teapot, would send her into a tizzy. Mother was fragile and had lived a sheltered and charmed life, in fact, I remember once I was sick in bed and I said the light hurt my eyes and asked her if she'd close the curtains and you know what she did? She rang the bell and got the maid to do it! I don't think she'd ever opened or drawn the curtains in her life. Imagine that.

Mother knew her place in life, and she also knew her place in her marriage. That's just how it was. She was above menial tasks but below the male members of our family and as I grew older, I saw it more and more.

Take Uncle Oscar for instance. Mother couldn't abide him, yet because he was her brother-in-law she was expected to tolerate him just like she did her boorish husband, my chauvinistic father.

I knew Oscar treated all our staff – especially the maids – appallingly, tweaking bottoms and being incapable of keeping his slimy hands to himself. I heard that via Old Cookie when I crept into the larder to steal some biscuits. I was such a little sneak but needs must, and how else would I have known what was going on in my own home?

Oscar was a gambler and a drunk, too. And I later learned he'd played fast and loose with the family finances and sailed close to the wind with his investments and the wives of his friends. No wonder his wife preferred to leave him to his own devices and live a quiet life in Berkshire while he did what he did in his Chelsea townhouse.

His visit during that summer of 1941 sticks in my mind for three reasons. One, was because there'd been a lot of whispering in Father's study and Mother had taken umbrage about him tipping up out of the blue, and refused to dine in Oscar's presence. The atmosphere was dreadful, and for once I was happy to be sent to my room.

Then, there was a bit of a to-do when Oscar was found passed out in the rose garden one morning by the gardener. Mother and I were taking breakfast alone, a rare treat for me and I suspected she wanted some female company.

When my uncle was discovered, Kingsley called for assistance and as usual I was ushered upstairs out of the way. Peeved, I cleverly escaped Miss Cleves by saying I needed the lavatory, and watched from the landing. It was the most entertaining thing that had happened for a while, seeing Oscar ferried to the front door in a wheelbarrow, clinging to a whisky bottle, shoeless, flies undone and bedraggled. Mother was mortified.

The third thing happened the day after Oscar went back to London and the house breathed again. I was summoned to Father's study where my pinched-faced Mother awaited. While she remained silent and obedient, I was told that Uncle Oscar had secured me a place at a very fine boarding school in Sussex. According to his contacts at the War Office, it wasn't safe living so near to Manchester and the threat of more raids.

I was *almost* ten years old. I spent most of my time being sent to my room or being told that 'I wouldn't understand' by everyone from Mother to Cookie. And Miss Cleves was permanently exasperated by my constant questions about everything under the sun. But even *silly old me* knew that living in the middle of the Cheshire countryside meant I wasn't in any danger and suspected they simply wanted me out of the way.

I suppose I was my own worst enemy and being inquisitive resulted in being shuffled off to school where I remained until the end of the war and beyond. I only came home for holidays and truthfully, as hard as boarding was at the beginning, I began to miss my parents less and less. The only person I did miss was Eleonora.

Her memorial service was held in 1946 and attended by my parents, myself, Uncle Oscar, and the staff, officiated over by the vicar. They erected a stone plinth and on it, was a gold plaque inscribed with the words – *in loving memory of Eleonora Agatha Louisa Chamberlain. Lost but not forgotten.*

That was it. My father didn't even say a few words. I remember being incensed by the meagre ceremony and inscription and seethed about it all day. It was as though they were paying lip service, the prayers, the gathering, a glass of sherry in the dining room then chop-chop, back to work. It was all a sham.

I'd learned by then that no good would ever come of approaching my parents with regards to Eleonora, so I kept my counsel and went back to school. I actually preferred it there with my friends, amongst women and away from obnoxious male family members and my fey, weeping wreck of a mother.

The effects of the war years rumbled on for a while. We were still hungry and missing those lost overseas, but slowly we got on with it and settled back into our everyday lives.

For my eighteenth birthday my parents bought me a beautiful thoroughbred. Apart from Eleonora walking through the door, it was the best present I could have received. Spirit became my soulmate. I spent every hour I could with him because he filled a huge void in my life.

Like my very special friend, Amelia, from school did. Amelia went home to India after the war and even though we corresponded for many years, I never saw her dear face again. And of course there was always the hole left by Eleonora. As for my parents, I don't think I missed something I never really had.

Spirit made up for all of that.

I won't bore you with the tedium of being a female member of the upper classes, only to say that, according to Mother, my main purpose in life was to find myself a husband. I had other ideas.

I secretly had ambitions to start a stud farm at Chamberlain, borne from my love of Spirit and the desire to have a purpose in life. Not to be a good wife and a baby making machine. I wanted more. Which was why I'd bravely mooted the idea with my father who promised to mull things over while I was on holiday in Switzerland.

Much to my annoyance Mother accompanied me to Verbier as my chaperone, like we were characters in a gothic novel. While I took to the slopes in order to escape, she entertained herself on the social circuit, one eye on the quest for a suitable spouse.

It finally happened on the green run. That's where, quite by accident and with a resounding wallop, I ran into the love of my life. Marquess Ursula Bonham-Jones, wife of Cyril, the Rt Honourable member of Parliament for Hampstead.

Once we were over the shock of the collision and had checked for broken bones, we made our way down the slope and headed straight to the lounge-bar. From the word go, there was something so magical and alive about Ursula. I'd never met anyone like her in my life. She made my heart and my world glow with just the sound of her laugh. The way she looked at me with glistening grey eyes. And when she ran elegant fingers through her ice-blonde hair I could only think thoughts that made me blush, all over, in every part of my body.

You will have guessed that we became lovers and she, being twenty years older, had much to teach me about so many things. Mother was also entranced by Ursula for a myriad of reasons, and none like mine.

During the month in Verbier, Ursula absorbed us into her 'set', and when the holiday ended, she invited me to stay in London where she would be my chaperone.

Obviously Mother was thrilled and agreed immediately. She also couldn't wait to get back and tell the Cheshire set all about our political connections with the landed gentry.

Even though Mother was a lady, her title would die with her. Therefore the Marquess as an ally was a gift because I was the Chamberlains' last hope. The only one left to bag another title when she bagged a husband and I had already decided that was never going to happen.

For the first time ever I was happy with my life. I commuted between Chamberlain and London where for almost two years Ursula and I conducted a very discreet affair.

Father had agreed to the stud farm and whilst I was over the moon at having what I considered to be a career of my own, it also gave me a valid excuse to see Ursula, who had no end of contacts in the equine world.

I was content and in love and had no reason to believe that my utopia would ever end. I played the game and was seen with plenty of eligible bachelors who were happy to wine and dine the heiress to a large estate in Cheshire, titled or untitled.

Mother was of course still eager that I'd find a match, but contented herself with photographs of me at Ascot in the Royal enclosure with Ursula and her glittering set. So apart from being forced into wedlock, what could go wrong?

Not so much a case of what, but who. Uncle Oscar.

I should have known by the look on his face during dinner. The sneer whenever I spoke and the chill in his eyes if I looked in his direction. The disdain in his voice was missed only by my father who spoke a similar language and was too interested in his food. My mother on the other hand became edgy, ate nothing and sipped water to quell her nerves.

At the grand old age of twenty-one I was actually allowed to join in the conversation and have an opinion which, along with my newfound life, was liberating. But with each comment I made, or question I asked, Oscar turned it around and made me sound foolish and naïve. Worse, the thing that caused my blood to cool was his frequent unnecessary references to Ursula.

Eyeing me closely he'd take a glug of wine, then say something like, 'Ah, I suppose you heard that from your dear friend the Marquess,' or 'sounds to me like you're spending too much time with Ursula and her racy set,' and the gut-twisting, 'Do you see much of Clive when you're in London? Such a good chap, don't you think so, Clarissa? I must arrange drinks with him at the club.'

I swallowed the spoonful of dessert I'd stupidly placed in my mouth and after forcing it down, it threatened to come straight back up again. I held my nerve, just.

Oscar knew something. I could tell. But whether it was the truth about me and Ursula, or he was hoping I'd misbehaved with one of the decoys I'd been seen with, I wasn't sure. I prayed it was the latter.

Mother retired to bed the second coffee was served and I followed suit but didn't sleep a wink. Which was why, when I was once again summoned to Father's study the following morning I looked dreadful and feared the worst.

CHAPTER 44

I will never ever forget that day. The things they said to me. The threats they made. How I was made to feel. But what hurt me the most was that *he*, Oscar, was privy to the conversation between my father and me. And that my mother hid in her room and didn't support me.

I sat in the chair in front of his desk. Oscar was to his right in the leather wing back chair, smoking a cigarette. Father stood as he laid out the facts as Oscar had no doubt gleefully reported them.

The rumours in London were rife about me and Ursula. We thought we'd been discreet but somehow someone, perhaps a maid, or one of her inner circle, had betrayed us. At first I denied it, but I've never been a good liar and they saw through me immediately.

The tears didn't help, or my trembling body. My cheeks burned with a shame I shouldn't have felt because right up until that moment Ursula and I had been beautiful, special, and pure. They made me feel dirty and cheap and worse, like a freak.

'So it's true then. Good Lord Clarissa how could you? Are you ill… did she force you?' I couldn't look at Father and I jumped when he banged his fist on the desk.

'No I'm not ill and Ursula didn't force me to do anything.' I was terrified but at the same time I had to speak out, because I would not betray us or what we had together, 'And we're in love.'

A roar like a wounded animal preceded silence so deafening that it made my head pound. Then I dared myself to look up. Father had his back to me and was staring out of the window. He didn't turn around as I spoke.

'Father, please listen. I didn't mean to upset you and we tried so terribly hard to keep our feelings secret.' I didn't apologise, even though I suppose that's what he expected but I wasn't sorry for what I'd done. Only that we'd been caught.

Still my father remained silent, so Oscar took it upon himself to speak on his behalf. 'Well you've done an appalling job because if the rumour has reached my ear, it won't be long before the press get hold of it and then you, your lover and her husband will be ruined. Worse, you will disgrace our family name. So I hope you're proud of yourself.'

When I turned in his direction I hope that the contempt I felt for him was plain to see. Never have I hated someone like I did in that moment. Even Mr Hitler came a poor second.

'Who told you? And does Clive know?'

'I'm not prepared to divulge my sources but as for poor Clive, perhaps he's being protected from the truth. Which is why we need to do everything in our power to quash these shameful, obnoxious and frankly sickening rumours and save this family's reputation.' He took a long satisfying drag of his cigarette and I had an incredible urge to lunge and push it down his throat.

My head spun as I tried to take in what they were insinuating. The underlying threat in Oscar's tone. The key words that held a clue to my fate.

Poor Clive. Sympathy clearly lay with the cuckolded husband.

More worrying, *everything in our power*. Meaning he and father had taken control.

Shameful, obnoxious, and sickening. That's how they felt about me.

And finally the one word that meant everything to the Chamberlain family and others of our class. *Reputation.*

Panic bloomed in me. 'I need to ring Ursula and tell her. She should know what's happened.'

I rose slightly but my knees gave way at the mere sound of my father's voice who rounded and marched over to where I sat. He loomed above me, so close I could smell pipe smoke embedded in the fibres of his tweed jacket. Spittle landed on my cheek, and such was his anger I feared he would actually strike me.

'You will do no such thing. From this moment onwards you will have no contact whatsoever with that disgusting perverted woman. DO YOU HEAR ME? If this gets out, we're ruined. Do you realise the impact this will have on your uncle, for pity's sake? He works in the city, has contacts in the government. And what about Clive? The scandal will ruin his political career and then there's your poor mother. The woman is distraught, and I doubt she'll be able to look you in the eye ever again. And neither will I. People will call you a freak... dear God Clarissa what have you done?'

Disgusting. Freak. Did Father not realise what he was saying? And I couldn't just cut Ursula from my life... how could he even think that?

Even though I was scared, I had to make him see sense. 'But Father, I simply can't just disappear from her life without an explanation. She might come looking for me and then there would be a scene...'

'STOP! Not another word Clarissa. It is all in hand.'

I looked from my father to Oscar and immediately averted my eyes from his smug face. 'What do you mean?'

A sigh preceded a tut. 'Oscar will deal with it. He's returning to London in the morning and will make an appointment to see Ursula and explain the situation. And I can assure you of this, Clarissa. Once the Marquess is aware of the jeopardy, she will drop you like a stone. So don't go getting any romantic notions about her coming to rescue you. Or the two of you running away together. It will never happen.'

I stood then. Enraged. My fists balled in anger.

'Father, you simply can't do this to me. I'm twenty-one years old and can make my own decisions and I will not have *him* speak on my behalf...' I cast Oscar a look to match those he'd given me at dinner '...or have you both run my life.'

That was the final straw and I swear I saw the red of evil in Father's eyes as he growled his reply, holding me in his stare like prey. 'HOW DARE YOU? How dare you speak to me like that. I'll have you know, young woman, that I am more than capable of ensuring you do exactly as I tell you. Do you hear me? Your sister thought–'

When Oscar cleared his throat it broke Father's stride, causing me to look in Oscar's direction. Even in my moment of utter desolation I spotted the warning look he gave my father which was heeded immediately.

'My sister thought what? Tell me. What were you going to say?'

The air was thick with malice and words left unsaid. There were too many questions left unanswered and my suspicions wouldn't rest.

'You didn't want Eleonora to leave and join up, but she stuck to her guns and got her own way in the end, and I shall follow her example. You can't make me give Ursula up like you couldn't stop my sister from leaving.' I stuck out my chin and curled my toes and scrunched my fist so tightly it hurt as I waited for my father to react, but the next voice was Oscar's.

'And look where that got her. Killed. The only reason your sister got her own way was because the war was on and your father was lenient, needs must and all that. So don't think for one moment that the same applies to you because believe me, Clarissa, he could disown you like that.' Oscar clicked his finger.

'And don't forget I have two fine sons who could take over here, should my brother decide to turf you out and leave you penniless. Because after all, dear niece, that's exactly what you would be without Chamberlain and your parents. A nothing. With nothing. A nobody.'

My mouth opened but no words came out.

Oscar wasn't afflicted so. 'So I suggest you have a good old think and consider your options. Do as you are told and hopefully the stain of your sordid behaviour won't stick to this family. Unless you choose the other option, in which case you will be cast out, destitute or maybe, like your sister, dead.'

The gasp that escaped from deep inside jolted my father from his place on the fence. 'Clarissa I hope you've heeded Oscar's words. Now go to your room and remain there. I cannot bear to look at you a moment longer. And don't even attempt to speak to your mother. Is that understood?'

For a second my brain couldn't take it all in and was unable to respond and then in a flash my legs were carrying me out of the door and towards my room where I obeyed Father and stayed all day.

I'm sure you can imagine what I went through in the hours afterwards. I refused to eat the food that was brought to my room on a tray and the pain of hunger somehow made me feel more alive. Each gripe of my stomach complemented the pain in my heart and reminded me that I had to fight for Ursula and what we had. I convinced myself that she too would fight for me and, somehow, we would find a way to be together.

The next morning when I found the door to my room locked from the outside I knew it was to prevent me from ringing Ursula. Oscar would be on his way to London to do his worst.

I didn't cause a scene or try to bolt when the maid brought my food which I ate because, for all my sins, I wasn't stupid. The die had been cast. So I didn't ask for my mother and she didn't come to see me. Instead I bided my time and made a plan.

Three days later my mother came to visit me. It was as though it never happened, and the previous few days were a silly dream. Because there she was sitting at the end of my bed, dressed in her twin set, smiling like it was Christmas morning. I remember wondering, as she spoke, if perhaps she'd lost her mind.

'Your father and I wondered if you'd like to take a drive to the coast. It's a glorious day and I think a brisk walk and a spot of lunch will do us the world of good, don't you?' She smoothed the silk of the bedspread as she spoke, not able to rest her eyes on my face for long.

All I wanted was to get out of the room and take the quickest route away from Chamberlain, down the footpath to the village. There was a public phone box outside the post office and from there I could ring Ursula and ask her what to do. I'd hidden all of my jewellery, which I intended to sell, and packed a small case, so I was ready to go once Ursula knew the plan. I would wait for her in Cornwall where she had a holiday home, unless she suggested her apartment in Monte Carlo, which was why I'd hidden my passport, too.

I answered my mother in the way she hoped for but perhaps didn't expect, who knows? 'That would be very nice, Mother. When would you like to leave? I'd like to have a bath and wash my hair first, if that's alright.'

At this I received a gracious bow of the head and a self-satisfied smile. 'Oh good. Shall we say ten-thirty? I have some paperwork to attend to in my room and your father has a meeting in his study. We will see you shortly.'

She stood and made her way to the door where she paused before opening it then turned to look me square in the eyes. 'I'm so glad you've seen sense, dear. It's for the best. We only have your interests at heart. Now hurry along.'

I didn't reply. I couldn't because if I'd done so, I think I would have put my mother in a sanitorium. Or sent her to her death bed. One or the other, and at the time I really didn't care which.

After scrabbling into the first pair of sensible shoes I found then grabbing a coat I took the servants' staircase and left the house via the tradesman's entrance. I then headed off across the fields in desperate haste. My only thoughts were of hearing Ursula's voice.

Thirty minutes later I was in the phone box asking the operator to connect me to the Belgravia number then waiting while Monroe, Ursula's sombre butler went to find his mistress. The waiting was a million times worse than the days I'd endured in my room.

When she finally came to the phone I heard it immediately. Her dismissal of me, us, was deftly done. In words of very few syllables. Without compassion or care. That's how I received the message loud and clear from a hushed voice I barely recognised.

'Please do not call again. It will only make things worse. Do you understand?'

'But Ursula... please... we need to talk.' When a moment of clarity reminded me that the operator could be listening, dread rushed through my veins as the threat of scandal loomed large.

So I simply said, 'I have to come and see you...'

'NO. That won't be possible. I don't have space in my diary. Please, do as I say and don't call again. Goodbye Clarissa.' And then she was gone.

I don't recall the walk home. If I cried or laughed hysterically like a madwoman escaped from an asylum, but for some reason unbeknown to me then or now, I did head straight back here, to Chamberlain. And as I entered the yard and saw father holding Spirit's reins, and the horsebox, my whole world felt like it was coming to an end.

CHAPTER 45

Clarissa paused and waited for the pain of that day to subside. Although it happened more than sixty years earlier, the events still tore up her heart and left it in shreds.

Reading the mood, Chuck made a suggestion. 'How about we have something a bit stronger than cocoa? Do you think it might help, because you've gone mighty pale.'

'I would love a brandy, a nice big one, please.' Clarissa rarely drank in the evenings, but needs must, and a stiff drink might help her brain to switch off when she went to bed. Her old bones looked after themselves.

Chuck didn't tarry and headed straight over to the drinks cabinet and poured them both large measures of brandy, settling beside her again once he'd handed her a glass. After taking a moment to savour the amber liquid Clarissa sighed. 'So now I have to finish my sorry tale, that's if you want to know the rest or have I thoroughly depressed you?'

Chuck rested his head back against the sofa before he replied, 'No, you ain't depressed me, more made me angry that they treated you that way and I have to know what happened to Spirit even though I'm kinda scared of the answer.'

Clarissa leant over and patted his arm. 'Don't worry. Spirit stayed, but my father's posturing worked a treat because he knew I'd do anything he said to keep my horse. He'd obviously worked out that I'd try to ring Ursula, that I wouldn't dare use the phone in the hall; so as soon as he found out I'd left the house he got the stable lad to bring Spirit round. It was all for show because he knew Ursula was going to break my heart, after all; Uncle Oscar would've made sure of it. No, the threat to sell Spirit was a warning that I should toe the line. So after I begged and cried like an obedient, chastened daughter, Father acquiesced, and the stable lad walked Spirit back to his stall.'

Clarissa had re-lived that scene so many times in her mind, imagining the worst-case scenario of losing Spirit, and even the thought of it made her feel quite unhinged. Had it happened, if he'd have been sold, Clarissa was sure she'd have lost her mind.

'So what happened then? Did you ever see Ursula again? And what was it like living here under a cloud and being controlled by your parents?'

Clarissa thought for a moment before responding. 'What was it like? It was like my earlier life, before I went away to school but on repeat, I suppose. I might as well have been nine again. My parents were here, in the house. We were perfectly pleasant to one another and passed the time of day when we were thrown together for meals. Apart from that I kept myself to myself.'

'I'd have done the same. I don't think I'd want to talk to them ever again, if you don't mind me sayin'.' Chuck sounded mildly angry but as always, polite.

'Oh I don't mind and you're right. I didn't particularly want to talk to them either. Conversation dried in my throat and as much as they didn't want to look at me, the feeling was mutual. And on top of that I couldn't rid myself of the shame. Not my own, because I will never ever feel that about Ursula. What we had was special and how she behaved in the end was through fear, which is why I respected her wishes and didn't contact her again. I can be very stubborn when I want to be.' She gave Chuck a friendly wink to make him smile because he looked so serious. It worked and she was glad.

'It was the shame they felt because of me that I found hard to bear. And I'm almost positive that the only reason they didn't turf me out or have me sent abroad or to a psychiatric hospital was so they could keep an eye on me. Damage limitation. And it worked but only because of Spirit. I couldn't leave him behind. Apart from some jewellery, I really was penniless in my own right, so I stayed and made the best life I could.

'There was never any mention of me finding an eligible bachelor simply because they were both too embarrassed to even bring up a matter that would remind them of what I'd done. Perhaps they thought it was a phase and were waiting for it to end. That one day a handsome chap would simply turn up, sweep me off my feet and we'd never talk about what a silly girl I'd been. My parents had plenty of rugs and anything unsavoury was sure to be swept under them.'

'So you carried on running the stud farm?'

'Yes, and rode Spirit, and read a lot, usually wrapped in a blanket in his stall. I felt happiest when I was with him.'

The rest of the tale was simple. Nine years after the scandal, her father died of lung cancer and in a strange way the day he took his last breath, it was as though Chamberlain sucked in a huge gulp of fresh air. Clarissa felt like she could breathe again, too.

At almost thirty years old she could've made a bid for freedom. Because her mother was weak willed and just as she'd been manipulated by her husband, it would've been just as easy for her daughter to do the same. Had she been cast in the same mould as her father – but thankfully, she was not.

And then there was Oscar. Who hovered, threatening to disrupt the equilibrium, always waiting for his chance to seize the estate and put one of his sons in Clarissa's place. Her mother's contempt of Oscar was a useful barrier, but it wasn't enough, so Clarissa had to tread carefully. And it was her desire to thwart her uncle that fuelled Clarissa and made her more determined to make a huge success of the stud farm and the estate. And she did.

'Did you ever meet anyone else? Didn't you get lonely?'

Clarissa tilted her head to one side and as always, had the urge not to make anyone sad, but she wanted Chuck to know the truth. It was important to her.

'Yes, I did get lonely because I'm only human, but I found that if I filled my days being the best I could be... and you have to remember that back then it wasn't as though we could swipe left, or is it right? You know what I mean.' She could see he was laughing, and it was about time after all the soul searching.

'And anyway, I'd been badly bitten once, so I was scared of taking the risk again. Rejection is simply dreadful no matter how many excuses you make for someone. Try to absolve them of the cruelty in order to feel a smidgen better about yourself.'

'Did you forgive Ursula, for cutting you off like that? I don't think I could've. When my girlfriend ran off with that guy in New York I thought I was gonna die of a broken heart. Didn't move from my room for days... so I kinda know what it feels like. I'd left my friends and my life behind for her and I felt so stupid. So I can't forgive her or forget how much she hurt me.'

Clarissa knew exactly what Chuck meant. 'Ah, the old, forgive and forget nonsense... well, just like you I have never understood how you can do that. I suppose one can look objectively at why someone acted in a certain way, my mother for example.

'She hurt me immensely by taking Father's side but that was the way of her world. He was in charge. His word was law. So I *am* able to forgive her to a certain extent, I think. Although I will never forget many things. I don't think it's possible. Unless I'm just being a stubborn old thing. Maybe it's in the genes, who knows.'

Chuck smiled, 'I guess you're right and that makes me feel like we have a connection, passed down through history, bringing me here to this moment because we mightn't have shared much together, but we *have* been through things that help us understand each other and brought us closer. Heck, maybe I can actually be glad for those things even though they were hell at the time.'

Clarissa had suddenly come over all emotional and couldn't quite speak so reached out. Her tiny hand was immediately entombed by Chuck's great bear paw. They sat for a moment in the quiet, listening to the wind outside as they watched the flames in the coal fire, the orange glow warming Clarissa as much as Chuck's words had done.

Pulled together again, she found some reciprocal words of comfort for the man beside her. 'That was such a wonderful thing to say, Chuck, and I will always feel very blessed to have spent this time with you. And I do hope you won't rush away any time soon. I'm sure we have some more adventures in us yet.'

'I'm happy to stay if you'll have me. Being here with you, and around animals and in the countryside soothes my soul and while I do miss Kentucky, I'd miss you too if I went home right now.'

Clarissa gave his hand a jiggle. 'Well that's settled then. Now, how about another mug of cocoa. And I think Jennifer may have dissolved in her bath or nodded off so would you do the honours and pop the kettle on?'

'I'll do that right away, and I'll check on Miss Jennifer too. See if she'd like one, and maybe some toast?'

'Toast it is.' Clarissa watched as Chuck gathered their empty glasses and mugs and disappeared towards the kitchen.

Once he was gone Clarissa plumped up the cushions and relaxed into the sofa. Talking about the past always exhausted her, but before Chuck returned she relished a moment alone, to pause and take stock of their conversation.

CHAPTER 46

More than anything, Clarissa hoped that one day others would look back and say she'd done her bit. Given back more than she'd taken through charity work and supporting trusts here and there. Making sure the estate thrived so those who worked there had an income and the tenants in the farms and cottages had decent homes. That was what counted.

Even though she lived a comfortable and, some would say, charmed existence, Clarissa didn't have a taste for the high life and fancy holidays or clothes. She was a country girl at heart. Happy at home, at Chamberlain.

The fact was that the good times began once her father died and she took the reins. Everything became so much easier then. Her mother left her to it, fading into the floral wallpaper of her private rooms where she seemed content to just be, as though relieved to be unburdened by the pressure of society and her marriage.

All in all, tumultuous events and having her heart broken aside, Clarissa would not allow herself to grumble about her lot. Also, tucked in a quiet corner of her heart, Chamberlain was a link to her sister, no matter how tenuous.

Was she still waiting for Eleonora to come back? Perhaps. For many years she had often looked down the long drive and imagined a lone figure, carrying a tatty brown suitcase, perhaps a beret set at a jaunty angle on her head. The figure would wave, Clarissa would gasp and realise who it was, race outside whatever the weather and then they'd be reunited.

Even when she was away at school Clarissa had harboured fantastical notions where Eleonora would track her down and, in between secret missions they would meet in the woods, clinging on to one another with only minutes to spare before her sister disappeared into the trees, off to do her bit.

But there was one more thing she had to do with her life. And talking with Chuck had only reaffirmed her fears that current events were mirroring those of the past. She still had to address the tricky subject of naming an heir and – like a scene on a television drama, the volume turned up high – she could hear echoes of her scheming uncle in her ear.

If she'd had suspicions in the past about Tristan Henderson, talking about Oscar had made the hairs on her arms tingle and unease creep up on her. Something had to be done, and soon.

Footsteps in the hall broke her concentration and, with the creak of the parlour door, Chuck reappeared announcing as he strode towards the fireplace, 'Miss Jennifer has survived her bath bomb and says she'll be down in five minutes and will make some supper and the cocoa.'

Chuck then stoked the fire and added a log to the orange-red coal. Once he was satisfied with the flame, he returned to the sofa, causing the cushions to bounce and the frame to creak as he re-arranged the blanket that lay over Clarissa's knees.

Expecting the arrival of Jennifer any minute, Clarissa decided to broach the Tristan subject, get it over with, otherwise even the brandy wouldn't help her nod off and she'd be going over and over it in her mind.

'Dearest Chuck, all that talk of Oscar has reminded me of the way he behaved leading up to the death of my father and it's bothering me, making me uneasy, so I'd like to get something off my chest. It has to do with you, the bad blood with my uncle, just so you know.'

Chuck's eyes widened, 'I'm guessing this is because I'm descended from Oscar's son, the one who married the heiress.'

Clarissa nodded. 'Let me explain, because it's the final part of my story, really.'

My father was at death's door, and it was only a matter of time. Time that had also run out where Oscar was concerned because, try as he might, he could not persuade Father to alter his will and name him as heir. He badgered, cajoled, ranted, and raved. Desperation oozed from his every pore. I could see it. He despised me.

Oscar was in terrible debt and needed to be bailed out, but this time it had to be big, not in the form of a Coutts cheque. He needed the estate. I stood in his way.

Ever since Ursula, I hadn't put a foot wrong, living my life as a paragon of virtue thus thwarting Oscar's grand plan. There'd been a terrible row in the study almost a year before. I overheard Father tell Oscar, with his own brand of brutish honesty, that he'd never allow the estate to be squandered on his many vices. Chamberlain was secure and in good hands – mine.

Old habits die hard, you see, and I was still an earwigger and heard it all. Oscar was dredging up the past, casting aspersions that once Father was gone I'd run amok and bring shame on the family.

Regardless of the ridiculous and lurid accusations, one of which was that I'd turn Chamberlain into a brothel for freaks like me, in the end, Father stood firm. He'd seen me as the safest bet and I took a small amount of pleasure from that, but it was getting one over on Oscar that had me dancing a little jig in the hallway.

Oscar stayed away until Mother made the call, saying he should come and say goodbye to Father. His absence until then had been a mercy because, whenever he'd visited in the past, I'd made myself scarce. This suited everyone because after all there's only so much awkwardness anyone, no matter how thick-skinned, can take.

That weekend was the longest of my life, waiting for Father to take his last breath and be released from the agony he was in. And for Oscar to go away forever. And when both occurred, and the estate came to me, I promised myself that I'd honour Father's dying wish. To care for Mother and Chamberlain and before I departed this earth, I'd make sure it was left in the safest of hands.

Clarissa was at the end of her story and there was an important parallel to draw.

'As you know, in the end my uncle and his long-suffering wife fell on the mercy of their son and went to live in Chicago because when he lost everything, over my dead body were they coming to live here.'

Chuck shook his head, 'Ain't no wonder my daddy was the way he was, comin' down the line from Oscar, but I hope you can see I'm nothin' like any of them. Not even my mama.'

She placed her hand on his arm. 'Dear man, I think nothing of the sort, and I might not have known you for long, but I can tell you haven't a bad bone in that body of yours. I've seen you with the horses, and around other animals and they know, as do I, that you're a good person. So don't worry about that.'

At this Chuck smiled and his shoulders relaxed, 'Well amen to that!'

'But there is someone in our midst who does trouble me and that's what I want to talk to you about.'

'Who?' Chuck had twisted his body and a frown creased his forehead.

'My solicitor, Tristan Henderson. Over the past few weeks I've been aware of a sense of urgency, a pushiness perhaps with regards to my affairs, and the fact he takes a great deal of interest in you.' She left that to settle and waited for Chuck's reaction.

'I can sure as heck agree with you on that! When he first got in touch I thought he would just be a go-between, kinda there to introduce me to you, but as soon as I arrived he wanted to be my best buddy, which is real weird seeing as the guy is nothing like me at all.'

Clarissa hummed and pursed her lips the way her mother used to when she was perplexed. 'My thoughts exactly. And like with Uncle Oscar, I suspect there's an ulterior motive to his urgency, and I must get to the bottom of it. I've always dealt with his father who is the polar opposite of his pushy – and dare I say rather slimy – son. That fact, and my other observations, have somewhat shone a spotlight on Tristan's behaviour.'

'Maybe he's just being thorough or too keen. He might really have your best interests at heart and mine, too.'

'Well it's very gratifying to see you playing devil's advocate and you could be correct, but I still want to be sure. Anyway, I trust my instincts and this time they're warning me about Tristan. And even though you don't like to think or talk of it, I'm not going to live forever and when I'm gone I won't be able to protect you, Jennifer and Chamberlain.'

'Okay... I hear ya. So do you have a plan?'

'Oh yes, I certainly do. You and I need to join forces and thwart the enemy. Fight the good fight and all that. What do you say?'

Chuck's eyebrows raised and he sounded wary when he replied, 'Hey, you can count me in... but what exactly are we going to do? I hope it doesn't involve any of those old pistols you got hangin' about in the place. I told you I'm a pacifist.'

At this Clarissa howled with laughter at his sincere yet unnecessary worries. 'I promise you no blood will be shed, but we might have some fun and make use of one or two hidden doorways about the place. We'll enlist Jennifer too.'

Hearing the turn of the door handle and noticing the unmistakable aroma of buttered toast as Jennifer entered the room carrying a tray, Clarissa clapped her hands. 'Perfect. The three musketeers are assembled at last.'

At this Jennifer gave Chuck a curious look and set the tray on the table. 'What are you two up to?'

Waiting until the supper had been distributed, and everyone was settled, Clarissa got herself comfy and explained.

CHAPTER 47

LEVI

One month and two days. In answer to his nana's question, that was how long he'd known Honey. He didn't even care if it wasn't a blokey thing to do, keep tally of how long you'd been totally smitten by someone. He'd even marked it on the calendar on his desktop and each day when he highlighted a box, it made him smile like an idiot.

The clock tower of the town hall building said it was almost ten, well past the Battette's bedtime. He was driving the Batty Bus back to Batty Towers after taking his Nan and Great-Grandma Pins to see the Christmas lights in Manchester. Even though it was only November! December was ten days away so surely they could have waited till then!

Still, it made them happy, so how could he refuse. And the German market did look really festive, and the aroma from the food stalls... actually...

Levi quickly wound up the window otherwise they'd have him parking on double yellows and running over to get them a big sausage on a bun like last year. Thankfully they'd forgotten, which was a Christmas miracle in itself, as was their preference to watching from the car rather than walking around St Anne's

Square. One would just about manage it and the other would have to be pushed in the wheelchair.

Instead they'd done five circuits of the square and Deansgate and Levi was starting to lose the will. Especially since he'd realised he was locked in a car with his two most nosey and persistent relatives. Had it all been a ruse so they could interrogate him? Probably.

It was now the turn of DCI Pins who, from the comfort of the second row back, wanted to know more about Honey's family. 'Well, her grandad sounds like a nice chap. I always wanted an allotment you know. Your great-grandfather let me dig up half of our garden so I could have a vegetable patch. Do you remember, Iris? We had the loveliest strawberries in the summer. Oh I do love a good strawberry and then we had runner beans and...'

While they both went back in time to an urban vegetable patch, Levi's mind focused on Ernie, who he'd met one evening at the café and found to be actually a nice chap. It had been Gospel's birthday, so Honey had arranged a little cake and wine celebration after work. She'd invited Levi and her grandad, saying that the latter would be more comfortable if the introduction was made less formally.

From what she'd told him, Honey's grandad Ernie was a complicated character and quite shy, preferring to keep himself to himself. She'd also told him about her aunt's revelations and how badly it had affected him. Expecting someone moody and gruff, Levi wasn't really looking forward to it. However, reservations aside, he and Ernie got on well. In as few, monosyllabic words as possible.

The following day, Honey had reported back that Ernie thought Levi 'were a nice lad'. Apparently it was high praise, so he'd been content with that and his life, which had changed for the better since the day his car had broken down outside 'Honey's Place'.

They had so much in common, yet the things that weren't in

perfect alignment didn't matter at all. Not that there was much. Who cared if she loved talent shows and never missed an episode of *Emmerdale*. And he wasn't the least bit offended that she'd never watched *The Big Bang Theory* and had no clue who Fleetwood Mac were. Anyway, he intended to put both of those things right. He wasn't watching Simon Cowell though. Not a chance! Love had its limitations.

Yes. He was in love. And intended to tell Honey when the moment was right. In between his work, her long hours at the café and her visits to Ernie, who she was worried about. And it wasn't as though they lived around the corner, either.

After the trek to the peak village, staying over meant a gruelling red-eye commute – but it was worth every mile, even though he didn't wake up properly until he hit the city ring road.

'Levi! Are you listening? Tell me about where he worked before he retired, this Ernie chap. You said the railways... did he drive a train? I love trains but not these speedy inter-city things. Proper steam locomotives are the best. Oh Iris, do you remember the journeys to your grandmother's house in the Lakes? I can still hear the whistle and the sound of the wheels turning...'

And then they were off again, chugging back in time while Levi thought about what Honey had told him. How Ernie had always aspired to university but his mother – or Molly as he now referred to her with a sneer – had thwarted his dreams and kept him close. Ernie's dad sounded like he was under the thumb, too, and doggedly worked his way up so they could move out of Manchester to Cheshire.

Levi imagined all the resentment that Ernie had built up as a child bubbling over when he found out what Molly had done. Not that he'd mentioned it to anyone. Honey asked him not to. It was bad enough without more people hearing about the baby-thief.

A tap on the shoulder from his nan reminded him about the Ernie question. So he spent the next ten minutes wondering why other people's lives fascinated them so much, while giving them as much detail as he remembered about the life and times of Ernie. His job on the railways as a maintenance engineer, his wife Nancy, and even that he was born in Manchester during the war.

For both his grandparents, that period was laced with sad memories. Nana Iris lost her mother and Grandma Pins her whole family so no matter how nosey they were, a swift change of subject was necessary.

'So, are we all set for the big party at the weekend?'

He watched from the rear-view mirror as Grandma Pins rocked her shoulders in excitement. 'Oh yes, we are. Everyone is coming. The whole table from bingo, all the neighbours, well the ones we like anyway. And everyone who comes in to look at us old fogeys and our failing body parts and I even invited the podiatrist who is a fiend and takes great delight in manhandling my feet. I do hate feet. Ugly things. Mine especially. And the psychopath who makes us do chair dancing. I mean really! Who invented that! Still, it humours your mother, and he has a lovely bottom, doesn't he, Iris?'

'Oh yes, a very nice bottom but don't let on to your grandad will you, Levi? He'll only take the huff.' Nana Iris gave him a tap to make sure he understood.

'Your secret's safe with me for now, Nana. But if you carry on eyeing up young men you'll have to sponsor another donkey to buy my silence, so behave!' Levi suffered a much firmer whack on his arm before they continued nattering about firm buttocks and iced buns.

This left his mind free to silently congratulate himself on a masterful avoidance of knitted Christmas presents or a Brut gift pack. His grandparents were more than happy to club together to buy him a donkey – that's what they thought they'd done no matter how he explained what sponsorship meant. This year, Santa would be bringing him a photo of Poppy. Along with

Venus, Polo and Fudge, three other orphans he'd decided to adopt himself.

Yep, he was a sucker for a donkey and the plight of the sanctuary. He'd already put feelers out and done some digging in the hope of finding them a new home because, according to Honey, time was running out. The same could be said for Ernie and the quest to find his birth mum.

Despite trying her hardest, Honey couldn't find any trace of Nora anywhere. Seeing how crestfallen she was, he'd suggested they enlist the help of a proper genealogist, but Honey wasn't sure and thought it could be a waste of time and expensive. Then again, it might be within his means, and better still, it would make a great Christmas present.

Why hadn't he thought about that before? He was more or less certain that Honey would prefer an experience or a service as a gift for Christmas, *and*, what if his gift to her also helped Ernie. Double brownie points!

Once his mind started ticking, Levi couldn't wait to get back to Batty Towers and then home to his apartment so he could start looking for someone to help – maybe they did 'Find My Family Gift Cards' online.

Fuelled by his idea and the fact his ears were literally starting to bleed because the Battettes in the back of the Batty Bus were now going through sandwich fillings, Levi put his foot down. He was on a mission. First, offload the Battettes then, do everything he could to help Honey find Ernie's long-lost family.

CHAPTER 48

MR TRISTAN HENDERSON JNR

Chuck had really pushed his luck with Tristan over the past couple of days, fobbing him off with excuses about trips to Rhyl with Clarissa and accompanying Matheson the estate manager to a cattle auction. Who the bloody hell did he think he was? Certainly not the lord of the manor yet so he could stop acting like it!

And he was late. Which was also bloody damn rude.

Tristan was in the dining room at Chamberlain where horse-features had left him earlier. In her snooty tone she'd informed him that Clarissa was having a nap, that she was off out, and that Chuck would be along shortly. Didn't even offer him refreshments before she slammed the door shut, and now he was stuck in a draughty room tapping his feet.

There was a lot riding on this meeting, and he had to find out how the land lay and, if necessary, enlist his father's help. Surely Clarissa would listen to her oldest legal advisor. Tristan bad-temperedly checked his phone for messages and was relieved to have none from Ion. Or his dealer, who was getting a bit arsey about the money Tristan owed him.

While Diana bemoaned the surging price of good virgin olive

oil thanks to the stupid Russians, if she knew how much a few grams of cocaine had gone up her eyes would water. Never mind if his dealer ran out of patience. Tristan's little habit was costing him a small fortune and his rainy-day fund was sorely depleted. Tristan gulped down the involuntary whoosh of bile that made his throat burn.

Finally, the sounds of footsteps in the hallway. The unmistakeable and unforgettable cowboy boots. Tristan straightened his back and flipped a file and pretended to be reading the contents when Chuck walked in and closed the door behind him.

Best foot forward old chap. Don't mess this up. 'Chuck old man, good to see you. Please, take a seat so we can catch up. I must say I feel rather neglected. I hoped we could spend some time together on the town like we planned.' Tristan reached out his hand and after a brief but friendly handshake, pulled out a chair at the table and indicated for Chuck to sit.

'I'm sorry about that but I've been getting to know the estate and Clarissa of course. There's a lot to see and I would've felt impolite, seeing as she's been so hospitable and all.' Chuck took a seat and as he did, placed a white envelope on the table.

Ignoring it, Tristan got down to business. Maybe Clarissa was sending Chuck on errands to the post office but whatever, there were important matters to tactfully discuss. 'Never mind. I just thought I'd pop by and see how you are. I feel rather responsible for you, seeing as I was the one who brought you here, so wanted to check you're happy and all that.'

'Yep, fine and dandy, thank you kindly.' Chuck then stared at Tristan and waited.

'Right, jolly good. Most reassuring.' A period of awkward finger tapping on the polished dining table followed where Tristan grappled with his temper and how to proceed. 'And has Clarissa mentioned anything about signing her will? It's all ready to go. She just has to say the word...'

Chuck interrupted. 'I don't know. I haven't asked her. We don't talk about things like that and I ain't gonna mention it, that's for sure.'

'Oh, well that's rather disappointing but not to worry...' Tristan literally wanted to scream.

'But she did give me this. I thought I should show it to you. Get your advice.' Chuck tapped the envelope.

'What is it?' Tristan prayed it was a family heirloom of immense value because that would be an excellent sign.

Chuck answered, 'A DNA testing kit.'

'A what?' This was a very bad sign. It meant Clarissa didn't trust Chuck and he'd said something stupid.

'DNA kit. It's to see if I'm really related to her. You have to take a swab...'

'Yes, I know what it is, Chuck. But why has she asked you to take one. I've provided her with a copy of your birth certificate and enough paperwork to make a giant origami horse, for pity's sake!'

'Search me.' Chuck shrugged. 'I don't mind doin' one. It'll only take a few weeks to get the results. I think she said three to twelve, somethin' like that anyways.'

Tristan had that awful feeling again, the one he had when he'd spoken with Ion and the kinky-whipping-desk came back to haunt him. He knew full well that ancestry results could take many weeks, time he simply did not have, and Chuck's casual attitude was really pissing him off. Maybe there was a fast-track option, he'd have to check. He was sure there would be, but it'd cost. Didn't everything!

Stay calm. Keep Chuck on side. 'Okay, not to worry. I'll make some enquiries and see if we can't speed this up a little. Perhaps we could do it now and then I'll post it off today. Save you a job and give the lab a ring. There'll be a number inside.'

'I think Miss Jennifer is going to do that, thanks all the same. And Miss Clarissa is takin' a nap. There's no rush.' Chuck took the envelope and placed it on his knee like a five-year-old who didn't want to share. 'And if you don't mind me saying, Mr Henderson, you seem mighty keen to get the will signed and it's makin' me kinda edgy. Is there something I don't know about? Miss Clarissa isn't ill, is she? And she's keepin' it from me?'

Tristan felt the nerve in his cheek pulse. Never had he hated anyone as much as he did in that moment. Not even Diana's mother, and that was saying something. Tristan sucked in and prayed for patience. 'Not that I know of.'

'Phew, you had me worried there, so if that's all I'll be on my way.'

Tristan dithered. Should he level with Chuck? It was a risk because he seemed rather fond of Clarissa but then again, what man would choose a doddering old woman he hardly knew over getting his hands on millions of dollars. And Chuck had zilch. No family. No home. Nothing. Tristan loved a good game of poker and in that moment, decided to show his hand.

Lowering his voice, just in case horse-features hadn't buggered off out like she said, Tristan leant a little closer to Chuck. 'Okay, I'm going to level with you. Between us, I have some very wealthy contacts in the business world and one of them is extremely interested in purchasing Chamberlain Manor. Which means, my friend, once the estate is yours I will be able to broker a very favourable deal and make you a ridiculously wealthy man. The problem is, we need to act quickly before my buyer moves on. He won't wait forever.'

At this Chuck looked confused but what could Tristan expect? The man was probably inbred. Still, after rubbing his chin and having a bit of a think, the Kentucky Kid found his voice. 'So, I'm guessing there's somethin' in this for you, and that's why you seem so keen. Am I right?' Chuck gave Tristan a sly wink.

Fair play, thought Tristan. At least the idiot was catching up. So he answered as honestly as he was able, 'Well naturally. I've negotiated my commission and bonuses et cetera but none of this matters unless we get this will signed.'

There, that sounded feasible. The moron should understand that concept.

'Okay, I get that but what if I don't want to sell. I like it here and I have nothing to go home for so maybe's I'll stay. Put down roots.'

Tristan really did think he was going to faint but held it together. 'But why on earth would you want to settle here when you could have homes all over America if you sold this place? Imagine a beach-front in Malibu, an apartment in New York, a chalet in Vermont, anywhere you fancied. You could even buy your own ranch! How wonderful would that be?'

When Chuck's face broke into a smile and his eyes lit up, Tristan could have wept.

'Well, I s'pose when you put it like that... but there's still something botherin' me.'

Tristan tried not to show his impatience and asked, 'Really, how so?'

Chuck folded his arms and screwed up his eyes, a quizzical expression complementing his question, 'Even if Miss Clarissa signs in my favour, it could be years before I get to inherit the estate. I for one hope she lives for many a long year, so if your guy is impatient now... then he's not gonna want to wait forever, is he?'

Tristan had had enough. There was only so much he could take. The coke-monster was at his door, not to mention how pissed off Ion would be and how incompetent Tristan would look if it all went pear-shaped.

But there was no way he could come right out and say to Chuck that the second his name was on the will, Clarissa's days were numbered. On the other hand, it could potentially put an end to the questions... No, it was too risky, so he had one more attempt.

'Okay, I get that... good point old man, so, let's just say we take it one step at a time. The most important thing is you're named as benefactor and then I can introduce you to my associate who will make everything clear. I'll hang around and we can do the DNA test when Clarissa wakes up. I'll take it with me and get it fast tracked. At my own expense. I'm sure Jennifer won't mind...'

The click, from somewhere inside the room interrupted Tristan mid-sentence and he was further distracted by what looked like part of the wall opening. And, oh fuck. Clarissa and horse-features appearing from within like a pantomime double act.

'I assure you that Jennifer will mind, and so will I!' Clarissa spoke as she was wheeled towards him her face like thunder.

Tristan was dumbfounded and looked towards Chuck who was rising from his seat wearing an expression to match Clarissa's. Jennifer stood beside her employer who hadn't finished.

'Yes, we heard it all. Every word.' She turned briefly to Chuck and said, 'Thank you, dear man. You did an excellent job of getting the truth out of this scurrilous individual. I'm so proud of you.'

Then once again her glare rested on Tristan, who was about to face-plant the parquet floor – and knew it was going to hurt. He didn't dare stand, because that would be further to fall.

'It seems clear to me, although you'd never admit it, *or* who your associate is, the grand masterplan was to wait until the ink was dry and soon afterwards, I'd meet a sticky and untimely end. Am I correct?'

Clarissa paused for a nano-second while Tristan's lips froze shut.

'Hmm, I thought so. Well, I can tell you now that once you have left my home, I will be speaking to your father and severing all ties with your practice forthwith. And had I proof that you were in league with those who sought to cause me harm, then I'd have Jennifer phone the police.'

Tristan was going to be sick.

'However, I have a much better way to deal with the likes of you. I will make damn sure everyone who needs to, understands why the Chamberlain Estate has sacked their most trusted solicitors. How your poor father deals with you is his own business. So goodbye Mr Henderson. You know where the door is.'

Tristan could barely move, but when the hulking giant took a step forward, his fists clenched, self-preservation kicked in. Moments later he was in his car, sobbing the length of the drive, not knowing which way to turn when he got to the end.

Left meant home, and back to Diana or right, towards the office to face his father.

Instead he went straight ahead, across the road, ploughing his Jaguar through the bracken hedge and into the field beyond. Past the grazing sheep who didn't even look up, not caring about the crazy man who was tearing up the grass. And seeing as his life was about to go tits-up, neither did Tristan.

CHAPTER 49

HONEY

The television in the background was distracting Honey from her nerves. She was being ridiculous because if Levi's family were anything like him, they'd all be lovely.

All she had to do was remember who they were because, to be fair, he had a right old crew of relatives living under one roof. Then, there were about a hundred aunts and cousins going to the party, too. Plus half the street, friends from far and wide, and every member of the care team that came in throughout the week.

It was overwhelming, though, because coming from a family with only three members – two really because she hardly ever saw her mum – facing the whole Robinson crew was daunting.

The thought of her mum made Honey smile and touch the photograph on the dresser, and she was glad that since their heart-to-heart weeks before, they'd turned a bit of a corner in their relationship. Keeping her word, after the headstone incident, Honey had called her mum and, during a soul-searching and honest conversation, they'd exorcised the phantoms that had blighted many years and made a pact to move on afresh.

If only her grandad could do the same. It had been a tough

month or so and it didn't look as though his mammoth brooding session was going to come to an end soon. Honey had tried to bring him out of himself, but it was clear he just wanted to be left alone either at his allotment or at home, where she imagined him staring at the photos of the parents he never knew.

Honey had the tiny images of the people in the locket enhanced and enlarged, then put into art deco frames, joined by a clasp in the centre so they looked just like they were inside the locket. Her grandad had come over all emotional when she'd given it to him, and the frames now had pride of place on his mantelpiece.

He'd also surprised Honey by giving her the locket and she'd been touched by the gesture, knowing how much having a piece of his mother meant to him.

'Lass, I want you to have this because I know how much you like antique bits and bobs, and it'd look right nice on you if you wanted to wear it. Seems a shame not to.' He placed the locket in her palm then closed her fingers around it.

'Grandad, no. I can't take it. You keep it here, close by. It was something your mum wanted you to have that's why she put it inside your blanket all those years ago. It belongs with you.' Honey tried to give it back, but he refused.

'No, lass. Please take it. I've got them nice photos to look at now and the ones in that locket are so tiny I have to put my specs on to see. Anyway I reckon your great-gran would want you to have it. It'll be yours one day so take it now.' He folded his hands around hers and gave it a gentle squeeze.

Honey always knew when to give in with Ernie, so agreed. 'Okay, if you're sure, but I'll keep it safe and hide it in my bedroom so if a burglar gets in...'

'Lass, stop worrying. It'll be fine. Now let's have a brew and one of them pattie things that Gospel made... they're bloody lovely they are but they burn my lips, and my bum the next day, that's a fact. It's them Scottish hat chillies I reckon.'

Even though it was far too much information, he'd made Honey laugh for the first time in ages so after fastening the locket around her neck, had followed her grumpy grandad into the kitchen.

That had been a couple of weeks back, and since then Ernie hadn't made her laugh again, but she was determined to forget about all that for at least the next few hours and enjoy meeting Levi's family. Checking the time, she realised she needed to get her finger out otherwise she'd be late.

She'd been watching a documentary about the industrial revolution and the local landed gentry who'd been part of it. They were currently chatting to an elderly lady who lived over in Cheshire on a huge estate, and she was telling them about her older sister who'd been killed during the war.

As much as Honey had immense respect for those who had laid down their lives during that time, she didn't have much truck with the upper classes, some of whom had more money than they knew what to do with. The camera was zooming in on a portrait of the older sister when Honey tutted, pointed the remote and clicked off the screen. She had a party to get ready for.

Levi hummed to a track on the radio while Honey fiddled nervously with the boho silk scarf she hoped was tied in a jaunty way around her neck. It complemented her ditsy maxi dress that just about covered her Converse. She was going for casual-chic, if that was even a thing.

Ziggy had assured Honey during a panicked FaceTime that her outfit was perfect and reflected her personality and *nobody* got dressed up anymore. Not even for weddings if the last one she'd attended was anything to go by. Before Ziggy could expand on her cousin's big-day-fashion-faux-pas, Honey, already running late, had ended the call, grabbed her overnight bag, and legged it to her car.

They were now in Levi's car, after leaving hers at his apartment, and on their way to Chorlton to meet the rellies.

'Stop fidgeting. You look gorgeous and everyone is going to love you, so please, could you not look so nervous.' Levi took his attention off the road for a second to side-eye Honey.

'I'll try. And thank you. I'll be okay once I'm there but it's just the anticipation that's making me all of a do-da. You know, meeting all those people in one place.'

Levi was watching the traffic lights. 'Well just imagine it's your café full of people and you're serving them egg and chips. That should do the trick. You meet new customers every day; you're a natural.'

Honey gave him a raised-eyebrow look and tried to relax, then felt her stomach flip when they turned in to a long street of houses of all shapes and sizes and Levi announced they were there.

Levi's old home was huge. A double-fronted Victorian detached house with ornate facias and a lovely open porch. The wide front door was guarded on each side by stone pillars on which was inscribed Melba Villa.

The first thing that hit her was the heat. Apparently the grandparents liked it warm. Then it took ten minutes to make their way along the hallway and through one of the lounges because Levi insisted on introducing every single person they passed by. When Honey finally met his mum and dad, who were both holding trays weighted down by glasses of prosecco, her nerves had been thoroughly banished.

It was a bit of a feat for Zoë, Levi's mum, kissing Honey on the cheek without toppling the tray of drinks but Mike, his dad, had it nailed and even managed a hug without spilling anything.

Zoë seemed genuinely pleased to meet Honey and after explaining that the food was laid out in the dining room, they'd find the birthday girl holding court over in the corner of the day lounge.

The rooms were cavernous, and Honey could easily imagine the house in the 1800s when it had been built to accommodate crinolines swishing around the place. Above her head were beautiful, moulded cornices and in the centre of the wall, what must have been the original fireplace.

Thanks to Levi's descriptions, she could also picture it as a boarding house where one lounge had been used for guests, the other for family. Back then everyone had eaten in the dining room at little tables set around the room and in her mind, Honey could almost see little Levi, running about the place and being spoilt by the guests and boarders.

It must have been a wonderful, homely place to live, especially when Zoë moved all of her relatives in. Only minutes in her company, Honey could tell she was one of those who loved people, and Zoë's next words confirmed that.

'It's so great to meet you at last because this one,' she inclined her head towards Levi, 'never shuts up about you, so I promise we'll have a proper chat later, once everyone's arrived and I can relax a bit, but you go ahead and say hello to the grandparents. They're dotted about the room so as to cause less trouble in one place... once you've met them, you'll understand.' Zoë winked, then glided away to welcome more guests who'd appeared in the hallway.

'Come on then, let's find Grandma Pins. We'll see the others in a bit.' Levi took her hand and guided her around the guests, resisting the urge to stop and chat.

They crossed the hall and entered the day lounge opposite. Some guests were seated on the sofas set against the wall, chatting or eating from plates on their knees. A hum of conversation mingled with music from the old stereo system in the corner. Honey recognised the deep tone of Tom Jones singing about a pussycat.

Her eyes scanned the room and found another huge fireplace on the chimney breast. There just to the right, in the corner, enveloped by a worn armchair made from brown velour edged with gold piping, sat the birthday girl.

The sight of her took Honey's breath away, and she almost gasped. She had no idea why the diminutive woman, with the ice white hair piled on top of her head, a bun having no luck taming a mass of curls, had such a profound effect. Only that her arms tingled with goosebumps and for some insane reason, Honey felt like they'd met before. But that was impossible.

Levi hovered for a second while his grandmother finished her conversation and Honey took the opportunity to drink in everything about her. She sat bolt upright, her spine ramrod straight, giving length to her lean frame.

In one hand, she held a walking stick, posed like Neptune with his fork. She wore a pale blue dress, tailored to the knee, like something the late queen would have worn. Her legs were clad in thick coffee-coloured tights, bumpy bony shins met patent black shoes, low heeled, adorned with a silver buckle. Everything about her oozed elegance and poise – from the simple strings of pearls at her neck and wrist, the liver-spotted skin on her arms, the wiry fingers that wound around the walking stick and clutched a handkerchief in her lap, to the glint of her wedding ring.

Honey suffered a momentary panic because she suddenly realised she didn't know Grandma Pins' name and she couldn't exactly address her as that so whispered, 'Levi, what do I call her? You've never told me her name and always say Grandma Pins, but I can't say that!'

Levi put his arm around her shoulder and replied just in time because the guest was moving away, 'Ellie, that's what everyone calls her, short for Eleonora, but she hates that name... come on. Our turn.'

When his great-grandmother's eyes met Levi's her whole face lit up and she reached out with both arms in his direction. 'And here he is. My very special boy.'

Honey stayed put and watched as Levi scrunched his knees

and body in a very uncomfortable looking pose so he could hug the birthday girl. The second he was released, an inquisitive face peered around his body and sought Honey.

'And this must be Honey. Come here and give me a hug. I've been so looking forward to seeing you.' Obeying the hands that beckoned, Honey also stooped and found herself encased by birdlike limbs that had the strength of an ox. And as their cheeks touched, Honey's brushing against peach-soft skin as she inhaled lily of the valley, tears pricked her eyes. What the hell was wrong with her?

Once the embrace was over, Honey found she couldn't escape, not that she wanted to, because Grandma Pins kept a tight grip of Honey's hand as she gave Levi instructions.

'Darling boy, bring over those two chairs, that's it, yes, put them there so I can see you both.' Levi shot off and returned with the goods and placed them to one side of his grandma. 'Lovely, now we can have a nice chat. I've already heard so much about you, Honey but I want you to tell me everything. I believe you have a delightful café. Do you have photographs? I'd love to see it.'

'Of course, just hold on, and thank you for inviting me by the way. Levi's told me lots about you, too.' With one hand, Honey tried to flip open the clasp of her handbag to retrieve her phone and the gift she'd brought but not had chance to give.

'Oh don't listen to him, it'll all be fibs.'

Honey stifled a giggle, maybe it was nerves or just a bubble of happiness had escaped, but whatever it was she knew one thing. That Levi was special, and so was his family. Especially the extraordinary, oddly familiar woman sitting by her side.

CHAPTER 50

In between interruptions from birthday guests wanting to say hello, Honey had filled in the gaps of her life story that Levi had missed or didn't know. To be honest, Grandma Pins – she'd insisted Honey call her that – was probably the most inquisitive and talkative person Honey had ever met and hands down beat her in the chatterbox stakes. And she really needed a drink because it was so warm.

The heating must've been on full blast and Honey dreaded to think what Mike and Zoë's bills must be like. It seemed that all of Levi's grandparents had an extra-sensory-laser-guided ability to detect when his mum had dared turn down the dial, so she'd given up and grew orchids in the conservatory instead. Two birds, one stone.

Levi must also have been waning under intense questioning and suffering from heatstroke, because he suddenly suggested he bring them some refreshments. Relieved, and unable to bear the heat any longer, Honey unwound her scarf as Levi took a drinks order from his Grandmother.

No sooner had the words port and lemon left her lips, Grandma Pins turned back to Honey to continue the conversation and as she did, seemed to freeze. Her eyes homed in on Honey's neck and after a few seconds, she pointed and asked, 'That locket. Where did you get it?'

Honey's fingers immediately went to the engraved silver necklace that rested at the base of her throat. 'It belonged to my grandad Ernie. He gave it to me recently. Why?'

'And may I ask where he got it, because I once owned something similar. In fact, I'd be very surprised if there were two identical lockets in existence. Mine was commissioned especially for my eighteenth birthday with my initials engraved on the front.'

Grandma Pins had spoken calmly, yet the air pulsed with electricity or was that the blood pounding in Honey's ears? She chanced a look at Levi whose eyes were wide. His thoughts perhaps, following a similar track to hers.

It couldn't be. This isn't possible. It can't be hers.

Honey could hear the tremor in her own voice as she answered, 'It was wrapped inside his baby blanket, on the day he was born. His mother put it there.'

It was at this point she knew. Honey could feel it in her bones and hear so clearly the voice that had been telling her for weeks to keep looking.

'He was born on the twenty-second of December 1940.'

Grandma Pins didn't react apart from asking, 'May I see inside?'

Honey nodded and with trembling fingers undid the clasp and passed the locket over and as she did, noticed that Grandma Pins hand had begun to shake, too. Once it was in her palm she clicked opened the catch like she'd done it a hundred times before. She didn't look at first. Instead she closed her eyes as though gathering strength and then opened them and looked down.

She didn't cry. Instead she smiled and said, 'Robert, my

darling Robert,' and when she looked up asked Honey, 'So my baby boy didn't die? He lived. And he still lives?'

Even though her lips were wobbling, and she could hardly see through the tears, Honey managed, 'Yes, he lived and still lives. And more than anything in the world he would love to meet you.'

When his grandma slumped in the chair, still conscious but looking like her bones had turned to mush, the colour drained from her face, Levi leapt forward and knelt by her side. 'Grandma, are you okay... shall I fetch you some brandy, or water? Grandma...'

The rest of the guests had stopped what they were doing, a hush had fallen. Tom Jones and the clanking of cutlery as forks hit plates was the only background noise. Honey was shaking from head to toe, wiping away tears as she watched and waited.

Within seconds the crumpled body in the squishy chair revived. 'No, no. I'm okay. But I... I don't understand. How can he be alive?'

Honey blurted out, 'I know... I know the whole story.'

Grandma Pins looked at Honey with a cautious expression but there was relief in her voice as she said, 'Oh thank goodness...' and then to Levi, 'But I'd like some privacy, so could you please ask the others to leave, then fetch Iris and your mother, and the others, my housemates.'

Levi shot off, muttering apologies as he herded everyone from the room, arms spread wide as if to shield Honey and his Grandma.

Then, in a movement so graceful, the woman in the armchair smiled, lifted her arm, and held out her hand to Honey and said, 'Please don't cry, my dear. It's all going to be just fine. And what a wonderful birthday present... meeting my great-granddaughter.'

On hearing this Honey sprang from her chair and knelt by what she now knew was her great-grandmother's side. Taking her soft, fragile liver-spotted hand and placing it to her face she said, 'I'm so glad we found you... I knew I had to look but didn't know where. I wanted to so badly, for my Grandad.'

'And now you have, dear girl, now you have.'

There had been a bit of a kerfuffle and mild panic amongst the gathered guests but once everyone was settled in the other lounge and their glasses refilled, they were reassured that Grandma Pins wasn't unwell, just a little overcome by the event.

The close family members were gathered in the day lounge. On the sofas sat Iris and her husband Bill, and on the outlaw side of the family as they were jokingly referred to, Levi's other grandparents.

By Grandma Pins' side on the floor sat Honey and next to her Levi, who had his arm protectively around Honey's shoulder. Zoë was perched on a chair next to Mike looking nervous, and for signs they might need to call the doctor. Levi reminded her that across the hall they had a plethora of healthcare professionals, so they had it covered.

Honey thought she was going to be sick because she knew what was coming, the big question, and all eyes were trained on her as Grandma Pins spoke.

'I'm sure you're all worried about me but there's no need. I've had something of a shock today because this young lady here has, quite by accident opened a window, or perhaps a door, to the past and now she has, there are things I need to tell you all. But first, and before I ask Honey to explain her side of things, I have a confession.'

Honey saw Zoë's shoulders rise as she inhaled, her breath held as Iris said, 'What on earth are you talking about, Mum? I don't understand.'

'Well if you wait and listen, then you will, Iris!' Grandma Pins tutted then continued but before she did, she gave Honey's hand a squeeze.

'My darling husband and I had such a wonderful marriage based on honesty and trust, not to mention the fact that he saved my life during the war. But out of respect for me and to save my feelings that had been badly hurt, he went along with the story I'd concocted. One that got me through the darkest days of my life.'

Honey saw Iris open her mouth but one look from her mother silenced her immediately.

'Over the years you've all known that I couldn't have children, and that I have loved my darling Iris and her brother Ian since the day I saw them and became their mother. However, the truth of the matter is, I suffered such grave injuries during the second night of the Blitz, that I was never able to carry a child again.'

Honey heard the key word 'again' and the gasp from the others told her they'd picked up on it too. Silence descended on the room, and she prayed Iris wouldn't speak because this moment belonged to Grandma Pins.

'On that dreadful night in 1940, I gave birth to a baby boy and to this day I believed that he'd died in my arms. Because when I awoke, after the longest night under a sky swarming with enemy planes, and found I'd been rescued and saved from the brink of death, I was told that my little boy hadn't made it. But it seems he did, and I have no idea why or how, but it now transpires that the baby I gave birth to lived, and I'm hoping that Honey here will be able to explain.'

All eyes were on Honey, and she thought she was going to cry, right there in front of everyone, such was the responsibility of telling the tale of Molly McCarthy. The true version of events that would no doubt have everyone in the room hating the woman who had stolen a baby.

Honey had no choice, though, because so many lives had been affected by the one snap decision. She owed it to the innocent woman seated by her side and strangely, Molly too, because it wasn't black and white. A case of right or wrong. It was down to Honey to give an unbiased, factual account of what happened. She wished she had the letter to read out, but it was at her grandad's.

She looked at Levi. His arm was still round her shoulder which he squeezed, encouraging and reassuring, the same as the look in his eyes. She could do this.

Taking a breath, she began.

It was time to be brave, tell the truth, share a secret and hopefully heal the wounds of the past. This was Aunty Beryl's and Molly McCarthy's chance to put some of it right. This was their moment.

CHAPTER 51

ELEONORA

Everyone was shell-shocked once Honey had told the story. Afterwards there'd been questions that the poor girl had answered to the best of her ability and Eleonora's heart went out to the pale-faced, bug-eyed woman seated by her side. And dear Levi had tried to help out too, but she expected that holding Honey's hand had been enough. Sometimes, that's all anyone needed, a hand to hold in the worst of times.

And amidst the hoo-ha, she'd wanted to laugh because really, she should have known. Or did she already? The minute she'd clapped eyes on Honey earlier, felt her skin against her cheek, their hands joined as one, she hadn't wanted to let go. It was the most curious feeling ever, like they fit.

And that hair, the exact same colour as Clarissa's. Not as deep-auburn as her own. Even now, she could remember sitting on the bed, brushing her little sister's long tresses as she told her a fairy story or sang a lullaby before bed.

Instinctively, Eleonora reached out and touched Honey's hair and smiled. Honey smiled back but her eyes were wary and tired. The recounting of the tale had taken its toll and throughout, even though she'd tried to be unbiased, Eleonora sensed that Honey had a sense of loyalty to the woman she regarded as family. Molly McCarthy.

That was to her credit and Eleonora admired Honey even more and felt the need to reciprocate in some way, to reassure. The eyes of the room were upon them, but she was holding court and now they'd asked their questions, she hoped they'd remain silent.

'You have exactly the same colour hair as my sister, you know.' Someone in the room allowed a gasp to escape and she understood why. Everyone thought her whole family had been killed by a bomb.

Eleonora continued, 'I'll tell you all about her when I explain my side of the story but first, I want to thank you for sharing what you know. It can't have been easy. Such a burden and a tough decision to make.'

Honey sighed. 'Well, put it this way, it wasn't what I was expecting when I opened the box. But it's your story I want to hear now. How everything fits together. You're the missing link.'

That was a perfect way to put it because, for the past eighty-three years, Eleonora had made damn sure she was missing. Dead to all those who knew her before. It was her coping mechanism. The only way she could move on with life.

'Yes I am, aren't I, and before I begin I want to say one thing. That I never meant to deceive any of you, but at the time I made decisions that were best for me and as the years rolled by well, my half-truths simply became fact. Reality, I suppose. Anyway, I need to tell you, otherwise Iris is going to explode over there. So buckle up. We're going back in time.'

After casting her eyes around the room, resting lastly on Levi and then Honey, Eleonora began.

CHAPTER 52

Manchester. 1940

My darling Robert had been killed more or less the minute his feet touched Belgian soil. Little did I know at the time, but our parting farewell had produced a baby. The grief at his loss consumed me and whether it was the shock, or just how my body behaved, when I dug my heels in and went off to join the army, I had no idea that I was going to be a mother.

I had to do something. Do my bit as we said back then. Rage and despair were churning my insides but then again, that could also have been the little seed that was growing within me.

When I did realise why my flat-iron stomach had a decidedly pot-bellied appearance, I really wasn't sure whether to laugh or cry, especially when the medical officer gave me my cards and sent me packing.

Common sense, or perhaps how I'd been brought up told me not to go running home and cause a fuss. That would never do, so instead I rang father and asked him to meet me in Manchester.

I waited for him outside Piccadilly Station on a late August afternoon and we walked to the Midland Hotel for lunch. That's where I told him of my predicament, in public, knowing that he couldn't bawl me out in front of nice ladies as they ate their soup.

Through gritted teeth and in a hushed tone he told me I was a disgrace and worse. Loathing was etched in the thick lines on his brow and his eyes... well, I'd never seen them full of such anger. He was disgusted. Simple as that.

According to him, the truth and consequent shame would kill my mother and I was a poor example for my sister Clarissa whose life would be tainted by my fall from grace. I'd never be able to be part of the season, and neither would she, thanks to my depravity. He actually used that word.

I didn't bother to point out to him that there was a war on and the last thing anyone cared about were debutantes being presented to the King, which was why it had all been cancelled. Or that secretly I hoped the whole ridiculous performance would remain so forever.

I remember he checked his watch and tutted and I knew that I was about to be dismissed. Definitely not invited to accompany him home on the next train.

When he managed to look at me, he was still grey with rage but held himself admirably while in a voice laced with contempt, he gave me one option. He would arrange for me to stay with his favourite cousin in Scotland, Aberdeen to be precise, and she would facilitate an adoption. Nobody would ever know apart from the three of us and afterwards I could return to Chamberlain. I can hear his voice like it was yesterday.

'I will tell your mother about our meeting today, but only that you were in transit to London and had no time to come home, such were your orders from Whitehall. She won't question my word. You will remain in Aberdeen until you've had *it*,' he glanced towards where the tablecloth concealed my stomach, 'and once it's gone, then I will allow you to come home. You can say you're on leave. Whatever. I will ask Oscar if he can use one of his contacts to fix you up with something in London. Office work perhaps, and he can keep an eye on you.'

What he was actually saying was that he couldn't stand the sight of me and once I'd done his bidding, after a short visit home he wanted me gone. Out of sight and mind.

It all sounded so simple apart from one tiny miscalculation on his part. I wanted to keep my baby because he was my last link to Robert, and I could never give either of them up. I thought he would explode, right there on the spot and oddly, I took pleasure from seeing him grip the edge of the table causing the white linen to scrunch under his fingers.

I was then offered an ultimatum. Do as he said or be disowned. It was my choice and knowing my father, he expected me to capitulate. He even wrote a cheque there and then for my lodgings in Manchester, where I was to wait until he'd made the arrangements, and then my onward expenses. Such was his arrogance he handed me the cheque and told me to ring him in two days' time. Then he stood, placed his trilby on his head, picked up his briefcase and without another word, walked away.

My legs shook so badly that I couldn't stand so I poured the last of the tea from the pot and added three sugars to my cup. My hands trembled as I stirred the little silver spoon and held back tears, averting my eyes from the people at adjacent tables who I knew were staring, so obvious was it that there'd been a scene.

As I sipped, taking nourishment for me and my baby, I had the strangest sensation of being seated on a perfectly round, white island, castaway and alone. All I had with me, all I had in fact, was the brown suitcase I'd taken when I'd left home to join up. That suitcase added to my humiliation. It sat on the carpet by my side, like a faithful dog waiting for its master to tell it where to go.

That's when I realised I was in charge of my own destiny, and I had a choice to make. By the time my cup was empty, and like a starving urchin I'd eaten every scrap of food left on the table, I'd formed a plan.

I walked straight to the bank and cashed the cheque. In a romantic gesture and to cheer myself up I bought a cheap ring from Woolworth's and decided to tell everyone I was a war widow. Then I wandered for a while, not really knowing where to go, until I came across a newsagents. In the window was a board advertising local services and lodgings. I asked the shopkeeper for directions and found a room in a clean but very basic bed and breakfast that only took women.

It wasn't this one, where we all live now – it was in Moss Side – but wouldn't that have been a lovely quirk to my tale. One of the other lodgers, Colette, worked in the munitions factory in Trafford Park and said she could get me a job there. I said yes on the spot.

Then, to prevent my father tracking me down I shortened my name to Nora and used Robert's surname, Jones. It was as though I'd started a new life and as much as I missed home and my little sister most of all, I got on with it like thousands of other women all across the land.

Because I was so tall and reed thin, I hid my pregnancy for months and even when it became obvious and I was summoned to the office, I wasn't made to leave. The supervisor was kind, and she took me off the line and away from the cordite and the fumes and found me lighter duties in the warehouse.

I wasn't the only one to have lost a husband or be alone in the world and expecting a baby, so we all stuck together, and that camaraderie spurred me on and made me feel safe. I believed I'd manage somehow, and it was the thought of Robert's baby growing inside me that gave me hope.

As for home, I put it out of my mind and told myself I had to be brave like the troops who were overseas and faced terrible dangers each day. My worst challenge was rationing and swollen ankles. I'd made some nice friends and had a clean bed to lay my head at night and my baby, who I couldn't wait to hold.

During autumn and into winter, my stubborn streak served me well, forbade me to open the door of every phone box I passed and ring my father to ask if he'd changed his mind. He wouldn't, I knew that really because my disobedience had probably tipped him over the edge. Hence why I couldn't bear the thought of speaking to my mother who'd have sobbed down the line telling me how woeful I'd made her life. As for Clarissa, hearing her sweet little voice asking me to come home would have dissolved any resolve I had.

I did wonder though, what Father had told them. Had he stuck to the story that I'd been sent to work in Whitehall? Mother would have loved that, telling her friends I was needed for important war work and hopefully, in dear Clarissa's imagination I'd be just fine.

And I was doing so well, right up until Christmas when perhaps hormones and the bitter cold got the better of me, that I desperately wanted to make some contact with my family. I'd been in the queue at the newsagents and spotted a lovely card on the shelf. A red candle surrounded by holly and ivy and the words *season's greetings*.

It was an irrational, spur-of-the-moment thing to do and as I'd popped the envelope into the post I didn't think about the postmark, not until later that evening as I shivered in my bed. It was too late to worry about it by then so I told myself nobody would notice and put it out of my mind. I was more concerned about the pains I'd been getting in my back, that the mother hens at the factory told me were just my body having a practice. They weren't though, and a few days before Christmas, my baby decided to make an appearance.

It could have been the horror of the night before when the German planes bombed Manchester and we'd been forced to spend the night in the shelter. We were on the late shift when the air raid siren went. The munitions factory was a natural target and as we made our way outside and then underground, being in enemy sights tightened the grip of fear around my heart.

Never had I been so utterly terrified, and I thought it would never end, but when we emerged into the smoke-clagged morning, and saw the devastation around us, we told ourselves we were the lucky ones. It took forever to get back to our lodgings because roads were closed, and the city was in chaos.

My waters broke just as I got off the bus, much to my embarrassment. Colette guided me towards the boarding house and made encouraging sounds, saying I'd better keep my promise and make her a godmother, and she'd ring the midwife the second we got back.

But the pains came quickly, and to my horror, so did the blood. Within minutes I could barely walk, and we had to stop so I could lean against a wall, anything that would hold me up. There was a pub opposite and Colette called out to someone to go inside and ring for an ambulance, and then it all becomes like a fuzzy dream.

My back of my legs resting on the cold pavement and Colette's hand cushioning my head, her kind voice, the clanging of a bell, white coats, blue uniforms, the most terrible pain. Sleep.

CHAPTER 53

When I woke up, I was in a little room in hospital and around me there was the most terrible noise. The air raid siren outside. People shouting instructions on the inside, footsteps outside my room, the sense of controlled panic. It's funny how you can hear it in someone's voice even if you can't see their face. But I could. I looked to my left and there he was, my baby. I hadn't even met him formally or if I had I couldn't remember. I had to hold him and see his face properly, so I got out of bed, a herculean effort but I had just enough energy and determination to lift him from his little cot and lay him by my side in the bed.

While I waited for someone to come for us, because I presumed we'd be taken to somewhere safe during the imminent raid, I just gazed at his beautiful little face and stroked his skin. He was perfect. Like a little peach swaddled in a blanket and if I thought I'd felt love when I met my Robert, it was nothing compared to what I felt for my son.

I was too weak to walk, to find help or shelter, in fact it took immense effort to lift and feed him, but I remember he suckled, and it was the most wonderful moment. Just the two of us, bonded by such a primal act.

We stayed like that, huddled together for what seemed forever but not long enough, and when the bombs started falling and nobody had come for us, I held him tight and prayed that we'd be saved. I told him about his father and how brave and clever he was, and so the two Roberts would be closer I took off my locket and tucked in inside his blanket, heart to heart.

That little capsule in time, those few precious hours with my son have stayed alive in my mind ever since and sometimes in my dreams I can still touch his skin, marvel at the length of his eyelashes, count his fingers one more time. I always wake up though and he's gone, just like I woke up and found we were covered in brick dust and debris, but little Robert was alive and after I washed his face with grateful tears I kissed his face in relief.

You know what happens next, from Molly's memories as written by Beryl. I do remember parts of it but it's such a haze because I was so dreadfully poorly. I didn't know it at the time, but I was haemorrhaging, so Molly's discovery when she moved the sheets is correct. When she thought I was dead, I was on the brink, and had I not been rescued I'd have faded away very quickly.

And this may surprise you, given what transpired afterwards, I can understand how someone untrained and in such a traumatic situation, no doubt suffering from shock, could make that mistake. Molly's baby had died in her arms, and she probably thought at points during the night she would too. So her actions on that day I have compassion for, I really do. She thought she was doing the right thing, for good reasons.

It's what she did later that I will find hard to reconcile but before all that, I need to tell you the rest. About the man who saved my life and gave me a new one.

After major surgery and many blood transfusions, I woke up

three days after The Blitz to the sight of a doctor asleep in the chair by my bedside. He was the one who'd patched me up and, even though it was touch and go, he'd spent every moment he could checking up on me. Rory.

The son of a doctor, he'd followed his father into the profession. After they dug me out of the rubble, I'd been taken to A&E in another hospital, still holding the body of my baby in my arms. He told me, much later of course, that the sight of me had left him so badly shaken that the sister on duty had raised her voice and told him to snap out of it.

His young wife had died a year earlier from pre-eclampsia and while their baby daughter had survived, the guilt at not being able to save the mother of his two children had almost finished Rory. When he saw me on the stretcher, with who I thought was Robert, he made a silent vow to not let it happen again. He wanted to save me and, in many ways, he did.

Our whole family know the story of how, after I was released from hospital weeks later, Rory came to find me at my lodgings and slowly, whenever he could find time, made good his vow. You see, I was a total wreck, mind body and soul. Moving, talking, eating and as much as I didn't want to, breathing, was too much of an effort. And it had as much to do with losing the two people most dear to me, as my father.

In one of my lowest moments, depleted to the core, when I'd run out of resolve and my stubborn streak failed me, I did a stupid thing. I rang home.

It was February 21st, 1941. Nine twenty-five precisely. I knew Father worked in his office every morning from nine till eleven, when he stopped to take tea with Mother. During that two-hour period he always took his own calls. The butler knew not to answer so I was unsurprised when my father answered in his habitual way with the words, 'Chamberlain Manor.' Ridiculous. That's what I was and how I felt because I should have known what to expect.

'Father, it's me. Eleonora.' My whole body shook.

'What do you want? I gave you instructions and you disobeyed so I have nothing further to say to you.'

And whilst I stood in the phone box dumbfounded and expecting him to put the phone down he surprised me with a question and killed me a little bit more with the use of one word.

'Have you had it?'

It.

He'd called my beautiful sleeping boy, *it.*

I was barely able to make my lips work but when they did, I made then answer honestly because there was no denying Robert, then or ever. 'Yes. I had a little boy and I named him Robert.'

And then the dagger to my heart, of which I have always been glad because as his words plunged deep into my body and soul, Father freed me of him and Chamberlain.

'Then you are dead to me. You are nothing to this family. Do you hear me? Never contact us again. Stay away from your mother and your sister or God help me I will not be responsible for my actions. You have shamed our family name and you are not worthy to call yourself a Chamberlain. Goodbye.'

Perhaps that was the day Molly saw me. I wandered for hours, around and around in a daze until I was too exhausted to walk any further. Perhaps I'd have recognised her, had I seen her first, but my memories of that night were like fog before my eyes and in my brain. I knew there was another woman there, but I never asked after her. I just presumed she'd gone home with her baby to her family.

The day she saw me, I may have stood and stared in shop windows or sat on vacant benches looking similarly so. All I do know is that I ended up back at the hospital and sat on a chair in A&E. To this day I have no idea why, but when Rory finished his shift that night he saw me, took me for a cup of tea, and the rest is a much happier history.

It was six months before I agreed to meet his children. One-and-half-year-old Iris and three-year-old Ian. I didn't think I would ever know love again until the day I saw them both in the garden. I watched from the gate and Rory waited, allowing me to decide if I'd like to go in and meet them. Or run away. Back to the cemetery where Robert's little casket lay in a spot I visited far more often than was good for me.

Iris was sitting on a blanket, wisps of blonde hair sprouting at all angles, chubby legged and shaking a rattle for all she was worth. Ian was flying a paper plane, all skinny limbs with a mop of fair hair that he flicked out of the way as he ran. Two motherless children and one childless mother and by her side, a man who would never let her down.

I didn't want them to be cared for by a nanny as I had been, or a housekeeper who saw them as part of her daily duty. And I wanted Rory to know he'd saved me and in doing so, could free himself of a burden too heavy for one as good as he to carry. He deserved to be loved. They all did. I did.

As for my other family, I wiped them out of my life the minute I became Mrs Rory Flynn, the doctor's wife. Nora Jones had never really existed, and I knew that somehow my father would have found a way to erase me, probably with the help of his slug of a brother Oscar. Mother would go along with whatever he said and believe whatever he said and dear little Clarissa, she deserved none of it. To have them for parents or me for a big sister. With the way our circle, our class worked, it was entirely feasible that my mud could stick to her. So I did what Father told me to do. To the letter.

Back then it was so much easier to disappear, blend into the background and become someone else entirely. People were neighbourly, and we had extended families but to a certain extent we kept ourselves and our private lives to ourselves.

Rory knew everything, of course, but he also respected that I wanted to start again and that it was my right. So he went along with my harmless story that all my family were killed during the blitz. Nobody ever came to look for me, and why would they?

As father said, I was dead to them. And they were dead to me.

And as time went by, they faded away and became people I used to know, whose paths I'd crossed and thought of occasionally.

And we had such a happy life, the four of us. After the war, Rory started his own practice, and we worked together. I ran the surgery, and he did what he did best and saved as many people as he could. But you know what Rory gave me – apart from a family I adored, and, I can safely say, adored me back? He gave me freedom to be who I wanted to be.

Yes, once I got my confidence back and society allowed women to speak that bit more freely I too found my voice. Rory didn't mind when I marched off to protest about whatever I'd got the pip about this time. And I know he rather liked it when I burnt my bras on a bonfire in the garden and it had nothing to do with my liberty. Oh I do miss him.

He was my rock and the fact that I couldn't have any more children didn't matter to him or me. I would always have Robert and the hours I spent with him and in my dreams, and sometimes in my daydreams I imagined him grown and what he would look like. What he would have done for a living. That type of thing.

It was as though he hadn't really gone, not completely. That his spirit had stayed close and wanted me to know he was still around; and if I reached out and closed my eyes that I could touch him. And now I know why. He'd been there all the while. Thirty miles away. My Robert. Just waiting to be found.

I often wondered what happened to my locket and reasoned that in my semi-conscious state I may have loosened the blanket while I tried to feed him during the night. Or it was lost when I was taken from the debris, up a ladder and into an ambulance. It's all such a blur. I mourned the loss of the only photo I had of my

Robert like I mourned the loss of his son. So to hold it in my hands again, after so long, is a gift.

But the greatest gift is knowing that my baby lived and that he still does. I will see his face again. I can tell him how much I loved him and have always done. And that he was never forgotten. All I want now is to hold him in my arms, even if it's just one more time. That will be enough.

CHAPTER 54

HONEY

Apart from when Levi changed gear, Honey clung onto his hand while they sped back to Marple. There were moments of intense silence where they plunged into worlds of their own. Then one of them would blurt something out and this time, it was Levi.

'I just can't get my head around it. It's like my brain is going to explode with it all. Is yours?'

Honey was resting her head but her eyes, tired, red from crying tears of sheer joy for her Grandad and Eleonora, were fixed on the road, willing the miles away.

'Yep, totally mashed, because as soon as I get one thing straight in my head another question pings up. I mean, Eleonora's dad for a start, just cutting her out of his life like that... it's so cruel. He sounds vile and I suppose she was better off without him. And I don't blame her either, for digging her heels in and doing the same in return. Imagine being bereft and alone and your dad turning his back like that. I'd have hated him forever.'

They'd stopped at some lights. 'Me too. And what the hell did her father say happened to her? That really freaks me out, that he somehow erased her from the Chamberlain family. And then there's your great gran, Molly. What a life she must have lived. Terrified she'd be found out and arrested and dreading ever bumping into my great-grandma again. No wonder she kept herself to herself and was the way she was. It's like loads of things fall into place, don't they.'

Honey sighed. 'They do and it's the little things, like where Grandad really gets his red hair from. And it's uncanny that his personality is so similar to how Eleonora describes herself, and then... this is so weird, how she's volunteered for charitable organisations all her life. And it's my thing, too. Is it what inspired you to do your job?'

The lights changed and they were off again, 'I suppose it is, although I didn't have career ambitions in that direction but when I saw the job advertised I knew it was right up my street. You know, because Mum and Great-grandma, even Grandma Iris, all had the mother hen streak in them. Wanting to look after people in one way or another. But really, we all got our values and morals from Eleonora. She's the one who always pointed us in the right direction.'

Honey smiled and wrapped her fingers around Levi's as their hands rested on the centre console. 'And this is another odd thing. We both knew... me and Eleonora when we met earlier. Not in a conscious way, more a feeling, a sense of something you can't describe. I'll never ever forget that moment when I saw her. I swear. I didn't recognise her from the photo in the locket because she's changed so much. Perhaps it was subliminal.'

Levi nodded. 'She said so, didn't she? Before we left. That when she held your hand she felt a connection but thought it was because she'd heard so much about you from me. God, it's just all so freaky but in a nice freaky way.'

'Not as freaky as the fact that we are now related! What are you, my step-cousin once removed? I can't even be bothered to work it out because my brain hurts.' It was true. Honey's head was crammed with so much stuff. Like she was about to sit an exam and had information overload.

Levi laughed. 'Well, let's thank our lucky but slightly warped stars that we didn't just find out we're brother and sister because with our lot, nothing would surprise me. But there's no getting away from the fact that my great-grandma is now your great-grandma! That's a proper mind bomb.'

At this Honey managed a bit of a giggle because he was right, and even though the blood connection didn't matter to any of Levi's family, the word 'step' had saved them from a world of pain.

As they headed further out of the city they once again lapsed into quiet. Comfortable and calming. Honey sorted through her mental inbox that was piled high with tatty pieces of paper bearing scribbled, haphazard notes to self. Then a question for Levi escaped.

'What about Clarissa? I wonder if she's still alive.'

Levi answered, 'I was thinking that earlier. Maybe we could look her up, but I bet she married some lord and moved away. Let's face it, I'd have wanted to get away from her father soon as, wouldn't you?'

Honey's answer was emphatic. 'Hell yes! I'd have married the frog prince if it meant escaping that horrible man. She might be dead though... she'd be nine years older than Grandad and not everyone lives as long as your great-gran. Poor Clarissa. I feel like she's the totally innocent party in all this because she was only little when Eleonora left and would have no idea her sister was alive, and what a total basta– nasty man her dad was.'

'Hmm, but what if she's still alive? She'd be about ninety-one, so you never know. I think we should look for her and once your grandad's been reunited with my Grandma Pins, perhaps she might want to make her peace with Clarissa, too. Before it's too late, because the way I look at it they've all been apart for too long.'

Again, Honey agreed. 'You're right. But from what I've heard and seen of Eleonora it will have to be her decision and we'd have to respect that, hard as it will be. I'm just so flipping glad I told Grandad the truth now... and met you obviously. It's like the fates were aligned. Do you believe they were?'

Levi lifted her hand and kissed it. 'I do now.'

And then from nowhere, in the middle of a tender moment came a surge of panic. 'Oh god, Levi. What the hell am I going to say to grandad...? How will I say it... Do you think I should make him sit down and get him some brandy... I don't think he'll have any... What about a can of pale ale? You know, for the shock. Would that work?'

He was laughing as he pulled onto a roundabout, 'I think you shouldn't overthink it and just say what comes into your head at the time because whichever way you look at it, you're taking him the best news ever. He's going to see his mum and once he gets over the shock... with or without a can of pale ale, he'll be the happiest man in Marple, I reckon.'

Honey relaxed a bit at Levi's words. He was right, this was good news. And then she thought of Eleonora and her answer to a very simple question.

It was Iris who'd asked, once the hoo-ha had died down and cups of tea were brought, and the other guests reassured everything was fine and all would be explained very shortly. As she'd passed Eleonora her drink, she'd asked, 'So, Mum. What do you want to do now? About Ernie, I mean.'

Eleonora placed her cup on her lap and answered, 'I want to see him. I need to see my son as soon as possible so,' she looked to where Levi and Honey were seated by her side, 'will you go and tell him that his daft old mum is alive. And if he wants to see me, will you bring him today? I'll wait up all night if I have to.'

A wash of panic and love and relief flooded Honey's body as she replied, 'Of course I will.' Then she looked at Levi. 'Will you come with me?' And of course he'd said yes.

They were almost there, climbing upwards, passing Marple Locks and, once they'd turned the next corner, they'd be on her grandad's street. Honey checked the clock on the dashboard. Had it only been three hours since they'd arrived for Grandma Pins' big birthday party? Because in that short space of time it felt like she'd lived another lifetime through the eyes of a woman badly wronged, yet so understanding and, in parts, forgiving.

Turning to Levi, Honey confessed that something that had been niggling away since they'd set off. 'You know after I'd told everyone about Molly, and they were all asking questions – perfectly natural and fair ones by the way – there were moments when I wanted to defend her. Do you think that's wrong, knowing what she did to your great-grandma?'

Levi shook his head. 'No, not at all, because Molly wasn't there and couldn't speak for herself and it's natural, especially because she's part of your family, that you'd want to protect her… or at least stick up for her. It's not a simple case of black and white, is it? There are so many grey areas and none of us will ever know what she was going through back then. And most of all, we can't change what happened, only what happens next, so let's focus on that.'

'How did I get such a wise and kind boyfriend? You always know how to make me feel better; but right now I think I need a sick bucket. I'm so excited to tell him you know, but nervous too. It's huge, all this, isn't it!'

They'd pulled up outside her grandad's house and she could see the lights on in the lounge and bizarrely hoped he'd had his tea. He hated his evening meal being interrupted and would grumble and tut when the doorbell rang.

Levi switched off the engine. 'Yes, it is. But it's not going to be like when you had to tell him about Beryl's letter. This is the *total* opposite.'

'Yes, you're right. I think I'm getting my knickers in a twist because I remember how awful that was, which is stupid.'

Levi smiled. 'Exactly. And if he agrees to come back with us, the rest of the night is going to be huge too, but happy. And this time we've got each other to lean on and Ernie to support. We'll be okay, okay?'

Honey nodded. 'Okay.'

'Now, I think you should go in on your own and I'll wait here until you've told him.'

'Why? Don't you want to be there when I tell him?' Honey had envisaged them both being part of a really special moment.

'No, because Ernie isn't one for a fuss, and if he gets upset he won't be too pleased about having an audience, will he?'

Even though Levi had got her grandad to a tee, she was adamant they told him together. 'No, he probably won't but if he does get upset you can sneak off and put the kettle on or something. But this is such a big part of us, our history because two families are about to become one, and we're the link. This is about me and you, as well as Grandad and Eleonora. So please come with me.'

Levi sighed and rolled his eyes but when she saw him pull the keys from the ignition, Honey knew she'd won.

The sound of the telly blaring in the front room was joined by the sound of the doorbell when Honey gave it a long hard push then waited. Levi was stood to her side but one pace back, her free hand in his. When she saw the blurry shape of her grandad through the panel of bubble glass in the door her heart did a giddy forward flip.

'Only me, Grandad,' she shouted and hoped he would hear above the telly.

The twitch of her lips meant the nervous giggles threatened but were soon banished the second she heard the slide of the safety latch. Next, a gust of warm air escaped from the hall as Ernie opened the front door and stood on the step, wearing a tea-towel tucked into his shirt front and a surprised expression.

'Honey, what are you doing here? I'm 'avin me tea. An' I

thought you'd gone to a party.' He then gave Levi a cursory nod and a quick once over. 'Alright lad. 'ope you brought me some cake?'

Honey sucked in the cold November air and blurted out, 'Grandad, we had to come and see you because,' she looked at Levi who with stretched eyes, told her to get on with it, 'we've got the most amazing news ever.' Honey paused and waited for him to react then in a moment of madness, wondered if he thought they'd got engaged or something.

In his usual unimpressed way, Ernie gave them a grunt and as he turned, said, 'Well come on in then. Don't stand there letting all the bloody warm out. I'll finish me tea while you tell me this amazing news, unless you want to stick the kettle on, and I'm reet disappointed you've not brought me some cake. I like a bit of birthday cake, I do.'

As he shuffled off back to the lounge with a very noticeable tut, they both stepped inside and Levi closed the door, at which point their eyes met and the nervous giggles took hold of them both. Once she'd composed herself and Levi nudged her along the hallway, Honey decided it'd be best to let her grandad finish his tea rather than annoy the grumpy old bugger. And then, all being well, she'd be able to make up for not bringing him a slice of bloody birthday cake.

CHAPTER 55

ELEONORA

She'd held many babies in her arms over the years. There'd been a time, however, shortly after she'd lost her own, that Eleonora didn't think she'd ever be able to look at, let alone touch a baby ever again. For a while she'd been consumed by such terrible envy whenever she was unfortunate enough to glimpse a pregnant woman, a pram even, and she trained herself to spot the enemy and take evasive action.

There'd even been anger, at having been saved and forced to live by Rory who refused to let her go. It would've been so much simpler if she'd been left to drift away, and then she could've been reunited in the afterlife she'd once believed in. Or if not there'd have been an end to the missing and wishing.

But she couldn't stay cross with the rescuers and Rory for long. Not once he'd told her about his wife and Eleonora accepted that by saving her, he'd saved himself, and she couldn't begrudge him that no matter how much she hurt inside.

It was his children who cured her. Wiped away the fear of allowing herself to love someone as much, even for a few short hours, as she'd loved her baby boy.

Iris, who would sleep in her arms for hours even though

everyone told her she was making a rod for her own back, but Eleonora didn't care. Her arms were full once more. And the little things, more precious than diamonds. Iris's face lighting up at the sound of Eleonora's voice, first thing in the morning when she peeped over the cot.

And then there'd been Ian. A whippetty-whirlwind who'd stolen her heart in a heartbeat by asking her one simple thing at the end of a perfect summer day when they'd first met.

He was three years old, doe-eyed like his father. Shyly standing by her side in his clean pyjamas he'd kissed her goodnight, soft as a butterfly on her cheek, his hair damp on his forehead, the clean smell of coal tar soap on his skin.

'Will you tuck me in and read me a story, please.' His little round face, nervous. Chubby fingers twiddling his pyjama button. How could she have refused?

And ever since both he and Iris had wrapped her round their fingers. Their lives became hers and she'd thanked the stars, that after losing one baby she'd been gifted two in return.

Eleonora had loved them like her own; they were her own and she'd ploughed her all into them and Rory and their life together. A full life at that. Where her husband had given her the freedom to be who she wanted to be. To believe in and support, to rail against whoever and whatever she chose.

And still, even when she'd been blessed by all that, there'd always been a hole. One that nothing and nobody could ever fill.

Every 22nd December brought with it such bittersweet memories that were embellished by images. For Eleonora, her son still lived in her mind where he grew and laughed and lived, because she simply couldn't let him go. So she'd survived on what-ifs. Making it up.

Her little boy looked so smart on his first day at school. And when he learned to read he would tap each word while his tongue poked out from the corner of his lips. He'd sat under a Christmas tree and opened his big present, a train set, that's what he'd have asked for. And he won so many trophies and when he got his first job, bought her a bunch of flowers with his wages. And he was married, happily with lots of children.

It was her secret and had seemed so ridiculous but as she waited patiently in the day lounge, with Iris and Zoë furtively watching her and the clock, Eleonora wondered if it hadn't been a sign. Had someone been trying to tell her something? Perhaps that night, when Molly had swapped their babies, her inner psyche, a part of her that kept vigil as she verged on death, had witnessed it all and for all those years had been screaming, *He's still alive, don't give up.*

Tutting at her own fanciful notions Eleonora told herself it was nothing of the sort, just love and a deep well of sadness that had conjured up a son to see her through the worst times, and in some ways it had worked. She had performed magic because he really was alive and any minute she would get her wish and see him, hold him, touch him one more time.

All she had to do was breathe, keep that heart ticking for a while longer. She'd waited this long so a few more minutes were a doddle. Even though the hand of the clock seemed to move in slow-motion ever since Zoë had given everyone a brief rundown of events. Following gasps and 'Well-I-nevers' her guests had kindly taken the hint. After waving from the door, one hand holding cake wrapped in a serviette, they'd left the family in peace.

When Levi rang to say that they'd told Ernie, Eleonora held her breath as Zoë related the conversation in real time.

'He's in a bit of a state, a happy state, and couldn't wait to get his shoes and coat on. We're setting off straight away and should be here within the hour, sooner depending on traffic. He can't wait to see you, and says he'll be with you soon.'

Zoë had burst into tears the second she put the phone down and then Iris joined in. Eleonora just straightened her back and waited. Like she'd been doing for eighty-three years.

Car headlights on the windows diverted all eyes from the clock that said 8pm, onto Eleonora. He was there.

Zoë and Iris almost sprang from their chairs, then turned, not really knowing what to do. It was Iris who asked, 'Do you want to be left alone, Mum?'

'Yes please, if you don't mind, love.' Eleonora watched as her daughter and grand-daughter hesitated then wordlessly left the room, closing the door firmly behind them.

She listened. The front door that stuck in the winter and banged shut in the summer was opened. The wind chimes always gave visitors away. The door shut. Voices, words muttered and too many all at once to decipher and then...

Eleonora's heart was putting in an extra shift already so when the door to the lounge slowly opened and a shaft of bright light illuminated the figure who stood, half in half out, it almost went on strike.

Neither of them said a word and she was aware of him stepping forward and the door being pulled closed behind him and all of a sudden he was there. She tried to stand but her legs had stopped doing that a long time ago, so instead she reached out and waited.

When their hands touched and he fell to his knees, she could see his face covered in tears which she wiped away, 'Shush now, don't cry, it's going to be alright, son. It's going to be alright.'

His shoulders heaved and he could barely speak but managed, 'I always knew, I always knew...'

And when he couldn't speak another word and fell against her chest, Eleonora wrapped her arms around him and held him tight. She'd heard his voice at last. And had touched his skin and seen his face again. No more imagining. No more what ifs.

Closing her eyes, they were back there once more. Just the two of them in a bombed-out hospital room covered in the dust of time. He was swaddled in a blanket and lay safe by her side. But this time things would be different. Eleonora would stay awake and guard him with every ounce of love and life that she had left, for however long that was.

Her baby, her little boy, the teenager who'd grown into a man had stepped out of her imagination and into her arms. Ernie had come home.

CHAPTER 56

CLARISSA

As always, Jennifer had taken control of the arrangements for Christmas and was giving Chuck very detailed instructions as to where she wanted the tree. And as was his way, he'd good-naturedly acquiesced to her every whim, even though she'd changed her mind twice already and was currently dithering over the alcove or by the window.

Thank heavens Matheson had trees sent up each year and Jennifer didn't have to choose herself, or they'd still be waiting on Christmas Eve. This made Clarissa chuckle, as did hearing Jennifer announce that the tree was definitely a bit on the wonky side.

Clarissa was busy sorting through the mail, a job usually undertaken by Jennifer, but seeing as she was occupied, she'd insisted on doing it herself, wanting nothing to do with trees or decorations or what they'd eat for dinner on the twenty-fifth.

It was bad enough that November was marred by another date in the calendar, her sister's birthday. One of those days you creep towards, like a snarling dog, and then after you've skirted around it, you run away as fast as you can, hoping it won't bite you on the bottom.

From the moment her eyes opened on November 23rd, Clarissa thought of Eleonora constantly. It had become a tradition that at the end of the day, before bed, she would leave two glasses of champagne in front of her sister's portrait and there she would drink a toast to Eleonora. And as her eyes closed on the day, like a child on Christmas Eve, Clarissa still courted a fantasy. Ridiculous really. Because just like she'd marvelled at the disappearance of a carrot and a mince pie left in front the fire for Santa, Clarissa had longed to find Eleonora's glass of champagne empty the next morning. A sign that never came.

Once November was over, the inevitable had to be dealt with: Christmas. She'd always found it to be such a disunion. On the one hand she respected those with faith who sought comfort in ritual and those without, who just wanted to have a jolly good time and a rest. Then on the other, it just reminded her of Eleonora and their last ever Christmas Day.

It had been wonderful, even though the country had been plunged into war, they'd been together as a family and she'd adored them, faults and all. The following Christmas was the worst ever because Eleonora was overseas and her mother stayed in bed for almost all of the festivities, if you could call them that.

Feeling herself being lulled by maudlin thoughts, Clarissa focused on her mail and sorted the junk mail from anything addressed to Jennifer, and then a pile for herself.

She would open the cards later and yes, of course she would hope for one with a red candle surrounded by ivy, but was brought up short and diverted from silly wishes by the envelope in her hands. She was just about to remark, then thought better of it, then further distracted by the phone in the hall ringing.

'I'll get it,' said Jennifer who shot from the room leaving Chuck underneath the tree tightening the screws on the stand and making huffing noises.

As she slid the envelope between the pile of Christmas cards, Clarissa strained her ears for clues as to who had rung the house phone. It was a rare occurrence these days because her friends were still savvy enough to operate mobile phones, as was she. The only person that had insisted on using the landline was Mr Henderson Senior, but that wouldn't happen anytime soon. Not now she'd sacked the lot of them!

Clarissa tutted and shook her head when she remembered the most awful scene that followed her ejection of Tristan Henderson from Chamberlain. Not only had the dreadful man been plotting to sell off her estate to some shady business associate, he'd gone doo-lally and tore across the bottom meadow, scaring the poor sheep to death, before ploughing into the little stone folly that had stood there for hundreds of years.

They'd been alerted by Yosef the gardener, who'd seen it all. So while Chuck and Jennifer raced down there, Clarissa had called the emergency services. By all accounts, even though he was squashed inside the crumpled car, Tristan's language when he saw Chuck was ripe. And the demeaning and cruel names he called the poor man had enraged Clarissa far more than the destruction of her folly. She was still livid about that, the hooligan!

Once the firefighters had freed Tristan from the wreckage of his car, they carted him off to hospital, but as soon as he'd been given the all-clear she'd pressed charges. He was due up in court soon for trespass and criminal damage. Served him right, the lunatic.

What got her goat the most was that he'd been manipulating Chuck all along for his own ends and it had made her so sad, that such a gentle soul had to listen to such derogatory and uncalled-for comments from someone who regarded themselves as well educated and a gentleman. Pah, Tristan Henderson was nothing of the sort and word had it that he'd fallen from grace at home and at the office.

So it couldn't possibly be one of that lot on the phone talking to Jennifer. No matter, all would be revealed soon, she expected.

Her attention was then drawn to Chuck who was reverse-wiggling from under the tree. She was so glad he'd agreed to stay on until the new year because Chamberlain just wouldn't be the same without him.

She was due to meet with her new firm of solicitors the following week, once they'd received all the files pertaining to the estate from the scurrilous Henderson and Son. Yes, she did see Jennifer and Chuck's point that it wasn't old Henderson's fault his son was an utter scoundrel, but she simply couldn't take the risk. If for whatever reason Tristan did take the reins, it would be tantamount to her father passing Chamberlain into the care of Oscar. And that was never going to happen.

Seeing Chuck and his spanner on approach, Clarissa scooped up the pile of mail belonging to her and placed it inside the box file on the table for later, and everything else of top of that. He flopped into the armchair opposite. 'That woman is a slavedriver!'

Looking over to the extremely straight Christmas tree, Clarissa raised her eyebrows and remarked, 'She certainly is, but thank goodness that one's done. Only two more to go.'

Chuck's head almost spun of his neck. 'Two more? Why does she need two more? I thought the ones outside were spare in case that one wasn't suitable.'

Clarissa laughed, 'Oh no, dear man. Jennifer likes to have one in the foyer and one in the dining room so, if I were you, I'd have a little rest because guess what you'll be doing this afternoon!'

Chuck feigned exhaustion and closed his eyes, just as Jennifer burst into the room, her cheeks flushed as she scooted around Chuck's long legs and plonked herself by Clarissa's side on the sofa. Something was up. She hoped it was good news for once. Maybe Tristan had been sentenced to a year of community service and banned from the golf club for life. From the wide-eyed look on Jennifer's face, and the way she took a deep breath, Clarissa was about to find out.

Placing both hands on her chest, Jennifer said, 'Oh my goodness Clarissa, I have the most incredible news.'

Definitely community service, thought Clarissa. *Picking litter in Chester town centre with any luck.*

Chuck recovered from his exhaustion and sat forward in his chair as Jennifer ploughed on. 'I've just been speaking to a young man by the name of Levi Robinson and… well there's only one way to say this, he's the great-grandson of your sister, Eleonora Chamberlain and… now you must stay very calm, Clarissa, she's alive and very well and living in Manchester.'

Nobody moved. The room stood still. As though time had stopped and while outside everything and everyone in the whole wide world moved on, Clarissa simply waited and listened.

'I asked him a hundred questions to make sure it wasn't a hoax. In case he'd seen the programme on the television but it's all true, I'm sure. He told me things that weren't mentioned on the show, about Robert Jones the teacher from the school who Eleonora was in love with, and she has the silver locket, the one on the portrait.'

At this Clarissa took a sharp breath and her hand rested on her neck. 'Go on.'

'It seems that someone wrote a letter, and that letter led this Levi Robinson's girlfriend to Eleonora. It all sounds rather complicated, but I do believe him.'

Jennifer fell silent, her eyes boring holes into Clarissa who was aware of nothing except the sound of her own breathing, which was good.

In, out, keep doing that, don't die now. For God's sake don't pop your clogs now!

Clarissa didn't know what to do or how to react so decided that she should check she'd heard correctly and wasn't dreaming. If it was a dream, it would be the worst one she'd had in her whole life.

'Could you say that again, dear?'

Jennifer reached over and took Clarissa's hands in hers. 'I said that your beloved sister Eleonora Chamberlain is alive and well and living in Manchester and would very much like to see you so she can explain where she's been for all this time, and at your earliest convenience. Is that clear enough? Oh, and he said Eleonora would expect you to be suspicious so said to tell you she hopes you kept all of her silly books that your mother banned very safe, because she'd like to read them again. Do you know what that means?'

When the room began to spin and Jennifer's hand felt like jelly, and Chuck's face dissolved before her eyes, Clarissa feared the worst and then promptly fainted, right there and then on the sofa, like a silly heroine in ones of Eleonora's silly books.

She came round moments later to find Chuck knelt by her side and Jennifer holding her hand and a tumbler of water. Once she'd regained her composure and allowed Chuck to settle in a more refined position, she took a sip of water and found her voice and, as she did, felt her face crease into a smile that made her cheeks hurt.

'I knew, I always knew he'd lied about her. So many things didn't add up, but I was so weak, and...' she looked to Chuck who knew her truth and after a squeeze of her hand she said, '... scared. I was scared of my father and his brother, so I went along with it all. That ridiculous memorial, Mother's silence. I never forgot Eleonora, though, and wished so hard that she'd come home to me.'

Chuck leant over and gave her a peck on the cheek. 'And your wish came true and now, we can all be together, maybe for Christmas. Wouldn't that be swell.'

Clarissa could feel the bubble of something inside and she wasn't sure what it was. Joy? Not tears, surely. She hadn't cried since Spirit died and that lasted for months and, afterwards, she had no tears left for anything or anyone.

It was seeing Jennifer wipe her eyes that ignited something in her soul, fire, action, determination but not tears. No, she hadn't time to weep. She needed to see her sister. Now. Later that day. Tomorrow. Quickly.

'Jennifer, you must ring him back immediately and tell him we will go today. All three of us. Please go, now, and make the arrangements and then I need you to fetch something from my room: Eleonora's books. I can finally give the ridiculous things back.'

At least she'd made Jennifer laugh and as they watched her race from the room, Chuck came and sat by her side. He didn't speak because there was no need. Instead he just gave her hand a gentle squeeze. In the space of minutes, Chuck's life had once again been pushed off course because they both knew that the discovery of Eleonora and the fact she had a grandson changed everything.

Clarissa's heart broke a little for Chuck in that moment as they listened to Jennifer's animated voice, and together, they waited.

Eleonora being alive was all that Clarissa had ever wished for and, seeing as luck was on her side for once, she thought it prudent to make another wish, for the dear man seated by her side. That one day, with a little bit of help from those who'd grown to love him, he'd find happiness too.

CHAPTER 57

HONEY

Chamberlain Manor. Eight months later.

Levi and Honey were taking a moment for themselves, seated on the wall that surrounded the lily pond, looking over the perfectly mowed lawn set below the terrace at the rear of Chamberlain Manor.

The wedding guests were seated at long tables under canopies to protect them from the blistering August sun and the hum of their voices carried on a much-needed gentle breeze.

Honey was also shaded, by an Edwardian parasol loaned to her by Clarissa for the special day. The cavernous wardrobes at Chamberlain, not to mention the attic rooms, contained a treasure trove of antiques, and Honey's wedding dress was one of them. Thanks to Clarissa's preservation of all things belonging to Eleonora, her bedroom was a time capsule, and everything inside remained exactly as it was on the day she left.

During one of their many long talks over the past months, where Honey learned all about her family history, Clarissa said that the only time she'd ever seen her mother dig her heels in was with regards to Eleonora's bedroom. Between them, they'd surmised that Clarissa's mother may have had her suspicions or was actually privy to her husband's deceit, but was powerless to intervene. Whatever the reason, maybe she too had lived in hope that Eleonora might be out there and would one day return. They would never know.

When Levi and Honey announced they were getting married, she, Clarissa and Eleonora had raided the wardrobe in Eleonora's room. There, amongst treasures that sent Honey into a retro frenzy, they found a beautiful Norman Hartnell gown and, after a few nips and tucks, she had her perfect wedding dress.

They'd been married on the lawn, in a simple ceremony attended by close family and friends – over a hundred of them. Gospel had insisted on doing the catering which was a rather quirky fusion of so many nationalities that they'd lost count. Honey and Levi didn't care. What mattered was all the people they loved were there to see them marry.

'Penny for them, Mrs Robinson.' Levi gave her a gentle bump.

Honey bumped him back. 'I'm just looking at our little family, Mr Robinson and feeling rather proud of them and us, if you must know.'

'I know what you mean. They're ace, aren't they. And so is this. Imagine us getting married in a place like this... and I'm glad we did the deed sooner rather than later. We've made a lot of people very happy today, me included, obviously.'

Looking up at Levi, who'd opted for more casual groom attire in his open neck shirt and extremely colourful canary blue waistcoat, she saw he was a bit on the pink side.

'Here, get under my parasol otherwise you'll look like a lobster and yes, I'm glad too. It would've been stupid to wait, and it wouldn't have been the same without them all here. I always imagined Grandad walking me down the aisle, and, as we've all learned since last year, nobody wants to live a life full of regrets.'

It was a sobering thought, not morbid, though, because facts were facts: nobody knew how long they'd have their two very senior citizens with them. Time was of the essence.

Going for a more cheerful vibe, Honey pointed, 'And Eleonora and Clarissa have loved being part of it all, haven't they. Look at them, like the two queens holding court. I need to remind the photographer to get a one of them together, a proper portrait that we can have made huge and keep forever.'

They both looked towards the terrace and there seated right in the middle of the table were her great-grandmother and her great-great-aunt looking every inch the ladies of the manor.

Rather than the bride and groom taking centre stage, Honey and Levi had wanted Eleonora and Clarissa to be the stars of the show. The newlyweds had sat at opposite ends of the trestle tables during the wedding breakfast knowing they'd have the rest of their lives side by side. Like they were on the day Levi proposed.

It had been a sunny March morning, as they sat outside Ernie's allotment shed, drinking coffee, eating their picnic and ticking off his very precise to-do list. And while it had come as a shock, Honey hadn't needed more than a nano-second to say yes. She remembered Levi's words, all of it, exactly.

When Ernie began spending most of his time at Melba Villa with Eleonora, both of them determined to make up for lost time, he'd been given his own room and often stayed for days on end. Levi, who was spending most of his time at Honey's by then, had offered to take care of Ernie's allotment and, after a bit of humming and hawing, Grumpy Grandad had agreed.

Levi threw himself into the task and bought a pair of wellies. He'd also invested in fold-up deckchairs. Which was where they were sat, side by side, when he said, 'Look at us, like an old married couple with our corned beef and piccalilli sarnies and Radio 4 playing in the background.'

'It's only on that channel because Grandad's transistor is so old that's all you can get. We could listen to something on your phone if you want and anyway, less of the old. And I'd quite like to be a married couple one day.' Once she'd said it, the words couldn't be scribbled out or rewound so cringing to the toes of her pink wellies, Honey hoped he hadn't noticed. But he had.

'I'm glad you said that because … well, when you know you know. Don't you.'

He looked at Honey who cautiously met his gaze and held her breath, and unusually for her, remained silent as Levi embellished.

'And I know that you're the one for me, and… well I was going to wait till your birthday next month but why wait when I can say it right now?'

She couldn't help herself even though she was sure what he meant. 'Say what?'

'That I think we should get married.'

In that wonderful memory, Honey remembered that Levi didn't look nervous. In fact she'd never seen him so serious and matter of fact.

Her reply was just as simple and to the point. 'I agree. I know I know, so yes. I think we should get married too.'

His face cracked into a huge smile and then he went all serious again and he was suddenly looking around for somewhere to put his cup and sarnie. 'Do you want me to get down on one knee and all that because I don't mind but it's a bit muddy and these jeans are clean on…'

'No, I don't want you to do that. I think it's cringe. Just give us a kiss and then stick the kettle back on. Grandad's got a bottle of whisky in the cupboard, so we'll have that in our coffee to celebrate.'

And that was that.

They could have waited a while, but neither of them could see the point, and the rest of the family were in agreement, especially when the hierarchy weren't getting any younger (and as his ecstatic mum pointed out, neither was Levi).

So there they were, married. Mr and Mrs Robinson. Sitting on a wall looking at their rather amazing family – because they were, Honey believed that more than anything.

They weren't perfect, not by any means, and there had been some bumps in the road where Clarissa and Eleonora were concerned because after their joyous reunion at Melba Villa came the questions and recriminations.

At first Eleonora was amused by the fact her father had reinvented her as some kind of war hero who'd been parachuted into France to fight the Nazis, when all the time she was working in a munitions factory a few miles north in Manchester. Her bitterness at being left childless and bereft, in shock at her father's words, losing her mind as half-frozen she'd wandered the streets of the city was never far below the surface, though.

It was Ernie who'd gone head-to-head with the second-most stubborn person in their family, and miraculously persuaded her to accept Clarissa's invitation and visit Chamberlain Manor. That momentous day, attended by Honey, Levi and Ernie, had ended in tears and an act of rebellion.

Following her banishment, Eleonora had sworn never to step foot on Chamberlain soil again, but as Ernie pointed out, those were her father's words. Clarissa was mistress there now, and Eleonora's return would mean a lot to a loyal sister who'd never given up hope.

They'd all lived under the cloud of Percival Chamberlain's bigotry and suffered as a result of his actions, so wasn't it time to put that right? Right some wrongs. Make the most of the time they had left by doing things their way.

It was all going so well, until Clarissa had shown Eleonora the memorial in the rose garden. When she'd read the words, barren of truth and emotion, she took another slap in the face and all the hurt and twisted lies came flooding back.

It was seeing her sister so distraught that made Clarissa act. 'Chuck, dear man. Would you run and fetch the largest hammer you can find. There should be one in Yosef's tool shed in the yard.'

Nobody spoke. Because the intention was clear and when Chuck returned she pointed to the stone memorial, 'Please destroy it. That monstrosity has no place here.'

In a surreal moment of respectful silence, everyone looked on as Chuck smashed it to pieces and it reminded Honey of how her grandad had reacted to another monument that was erected on lies. The destruction of Eleonora's fake memorial had been so moving and symbolic it had taken Honey's breath away.

It wasn't a one-way street though, where hurt and confusion were concerned, because Clarissa had things she needed to get off her chest, too. Why and how could Eleonora have wiped her own sister out of her life? She could have made discreet enquiries, waited until their parents were dead even, then written a letter to explain everything. Had Eleonora never been curious? Had she even missed Clarissa like Clarissa had missed her?

Whatever was said during that meeting, the reasons or excuses Eleonora gave remained between the sisters. But from what Ernie had told Honey, his mother thought it was for the best where Clarissa was concerned. She'd even seen sense in some of her father's words so allowed her to get on with the life she'd been accustomed to.

Having a fallen-from-grace sister, married to a lowly doctor, an ex-factory worker with two step-children and one dead baby she'd had by the local schoolteacher, turn up out of the blue wasn't the upper-class way.

The greatest stumbling block, the one thing Eleonora simply couldn't surmount, was a very primal emotion called hate. And from raw hate was borne a simple fact. She could neither forgive nor forget; and the casualty of that sorry state of affairs was Clarissa.

In the end they'd agreed that their past was a hornets' nest of whys and what-ifs and that regrets were a waste of energy that both of them preferred to reserve for the here and now. The Percivals, Francescas, Oscars and Mollys were ghosts and should have no grip, no presence, or space in their minds. Not anymore.

So together Clarissa and Eleonora were reunited and resolved in one last mission. To enjoy what time they had left together and make sure that those who would carry the Chamberlain legacy forward were people they trusted.

CHAPTER 58

They spotted Ziggy and Chuck sitting on the terrace steps, surrounded by Levi's little cousins from the outlaw side of his family, who were playing with the croquet set on the lawn.

Chuck was laughing at something Ziggy was saying and it made Honey smile, too. He was wearing a similar outfit to Levi, plus a Stetson which everyone thought was very sensible considering the heat of the day.

Ziggy looked completely lovely in her column bridesmaid dress, and it matched Levi's waistcoat and the tinted dreadlocks in her hair. It also matched her and Chuck's identical blue cowboy boots. Apparently they'd had a pig of a time finding some and eventually got lucky on eBay. They were like peas from the same pod.

Thankfully, Clarissa and Eleonora didn't bat an eyelid at the less formal wedding arrangements and attire, or at Ziggy when they first met. In fact they were smitten, and the sentiment was mutual.

Ziggy was just Ziggy and treated everyone the same, because according to her, no matter where you came from everyone's got bum-holes, boobs and willies and grim things going on with their bodies and down belows. Poo was poo and sick was sick, and if you wanted to do things with the hoover pipe and end up with it stuck to your pecker, who was she to judge.

Her gung-ho attitude to life and getting the fuck on with it, as she'd told them both while they ate a Greggs' meal deal on the dining room table at Chamberlain, had caused near hysteria and a full-fat Cherry Coke cheers.

The duchesses, as Ziggy called them, loved their loony friend so much that Honey wouldn't be surprised if they'd go through with their plan to get matching tattoos. They'd discussed many options, some of them rather rude and others a bit odd, well for one pushing a hundred and the other well over the line. Eleonora wanted the CND symbol and Clarissa opted for the name Spirit.

Nah, they were winding everyone up... but then again...

'I think Ziggy's got a crush on Chuck, don't you?' Honey twiddled the stem of her parasol as she watched her friend laughing with her many times removed cousin.

'I'm not surprised, he's a nice bloke and it's a shame he's going back to the states... do you think he'll come back? I want him to, don't you?'

Levi was rolling the cuffs up on his shirt and Honey thought it was time they headed back otherwise they'd melt, and everyone would think they were being rude.

'I really do because you can tell he's happy here and Clarissa adores him, but she's right. He has to decide for himself where he wants to be, and the only way he'll know is if he goes home and gives it a go. I hope he hates it because I want him to be a part of all this and our family... is that selfish and bad?' Sometimes Honey wished she could keep some of her thoughts in her head and not just blurt them out.

'No, you're just being honest, and I get what you mean about Chuck but, either way, he'll be okay. Clarissa has seen to that so don't worry, and we'll Zoom him all the time.'

They lapsed into silence while Levi fiddled with his other cuff and Honey watched Chuck and Ziggy as her mind went into overdrive imagining alternative futures for them both.

One had Chuck becoming a huge success in the states. Using the money Clarissa had gifted him to start a new life, he would open a chain of Blue Grass bars and restaurants across the state of Kentucky.

It had been Clarissa's way of softening the blow when it became clear that he wouldn't be named heir to Chamberlain. Not that he seemed to care. He was more than happy with being part of the family, which was why, after he'd embraced Cheshire life and become part of the furniture, something was drawing him back home, to Kentucky.

Clarissa understood and, having had her wings clipped and her dreams shattered, was adamant that Chuck wouldn't suffer the same. But he needed to make his own mind up so in giving him funds to achieve his dream, she'd set him free. On one condition: that if he changed his mind, or was unhappy, he would come straight back to Chamberlain. There would always be a welcome and a home for him there.

And that was Honey's alternative scenario for Chuck. That he would hate Kentucky so much he'd come straight back, fall in love with Ziggy and they'd all live happily ever after. The end.

She didn't realise she was smiling but Levi had noticed and placed an arm around her shoulder and pulled her close.

'I hope that cheeky grin on your face is because you're thinking of me, Mrs Robinson.'

'You, Mr Robinson are such a needy attention seeker, but I do love you. Although I was actually making up happy endings for Ziggy and Chuck. I've not even got started on Gospel and the plans for the café yet, but having seen how magnificent he's been today, I think it's time I let him loose to do his own thing, don't you?'

'I do indeed. So you're going to let him open the café at night, as a restaurant?'

Honey nodded. It was the fair and sensible thing to do because once Levi had set them up as a not-for-profit charity, things had moved quite quickly and, thanks to a grant, they'd soon be knocking through to next door and Honey's school-holiday-club would be born.

They'd already been able to take on another trainee chef and now it was Gospel's time to fly. Not far though, just swap his daytime shift for the evenings and let him live his dream.

Thoughts of opening a Caribbean-themed fusion restaurant in the village were interrupted by new arrivals on the lawn. 'Ooh look. Here come the donkeys. The little ones will love this.'

Levi and Honey watched on as a couple of volunteers brought their wards to say hello. Clarissa, the patron saint of good deeds, had stepped into the breach when she heard that the sanctuary had run out of time and options and offered them a new home at Chamberlain, rent free.

It was a bit of a contrast, a donkey sanctuary housed next to the stud farm, but the equids on both sides of the fence were getting on fine. And the locals loved coming to see the little donkeys and the regular volunteers had been joined by fresh eager faces, so it had all worked out well.

They were watching the little kids feed and pet the donkeys when Levi spotted something and grimaced, 'Oh bloody hell. I hope Yosef isn't going to lose his mind when he sees what Sharon's just done on his lawn...'

Levi had become something of a donkey expert since the sanctuary had been re-housed, and he knew the names of every single one. Sharon was one of his favourites because, as she'd just proved, she was the naughtiest.

'Oh no, that's a big one. I suppose it's good for the plants... but no way am I offering to scoop... oh lordy, one of the kids has stood in it. Look away, look away quick and pretend we haven't seen.' Honey wasn't like Ziggy and didn't do poo or sick of any kind.

Levi stood and averted his eyes, holding out his hand to Honey. 'Come on, Mrs R, lets walk the long way round and make our way back to the terrace and with a bit of luck everything will be sorted and smelling nice by the time we get back.'

Knowing a good plan when she heard one, she linked his arm and began to stroll around the edge of the lawn, like the lord and lady of the manor, surveying all they owned, or would do, anyway.

Once all the fuss had died down and everyone had met up and caught their breath, Eleonora and Clarissa had convened a pow-wow. A private conversation between the two of them where together they decided the destiny of Chamberlain and more to the point, Levi and Honey.

Even though there were more senior members in the family pecking order, Clarissa was adamant that Levi as the youngest and most able, should be named as joint beneficiary along with their one direct descendant, Honey. Eleonora wholeheartedly agreed.

It made perfect sense that when the time came, Levi and Honey would take the reins. And while they were grateful and humbled by the gesture, both she and Levi hoped that it would be many years before their time came. Clarissa was a Chamberlain and not only was she dearly loved by them and many others, hers were big boots to fill.

They'd discussed it until the wee hours many times, the potential that Chamberlain had. The good it could do and for them it would never be about private wealth. It would be about giving back more than you took.

It was still daunting though and, as they stopped at the corner of the rose garden, the sun began to dip behind the manor, casting it in a peachy-pink glow. Honey wished she could capture it in that moment, because it was perfect. Like the day had been, and like their imperfect, semi-dysfunctional but joined together family.

'It's beautiful isn't it. When you see it like that. Despite the secrets it kept and the things its seen. I hope when it's our turn we can do something spectacular with Chamberlain and really do it and Clarissa justice. Do you think we can?'

Honey felt Levi's arm slip around her shoulder and pull her close before he kissed her hair.

'I do. Because you know what, Mrs Robinson? Me and you are a team. We share the same vision, principles, a family so I have absolutely no doubt at all that together, one way or another, we'll think of something.'

CHAPTER 59

Chamberlain Manor. Present Day

Clarissa was alone in the parlour, warming herself beside the fire. October had started with a damp chill to the air, so Jennifer had done the honours.

'There, that should keep you toasty while I pop out now, is there anything you need from town?'

Clarissa was in one of her funny moods so shook her head and, not wanting to bring Jennifer down too, feigned a smile. 'No, I'll be fine, dear. You get off, but pass me my box file and I'll do some sorting out. I can chuck all the rubbish on the fire and keep it going.'

Jennifer paused then turned to fetch the box that contained Clarissa's correspondence. When she returned and placed it on her knee, Jennifer's words were meant to reassure.

'It's only been three weeks and it's too early for him to have made up his mind, so don't worry. He'll call you tomorrow like he said. Maybe then you'll be able to gauge how he's feeling – or just ask him.'

Clarissa could only manage a weak smile as she gave Jennifer the hint. 'Yes you're right, dear, now off you go otherwise you'll be stuck in traffic.'

She heard Jennifer's sigh, but was relieved when she took her leave and left Clarissa alone to her thoughts with one final suggestion, 'Why don't you give Eleonora a call and have a chat? That always cheers you up. Toodle-pip. Back soon.'

Finally she was gone, and Clarissa allowed her body to relax and ponder Jennifer's words that were in fact correct. Chuck had been gone a short while and she couldn't expect him to make a life-changing decision in such a short space of time. And yes, he'd call her on the dot of seven like he had every Friday since he'd left so they could catch up.

And it always cheered her up, chatting with her sister even for a few moments each day. It did her soul good to hear a voice that for so long had only lived in her dreams. But there was something Clarissa needed to do first. A task only she could take care of.

The night before, Clarissa had lain in bed going over all that had transpired between herself, Eleonora and a stranger named Molly McCarthy.

Eleonora had told Clarissa that while Ernie would forgive none of it, she was caught in that grey area between right and wrong. And that was where Clarissa found herself, right up to the point where Molly had passed the buck to Beryl and then Beryl had done the same to Honey.

Clarissa's foot was teetering on the edge of the black zone where dereliction of one's duty was concerned. And now, a similar task had fallen in Clarissa's lap because she too had a family secret, and it was her turn to decide what to do with it.

Opening the box file that Jennifer had placed on her lap, Clarissa found the envelope that lay right at the bottom and slipped out the contents. Jennifer had no idea it existed because the day it arrived; she'd been fussing over the Christmas tree with Chuck. Then Levi rang and the balloon went up and it was days later before Clarissa remembered to open it.

Unfolding the sheet of paper that contained the DNA results she'd had expedited, Clarissa read the words again, that confirmed a stark and unexpected truth. Chuck was not a Chamberlain.

How she wished she'd not been persuaded by a dear man who'd just wanted to prove his sincerity. On the day she'd given Tristan his marching orders, Chuck had insisted he took the test. Jennifer suggested that there was no harm in it. That at least the results could go on file, and nobody would be able to challenge Chuck's claim to his inheritance. That's how sure she, and Clarissa were of him.

Clarissa could have wept when she'd read the report.

Weeks later, to be on the safe side, Clarissa had fobbed Jennifer off with a fact and some fiction.

'Oh, I forgot to tell you. The DNA report came back while you were out. Yosef signed for the post and brought the bundle to me. Everything was fine and Chuck is one of the clan. I knew he was, but it doesn't matter now does it, because we've found Honey and Levi. I'll give the report to the new solicitor next time he comes.'

Jennifer had smiled and said that she was pleased and knowing that her aide was never present during legal meetings, she would presume everything was in order. Clarissa told Chuck exactly the same thing later that day. That everything was as it should be and being a trusting soul and polite with it, he hadn't asked to see the letter. Why would he? He adored Clarissa and trusted her. Which was why she'd got away with it.

And then came a bigger decision because somewhere along the line, Chuck's mother had cheated on his father and passed her baby off as another man's child. The story had a familiar ring to it, and just like Ernie had been an innocent in his, so was Chuck.

The difference was, Chuck had lived the worst kind of life and with two terrible parents, who as far as Clarissa was concerned, didn't deserve him. And even if he knew that his birth father was somewhere out there, would his mother be in any fit state to tell Chuck who he was?

Chuck was alone in the world, just like Eleonora had been. She'd found Rory who gave her a home and a family and love, a future.

Clarissa couldn't bear the thought of him going through life without an anchor, someone to call family, a place to rest his head, so she had to put that right. Which was why she'd gifted him more than enough money to start a new life of his own, a fortune in fact. But she hoped the greatest gift was worth more than money could buy. That being a Chamberlain, and related to her and Honey and Levi, and their extended family, he'd have his anchor.

Clarissa cared not a jot about whose blood ran through someone's veins. There was more to a human being than that. What was in their heart mattered more. If they had a good soul, morals, principles and loyalty. Chuck had all that in spades.

Just like Eleonora had loved Iris and Ian as her own, and they'd loved her right back. That was priceless and pure.

Since she read the results, Clarissa hadn't told a soul about them and never would. She would take the truth to the grave and not make the secret someone else's problem. Unlike Molly McCarthy.

She'd decided in the early hours of the morning that sometime in the future, when she was long gone and they were sorting through her things, nobody would stumble upon an envelope whose contents had the potential to rip someone's life and world apart, to make them sad, or bitter. To have to choose whether to forgive and forget.

A part of Chuck's story would end there and whether he came back or not, he could make up the ending to it however he chose.

He would always have Honey and Levi in his life, and their children – if and when they came. They'd promised her that.

He could hold his head up high and say, 'I'm a Chamberlain and I have family in England.'

Placing the report inside the letter, Clarissa kissed the envelope then leant forward and flicked it into the fire, watching as the paper curled and browned. Within minutes, the words of the report had turned to ash.

Smiling, her body awash with relief, Clarissa was reconciled to what she'd done. Content. Because when she closed her eyes to sleep, or even for that last time, she would rest easy. Knowing that her secret, and Chuck's secret, would forever and all time remain a family affair.

THE END

AFTERWORD

The story of Molly McCarthy is inspired by true events. My very own family affair.

I wanted to share some of my personal history with you and explain why this book is dedicated to Grandad Charlie and Grandma Nellie.

My late grandparents, who I loved dearly, are embedded in my happy childhood memories. Growing up in the sixties and seventies, I knew their back door was never locked, and the kettle was always on the boil.

Their lives, however, were cloaked in a veil of mystery and never fully resolved despite my efforts. Their story has always intrigued me and the urge to get to the truth will never go away.

I will also never understand why my mother didn't ask more questions when she could. Because believe me, in her final years the missing piece of the puzzle, the Irish connection, troubled her deeply.

Perhaps her generation, or her family, just accepted what they were told and never rocked the boat. Was it the British way? That stiff upper lip. The fear of scandal and stigma tainting a simple life. Least said, soonest mended.

Also, thanks to the lack of social media and access to the internet, relying on what the BBC and the papers said, our ancestors were to some extent able to keep their lives private, their secrets well buried. And if they were lucky, stay under the radar.

Just like my grandparents.

Grandad Charlie was of Irish heritage. His father was born in Enniskillen and emigrated to England. Manchester to be precise. Raised a Catholic, Grandad was married with seven sons. When he met another woman, my grandma Nellie, and left his family to start another, his life was never going to be easy. Outcast and penniless they moved away, not millions of miles either, just to the next town, but back then it was probably far enough.

Tormented by his faith, shame and guilt, Grandad was plagued by visions of his dead mother standing at the top of the stairs, giving him the evil eye.

In another more curious thread, at his funeral, one of the sons from his first marriage presented my grandma with an orange sash. It's a conundrum I've never been able to fathom. What were his links to the Protestant Orange Order? I believe it has strong ties to Enniskillen where his family are from.

In his darkest moments, he would begin to tell my mum a tale, saying to Grandma that she needed to know the truth, but Grandma always stopped him, saying mum wouldn't understand. I wish he'd told her that story.

For many years my grandparents lived 'in sin' and one step away from being discovered by whoever they were hiding from. The burden of whatever he'd done weighed heavy on his soul. They finally married in the fifties, and in my memories of them, through a child's eyes, they always seemed happy. My mum remembered things differently.

I was around eleven or twelve years old when I learned of our family secrets, just after the death of my grandmother. I can still remember how incredulous I was when Mum told me this story.

During the second world war, Grandad Charlie worked away as a steel-erector. Grandma Nellie was left at home to care for her six children, the youngest being Ann, my mother, who was born in June 1940. Later that year in December, during the Manchester Blitz, the family was bombed out and life became even more difficult.

It was around this time that Grandad wrote to Grandma. He suggested that to ease the burden, their eldest son, Terence, who would be nine or ten years old, should go and live with Grandad's sister, Janey. She lived on the other side of Manchester in a place called Belle Vue. She and her husband were childless so, in wartime Britain, it probably made sense. With a resolve inherent of that generation, putting her feelings aside, Grandma Nellie agreed.

When the war was over and my grandparents were re-housed, naturally Grandma asked that Terence came home. Almost six years had passed, and during that time Terence had never been to see his mother and siblings. Janey had also become attached to her nephew who she looked upon as her own.

With another baby now on the way, and as times were still tough, Grandad in his wisdom, or maybe influenced by his sister and having many mouths to feed, decided it was best if Terence remained where he was, to be brought up as Janey's son. He never returned.

My mother had no clue that Terence was her brother, or that his existence was known to her two elder siblings, but never mentioned. It was as though he didn't exist. Uncle Charles became the eldest son, Terence was safe and cared for; life went on. It is hard to believe that only five miles away, a two-bus ride, lived a brother my mum regarded as her cousin. Four more children came along, and they were also unaware.

When Mum was old enough to travel alone, every now and then Grandma would send her over to Belle Vue on an errand, saying that if she saw Cousin Terence, to say hello from Aunty Nellie.

When Mum returned, Grandma would want to know if she'd seen Terence and if he was okay. Of course Mum didn't understand why, and it wasn't until Grandma died that the truth about Terence was revealed and the dots of her family tree were joined up.

Mum's eldest sister had decided it was time to tell the truth and re-introduce Terence to the family, just before Grandma's funeral. As you can imagine, it came as quite a shock to the younger siblings and Uncle Charlie was not happy about it at all. Perhaps he felt his position in the family was destabilised. The others were shocked and wary but welcoming. I believe the funeral was rather awkward, as you can imagine.

Terence also had his issues. Having spent most of his life feeling rejected and no doubt harbouring many wounded thoughts, he was still the outsider. Despite my aunt's efforts to integrate him into the family and start afresh, it didn't go well.

After all those years, it was too late for him to ask questions of the one person who could explain – his mother. Instead, the blanks had to be filled in by others and I cannot imagine the frustration he would have experienced. He'd missed out on having siblings, being loved by his natural parents, feeling part of a family.

The relationship between the brothers and sisters continued to be awkward, a combination of many factors, I suppose. My aunt persevered, and for whatever reasons, my mum, other aunts, and uncles didn't.

When I met Terence in the nineties, the best way to describe him was having a chip on his shoulder. He exuded an aura of resentment, and seemed very bitter, angry at the world, and as though he was trying to reinforce his position in the pecking order. Needless to say I didn't warm to him, but with hindsight I wish I'd taken the opportunity to get to know him and ask him some questions of my own.

I've also wondered about Grandma's role in all of this.

Why, when Grandad died, did she never reach out to her son? Perhaps she thought it was too late or just couldn't face Terence. More than likely, she simply didn't want the secret to come out. Maybe it was just too painful for her. And why didn't she make a stand and get Terence back, go to see him? That question is somewhat easier to answer.

Grandma was a petite, shy, woman, who kept herself to herself for the reasons stated at the start. What went on in the home stayed there, buried under the carpet, only the cuckoo in the wall clock privy to the intimacies of her complicated world.

She was married to a dominant, giant of a man prone to melancholy and guilt-fuelled bad temper. That's all I shall say on that matter, but you can imagine the rest.

From talking with my mum, I know Grandma's life was sometimes difficult, living in a post-war era, following the rules set by a male-led society, living under the radar in times of great hardship. Times that women nowadays might struggle to comprehend. Or maybe not.

Through my research I've heard many stories that confirm our family affair isn't unique. Babies born out of wedlock, then brought up by the maternal grandmother as their own, never knowing their sister was actually their mum. Women sent to stay with aunts for a while, then returning home without the baby they'd secretly given birth to. Children sent away for their own safety to far-flung corners of the globe, the countryside, to strangers, never to return.

Who knows how many secrets remain buried to this day. Maybe there are some in your family, too.

When I first heard the story of Terence, I couldn't take it in, but with the passing of years comes understanding. That often, the complicated dynamics of life and family force people to make challenging choices; unwise decisions; hold on to secrets; live a life of regret.

How terribly sad it must be if you are unable to right a wrong, turn back time, take a different path.

It must make life such a hard road to travel. A journey you long to end. Then it's done, and you can rest.

I hope with all my heart that Grandad Charlie and Grandma Nellie sleep well now. That their dreams are kind. And they don't mind that their story is the inspiration for *A Family Affair*. I wish that I could tell them that I still love them no matter what. And that is why I shared some of their history with you.

Maybe in the words of this book there is some resolution. Not just for me, but for anyone out there with questions still to ask. I may never fully make sense of the past. But I can write a happier ending for the troubled souls who live on in fiction, and those who rest in my heart and in my memory, always.

x

ACKNOWLEDGEMENTS

Dear reader.

I hope you enjoyed the story, and that the Afterword has shed some light on why I felt inspired to write it for you.

In this book there are so many nods to relatives long gone. Little memories that remind me of my childhood and heritage. Pea and ham soup, my city being bombed in the blitz, a cuckoo clock and a little budgie that gave my Grandma and Grandad Birdie their name. Pins the Knicker Ripper really was a very naughty black poodle, hence my paternal grandparents' moniker. The Hat and Feathers pub in Ancoats is no longer there, and neither is the steelworks in Openshaw. The donkey sanctuary is thriving, thank goodness, and a few minutes from where I live. All of these, plus the events that I mention in the Afterword helped to build a picture of the McCarthy family. I can honestly say this story and the journey it took me on was the most enjoyable for a long time. I was really sad when I had to say goodbye to all of my characters, like I was waving off family.

There was also something else I needed to get off my chest and even though it's been a couple of years since it happened, it's still raw and was quite painful to write. I'm glad I did it though.

The part of Ziggy is based on the experiences of our wonderful grandson Harry who, in 2021, was diagnosed with T1 Diabetes. Just like Ziggy, Harry had wanted to join the military, following his uncle into the RAF. After diagnosis, his dreams were shattered, and he too suffered everything my imaginary dreadlocked nurse experienced in the book. Yet two years later we couldn't be prouder of him and all he has achieved. He continues to amaze us with his resilience and his bravery when there's a blip, but he's determined that, powered by insulin, his condition won't hold him back. I just wanted to say here in black and white, that I love you, Harry. *Per Ardua Ad Astra.* Through adversity to the stars.

Now it's time for thank-yous.

To the fabulous team at Bloodhound Books who bring my stories to life. Betsy, Fred, Clare, Abbie, Tara, Maria, Vicky and Katia, thank you from the bottom of my heart.

To Jon King, who in his day job is the character, Levi. Jon patiently explained to me all about not-for-profit, and his ideas and enthusiasm for charitable enterprises inspired me to write Honey's character. In his other job, he is a superhero who gives back and trains kids and adults in mixed martial arts. He is a fabulous mentor, inspiration and friend to Harry who, because of Jon is now a First Dan black belt. Thank you, Jon.

Another thank you to Linda Rhead genealogist extraordinaire. The things you discover blow my mind... and I have a feeling we're not finished yet!

To my wonderful, dedicated, loyal and a bit bonkers ARC group who make me laugh, cheer me on and support every single one of my books. Your willingness to help but most importantly your friendship, is priceless. If I could, I'd list every single one of you here, but you know who you are. Thank you.

To all of my readers and friends who take the time to buy and review my books, again your friendship and support is much appreciated. I wish I could name you all individually, too.

To Keri and Nathan for taking time to read the book during its incarnation and offering their erudite advice. And for the rest of the time, thank you for chatting mainly rubbish and making me laugh, a lot.

And finally, as always, to my family.

In every book I write there is always something of us. The essence of who we are and where we are from. The lessons my parents and grandparents taught us, their wisdom and mistakes, the memories of 2 Franklyn. Within each line and chapter, there are things that only we understand. An undercurrent of pure love and without you, I wouldn't know what that was. The six of you are my world and in it, we speak our own language, follow our own codes and together, we will be okay. Always remember that.

I love you. x

ALSO BY PATRICIA DIXON

PSYCHOLOGICAL THRILLERS/SUSPENSE/DRAMAS

Over My Shoulder

The Secrets of Tenley House

#MeToo

Liars (co-authored with Anita Waller)

Blame

The Other Woman

Coming Home

Venus Was Her Name

A Good Mother

WOMEN'S FICTION/FAMILY SAGAS

They Don't Know

Resistance

Birthright

The Destiny Series:

Rosie and Ruby

Anna

Tilly

Grace

Destiny

A NOTE FROM THE PUBLISHER

Thank you for reading this book. If you enjoyed it please do consider leaving a review on Amazon to help others find it too.

We hate typos. All of our books have been rigorously edited and proofread, but sometimes mistakes do slip through. If you have spotted a typo, please do let us know and we can get it amended within hours.

info@bloodhoundbooks.com